Dear Reader,

1492 marks perhaps the greatest turning point in Western history. The Catholic monarchs finally conquered the last Muslim kingdom in Spain and sent Christopher Columbus off to seek the New World. The Alhambra, where the young sultan handed over the keys of the city of Granada, remains one of the world's most-visited tourist attractions.

This 13th century palace described by Muslim poets as "a pearl set in emeralds" has beguiled the millions who have walked beneath its graceful arches and gazed upon its serene pools and lacy, geometric stonework, including me. I first visited the palace 20-odd years ago, and it cast its spell over me. I knew that I would set a novel there, and at last the idea for *Court of Lions* came—as ideas do—out of that lovely mixture of imagination and serendipity that novelists cherish.

A movie producer working on *The Sultan's Wife* told me a story, out of the blue, about restorers discovering an ancient love letter hidden in a palace door in the Alhambra. I remembered Lorca's quote, that "In Spain, the dead are more alive than the dead in any other country in the world." And suddenly I could see how the eternal force of love might arc powerfully back and forth, connecting past and present.

This terrible clash of cultures, as relevant today as it was in the 15th century, is usually told from the viewpoint of the Spanish, but I decided to tell it from the Moorish side, and to counterpoint the epic with the intimate. And so the modern story of Kate Fordham—a young woman escaping oppression in her own life who finds a similar scrap of paper in the grounds of the Alhambra—wrapped itself through the tale of the young sultan growing up in the most beautiful palace on earth, yet at the heart of a terribly fractured family.

The result is a sweeping historical epic told through two deeply romantic love stories set 600 years apart, yet connected by a delicious mystery. I hope you enjoy it.

Jane Johnson
Cornwall, January 2017

Court of Lions

Court of Lions

JANE JOHNSON

Doubleday Canada

Doubleday Canada and colophon are registered trademarks of Penguin Random House Canada Limited.

Library and Archives Canada Cataloguing in Publication is available upon request.

ISBN: 9780385682657
eBook ISBN: 9780385682664

[insert design/art creds]

Printed and bound in Canada

Published in Canada by Doubleday Canada, a division of Penguin Random House Canada Limited

www.penguinrandomhouse.ca

10 9 8 7 6 5 4 3 2 1

Penguin
Random House
DOUBLEDAY CANADA

To Hani and Christina,
You know why

Renaissance Europe 15th Century

SCOTLAND

IRELAND

ENGLAND

TUETONS

RUSSIA

MANY
SMALL
INDEPENDENT
STATES

POLAND

LITHUANIA

BOHEMIA

FRANCE

MILAN

AUSTRIA

VENICE

HUNGARY

NAVARRA

PORTUGAL

ARAGON

GENOA

OTTOMANS

CASTILE

Córdoba

PAPAL
STATES

NAPLES

OTTOMANS

Granada
GRANADA

TLEMCEN

TUNIS

MOROCCO

• Fez

Iberian Peninsula

KINGDOM OF NAVARRA

KINGDOM
OF ARAGON

KINGDOM
OF
CASTILE

KINGDOM
OF
PORTUGAL

EMIRATE
OF GRANADA

BARBOURY COAST   TLEMCEN

SULTINATE OF MOROCCO

Emirate of Granada

Córdoba   • Porcuna   Huescar
                                      • Velez Blanco

• Sevilla   GRANADA

CASTILE   • Lucena   • Guadix

Loja   • Granada

Velez Malaga   Almeria
Malaga

Though the shadows of these walls have long
since gone, the memory of them will live on as
the final refuge of dreams and art. And then the
last nightingale to breathe on this earth will build
its nest and sing its farewell song among the
glorious ruins of the Alhambra.

FRANCISCO VILLAESPESA

Molten silver flows through the pearls, which it
resembles in its pure, white beauty
Water and marble seem to be one in appearance, and
we know not which of the two is flowing.
Do you not see how the water spills into the basin,
but the hidden spout hides it immediately?
It is a lover whose eyes brim over with tears, tears that
it hides for fear someone will reveal them . . .

IBN ZAMRAK

Dramatis Personae

KATE'S STORY

IN SPAIN

Kate Fordham, Englishwoman working in Granada under the name of
  Anna Maria Moreno
Jimena, owner of the Bodega Santa Isabella in Granada
Juan, Axel, Leena, Giorgio, Kate's co-workers in the bodega
Hicham, Moroccan man working in an Internet café
Dr. Khadija Boutaki, expert in Islamic gardens
Brahim Boutaki, her husband, a retired *zellij* worker
Omar Boutaki, Brahim's brother, working in restoration at the Alhambra
Abdou, a *ma'allem*—master—*zellij* worker
Mohamed Boutaki, Omar's son, a *zellij* expert from Fez

IN ENGLAND

Jess Scott, née Fordham, Kate's twin sister
Luke, Kate's son
Evan Scott, Jess's husband
James Foxley, antiques dealer
Yusuf, corner-shop assistant

BLESSINGS'S STORY

GRANADA IN THE FIFTEENTH CENTURY

Blessings, child from a desert tribe sold into the Granada court as a companion to

Prince Abu Abdullah Mohammed (Momo), soon to be Mohammed XII of Granada, known by his enemies as Boabdil

Abu'l Hasan Ali, sultan of Granada, known also as Moulay Hasan, father to Momo

Abu Abdullah Muhamed al-Zaghal, his brother, called usually al-Zaghal

Lalla Aysha the Pious, the Chaste, the sultana, married to Moulay Hasan, mother to Momo

Rachid, the younger son of Moulay Hasan and Lalla Aysha

Qasim Abdelmalik, the vizier (chief minister) at the Granada court

Dr. Ibrahim, court doctor

Isobel de Solis, war captive, convert to Islam, married to Moulay Hasan and renamed Zoraya, Star of Morning

La Sabia, the Wise One, her servant

Ali Attar, pasha of the town of Loja

Mariam, his daughter, wife to Momo

Ahmed, the elder son of Momo and Mariam, known also as Alfonso

Yusuf, the baby son of Momo and Mariam

Musa Ibn Abu'l Ghrassan, chief of the Banu Serraj (Abencerrages) clan, allied to Lalla Aysha

CASTILIANS AND ARAGONESE

Queen Isabella, queen of the conjoined kingdom of Castile and Aragón

King Ferdinand, her husband and king of the conjoined kingdom of Castile and Aragón

Don Diego Fernández of Córdoba, the Count of Cabra

Don Diego, his nephew, a knight

Don Gonzalo Fernández of Córdoba, known as the Great Captain

Don Rodrigo Ponce de León, the Marquis of Cádiz and King Ferdinand's general

Cristoforo Colombo, also known as Cristóbal Colón and Christopher Columbus, adventurer

Kate

GRANADA

NOW

K ate didn't consider herself a vandal. She had never wilfully damaged anything in her life (apart from herself),
let alone a World Heritage Site. Intrigued by a plant that
resembled a familiar English weed she knew of as the Mother of
Thousands or Kenilworth ivy, she had been taking a closer look,
and glimpsed something that shouldn't have been there. Winkling
it out, she'd triggered a little cascade of debris.

She glanced around, hoping no one had seen. The Alhambra
palaces, constructed by the medieval Moorish kings of Granada
and wrapped around by their majestic gardens, represented to her a
sort of perfection: a paradise on earth. To get thrown out would be
like getting expelled from Eden. She managed to fiddle the object
into her palm and sat back, trying to look innocent.

No one appeared to have noticed, not even the group of tourists
she'd come in with, who were now standing in a knot, poring over
a guidebook, then staring across the gorge to the summer palace,

their sun visors glinting in the low afternoon light and their Nordic walking poles tucked under their arms. She'd watched them striding purposefully up the hill from the Pomegranate Gate, their poles clacking on the stones, as if they were making their way to Everest Base Camp instead of a sunlit garden in Andalusia.

Turning slightly away from them, Kate tucked her hair behind her ears to examine what she had found, feeling an unexpected simple pleasure in the act. Her hair had taken its time growing back, as if nervous to be seen out in public, but now it brushed her shoulders. Perhaps it marked the extent to which she was being restored to herself.

She opened her hand. It was just an old screw of paper, probably a scrap of rubbish crammed into the crack in the wall by a visitor. Habit dictated that she painstakingly unroll it. (She did this with used wrapping paper, peeling off the tape, trying not to tear it. As a child, she had frustrated her family at Christmas by holding up the gift opening with her mildly autistic patience.) Inside the scroll of paper was a layer of coarse white grains, and beneath this was inked a series of symbols.

Her brain buzzed at a sudden memory: sitting with Jess on a long-ago wet Sunday afternoon with a book on the floor between them.

They were twins. Non-identical, but if they made the effort, it could be hard for people to tell them apart. They had been taking turns reading to each other, but she had been interrupting Jess, driving her mad with a typical eight-year-old's questions. "Yes, but what sort of spiders are they? Where did they come from? How did they get to be so big? Are there spiders in our woods that cocoon people and eat them alive?"

Infuriated, Jess had put the book down flat as if hiding its contents from Kate, who had spied something she had never noticed before: that the pattern on the front cover also ran across the spine and onto the back of the book. And not just any pattern: symbols that looked sort of like an alphabet but were a type of writing she couldn't quite understand. She had touched the border in wonder. "Look," she'd said. "Letters!"

Jess had sighed. "They're runes, stupid," she'd declared with almost adult condescension. "It's another language." She pointed to a section of the border. "See, there? You must be able to work that out."

It was a sort of spiky double *B*. In a flash of revelation Kate understood how the letters grouped around it made up a name. "It says '*The Hobbit*'!" she squealed. It was a glimpse into a secret world. "What does the rest say?"

They had spent the remainder of the afternoon transliterating the code and making up messages to each other. Over the years it had become their thing. Different codes, different games. Kate would receive postcards from Jess when she was travelling through Europe on a student rail card in her gap year: a few lines of neat runes, followed by a heart and a *J*, notes that remained cryptic even when decoded.

Boys like wolves roam. A lick or a kiss?

This, with an Italian stamp and a picture of a statue of Romulus and Remus. From Spain, a postcard showing a statue of a mounted hero named Rodrigo Díaz de Vivar in Burgos. *C Heston's steely gaze and* auto da fe *hair*, she translated from Jess's code. *Reader, I swived him.*

Swived was one of their code words, gleaned from reading Chaucer's tales. The moment Kate had translated that fourth letter she'd burst out laughing and their mother had demanded to know why. Of course she hadn't told.

Remembering, Kate smiled as she examined the paper further. The symbols on it resembled Tolkien's runes: but unlike them, she could find no simple guiding principle, could not even tell if they ran from left to right, right to left, top to bottom. They were a series of tiny markings, as if to save space, or to make the secret they contained even more obscure.

Perhaps this was a note left for an illicit lover, admitting to jealousy or betrayal or everlasting adoration. But more likely it was just a game, or a shopping list; or her imagination running away with her. A meaningless bit of garbage crammed into this crevice because someone couldn't be bothered to find a bin to throw it away in. Which was probably what she should do with it.

But instead, she tucked it into her jeans pocket. Perhaps it was just in a language she didn't know, like Hebrew or Cyrillic. Maybe she should show it around at the bar and see what anyone there could make of it. They were a cosmopolitan lot. She glanced at her watch. Nearly five o'clock. She was on evenings this week, which was better for tips but played havoc with her sleep. She pushed herself to her feet, grimacing as her knees cracked. *Showing your age, Kate. Creaking knees and a watch.* No one else at the bar even owned a watch: smart phones had taken over. This thought triggered another: *I must phone Jess and Luke.*

The idea of reconnecting to the world should have warmed her, but it was as if a cloud passed across the face of the sun.

"Anna! Anna Maria, I'm talking to you—did you hear a word I said?"

Kate looked up with a start from the chalkboard on which she was writing—in Spanish on one side, English on the other—that night's specials: *patatas a lo pobre*, poor man's potatoes; *piquillos rellenos*, stuffed peppers; *boquerónes*, Spanish white anchovies. "Sorry, I was a million miles away." It took her a moment to find a suitable Spanish phrase. *"Un millón de millas."*

Jimena shook her head wearily. "Sometimes it's as if you're in another world. When I started working, if I didn't leap to attention as soon as Paolo called my name, I'd have been out in the gutter, doing *trabajo de negros.*"

Black man's work.

Jimena's tales of her hardscrabble life before she clawed her way up to owning the Bodega Santa Isabel were always colourful; her racism, however, was highly unpleasant. Kate bit her tongue and held up the finished chalkboard. "There—is that okay?"

Jimena ran her eyes over the Spanish text, her thin face as intent as a hawk's as she concentrated. "Two *r*'s in *chicharrón,*" she said, focusing on the single error, handing the tablet back without a word of praise. "And as I was saying, table seven is filthy and the candle on table five needs to be replaced."

And she was off to berate someone else.

Kate watched as she headed for Leena and Giorgio, standing together with their backs foolishly to the bar as they laughed about something, their heads bent in joyful complicity. She wished she could warn them, but seconds later they jolted upright like guilty children, away from the phone they'd been craning over, and in an instant Jimena had it in her hands like some sort of wicked stepmother, confiscated for the rest of the night. Kate fingered the scrap of paper in her jeans pocket, and left it there.

She moved deftly between the tables, setting chairs and placemats straight, aligning a knife someone had put down askew. She replaced the candle on table five and wiped down the plastic cloth on table seven, going through her paces on automatic. But all the while she was thinking: *I must call Jess.*

It had been less than a week since they last spoke, but something was niggling at her. She hoped Luke wasn't ill. A stabbing pain went through her at the thought of that.

"Hi, Anna!" Axel called through a cloud of steam. Beside him Juan was peeling and chopping potatoes.

"Drink later?" he asked.

"Maybe." Sometimes they sat out on the back step after service, drinking beer: the two lads were good company, though she did feel old enough to be their mother.

Axel had blond, blunt Swedish features; Juan was dark and aquiline and Spanish, from Madrid. They were like flip sides of the same coin: in their twenties, working their way from town to town, devouring life as they went. Kate was thirty-nine. She envied them their unmoored lifestyle. Yet here she was, cast away with no anchor, a long, long way from the life she had known. But she did not feel blithe and carefree: far from it. Perhaps that was the difference between thirty-nine and twenty-five.

Try to live in the moment, Kate, she told herself fiercely. She took a few deep breaths. *You only get the one life.* "Okay," she amended. "If we don't finish too late."

The crowd in tonight was varied. The Alhambra, and the city that had grown up around it, attracted all sorts of visitors. Youngsters making the rounds of the sights of Europe, too full of narcissism and hormones for its majesty and tragedy to touch their hearts; academics who carried notebooks with them, looking, looking, but never really seeing; couples on honeymoon, come to sigh over the sunsets and the romantic courtyards; seasoned travellers who walked briskly through the gardens, eating the ground away till they could get to the Nasrid palaces and tick off the most famous marvels from their itineraries; batty old women who touched the walls when they thought no one was looking as if they might raise a ghost or two; dark-eyed men from North Africa, glowering at all that was lost, when once they had been kings. They all came in here for tapas, for the deep red local wine and for *cerveza*.

Well, that wasn't entirely true. When Jimena was front of house, the latter group got turned away with a curt "We have no tables"; unspoken: "for the likes of you" — even though the place was patently empty.

To say her boss was racist was too simple a statement. It was as if Jimena felt she was the last bastion of Catholic Spain, a holy inquisitor holding back the Moorish hordes. Arabs were not welcome in the bodega under Jimena's regime and woe betide you if you let one in. "They're terrorists, all of them. You think they wouldn't kill you in an instant if they could get away with it? I lost a cousin in the Madrid bombings. It's what their kind has been doing for centuries. It's in their blood. They hate us for what we took back from them, and they're planning all the time how they're going to get it back, or destroy it if they can't. They are the enemy. They have always been the enemy. I may not have the power to keep them out of my country, but by God I'll keep them out of my bar!"

The first time Kate had heard this tirade—levelled at a newcomer who'd had the temerity to seat a pleasant family of Moroccan tourists—she'd felt something inside her shrivel. Once, she'd have called Jimena to account, but she'd lost that earlier confidence, found it hard to summon the courage. And she hated herself for that.

There were Swedes and French, Germans, Japanese and Danes in tonight; she heard Leena greet the latter group with a cheery "*Hej hej.*" No English, which was something of a relief. Kate felt herself tense whenever she heard an English accent, no matter how unfamiliar it might be. It was absurd, she knew, but she couldn't help it.

Taking a short break at half past eleven, she stepped out into the street to get a better phone signal and called her sister's landline. There was a long pause before the dial tone kicked in, and then the ringing went on and on and on. For so long, in fact, that she thought she must have keyed in the wrong number. She kept no stored information on the phone—it was a cheap one loaded with a local sim card that she topped up with cash—and she was tired, so a wrong number was quite possible. Concentrating, she punched the number in again, but still there was no response, not even from the answering machine. Kate's skin prickled. Probably Jess was out for the evening and had forgotten to set it. But wouldn't the baby-sitter have answered in that case? She tried Jess's mobile; it went to voice mail. Jess must have had an early night, Kate told herself firmly. She would try phoning again in the morning; nothing to worry about.

Even so, she felt a tug of anxiety for the rest of her shift, despite playing her part with professional smiles and small talk.

By the time the party of Danes had finished their drinks and finally departed with a promise to return before the end of the week, it was long past one and Kate was suppressing yawns that felt as if she might dislocate her jaw. The youngsters didn't seem to care at all that it was so late: they just slept in the next day. But Kate had a routine and breaking it made her uncomfortable. She thought: *If I hurry, I can get six hours' sleep.* So when Juan approached with a pair of beer bottles swinging between the fingers of one hand, she shook her head. "Actually, I changed my mind, Juan. Not tonight— I'm too tired."

He shrugged. "Maybe tomorrow, huh?"

"Good night, Anna!" Leena kissed her on the cheek. "See you Sunday." Lucky Leena: two whole days off.

Kate said her farewells and slipped into the night. She'd arrived in Granada the previous summer, during a particularly sweltering July, but she still couldn't seem to catch the relaxed local vibe. Her heels rang on the uneven stones of the narrow road down to the Plaza Nueva, the sound echoing off the metal-shuttered shopfronts. As she crossed into the Arab quarter, known as the Albayzín, some-thing shot out of the shadows and scurried through a patch of moonlight and into the obscurity of the undergrowth at the foot of the Sabika Hill. She jumped, startled, and then chided herself—a cat, she thought. Or maybe a fox. Silly to feel so shaken up because of some small creature that was no doubt a lot more scared of her than she should be of it.

She followed the course of the River Darro along the main road for a while, then turned left up the Calle Zafra and climbed the narrow street steadily, the pebble mosaics underfoot made slippery by centuries of walkers, lethal when it rained. Approaching the Calle Guinea at last, she dug out her key, clutched it in her palm, letting the tang protrude between her fingers as she'd been taught in self-defence classes. It really wasn't that sort of place, the Albayzín, though it had an edge to it sometimes, but she was always careful. At that moment she saw the bit of paper she'd taken out of the wall that afternoon fluttering to the ground. She'd forgotten to show it around at work to see if anyone recognized the markings on it. Never mind. There was always tomorrow.

Crouching, she retrieved it and was about to stand again, when someone said her name. Not a shout but a quiet statement.

"Kate."

Here, no one called her Kate. No one. Here, she was Anna. Anna Maria, to be precise. Her surname Moreno. It was a common name, meaning dark haired. A small private joke. Even a clue . . .

She sprang upright, heart beating wildly, the key in her hand ready to jab. She thought the voice had come from behind her. Her pulse raced. She interrogated her surroundings at speed. But nothing moved in the darkness.

Stop it, Kate.

Forcing herself to ignore her terror, she ran down the alley to her door.

As she reached for the lock, moonlight picked out the web of tiny, pale scars on her forearm.

2

He was nearly on her. She could feel his hot breath on her naked back. Her legs felt like lead as she forced them to run, but he caught her and—

The bleep of the phone on the bedside table woke Kate just as the hand closed on her shoulder. She lay there, heart thudding, and tried to push through the membrane of the dream, tried to puzzle out why she had been running naked down an alley. The return to reality came slowly, as if the dream were in league with her pursuer. She realized it was still fully dark, not even a hint of light flickering around the edges of her closed curtains. Nervously, she picked up the phone and stared at the text message. From Jess, of course; the only person who had this number:

At Sarah's. Just walked up the cliff for signal—none in the house. Will email tomorrow am. Love you. Jx

It was 3:28 a.m. and Jess's friend Sarah lived in a remote cottage in North Cornwall. What on earth had driven her sister to be walking up a Cornish cliff in the middle of the night to send her a text? She rang back at once, but there was no reply. Beset by anxieties, Kate swung her legs out of the narrow bunk and walked barefoot over the cool tiles to the window. She pushed back the drapes and gazed out across the Darro gorge to where the moon limned the roofs and walls of the ancient fortress. What was she doing here, a thousand miles away from her real life? She leaned her forehead against the window, watched her breath bloom and evaporate upon the cold glass. *Breathe in and out, keep breathing.* Sometimes it was all she could do.

Eventually, she got back into bed and lay there, trying to summon sleep, reciting the common names of wildflowers she and Jess used to find in the hedgerows on their walk to school instead of counting sheep:

Yellow archangel
Alexanders
Queen Anne's lace
Charlock
Bird's-eye speedwell
Kenilworth ivy

When this proved ineffective, she started on their botanical names:

Lamium galeobdolon
Smyrnium olusatrum
Anthriscus sylvestris
Sinapis arvensis
Veronica chamaedrys
Cymbalaria muralis

Her love of plants should have carried her into a career as a botanist. Instead she'd ended up as a data analyst. She used to think that by applying logic she had some control over her choices, but life seemed determined to prove her wrong. For where was she now? No longer a well-respected analyst on a good salary but a waitress living in a foreign country under an assumed name, having lost everything she cared most about in the world.

Kate woke again to the sound of a phone ringing, but when she grabbed her mobile to answer it, the wretched thing died, its battery flat. She'd forgotten to plug it in overnight, something she did religiously, part of her pre-bed routine. She *had* been spooked last night.

She paced the apartment while she waited for the phone to charge, made some coffee, took a cup of it out and sat to drink it in a pool of sunlight on the edge of the terrace wall. She loved this view looking over the undulating terracotta rooftops that had sheltered the houses beneath for hundreds of years in some cases, to the presiding grandeur of the Alhambra on its great platform of rock across the gorge, with its massive tawny walls, its turrets and towers. How extraordinary it must have been to live in such magnificent surroundings. She wondered if anyone raised in a palace could ever be a normal person, could even begin to function as an understandable human being. In her small experience of the world, luxuries spoiled people; made them increasingly less human, less accommodating to others; made them think too highly of themselves. Made them cruel.

She shuddered, and turned that thought aside.

The phone had some charge now. She rang Jess's number, but it went to voice mail and all she could do was to say she had called, that she hoped Jess and Luke were okay, and that she would call back. She plugged the phone back into its charger. Made another cup of coffee. Drank it. Shook the phone, stared at the message again. Left another voice mail:

Call me, Jess—I'm really worried now!

Then she wished she hadn't. Another ten minutes passed with no response from her sister. This was ridiculous. She couldn't spend all day waiting for the phone to charge and Jess to call; she had a life to live, even if that did mean such mundanities as dealing with laundry and grocery shopping.

It was a Friday and approaching eleven by the time she'd walked up to the Calle Charca to drop her laundry off with Rosita, a cheerful, tubby Spanish woman whose husband made the deliveries to the bodega and who washed three times a week for those with no machines, like Kate. Picking up fresh laundry a day later was one of Kate's pleasures. Nothing smelled as nice as sheets that had been dried in the Albayzín sun: it seemed to imbue them with a whiff of the incense of ages past, with bitter oranges and a little spiced brandy. Then it was on to the little supermarket on the Calle Panaderos and the market in the square for beautifully organic fruit and veg. And still Jess hadn't rung!

As Kate was making her way back home with her groceries, she thought she heard the muezzin at the mosque, the Mezquita Mayor, just a few streets away, starting to call the Muslim faithful to prayer. She strained her ears toward the fragile sound, but a truck came rattling along the narrow street, making her flatten herself against the rough wall, and by the time its roar had passed, the muezzin had fallen silent. The mosque had been constructed less than twenty years ago, the city finally bowing to the pressure to provide its significant North African population with somewhere to worship other than out of sight in garages and private houses. Catholic Spain might have expelled its Moors at the end of the fifteenth century, but it seemed they had been allowed to return more than half a millennium later, and be woven back into the rich warp and weft of the country they had done so much to civilize. Even if they hadn't been permitted to give the muezzin a loudspeaker.

She dropped into the Internet café to send Jess an email. Hicham, not Saïd, was on duty, and he did not meet her eyes when she greeted him, or hold his hand out for the money, but instead waited for her to put the coins down on the counter, as if her touch might contaminate him. The place was usually stuffed with young men, but when Saïd was here, she never felt uncomfortable coming in on her own. The way Hicham treated her, though, made her clumsy. Trying to fiddle her change back into her bag, she dislodged a slip of paper, which spun across the melamine countertop toward him. Hicham stopped its progress with a stab of his finger.

"Sorry," she said automatically. Then added, "*Perdón.*" She reached out to take it back, but he put his hand flat over it. His black eyes challenged her.

"Why you have this?"

"What?"

He repeated the question. Flummoxed, she shrugged. "Sorry, it's just a bit of rubbish. I should have put it in a bin. But there's never one around when you need one, is there?" She laughed awkwardly. Had she unleashed some sort of obscure insult: dropping a bit of waste paper in front of a Muslim man? She had no idea.

"If it just rubbish, why you want it back?"

There was no answer to this. She watched Hicham pick up the paper to scrutinize it. Then she realized what it was. The scrap of paper that she'd winkled out of the wall in the palace gardens yesterday. "Oh. Please, I do want that back."

Hicham's lip curled. "I don't think so. It not yours."

For a brief, embarrassing moment Kate thought she might burst into tears. What on earth was the matter with her? When had she become so pathetic? He was only a local café worker playing a game with her. A rather nasty, dour little game, exercising a bit of power over a woman: she should recognize that sort of thing by now. And really, did it matter so much? All this fuss over a scrap of rubbish. She rallied herself. "Keep it, then."

For a moment he looked confused. Then he shoved the paper back across the counter at her. "You don't trick me like that." He turned and made for the back room, his mobile phone already to his ear.

She slid the scrap back into her bag. Hicham had truly rattled her; how dare he be so rude? Saïd was always so nice, so easy to talk to, even a bit flirty. He had a Spanish girlfriend, though, a handsome woman called Pilar, who worked at a museum. At least, she thought Pilar was his girlfriend. Did men from his culture even have girlfriends, or were they expected to marry to have a relationship? Really, what she knew about Muslim men—indeed, any sort of men—she could fit on the back of that sweet wrapper, or whatever it was.

She found an unoccupied monitor along the back wall between a group of giggling teenagers and a quiet young man who swiftly angled his body to shield the screen of his monitor from her. As if she cared that he was looking at pornography at midday on a Friday. Except . . . it seemed she did care. Unwelcome images swam up from the depths of her memory, cutting through dark waters with sharp fins.

No. She would not think about any of that. She would not. She must find out why Jess had left her a message in the middle of the night, see if the promised email had arrived yet.

She logged into her anonymous email account, but there was nothing from Jess. A couple of bits of spam from addresses she didn't recognize. Not opening those. Sighing, she clicked out of her emails and onto a news site, her mind whirling. A terrorist bombing in North Africa. The breaking of a ceasefire in the Middle East. Drone strikes, drowned migrants, a volcano erupting in South America. Death and disaster all around.

Why hadn't Jess returned her call? Perhaps it was the signal at Sarah's. The area was pretty remote: on the north coast of Cornwall, at the tail end of a narrow valley leading down to the sea. Amid the ramsons and nettles on the overgrown path were standing stones of mossy granite covered with ancient carved spirals. Kate and Jess had helped Sarah to move in. Getting the fridge down that track had been a nightmare. In fact, the whole experience had rather freaked her out. She found the place eerie, the only consolation for that being that she had spotted the glowing lights of fireflies darting between the trees on that first night, and on the heathland at the top of the cliff she had climbed, desperate for some sunlight, had come across a *Dactylorhiza maculata*, a heath spotted orchid, its whorls of lilac and white as intricate as a printed paisley pattern.

But something was definitely up with Jess. What had made her sister drive all that way without warning? Kate thought of Luke bundled in a blanket in the passenger seat of the ailing Fiat as Jess drove fiercely through the night, all the way to Cornwall, which was pretty much the end of the world.

Kate felt her stomach clench with anxiety.

She went back to her emails, checked her phone again. Still nothing. She was about to click out of her session, when she realized one of the spam emails might not be what she'd thought.

remaker@google.co.uk

Suddenly she remembered that was the name Sarah used for her refurbishing business. She clicked on the email. It took an age to load, and when it did, the message was in code.

Kate felt a frisson of terror tinged with excitement. Terror, that Jess had felt the need to obscure her message. Excitement, that there was a puzzle to be solved.

She burrowed in her bag for a pen and something to write on. There was only the scrap of paper that had come out of the wall. She couldn't write on that. The symbols taunted her: the inverted triangles and dotted circles, the stick figures and sideways *E*'s. One symbol looked like a trestle table, another like a wide-armed *Y*. It was clearly as much of a language as the code she and Jess had devised. And it might be old, and important. No, she couldn't use the scrap of paper for her workings. Yesterday's newspaper lay on the floor. She picked it up. On the sports pages was a huge photo of Cristiano Ronaldo. The wide, blank planes of his face offered plenty of room for the code working. After all, the message was not, she was disappointed to see, a long one.

$G3.E2D4.D5A3B4 \ldots$

Kate couldn't help but smile. It was an easy code—with a twist. She didn't even have to draw the grid: she could picture it quite easily.

HE FO—

By the time Kate had reached the fifth letter her heart was thudding. No. It couldn't be. He couldn't— She felt coffee begin to come back up her throat, had to swallow it with a choking gulp that caught even the attention of the teenagers, who turned dark-eyed stares upon her. For a moment she felt light-headed. She gritted her teeth, fought for control.

When she opened her eyes, she found one of the boys peering at her. Had she chanted aloud? He would think she was a madwoman. Or a penitent, praying. Or a witch, making an incantation. He said something and they all turned to look at her, leering. Then suddenly they were off out the door, shouting and laughing.

Kate was shaking. She took a deep breath to steady herself and went back to the coded message, praying she had made a mistake.

She had not.

HE FOUND US, KATE.

3

Blessings

GRANADA
1476, OR IN THE HEGIRA SHA'BAN 891

He stroked the tiled skin of the palace wall, and I wished suddenly, fervently, it were my skin he touched with such tenderness.

"Look, Blessings," he said again. "Really look. What do you see?"

I was bored now. "Patterns," I said, deliberately obtuse. "Just patterns."

Prince Abu Abdullah Mohammed, heir to the throne of Granada, known to me as Momo, sighed. Sometimes he was so patient it made me want to break things. "Spiderwebs—can't you see them? Hundreds of spiderwebs, thousands of them."

They didn't look much like spiderwebs to me, who had seen real ones stretched between cactuses in the desert, their fragile filaments barely catching the light. These webs were green, and gold, and red, and white. I supposed the craftsmen had used their imagination and jewelled them up. Sultans didn't want their palaces adorned with real webs: they employed a battalion of slaves to get rid of all such traces of reality.

"They represent the webs the spiders made to protect the Prophet when he was fleeing his enemies on the road to Medina," Momo went on.

He liked to educate me in such matters, since he regarded me as a heathen, a wild little savage. Both were pet names for me and I had allowed them to define me.

"The Prophet, peace be upon him, hid in a cave in the mountains and the spiders worked furiously to spin their webs across the entrance. When the murderers came upon the cave in which he hid, the webs were so thick they passed by, convinced no one could have been there in years."

I yawned. I had heard the story before. "Can't we go outside?" I whined.

"In a minute. The men who made this *zellij* were the finest craftsmen in the world. Imagine the care and patience it must take to cut each piece so precisely." His finger traced the design of the intricately pieced together tiling. There was such awe in his voice. It might seem mad to be jealous of a wall, but I was.

When they brought me to the Alhambra, it seemed so massive I was scared of it. The ceilings, so high, so heavy with detail in carved and coffered wood; or worse, the lacy plasterwork, cascading like frozen water or giant honeycombs. It all simply terrified me. I was so sure they would fall on me in the night that I could not sleep and would creep out into one of the courtyards and curl up in a niche there. Before I came here, I had only ever slept under a low camel-hide tent or a canopy of stars. It took me months to get used to being indoors. If it hadn't been for Momo, I would long since have run away.

He clasped my hand and led me into the next room. "How's your Arabic coming along? Can you read this inscription yet?" he persisted. The stylized calligraphy ran in a frieze across the fretted plasterwork. I sighed. It would be about God. It was always about God, and in Classical Arabic, which had no connection to my language. Reluctantly, I raised my eyes. The thought of sunshine and oranges, of fountains and wet skin, was calling to me. Working from right to left, I gabbled it off by memory:

> *I am a garden adorned by beauty:*
> *I will know whether you look at my beauty*
> *O, Mohammed, my king, I try to be equal to*
> *the finest thing that has existed or will ever exist.*

A more personal connection with these words suddenly struck me, and I found myself blushing. But Momo did not notice. His intense amber gaze had gone distant.

"A king. One day I will be sultan. I will sit on the throne of Granada and dispense my kingdom's laws and defend its people." His voice was dreamy. He blinked and looked back at me. "What do you think about that?"

I made a face. "Sounds boring. Who in his right mind would want to be a king?" I grabbed him by the hand and dragged him outside into the light of day.

The heat had channelled itself into the palace's hidden courtyards and secluded gardens, driving everyone into the cool interior. On days like this, when our teachers drowsed, Momo and I could escape their strict regime.

We spent an hour splashing each other with water from the fountains, trying not to shriek or laugh too loudly. We walked only on the blue tiles so none of the djinn could catch us, with Momo's little brother, Rachid, getting in our way. To avoid having to play with him, for he was a nuisance, we ran faster than he could, through the speckled shade of the vine-covered path over the ravine to the Hill of the Sun, where the gardens were more overgrown and chaotic. Rachid's wails followed us like the cries of a bird, until they were lost in the hazy air.

These were the gardens where fruit and vegetables for the palace were grown among a riot of lilac and lavender, white poppy and blue stock. When the pea pods were ripe, we would steal armfuls while the gardeners' backs were turned, popping the cases and gorging ourselves on the sweet contents. There might be grapes or pears to be filched; apples espaliered along one terracotta wall, apricots along another. Peach trees and pomegranate trees heavy with fruit.

As we made a careful detour to avoid a pair of gardeners, we heard high-pitched mews coming from the herb beds. Among the parsley and lavender a female tabby lay on her side. Seven forms squirmed against her belly. As we parted the stems, the tabby regarded us with slitted golden eyes but did not seem alarmed. Momo, entranced, dropped to his knees.

We had no cats in the desert, but the palace ran with them. I did not know what to make of these semi-tame creatures that took food from the hand and slipped away, but I admired their dignity and that no one thought less of them, or tried to punish them, for the coolness of their nature.

One kitten squirmed with its eyes shut, calling feebly. The way it just lay there, complaining about its plight rather than trying to do something about it, sent a sudden flare of anger through me. It was just like Rachid: so annoying. But Momo scooped it up, his thumb running tenderly over its trembling body. "Poor little thing." He pushed its nose toward a teat, then sat back on his heels, waiting for it to latch on. I stood up, impatient, but Momo stayed kneeling, his head on one side, his expression tender. Then, as if aware of my eyes on him, he shot a look at me, an anxious glance as if I might tease him for being so soft. That glance—both vulnerable and bold—pierced me through. Then, with a change of heart, he sprang to his feet and tagged me on the arm. "Race you to the orangery!" He sprinted away, as fleet as a gazelle.

Usually, I would dash after him, but something seemed to have come adrift in me. Where he had touched me, it felt as if my skin had burned away. For a moment I felt dizzy; as though my soul had been expelled from my body, made naked to the world. It took immense effort to summon it back again, to push away the weakness and run after him.

Later, we sat under the fruit trees with our booty. Too hot after all the running, I had removed my tunic and was wearing only wide-legged cotton pants, thinking nothing of it. But when Momo followed suit, my heart skipped like a stone set skimming over a pool. I applied myself to the oranges. Puffs of fragrant zest scintillated in the sunlit air as we broke into the stolen fruit. I felt the little explosions cool against my hands. We ate like children: to excess, though I had no clear idea of my own age—there had been no one left to tell me. Momo was thirteen and said I must be younger because I was smaller.

As I bent over to hug my knees, Momo poked my chest, not gently. "You're getting fat."

"I am not." I was indignant. "It's just the way I'm sitting. Look." I unfolded my legs and lay down, the earth scratchy beneath my back. "See?" Stretched out, I was as flat as the page of a book.

Momo lined himself beside me, hip to hip, and for a moment I felt we might clang together: he was a magnet and I a fragment of metal caught in the thrall of his attraction. But we did not touch: he just looked from my torso to his own and back again. "My skin is much lighter than yours," he said with quiet satisfaction. "Mother says that's a mark of pure blood."

"Where I come from people are darker. It's because of the sun."

"It's because you're Sanhaji."

It sounded like an insult. "I am not."

"Banu Warith." He grinned.

Banu was a tribal designation. Momo's tribe was the Banu Ahmar, the Red Ones, but our tribes prefixed their names with *Kel*. Kel Tamasheq—Those Who Speak Tamasheq. Kel Ahhagar—the People of the Hoggar. Kel Adrar—Those from the Mountains. I had no idea what the Warith was, but it sounded bad. I frowned and he laughed.

"See, you are fierce. Banu Warith, without a doubt."

That pleased me. I was fierce. I felt fierce, like a lion, a small brown mountain lion reduced to muscle and sinew and appetite by hard desert living. Except that he thought I was getting fat. It was true that I ate like an animal; everyone said so. I was perpetually ravenous. Perhaps you never get over famine.

I paused, thinking it over. "Well, I might be Banu Warith," I conceded at last, wanting to please him. "I don't know."

"Isn't it strange not knowing your lineage?"

I had been born after my father died. To never have met your father was regarded as bad luck. It was one of the reasons I'd had to leave.

"Not really. I like it. I can be what I want."

He frowned at this, his beautiful face troubled, and I saw how his downcast lashes spread upon his cheek, how the line of his straight nose pointed like an arrow to the ground, how his lips pressed together as he concentrated. I loved that I could say things that made him think this hard; I, a fatherless nomad child; he, the son of a king.

"You are lucky to have such freedom," he said, suddenly sombre. "I am bound by duty."

As if on cue, the call to prayer trembled through the hot air. Momo pushed himself to his feet and the spell was broken. "Are you coming?" he asked, his voice muffled as he struggled back into his tunic.

I shook my head. "I'm going to see the sick kitten again." It was the best temptation I could offer. He wavered for a moment, then headed back along our earlier path, feet dragging with reluctance. When he was out of sight, I lay there, considering this feeling of my heart being pulled on a wire behind him, but within moments I fell asleep.

By the time I awoke the sky had gone pale lavender and I was cold. It was late, and I scrambled up, uneasy. Something, somewhere, felt wrong.

Because I knew he would ask me, I went back to look at the runt kitten. The mother cat lay in the last patch of sun, her tabby fur a mystery of light and shade. She blinked at me and then rolled away, making a barrier of her back, leaving one kitten—the runt— exposed. As I looked at it, a fly buzzed lazily out of its open mouth, startlingly blue-black against the pink flesh. It was dead.

I'd seen enough dead things in the world not to be shocked by one more. But somehow the sight of it, abandoned and rejected, opened a wound I had not been aware of, and my eyes filled with tears. Tears I would never show or shed. I [picked up the little body and ran with it back through the gardens toward the palace. Momo would want to bury it, with full ceremony, before the last light went out of the sky. But as if the warmth of my hands awoke some deep spark inside it, the kitten twitched and gave a wheezy cough. I was so surprised I almost dropped it.

I looked back. I should return it to its mother, except servants were converging on the herb garden, walking the tiled paths with baskets over their arms. That decided it. We could take care of it. The kitten would be our secret, mine and Momo's. I would make a gift of it to him, an offering of love.

But as I made my way through the corridors to the private quarters of the palace, something in the quality of the air changed. I was excited about bringing Momo the kitten, worried about how I was going to smuggle it into our apartments, yet it was not just that. Those were minor concerns, thoughts like delicate clouds drifting across the sun: this was the quiet before a thunderstorm, the time when all the birds go silent. In my hands the runt curled tighter, sensing danger.

I slipped into the palace by a door where the guards knew me well enough not to go through too many annoying formalities, then ran through the labyrinth of arched and decorated passages that brought me at last, panting, out into the pillared arcade surrounding the Court of Lions, which lay at the heart of the palaces. Aromatic shrubs had been planted in profusion here around a great lion-ringed fountain: jasmine and rose and myrtle all gave up their scents to the heat-heavy air. Around the courtyard the great wooden doors to the royal apartments had been thrown open to allow the passage of this water-cooled, perfumed air. I was about to run out onto the path between the plants, when I heard raised voices: a man and a woman locked in a battle of words. It could only be the sultan and his wife. Something inside me clenched, sorry for my friend. The furious arguments of Momo's parents drove him to melancholy.

I supposed this was what happened when people were pushed together without love or choice. Where I came from, women led the men they chose to partner with to their tents and laughed with them through the night. There was no secret about what went on. But they had no kingdoms or walls to defend, nothing but the shifting sands and the salt roads that ran through them. Sometimes there was jealousy and anger, then jeering till there was good humour again. But this was the sultan—Moulay Hasan—and his wife Aysha, and no one could jeer at them, or tell them to behave, or say that if they were going to row, it was best not to do it in public, or in front of children.

In the shadows of the slender pillars, I decided to wait their argument out. But they raged on, their voices audible even over the tumbling of the water from the seventh of the spouting lions that ringed the central fountain.

I hazarded a look. The sultana's neck was thrust out, her veil had fallen off and her hair had sprung loose: I saw her square jaw and those fiery black eyes beneath a single dark eyebrow. Court poets skirted flower images when they wrote songs for her; instead, they spoke of eagles and hunting cats. She was older than the sultan, the widow of a previous king, and claimed descent from the Prophet, thus thought herself better bred than her current husband.

Moulay Hasan stormed away from her toward me and I fiercely wished myself invisible. When I summoned the courage to glance around, I found him standing not five yards off, with the setting sun catching the jewels in his turban. For a moment he seemed almost magnificent: but in reality he was as wiry and twisted as the root of an olive tree, as if he had been left out in the sun and reduced to his most unpleasant essence. How these two could have produced a son like Momo I had no idea.

The sultana was shrieking something about a foreign woman and he shouted back. Bad words, designed to wound: her age, her lack of beauty.

I was not alone in witnessing this shameful scene. Up in the women's quarters there were flickers of movement behind the fretted windows. On the other side of the court I spied the sultan's chief minister, the vizier Qasim Abdelmalik, his turban like a gigantic onion. And Momo, ghosting between the pillars in his white mosque-robe.

The sultan must have said something truly insulting then, for Aysha launched herself at him. He caught her hand just before her nails touched his face, and closed his fist hard over her fingers. The sultana bared her teeth, then spat at him. He let go, shocked; then raised his fist. It connected—not with his wife but with a pale shape that had flown between them. The shape spun across the courtyard and slammed with terrible force into the stone lions around the fountain.

There was a moment of silence and then women were screaming, men shouting. Even before the thought was fully formed I was running. As I fell to my knees at Momo's side, by accident I dropped the kitten in the fountain and tried to turn Momo over, but he was like stone. All around me moved bare feet, sandals, robes, embroidered slippers, marking out the steps of a dance I couldn't understand. Someone caught me under the arms and pulled me away, and some of the noise went with me and I realized that I was screaming too.

"Being of royal blood does not improve people's behaviour," the vizier, Qasim, observed quietly as Momo was carried inside, his hanging arm as limp as a corpse's.

I twisted in his grip. "Is he dead?" I managed to choke out.

"Let us hope not. A dead heir would give us all a headache."

He drew me across the courtyard with him. Slaves with cloths were already scrubbing the patio stones. One picked the sodden kitten out of the fountain and stared at it. "A rat," he said, holding it away from him. They put it in a bucket and took it away.

The muzzle of the midnight fountain lion was red, as if it had savaged its prey. I could not stop looking at it. I bent and touched the blood, and suddenly everything in the world seemed red. "If he dies, my world is ended." My voice hardly sounded like my own as the prophecy passed over my lips. "But if he lives, he will lose everything he loves."

4

No one could have kept me away from him. I was a twist of shadow, a nighttime breeze. Like a change in the air I slipped into the alcove where he had been laid out and hunkered down in a corner, making myself small. No one noticed me. There was much coming and going of servants and doctors, so it seemed he lived still. I comforted myself with the barely perceptible draw of his breath, the smallest movement of his covers.

When at last everyone went away, I wormed myself into the space between his divan and the wall and stared at him, trying to remember how he had looked, shirtless, in the dappled shade beneath the fruit trees—golden and robust and full of quiet mischief, as if by thinking it hard enough I could restore him.

The sight of him lying there, his head swathed in a bandage as big as the vizier's turban, his skin as pale as the cotton, filled me with a sort of frustrated, helpless rage. I wanted to shake him, to shout at him, to make him wake up. Then his breath caught and seemed to stop and the rage left me. Suddenly I was praying, in a way I had never prayed before, not for my mother, not even for myself. *Let him live, just let him live.* It was all I asked, just that he survive. Not that he would love me or that we would be together always but just that he would live.

Let him live and you can take anything from me that you wish. My arms, my legs, my eyes. Even my life.

I did not even know to whom this fervent plea was addressed. I had no real belief in a god or gods. It had been made clear to me that if there was such a higher being, he had no interest for the welfare of children.

Just before dawn someone entered the room. I thought, in the moment before I hid myself, that it was the sultan. But when he spoke, I knew it was not.

"So. There you lie. Heir to the throne that should be mine. Look at you, so feeble and girlish. What sort of warrior will you ever be? How will such a worm defend us from the unbelievers? I heard them read the auguries at your birth: they foretold you would lose our kingdom, even though your mother had the astrologers killed before word got out. We are the last bastion of Islam against these *kafir*, who would see us all killed or driven into the sea. We cannot fail. We cannot!"

I lay listening there in terror. It was Momo's uncle, Muhamed al-Zaghal. If the sultan was an olive root, his brother was iron.

"It would be best for all of us if you were to die right now. I should have the guts to destroy you myself. Put a cushion over your mouth and finish the task my brother started. And he is no better, sniffing after Christian women like a dog. I am the only one fit to lead our people against the unbelievers. I should do it. Take the necessary action."

What could I do? I had no weapon and Momo's uncle was the fiercest warrior in all Granada. I should launch myself at him, screaming, sacrifice myself for my friend. After all, I had just promised that very thing. My muscles trembled with intent, but when I stuck my head up, it was to see the sultana sweeping into the chamber, Dr. Ibrahim in her wake. She stopped when she saw her husband's brother, and I ducked back down.

"What are you doing in here?" She had no fear of anyone, that woman.

Al-Zaghal looked as guilty as a jackal in the sheep pen. "I came to see how the boy was."

"That's more than his father has done," the sultana said grudgingly.

I heard shuffling, the movement of fabric. Then the doctor said, "His breathing is easier and his heart is beating more strongly. I think he will live."

Al-Zaghal muttered his excuses and slipped away. Dr. Ibrahim and the sultana stayed awhile, talking quietly. Then I heard the sultana dismiss him and the scrape of wood on tile as she pulled a stool closer to the bed.

"My son, all my hope resides in you. All the hope of the kingdom rests on your shoulders. You must come back to us!"

All this talk of kingdom, I thought. *But none of love.*

Momo did not stir. Soon she was striding around the room again. "And Hasan, what is he thinking, bringing that bitch-whore into my palace?" The stool, kicked hard, skittered across the floor. "How he disrespects me. Me! A woman of the Prophet's line. He married me only so he could grab the throne. If there were any justice in the world, I would rule here. They say the Castilian queen holds the reins of power, this Isabella. So why not me? I cannot even rule my own palace! I will not have that woman under my roof. An unbeliever, a *kafir*. How dare he? If I were a man . . ."

If Aysha were a man, I thought, *the whole world would cower in terror.* She frightened me even more than al-Zaghal. I had once seen her backhand an unfortunate slave who had been clumsy with the hot sugar paste used to remove her mistress's moustache. The slave had cracked her skull. I never saw the girl again, and no one even spoke her name.

The clicking stopped. Into the silence dropped a long, deep sigh.

I held my breath till I thought I might burst. Then her footsteps recommenced, at last dwindling as she left the room. Even so, I did not move. If she caught me, she would be furious at what I had overheard. Her bitter anger, her sharp jealousy.

I did not understand then how jealousy can poison a heart.

Finally I felt safe enough to crawl from my hiding place and lie beside Momo. His chest rose and fell, rose and fell: it seemed my wish had been granted. But we are never happy with our bargains, are we? For now, I did not just want him to be alive but to open his eyes and speak to me, to embrace me as his dearest friend.

I propped myself up on one elbow and looked down at him. Beneath the bandage his face was so beautiful I felt a tightness in my chest. This was perhaps the only time I would have the chance to do what I knew I had to do. Only I would know. It would be a secret that I hugged to myself in the darkness, that would give me hope when there was none left in the world.

I bent my head and kissed him on the lips.

His eyelids fluttered, then flew open, and I saw myself reflected in the widening dark pools of his pupils—small, thin, anxious, all nose and eyes, like a scared bird.

"What are you doing?" he croaked.

"Nothing." The age-old denial of children everywhere caught in the act of trespass.

"Blessings," he said, and smiled.

I had never been so happy.

Momo's miraculous return to consciousness was soon blared about the palace. Doves were gathered and released, trumpets sounded, drums beaten: it was a great to-do. But something had gone out of him—whether from the blow itself or the circumstances of the injury; or that his father never showed the least regret over it. Not that he remembered anything about what happened: he made me tell him all I had heard and seen. He latched on to the mention of the Christian woman who had made his mother so furious. It was, perhaps, easier to focus his woes on a stranger than to look closer to home. He became obsessed with her. And maybe he was right to be.

"This captive is a new player on the board," Qasim said thoughtfully when I went to make my weekly report to him. "And she could be dangerous."

"To Momo?" I stared at him.

"Maybe, in time, to all of us. Or maybe she's not important at all. Perhaps . . ." His black eyes regarded me beneath their heavy lids. "Perhaps you might go into the women's quarters and tell me what you hear, what you see, what she says."

"Me? How can I enter the women's quarters?" It was forbidden for anyone except the sultan himself to enter there.

"A bit of kohl, some earrings, the right outfit: you'll make a lovely girl."

Momo watched me as I drew a long line along the base of my eyelid, extending it to a wing beyond the outer corner.

"How do you keep such a steady hand?"

In all honesty, I did not know: his proximity was distracting.

"You've done this before!" he accused.

I had. But that was a tale for another time.

"You will tell me everything, won't you? I can't bear to see Mama so unhappy."

And so, I was to be paid twice over for my single task: once in coin by the vizier and once in gratitude of my friend, which seemed a good bargain to me at the time. Clothes from the washing line, one of the sultana's head scarves and some earrings I had kept of my mother's, and the transformation was complete. Momo tilted his head to consider me, then laughed long and hard and led me out to one of the still pools in the courtyard, where I stared at myself in wonder. A girl. I was a girl.

The courtesans' quarters lay directly above the main living area of the royal harem, just a few corridors and some stairs from where we ran and played. But despite the easy entry past the guard, it might as well have been a world away.

I thought the women's quarters would be quiet and dull, full of quiet, dull young women. I thought to slip among them, watching and listening, committing to memory a swaying walk or a fat waddle: embellishments to my spying mission that would entertain Momo when I returned. I was so stupid.

There were some very ancient women here, bent backed and white eyed, their faces as wrinkled as old fruit, their hands and nails orange with henna. Some had lines tattooed on chins and foreheads or to the side of their noses. And all wore kohl, just the way the women from my tribe did, to protect them from the spirits and the evil eye.

Their eyes were watching me now. I had not realized then how every change and arrival in the harem is immediately examined for messages about the state of the outside world, in the way our trackers interrogate the landscape through which they move for signs of wild beasts, quicksand and water.

"What is she thinking of, coming in here with no henna?" one of the old ones said.

"She will bring the djinn in with her."

They made signs against that.

"She must have come with the *zahira*."

I knew that word: it meant "witch."

They made signs against that too.

"Who do you serve?" one of them asked me.

"Why, God, of course."

They laughed, but indulgently. "No, dear, who is your mistress?"

"The sultana, Aysha the Pious," I said promptly.

"Then why are you here and not in her apartments?" The sultana had separate quarters in an exquisite pavilion whose windows overlooked the gardens and the city beyond.

I bent in conspiratorially. "She sent me to take a look at the new arrival."

"She is not here, the infidel." An old woman spat, expelling an olive seed with such force that it rebounded against the wall. "The sultana, peace be upon her, decreed she be placed in her own quarters adjoining the baths rather than in here, polluting our air."

A slave girl carrying linen said, "Come with me."

She wove a convoluted path down winding corridors, narrow stairs and through sunlit courtyards. I had not realized how much of the Alhambra had been hidden from me. All the courtyards were enclosed: I did not once glimpse the wider gardens or even the pavilions of the main palace, though they could not be far away. It was such a labyrinth I began to wonder if I would be able to find my way back.

At last she stopped at a doorway to a *hammam* I had not seen before. "In there," she said softly, and gave me the linen.

Inside, it was hot and steamy. There was so much perfume in the air that I sneezed, which cleared enough of an eddy in the vapour for me to make out a figure in a marble tub. If this was the Christian witch, it seemed to me that a lot of fuss had been made about nothing. Where I came from the women were strong, with black hair and eyes like the night, their sun-baked skin as brown as bark and about as tough. This one was as pale as a wraith. I almost walked away then, to report back to Qasim with a sneer.

I wish I had.

For when Isobel de Solis rose from her bath, every impression of weakness vanished like the coiling vapours from which she emerged. She stood with her shoulders back and her chin high, making no attempt to hide any part of herself.

I had never seen a woman naked before, bathing opportunities being limited in the desert, and never having acquired this peculiar habit of stripping and steaming and scrubbing, I never used the royal *hammam* but instead confined my efforts at cleanliness to dabbing dubiously at myself out of view of everyone, with a cloth dipped in wash water. Which merely added to Momo's view of me as a little heathen. So I regarded her with curiosity, even though I had no appreciation for the aspects of her that appeared to have driven the sultan wild. To me, breasts were appendages like camels' humps for storing sustenance—and hers seemed unimpressive. The rest of her was slender and girlish. But then her eyes came to rest on me. They were the green of a flame that changes its hue when a charlatan throws mineral powder into the fire.

She clicked her fingers and spoke in a foreign tongue. One of the women scuttled like a big black beetle to stare at me. "Lady say you her slave now," she rasped in horrible Arabic.

"What?" I laughed nervously. "I'm not her slave."

"She choose you."

"She can't choose me. I'm the sultana's servant."

"You belong Lady Isobel." The old woman dug her fingers into the meat of my arm. I caught a whiff of her, bitterness distilled. *Sheeba*, grown in the kitchen garden to ward off parasites. Who would wear wormwood as a perfume?

"What your name?" she demanded.

"Jihad," I told her defiantly. *Struggle.*

She gave me a hard stare, then conveyed my insolence to Isobel. I saw a frown pleat a deep line in the perfect brow and thought: *She is really quite old. Nineteen, at least.* Then she responded to the crone with a stream of harsh-sounding words.

"The lady will call you Gatita," the crone said. "'Little cat.'"

A drowned kitten's corpse being carried away in a bucket. I shivered.

"And I am La Sabia—the Wise One. I earn my name. Do not forget."

"I earned mine too," I said, hardening my muscles against her fingers. "It's a Muslim name and you are in a Muslim kingdom, so maybe you should get used to that."

Her expression did not change by so much as a flicker, but abruptly I was lying on the wet tiles and blood was singing in my ears. I was just getting used to the unlikely idea that the old woman had put me there, when she kicked me in the stomach. Even though she wore nothing more substantial than a soft leather slipper, the blow doubled me up like a dying wasp.

Her voice seemed to come from a long way away. "*¡Pequeño demonio!*"

In my two years at the palace I had been treated with if not kindness, then something that to my love-starved self seemed close to it. No one here had ever hit me, not even the vizier. No one except the gardeners had even shouted at me. I lay there, stunned.

La Sabia took my lack of movement as further insubordination. "Get up!" When I did not immediately leap to my feet, she gave me another kick in the small of the back.

This time injustice and pain drove me upright and I flung myself at her, biting, and thrashing my arms: a desert dervish of hate and panic. Someone pulled me off her at last—but only after I had her down on the floor and had ripped a hole in her dress with feral teeth, trying to get at her flesh. Isobel de Solis sat back on the edge of the marble bath with her fists held to her mouth. "*¡Bravo, bravo!*

¡Vamos; Gatita." And when the old woman struggled to her feet with murder in her eyes, she laughed even more.

I was hustled away into a cell-like room and locked in with nothing but an enormous brown cockroach that scuttled out of the pallet, the only other thing in the room.

On the first day, I sat there devising ways to kill them all, including the cockroach. By the second day, I was weeping with hunger, convinced they would starve me to death and bury my body in the kitchen gardens to nourish the quince trees. By the third day, I was talking to the cockroach.

The door opened, and light streamed in around a silhouetted figure. For a moment I thought it was Momo and he had come to save me. Then it spoke. "So, Gatita, you lie. The sultana has no slave called Jihad. *¡Qué extraño!*"

My hope fell away like a stone down a well. I had been abandoned. I sat very still and small, trying to show nothing of myself to her.

She took my inaction for submission. "Aha, no more tooths, *diablita*. Maybe you learn. Come!" She took me by the arm. "You teach lady Muslim court manners. Ha!" She spat to one side. "As if savage understand such things. But lady like you and she determined, want speak good to sultan when he return."

My ears pricked up. "The sultan is away?"

"No concern of you." The fingers pinched tighter. "Hurry."

"You can't treat me like this. I am the prince's friend—"

She laughed. "Prince no here. Sultan and brother take him away, learn fight, be a man, not mother-boy."

Cold dread washed over me as I recalled al-Zaghal's threats when Momo lay unconscious. It would be so easy for my friend to have an accident: to fall from a horse, to slip during sword training, for a blunt practice-blade to be replaced by a honed weapon. Or poison: silent and unseen, easily administered by the enemy's servants . . .

And if Momo died, what would happen to me? My entire existence was defined by my relationship to him. I was a royal companion, a slave purchased precisely for the purpose of providing the young emir with a friend. I shadowed him, took lessons with him, was treated like a little lord, living a life of such luxury neither I nor any member of my tribe could even have conceived of it. But without him I was nothing, just a bit of human rubbish that could be thrown away, tossed back into the filthy, dangerous streets from which I'd come.

As soon as I was able, I stole a scrap of paper and fashioned a pen from a pigeon's feather, dug the sharp end in my wrist and used the blood as ink. On it I wrote four lines of text. When the blood was dry, I scattered salt grains on the paper to keep the djinn away from it. Then I spat on it and hid it in a wall outside, moving aside the creeping carpet of the protective Mother of Thousands plant. Now water, earth and air, all bound by the salt, would surely keep him safe.

5

It was one of those late-summer days when it felt as if the earth had soaked up a whole year's sunshine in a single day and was giving it back in stupefying bursts of heat. It was also Ramadan: most of the staff were asleep, eking out the long hours till sundown. I had been in captivity for six weeks and could now understand and speak passable Castilian, and still Qasim had not reclaimed me and Momo had not returned.

Bored with the way her mistress consistently mangled the Arabic language during our long lessons, La Sabia took herself off to find some refreshments, there being not a single slave around, a fact that had made her curse. As soon as the old woman was out of sight, the witch clutched my hand. "Now, Gatita, we can talk freely."

This sudden complicity shocked me: there had never been a chink of light between the two of them before. They had always appeared to me to be two aspects of the same being: Foreign Woman, turning the beautiful side of her face to me one moment and her withered side the next.

"Tell me quickly, Little Cat—how do I say to him 'Great One, your cock is so vast, how will I ever be able accommodate it'?"

I was lost for words.

She laughed: the throaty gurgle of a washerwoman. "Don't you understand?" The pressure on my hand increased. "Have you not experienced the pleasure of a man between your legs, Gatita?"

The words *But I am only twelve* trembled in my mouth. I said nothing. Some memories you bury deep. Some you dig up again uncontrollably to get a good whiff of their putrefaction. But no matter how long they have been buried or how often you exhume them they retain their power to poison your life.

Fez: a moonless night. My face pushed down into the stones at the river's edge in the dry season, the smell of goat dung and rotting vegetables. A hard hand on the back of my neck, the other under my robe.

"No," I said flatly now. This conversation I would not be reporting back, I decided.

She gave a disappointed pout. "Well, you can still help me with the words if I explain them. So, Great One . . . ?"

"*Malik*," I said without expression. We went through the rest as best I could manage. She repeated each phrase to me with perfect intonation.

My expression made her laugh. "Such an innocent! Did you really think I was too stupid to learn your language?"

It isn't my language, I thought but did not say. I wondered why she would use such deceit, then realized it had been to bore the old woman till she went away.

"Why do you think I am here?" she asked then.

"Because you were captured by the sultan."

"Wrong. It was his brother who took the town of Martos. It was al-Zaghal who captured me."

I waited for her to explain.

"Al-Zaghal has no interest in women, Gatita. I can tell you that much. I tried all I knew with him."

I closed my face to her, feeling trapped in that baking heat, hemmed in by dangerous words and memories. How I wished I might escape while La Sabia was away. The *zahira* was barefoot. Her embroidered slippers lay abandoned on the floor, the gold thread in their embroidery catching stray shafts of sunlight. I was sure I could outpace her. But I already knew the courtyard wall was unscalable: I had failed to climb it while they dozed one afternoon.

At last she stopped. "Why are you eyeing me like that? Did you think I was some silly girl who would faint at the sight of a naked Moor? You look as shocked as my father did when he found me with Alfonso."

And then she proceeded to tell me about the *caballero* who had come riding through her town on a fine bay horse; his long dark hair like a flag; his guards all in livery, to show he was a rich man. How her father had housed the men and stabled the horses, since he was the mayor of the town and had the largest house. How Alfonso had told her she was lovelier than the moon, that he wished he was a cloud so he might cover her at night; and then her father caught him doing just that. "I begged Alfonso to take me with him. But he was a coward. He pretended he had urgent business and rode out. And that's how I ended up here."

"Your father sold you to al-Zaghal?"

"No." She tutted. "He tried to sell me to God. To send me to a nunnery, but I refused to go."

"Nunnery?"

She placed her hands together as if praying and made a pious face. I had seen captured slaves in the square with their hands pressed together like that as they called on their god to save them.

"My father refused to ransom me back from al-Zaghal because I had defied him." She laughed bitterly. "Nun or whore, what a choice! Still, I'd rather spend my life on my back than on my knees. The sultan will become my slave: mark what I say! Once I finally give myself to him, I will make him so crazed with desire that he will give me the world!"

I stared at her, taking this in. Perhaps, if he ever reclaimed me, this information would earn me a bonus from Qasim.

La Sabia returned with a tray of sweetmeats and a jug of citrus water. I could see the ice crystals floating in the liquid as she poured a tall glass for her mistress: snow gathered from the mountains of the Sierra Nevada and kept in the ice pit beneath the kitchens. I could imagine it cooling my throat. But I refused it all the same. "It's Ramadan," I reminded her. "You're not supposed to eat or drink till sundown." Another morsel to report.

Isobel shifted languorously onto one elbow so that her breasts fell together under the sheer silk of her tunic. She caught me peering and rearranged her contours subtly so that her upmost hip jutted in a sinuously seductive curve. She craved admiration wherever she could find it, each admiring glance another coin to add to the treasury of her self-worth, even the meagre tin dirham of a slave's gaze. But I would not give her even that small satisfaction. "The sultan is very strict about the observance of Ramadan," I said steadfastly. "Were he here, he would punish you for breaking the fast."

Isobel reached for the glass. "Well, he's not here, and when I get my hands on him, he won't care what day it is, or whether he's Muslim or Christian, Castilian or Moor. I shall make him forget Ferdinand and Isabella: he will think only of Isobel!"

Momo and I were running through the orchards at dawn, our bare feet wet with dew. The air raced past my shoulders and I was laughing, my mouth wide with happiness, as I bolted toward the quince tree beneath which we had hidden our treasures—some little soap-stone animals, a ball of polished marble, a flute we were not allowed to play inside the palace. I touched the tree first. I had won! I turned to crow, and in that moment he caught me around the waist, pulled me down and kissed me.

I lay there in a daze, my entire body suffused with a sweetness that made me want to cry. And that was when the muezzin's call came, breaking into my dream like a thief to steal it away.

I rolled over and reached for the memory of the clean planes of Momo's face, the long, fine nose. His limpid eyes, flecked with gold . . . Gone. All of it, gone. My brain hurt with the effort to remember, but he had been erased from my memory like marks on a wax tablet wiped smooth.

Desolate, I stared at the ceiling. There were seventy-seven cedarwood strakes up there. I had counted them. Every patch and dimple in the walls, every crack in the tiles on the floor, I knew them all. And now their dull detail had replaced Momo. I cursed my existence. It was not only Momo I had lost. Some days when I awoke I no longer knew who I was. Some days I didn't care. When I thought about myself and my journey to this point, I felt my past had belonged to someone else. The routine and the boredom that went with it eroded my spirit, stole me from myself, made me as dull as a stone. By the end of the summer, one day ran into the next, indistinguishable from the last, one week from another. My horizons had lowered till I was looking only at the ground, shuffling my feet. Any belief I had in possibility, and escape, had slipped away. Looked at one day at a time, the change to my world seemed innocuous, unremarkable. And yet in the space of four months, I had become a completely different person.

In the desert, they say the big dunes are always in flux, the grains of sand that build them ever shifting with winds that lift a layer of dust one day and settle it the next, the dune moving its position by increments so tiny you would never notice it unless you left one day and did not return for the year—to find the entire series of sweeping scimitar dunes had crawled ten camel lengths from where it was.

And so, as I changed the incense in the brazier, my mind inured to the foreign chatter of my mistress and her evil old maid, I almost missed the reference to my beloved. But then it came again, the words *Prince Mohammed*. My heart lifted like a lark soaring into a clear blue sky. "The prince has returned?" I asked, suddenly alert.

"Nothing to do with you." La Sabia turned her back to me.

Isobel twisted her braid in her fingers, examining the smooth snake of hair for split ends. "How old is the prince?" she asked nonchalantly.

The old woman shrugged. "Who knows, or cares?"

I know, and I care. As La Sabia poured the herb tea with which Isobel always started her morning, I saw in the twining thread of golden liquid the column of his throat. Suddenly I could not stand still. I dropped a spoon on the tiles, where it fell with a resounding clatter. The old woman gave me the sort of shake a dog gives a rat. "Go and fetch a clean spoon, you fool!"

I didn't need to be told twice. My brain had come to life. I was Blessings, and I was going to escape!

I slipped out into the baking sun, to find area the behind the *hammam* deserted apart from a thin palace cat batting the body of a bright blue dragonfly from one paw to another. When it saw me, it abandoned the maimed insect and, leaping up the woodpile used for heating the water, disappeared up the wall and over the roofs.

I would do the same! I grabbed the handle of a big metal bucket by the door and set it down, inverted, on top of the woodpile. I pulled the hem of my robe up till I could hold it between my teeth, and clambered up onto the bucket, which at once rocked. *No,* I told it fiercely. *No!*

Concentrating on the wall above it, I grabbed at where a brick had crumbled loose, skittered my feet up almost to the same height and slapped for the brick edge. For a moment I hung there, feeling the inadequacy of my arm muscles after months in captivity in the *hammam*, my breath soughing out past the damp cotton in my mouth: then desperation drove me upward onto the top of the wall, and I was aware of the space yawning away below me.

I spread my hands on the roof tiles, trying to get my balance. They were round backed and slick. Feeling horribly exposed, I inched sideways toward the corner, my heart beating in my throat, set my foot in the mortared angle and reached up to the roof tiles to either side. Bringing my second foot up felt terrifyingly precarious. I executed three heart-stopping moves and had the top almost within grasp, when my slipper parted company with my foot. I made the mistake of looking down to watch it spinning toward a slave girl carrying a heap of linens.

Fighting the urge to vomit on her head, I caught the brass spike at the apex of the roof and swung myself over, pressed myself flat to the tiles on the other side. I risked a peek and saw the girl pick up the slipper and turn it over, as if the mystery of its wild flight might be read on its sole. She looked up. For a piercing second our eyes met and hers widened; then the spike gave way and I fell down the other side, the tiles ripping my robe and the skin of my legs. Then I was airborne.

In the desert, life is lived low to the ground. I had never even seen stairs until I got to Zagora, the first town I reached when I left the desert, and entered a rich merchant's house. The first sight of them made me cry. I could not conceive of how anyone could bear to sleep in an upstairs room. I crouched in the courtyard all night, waiting for the djinn to come and get me. Until then the greatest height I had ever experienced had been on camel back, with my *anet ma*, my maternal uncle. He had wedged me between him and the tall-cantle wooden seat the men use for long desert trips, high at the front and back so they can sleep in the saddle as their animal paces across the great emptiness. I had not much enjoyed the experience: the ground had seemed a long way off, the sky too close for comfort. And when I did inevitably fall off, the air had rushed past in just this way. But sand had provided a much kinder landing than now.

I felt the impact as if a mountain had fallen on me. My leading leg buckled and pain jolted from my ankle to the top of my head. Someone was shouting—several someones. I tried to pay attention to their words, but the pain came at me like a million burning ants setting fire to everything in their path. I opened my mouth to scream, but it was stuffed full of cotton. And then there were hands on me, hands rough and hands smooth, against my skin, and the memory of that night in Fez began to engulf me again.

The robe swallowed all my cries and then, mercifully, I passed out.

Old men, sombre faced and long bearded, in caps and black robes, chased me with knives. Sometimes, as I tried to escape them, I climbed a roof and fell endlessly, through time and skies, the world spinning. Sometimes I was on the ground and they were advancing on me. But I could not run. The panic filled my legs with urgency, but they did not work anymore. Sometimes the old men had the face of the vizier, sometimes of La Sabia. "I've got you now!" she gloated. Sometimes Isobel de Solis leaned over me. "Let's find out what you've got under there, shall we?" She pawed at my clothes.

I awoke sweating and trembling. No cedarwood strakes in this ceiling, but a thousand plaster teeth coloured with lapis and gold. A small candle lantern cast dancing sprays of light off patterned wall tiles. These were no slave's quarters. I lay still, remembering the fall and the landing. My right leg felt full of molten metal. I moaned.

Wood scraped on stone and Momo came into view, older than when I had last seen him, his hair close cropped, his cheeks hollowed, a refining of skin over bone, as if his boyishness had been burned out of him.

"Blessings!"

The body is always aware of change; it is the head that resists the knowledge of difference. Without understanding why, I began to shake.

"I'm so sorry," he said, which did not help.

"What is it?" I croaked.

He took my hand in his. This was the moment I had yearned for so long, but now I was terribly afraid.

"Ah, Blessings, what were you doing? Dressed like a girl, climbing out of the harem . . ."

Could he really have forgotten? "I heard you were back," I whispered.

"It's all my fault. Your poor leg . . ." His eyes were filling up.

"Oh, that." I managed a grin. "It was not my best landing. But my leg will heal." I had to be brave: princes should not weep.

"I asked them to let me tell you," he choked out. "But I . . . can't." He rubbed his hand across his face. "They tell me I am a man now and that I must behave like one. My uncle . . ." He shook his head. "No, this is about you, not me. Oh, Blessings . . ."

All this apologizing.

"They dosed you with poppy. You were delirious. For a lot of that time. I worried you'd lost your mind."

Flickers of the dreams came back to me. The old men, the knives . . . Panic seized me. I pushed myself up on my elbows.

"Dr. Ibrahim did the best he could with poultices and drawing pastes. But they didn't work, and then he said you would die. And my mother said the hand of death was upon you, that it was Allah's will. But I could not believe it. I . . . I sent to Córdoba, for better doctors. Qasim went for me: he had contacts there, he said. I sold the sword from my uncle to fight the infidels with to give Qasim the money for the doctors. I daresay they will punish me for that when they find out. But I don't care. And they saved you. Oh, Blessings, I'm so happy you're alive. But I have to tell you . . ." He drew a deep breath. The anguish in his regard was unbearable. "They had to . . ."

His words were lost in the storm surge of blood in my ears. I tore at the rich bedcover with brutal strength and it fell away. There, spangled with the light of the candle lantern, was my left leg, bandaged where the roof tiles had ripped at me. But as to the right . . . There was my thigh, my knee and then— "Where's the rest of it?" I wailed.

"Your foot was smashed to pieces. It started to rot, and the smell . . ."

"My foot rotted?" Dead rats rotting in Fez drains, sick sweet and carrion stench, maggots swarming over them . . . Bile rose in my throat. I swallowed it down. "But how will I run?" Stupid question. How would I walk? How would I do anything at all? I had seen cripples in the marketplaces of Morocco, gimping along on sticks or pushing themselves around on wheeled trolleys, begging for coin. Was that my future? Would this grown-up prince, who had come back with stubble on his chin and a deeper voice, who spoke of swords and being a man, send me off now that I was broken? I turned away so he would not see my loss of composure. The concept of *asshak*, the dignified acceptance of even the worst fate, was the bedrock of my people.

"Don't, Blessings, don't. If I could take your pain and bear it myself, I would."

I lay there, shamed by the desperation in his voice. He had sold his sword, risked his uncle's fury, sent his father's vizier to Córdoba for better doctors, saved my life. But for what? To be a palace cripple? Self-pity welled up again. I forced it down, like the bile. Then I showed him a mask of my face. "I will survive this," I told him, and watched as his grimace relaxed. "Thank you for saving me, my prince."

"Oh, Blessings," he said, choking. "If I hadn't encouraged you, this wouldn't have happened. Everything they say about me is true: I am cursed."

"What do the stars know? They're just there help us navigate a course in the darkness. They can't tell you your future. But I can."

"Can you, Blessings?"

"I was taught by my mother: our people believe that the power of seeing is passed down the line, from mother to son. Or daughter."

"How do you do it? By numbers, or lines of the Quran? Or with chicken entrails, like the ancients?"

"Every man's fate is written in his hand, not in the stars," I said, taking his into my own. So warm, but more muscled than it had been, some coarseness on the pads of the fingers, calluses in the palm. He was no longer a boy: they were making him into a warrior, and if he went to war, I knew I would lose him. "Look here," I said, tracing a vertical line. "Such an old man you will grow to be, though there is suffering to bear on the way. Here is where your heart lies." I touched the spot just above the centre of his palm. "Love is always with you, closer than you think. Be careful to keep it close."

He laughed and tried to pull his hand away. "You're such a little heathen."

I held on to him. "Don't put me aside because of my leg," I said fiercely.

Momo looked as if I'd struck him. "Do you think I'm some sort of monster?"

"I won't be able to walk or run, or do the things we used to do. I won't be able to do anything much at all."

"You will," he said. A deep line formed between the hawk's wings of his eyebrows. Then he said, "Blessings, you shall be my Special Guardian, always by my side. You will be my guard, and I yours: by Allah the Most Mighty and Merciful I swear it."

I almost laughed and spoiled the moment. I could not even stand, let alone defend him. "Should we swear it in blood?" I nodded to his belt-knife.

He looked shocked. "Make a blood covenant? Blood is *najis*, unclean. That would be an affront to God."

He had changed in more ways than appearance, I thought. I bowed my head. "Prince Mohamed, I will be your Special Guardian."

The hug he gave me stole my breath. It was worth almost losing a foot just for that.

Almost.

6

Kate

ENGLAND

FIVE YEARS EARLIER

Kate's visit to Hampton Court had been a belated gift to herself after finally biting the bullet and breaking up with Matty, who had never had the least interest in anything older than the musical revolution of the sixties. Or indeed, for the past few years, an interest in anything other than the bottom of a glass or any substance that detached him from reality. In all that time she had been trying—and failing—to persuade him to get sober. She thought of herself as a trier, someone who did not give up easily, but in the end she had had to walk away before she was sucked down into the vortex of chaos Matty created around himself. She still felt guilty. When she'd said she had had enough, he'd looked even more hangdog than his springer spaniel, Dylan, did when caught peeing on her best rug.

It had taken her a while to wash Matty out of her thoughts, although having to wash the traces of him and his wretched dog out of the carpet, sofa and the cork tiles in the kitchen soon hardened her heart. She had really loved Matty at the start, had fallen for him in a gorgeous, mad tumble of desire and delight. It troubled her terribly that she could have made such a grave mistake of judgment. She was usually so good at working out problems, seeing potential pitfalls; yet with Matty she had fallen in one up to her neck. But at least, she told herself brightly, she had got out and saved herself: she was a survivor. Visiting the palace of England's most carnal and gluttonous king—a place that celebrated the heights of hedonism—was a special treat to herself after remaking her life. She felt strong and empowered and ready to take on the world again.

The sense of freedom to be able to wander where she wanted, to stop and take in the intricacies of a carving, the glories of a fine tapestry, without someone's bored sighing behind her, was a great pleasure. Arriving in one of the royal bedchambers, she gazed up at the painted ceiling where a beautifully muscular god of war, exhausted by battle, lay asleep in the arms of Venus, while some chubby cherubs carried off his armour, and was dismayed to realize he looked a lot like a beefier version of Matty, passed out after one of his long drinking sessions. "Love disarming Strife," she read in the guidebook, as if it were that easy. *Lucky Venus*, she thought: all those cherubs to help put matters straight. Clearly Mars had not been hitting the bottle, then passing out on the sofa covered in sick.

The image had quite changed her mood. She needed to get outside, away from all the stern Biblical scenes, from the portraits of meaty-faced men and their women in French hoods, who were in their lives only to look ornamental, to breed and be silent and subservient.

She strolled back across the bridge into East Molesey to find somewhere to have a late lunch, and an antiques shop next to one of the many awninged restaurants nearby caught her eye. The particularly lovely chaise longue in the window seduced her into the shop. She had secretly always fancied herself as the sort of woman who might own a chaise longue, but up till now one like this—covered in a delicate cream damask—would have died a slow death from wine stains, vomit and dog prints.

She had gone in just to get a better look at it. To run an admiring hand over its impeccable upholstery and its shapely wooden back. She was lost in a moment of dreamy self-indulgence, when someone spoke beside her. "It's a nice piece, isn't it? William IV, dating from around 1830. All the mahogany is original. You can sense all the character, all the years it's seen, in that deep patination, can't you?"

Shocked out of her reverie, she had turned to find an austerely handsome middle-aged man in a button-down shirt and chinos beside her. She smiled at him. "It's beautiful."

"I restored it myself."

"You did?" She stroked the seat cushion as gently as if it were a cat. "That's amazing."

"It's such a pleasure to meet someone who appreciates true quality. I could tell you were discerning the moment you walked in."

Good sales patter, she thought. But still, she was flattered.

"James Foxley," he'd said, holding out a hand.

His fingers, dry and cool, closed over hers. Was it her imagination or did his grip linger longer than was entirely polite?

"It's really lovely, but probably not very practical," she said.

"I'm not sure practicality is the point of a chaise longue," he said with a grin, and she found herself thinking how attractive he was, with that sweep of dark hair and those cheekbones and deepset brown eyes. Ridiculous: he was too old for her, even if she hadn't sworn off men for all time.

She cast another wistful glance at the chaise. It would look perfect beneath the window in what she had now designated as the dining room, which Matty had turned into a dark and filthy den. She had jettisoned the ruined carpet, bullied the floorboards back to cleanliness with a sanding machine, repainted the walls a lovely cool grey, but still the room appeared rather soulless and unloved. Something impractical might be just what it needed. "How much is it?" she asked, and was shocked by the price he quoted.

Ten minutes later they had reached a sort of compromise and she was feeling light in the head, as well as in the wallet. The power of doing something so mad, so impulsive, just for herself, was intoxicating. She felt quite giddy with it. The world spun, and all of a sudden she was sitting on the floor, alongside an intricately engraved wooden boot that she had managed to knock over, spilling cigarette ends and ash all over.

"Oh no, I'm so sorry. I hope I haven't broken it." She set the boot upright again.

"Good Lord, are you okay?"

"I . . . Yes, yes, of course." She scrambled to her knees and started scraping the scattered butts into a pile. "I've no idea what's the matter with me. I've never done anything like that before."

"Let's get you up. Don't worry about that old thing. Just a bit of Moroccan tat."

"Poor thing: it's much too nice to be used as an ashtray."

He helped her up and rather presumptuously dusted off the seat of her jeans. Taking her by the arm, he steered her to a Queen Anne chair and pushed her down into the plush velvet. Kate struggled to stand up, but he kept her pinned. "You are going nowhere till you've had a cup of tea and at least two chocolate Hobnobs. Just stay there. I'll be right back."

Kate's cheeks were aflame. Had she really fainted? It was just a bit of dizziness, an inner ear thing, a virus maybe. It was only when James returned with the tray bearing a silver teapot, a pair of porcelain cups on saucers, a matching milk jug and sugar bowl, a pair of silver sugar tongs and a vast slice of cake that her stomach rumbled like thunder and she remembered she had eaten nothing all day.

"Sorry, ran out of the promised Hobnobs," he apologized. "Had to pop to the café for the next best thing."

"I can't eat all that," she protested, staring at the gleaming slice of chocolate torte. But she did. She could not remember the last time anyone had brought her a cup of tea, let alone such a treat. Self-pitying tears, something she never allowed herself, welled up, and suddenly she was snuffling. "God, sorry, sorry, I'm such a mess." She dug in her handbag for a tissue, and of course couldn't find one. Snot was tickling the tip of her nose. She raised a hand to wipe it away before it could fall and unexpectedly a crisp white handkerchief appeared in front of her. She stared at it. Someone had ironed it into perfect quarters. There was a *J* embroidered into one corner. It was far too smart to wipe a snotty nose on.

"Please," he said, pushing it at her. "I have hundreds of the things. My aunt lacks imagination when it comes to Christmas presents."

She laugh-snorted into the hanky, then refolded it to hide the contents and put it down on the tray. "You're very kind."

"It's not every day I have a beautiful woman with a fine eye for quality coming into the shop."

It was probably the tea, but Kate felt herself go warm all over. In all their time together Matty had never once called her beautiful. A few minutes later she had agreed to go to dinner with James Foxley.

She was halfway out the door, when he called her back.

"Close your eyes and put your hands out."

In a bit of a daze, she did as she was told, and nearly dropped the object he put there, it being far heavier than she had been expecting.

"Just give it a rinse: it'll make an excellent doorstop."

She looked down. In her hands was the decorative Moroccan boot. Except, she realized in a moment of sudden clarity it wasn't a boot at all but a sort of artificial leg.

Some weeks later, in a riverside pub, she sat drinking red wine with James. It was their third date and they were getting down to the nitty-gritty.

"I never meant to get involved with an addict," Kate said. "Matty was very cunning at hiding his vices from me. I just thought he was great fun when we first met."

James listened without interrupting, which she liked. His eyes never left her face, even when she recounted the more unsavoury details—the hidden bottles, the chemical lows brought on by the chemical highs of the night before, the cryptic phone calls and sudden disappearances. The late-night weeping and manic, red-eyed laughter; the disturbing periods of unconsciousness. All hidden from everybody but her.

"Everyone thought him a grand fellow, the life and soul of every party. They thought I was a miserable old cow for reining him in."

"How very unfair on you," he said sympathetically. "What a good job you didn't marry him."

Matty had asked her, but Kate knew by then she couldn't do it. When she'd said no, Matty had shut himself in the den and drunk an entire bottle of whisky, then smashed his favourite guitar, leaving angry holes in the plaster.

"I was always clearing up after him," Kate said. "I felt more like his mother than his girlfriend." She looked past James to where a young couple were twined around each other, laughing and kissing. "When we met, I thought I wanted a child," she sighed at last. "But not a forty-year-old one."

James touched her hand lightly. "Plenty of time for that."

She smiled. "Not really."

"But you can't be more than twenty-five?"

Kate swallowed her mouthful of wine before she blew it out all over the table. "I'm nearly thirty-four."

James sat back, looking poleaxed.

Kate had never actually asked him how old he was. She hadn't had to; he'd left his wallet open on the table one evening when he went outside for a cigarette. She felt guilty for snooping, but there were two photos tucked into the card slots: one of two women smiling in the sun, the other a black-and-white picture of a solemn little boy in the same place. On the back of that one was pencilled "James, aged four. Porth Clais, 1964."

Once he knew her age, though, he seemed disengaged, less forthcoming. After a series of monosyllabic answers she said, "You're being a bit moody."

His eyes flashed at her. "I am not!"

Uh-oh, she thought. She bent down, picked up her handbag, slipped its strap over her shoulder and got up. "I think it's time I went home. Thanks for a nice evening."

He shot to his feet. "Don't go." He wiped a hand across his face. "You must think I'm so rude. It's just, well . . . My wife was thirty-four when she died."

She should have said, *Oh, I'm so sorry. How terrible for you.* But instead she said, "Your wife?" It came out accusatory.

"I should have mentioned her before now, but I didn't want to put you off. Older man carrying a ton of baggage, you know."

Kate sat down again, tucking her feet under her chair, her elbows close to her sides; she felt ashamed. "I'd rather know," she said quietly. "It's not like I don't come with baggage of my own."

He took out his wallet and thumbed out the first of the photos she'd seen. "There she is. Ingrid, with my mother." Two women standing outside a tiny whitewashed cottage.

Of course she didn't admit to having seen it before. This time her eyes went straight to the younger woman. Her first thought was: *She's so pretty.* Her second, with some surprise: *She looks a lot like me, but with different hair.* They could easily have passed as sisters. Weird. "Can I ask what happened to her? Was she sick?"

"There was an accident. An absurd accident. We were on holiday, in Cornwall. It was a beautiful day, early June, the cliff path full of wildflowers, and Ingrid— She was always a bit more adventurous and a bit fitter than me. She'd gone on ahead after teasing me that I was getting to be an old man—I suppose I was huffing and puffing a little. And she just . . . vanished."

"Vanished?"

"I walked round a corner where there was a clear view of the path for miles, and there was no sign of her, in any direction. I thought she was playing a trick on me—hiding in the bracken or behind a rock, ready to jump out at me. I walked on as fast as I could. I even ran, out of panic. But I couldn't find her. I kept shouting her name, getting more and more terrified. I even made myself peer over the edge, where the path was close to a drop. I lay on my stomach and forced myself to look down, but I couldn't see her. In all that time no one passed me at all. And there was no phone signal." He choked. "Her body washed up along the coast a fortnight later. I—I had to identify it." He put his face in his hands.

Kate sat rigid, silent and paralyzed. She wasn't sure how she felt about this, about him. They had kissed a couple of times, but his kisses had been decorous, rather than the clothes-tearing, giggling rampages she'd experienced with Matty at the beginning. And she was being careful with her feelings, trying not to get too involved too quickly. Even so, she felt her heart contract in sympathy for him. "When did this happen?" she asked softly.

"Seven years ago."

Seven years? That seemed a long time for the grief still to be so raw. And still to have her photo in his wallet. But it was a terrible thing to lose your wife in such a mysterious way and then to have to view what the sea had done with her. Kate chastised herself for being cold. "I'm so sorry, James. How utterly dreadful for you."

He managed a wobbly smile. "It was a hard time. If it hadn't been for my mother . . . well." He ran a finger across his throat. "I doubt I'd still be here. I was in a bad way."

Kate regarded the photo again. "She looks lovely, your mum. You must be very fond of her."

"Oh, she's dead," he said. "Only last year. I've had a rough time of it. I wouldn't blame you if you ran a mile," he said.

Of course making it quite impossible for her to do so.

7

Over the weeks that followed James took her to the cinema, to dinners in fancy restaurants—including once, memorably, to Le Manoir aux Quat' Saisons, where he insisted on buying such an expensive bottle of champagne that she could hardly bring herself to drink it. He bought her peonies because she had once mentioned she loved them, and antique vases to put them in. A set of antique Wedgwood to replace her Marks & Spencer crockery; framed paintings instead of her student-ish posters; little *objets d'art*; a pretty Victorian dresser on which to display a set of crystal glasses that had come into his possession. He repositioned the sofas so that the sitting room seemed more spacious, helped her repaint the kitchen and bathroom, brought a pretty embroidered cushion to decorate the chaise longue. Soon her flat was looking so elegant she hardly recognized it. And all the while the Moroccan foot sat by the front door, ready to prop it open for the world to come in and out.

One day James bought her a beautiful antique crucifix on a fine chain, and when she demurred that it wasn't her sort of thing, he insisted on fastening it around her neck and propelling her to the hall mirror. "See? It looks beautiful on you."

Kate lifted her long hair and turned her head to admire the

smooth column of her neck and the glint of the gold against her skin. In his reflection in the mirror James was regarding her critically. "If you cut your hair shorter, it would enhance your jawline. Add a few reddish highlights for some warmth—"

"No, thank you. I like my hair just the way it is." She watched his face register disappointment. "I'm sure it would look smart shorter," she admitted, "but I'm used to it long. And you shouldn't spend so much on me. This is too expensive." He kept saying the shop was not doing as well as he would like, so how could he afford it? One part of her loved having a man lavish such care and attention on her, each gift a gesture of a yet unspoken love: but another part rebelled against what the necklace stood for.

In the local café he'd leaned across the table and taken her hands between his. "Tell me where you were baptized."

She'd frowned. "I haven't the faintest idea."

"Well, surely you were?"

"I honestly don't know."

He looked alarmed. "Call your sister. Perhaps she will know."

"Is it important?"

"For me. Do it for me."

His regard was so full of concern that she did: she called Jess. A few minutes later, she put the phone down. "Well, there you go. At Saint Peter's Church in Huddersfield. Religion was never big in our family. I'm surprised Jess even knew."

Was that relief she read on his face? It seemed absurd, but after that a cloud appeared to lift. That evening they slept together for the first time.

It had been a while since she'd had sex with a partner: toward the end of her relationship with Matty, she'd withheld herself from him as a sort of punishment. She'd despised herself for doing it, but she despised Matty even more, and it was hard to feel desire for someone you'd lost all respect for. James had taken her out to a

French restaurant in Chelsea and plied her with champagne: she'd been quite tipsy by the time they left. As the taxi stopped outside her flat, he'd leaned across and kissed her with such intensity that she'd felt light-headed. And at that moment she wanted him, with a greedy ferocity: she'd hauled him up the steps and already had his shirt off by the time they got to the bedroom. His chest was pale, contrasting with the tan on his arms from where he'd rolled his shirt sleeves up in summer: the sight of it—vulnerable, private, hidden away—was somehow erotic. James never wore T-shirts, unlike Matty who never wore anything else: it made James seem so grown-up and manly by comparison. She could feel his erection pressing into her stomach and it made her feel both desirable and desiring. She flung off her own clothes with abandon and, stepping out of her knickers—the good ones that actually matched her bra, put on this evening to boost her confidence—she stood naked before him for the first time. His gaze travelled over her and he looked suddenly intent and alert, like a ravenous animal taking in a fresh kill. The bright, almost dangerous, gleam in his eyes made her want to lie down for him but also run away. Uncomfortable under his gaze, she stepped toward him.

James reached out and cupped one of her breasts in a sort of wonder. "So beautiful," he said.

Then he bent his head to her nipple, and Kate felt her knees go liquid and a determined pulse beat between her legs. She pulled him toward the bed and they fell together in a tangle, with Kate tugging at his belt. At last it was undone, and his trousers and underpants were out of the way and she could feel the smooth, hot skin of his penis against her.

She twisted and reached for the drawer of the bedside table, where the condoms were kept, but James pulled her back toward him. He was so strong, she realized, stronger than she'd expected, and that too delighted her and made her brain go fuzzy. She had to insist on using protection, she knew it: but just now she couldn't seem to form the words, and instead became quiescent. She allowed him to hold her, and didn't move when he pushed himself up on his hands to look down the length of her, taking her in, his gaze lingering on her breasts, her belly, her cunt as she opened her legs. There was a sort of power to be had by showing herself to him, she thought: it was as if he was worshipping her with his eyes.

And then he reared back from her onto his haunches, and taking his cock in his hand, he muttered, "*Benedic, Domine, nos et dona tua, quae de largitate tua sumus sumpturi,*" which even Kate recognized as a form of Latin grace. A few strokes later he ejaculated all over her stomach.

The experience had left Kate feeling confused, frustrated and in need of discussion, since James refused to talk about it, saying only that sex before marriage was sinful. This seemed medieval to Kate, whose background had been rigorously secular. Surely not all Catholics shared James's strange predilections. Though wasn't it rather nice that he solemnized things so? At least he wasn't a fuck-and-run, one-night- stand merchant: he was serious about her; he cared. A lot. But even so, it was . . . weird, and she needed some guidance. Her colleagues were not the sort of people with whom she shared confidences of a sexual nature and somehow she'd let other friendships drift over the past months. So at last she called her sister, only to have Jess cry down the phone at her.

"Evan can't understand why it matters to me so much," she sobbed. "Hardly any of his friends have kids, and those who do just seem to moan about all the trouble and expense. He says he doesn't feel that his job is secure enough for us to start a family yet, but if we don't do it now, it'll be too late!"

Evan was the same age as Jess and Kate but behaved as if he were ten years younger, going out on benders with his mates, not turning up to medical appointments, disappearing at weekends.

When Kate had been with Matty, Jess had been furious with her. "For God's sake throw him out! He's a parasite!" Kate now wondered whether Jess's vehemence had had more to do with the frustrations in her own marriage. They had been so close as children, proper twins, but ever since Jess had got involved with Evan, she always seemed so angry and critical. It hurt Kate in a way she could hardly articulate, as if a part of her own body had gone rogue and begun to attack her. But Jess was obviously hurting now, and it made her own concerns seem pathetic by comparison.

"Can't you sit down and talk to him?" she asked gently.

Jess snorted. "Evan doesn't 'do' talking. Every time I try, he acts like a dog that's been hit for no reason. Or he gets defensive and angry. Anyway—" she blew her nose "—what's up with Prince Charming?"

"Don't call him that." Kate felt herself bristle. "Look, it's so trivial . . ."

"I could do with some distraction."

And so Kate found herself listing the treats and gifts, the texts and compliments. Even to her own ears it was an absurd whine, but she had to build up to what had happened last night.

At last her sister cut in.

"Honestly, Kate, I can't believe you're complaining about a man treating you like a princess," Jess said. "You're so used to being treated badly you don't know a nice guy when he comes along."

Kate laughed. "I know. He *is* nice," she conceded. "But . . . here's the thing, and promise you won't laugh. No, really—promise."

"Okay, I promise."

"We slept together last night. But he wouldn't . . . penetrate me."

There was a long silence at the other end of the line. Then Jess burst out laughing. "Sorry, sorry. He what?"

Kate went over the events of the evening, her cheeks burning. "After he came the first time, I tried to get him hard again, but he just sort of fended me off, made me feel like some sort of wicked temptress intent on my own pleasure. He kept saying, 'Not yet. It would be wrong.' Look, I know it's weird, but there isn't really anyone else I can talk to about it."

"Well, maybe it's just his thing, deferring pleasure. They've all got some strange kink or another. That's what sex is all about, isn't it? Strange kinks?"

"No, it's more than that. It's like . . . it doesn't count if he doesn't come inside me, as if he's denying himself. Or as if he's waiting for something."

"Waiting? For what?"

"I—" Instinctively her hand went to the little crucifix. "I really don't know."

Funny what you got used to. Kate found that although penetration remained taboo, it was perfectly acceptable to James if she masturbated herself to a climax in front of him: indeed, it seemed to excite him inordinately, and so they continued as a couple on a reasonably stable footing: going out for walks, to dinner, to the cinema. Then, about five months into the relationship, James went missing. His landlines at the shop and his flat went to the answering machine, and his mobile straight to voice mail when Kate rang. He did not reply to her texts or respond to any of the emails she sent him, which started with gentle inquiries about his health and became increasingly anxious.

It wasn't like James to be out of contact. If anything, he was too assiduous at keeping in touch. Sometimes he texted or called her several times a day. Once, she had failed to reply to him for a whole four hours and he'd contacted her office colleagues to make sure she was all right. "I was worried she might have had an accident on the way to work," he explained, sounding rather sheepish when they said no, she was fine but stuck in a long budget meeting. Now she pictured James lying dead on the floor of the stockroom with blowflies buzzing over him.

It was odd that she was so stricken: there were times when she wasn't even sure she liked him that much. The last evening they'd spent together they'd argued about the Charlie Hebdo atrocity. "Yes, of course it's crucial that we defend free speech," she had said, "but I do feel sorry for all the ordinary Muslims in Paris. Wherever they go, people will stare at them and wonder if they sympathized, if they are terrorists at heart."

"All Muslims are terrorists," James said with such vehemence that she choked on her wine.

She wondered if she had heard him correctly. "Say that again?"

"All Muslims are terrorists," he enunciated with patronizing clarity. "Their religion is based on violence and intolerance."

Kate was stymied. "You can't possibly mean that," she said at last. "Islam is a religion of peace—it's only fundamentalist nutters who twist it to suit their agenda."

He sneered at her. "A religion of peace? You must be joking!" He ticked off names on his fingers: "Saladin, Saddam Hussein, Yasser Arafat, Osama bin Laden, ISIS and the Taliban. What have they all got in common?"

Kate laughed and tried to muster a counter-argument. "Um, well, what about the Spanish Inquisition, Bloody Mary, the Ku Klux Klan, the Nazis and the Lord's Resistance Army?"

"You really don't know what you're talking about. Didn't you learn anything at university?"

Kate felt the insult like a blow. He knew she hadn't been to university, unlike Jess: she'd told him so. Had he forgotten, or was he twisting the knife? In her family, Jess had always been "the clever one" and Kate a sort of plodder, the one who always got things done, quietly and stoically, with her head down. In retrospect, Kate had realized this was unfair: it was just that Jess was more emotional and made more fuss, so people took more notice of her. But when you're a twin, you tend to adopt roles to differentiate yourself from your sibling, and she and Jess had each formed their own stereotype. She didn't, generally, mind not having been to university: no one in her social circles made her feel stigmatized or lacking education, and she'd been earning ever since the summer after A-levels and had bought a flat before Jess had. She saw herself as a worker, and a successful, confident woman. But now here was James reminding her that she was—in his terms—uneducated and, by extension, of a lower order. James didn't boast about his upbringing, but he'd dropped enough snippets for Kate to gather that he had been to prep school and then to Eton; and he had the bearing and accent of the truly privileged. She did know that he'd taken a first at Cambridge and she suspected he had been a member of a debating society, for now he started using all manner of rhetorical tricks to knock down each of her arguments, quoting from learned sources and dropping Latin phrases. On the last occasion, unable to muster any cool logic, she'd yelled, "Stop it, stop it!" She'd slammed the table with both hands and her glass shuddered and fell over, breaking immediately and spilling the scant dregs onto the table. It was an expensive glass, one of the crystal ones James had bought for her.

James reeled as if she had physically assaulted him. "Now look what you've done. Don't you see how destructive you are? That says everything—" He waved at the broken glass. "You insult me and break the beautiful things I give you. Do you even care for me at all?"

Her own violence had surprised her: she felt suddenly very much in the wrong. Was she turning into a female version of Matty? That would be awful, and James didn't deserve such treatment.

"I'm sorry," she said, placing a mollifying hand on his arm. "I do care for you—of course I do."

He looked her in the eye. "Care for, maybe. Not love."

His eyes held her, pinned her. The air between them was charged with expectancy, but Kate couldn't bring herself to say the word. She wasn't ready yet, didn't think that her feelings for James were strong enough to make this irrevocable statement. Sometimes she thought she might be falling for him, but often she wondered if her yearning for a stable relationship had more to do with her own inadequacies than with what she felt for James. The atmosphere became oppressive, more so even than during the argument, but an adamantine part at the core of her refused to be cowed. Even if it meant the end of everything.

And when it became clear that she wasn't going to say she loved him, he'd shaken her hand off and got to his feet. "What's the point of this? There's no point, is there? I might as well kill myself: then we'd see how much you cared."

At the time Kate had almost laughed at his dramatics. Then she had felt angry at being on the end of such blatant emotional manipulation and told him he'd better go home. And so the evening had come to a rancorous ending. That had been the last time they'd spoken, and since then she'd felt increasingly guilty. An awful thought occurred to her now. What if he'd really meant it? What if he'd taken an overdose or something? It was, she told herself, a ridiculous case of catastrophic thinking.

But it *had* been three days . . .

In the end she couldn't settle to anything. At lunchtime she excused herself from the office and took the train to East Molesey. It was November and the streetlights were already coming on by the time she reached the shop. People were muffled in scarves, heads down against the chill. The shop was locked and there was a CLOSED sign on the door. She cupped her hands against the window. Inside, the place looked gloomy and ramshackle without the glamour lent by the sparkling chandeliers. It looked like a junk shop, tawdry and untidy.

She stepped back. No lights were on in the flat upstairs, and she had no door key: James had always been unwilling to let her in there. "It's a mess," he would say. "I've got deliveries every-where—there's nowhere to sit down." She tried the flat phone again and heard it ringing in the distance, echoing and mournful. His mobile went to voice mail.

Just down the road was a twenty-four-hour convenience store. "Hello!" she greeted the man behind the counter. "I was looking for James from the antiques shop?" She gestured vaguely to her left. "I don't suppose you've seen him?"

The man was in his early twenties, with a curving, hawk-like nose and very white teeth. "Hi, I'm Yusuf," he said with a grin. "Lucky James." When she didn't smile, he added, "I haven't, not for a few days."

Kate's heart thumped. "He's not answering his phone. I'm worried about him."

"Right," Yusuf said. "Hang on." He came out from behind the counter, locked the door and flipped the OPEN sign to CLOSED. "Come on."

She followed him out through the back of the shop, past towers of toilet rolls and stacked boxes, into a small courtyard brimming with potted herbs and heathers. At the far end a wooden door gave onto a grassy alleyway that led behind the other premises on the road. When they reached the back of what must be the antiques shop, Yusuf tried the gate, but it appeared to be bolted. "Okay, here goes." He launched himself up and over the fence, which shud-dered briefly under his weight with the groan of an old man who had creaky knees. Then he was across the yard and rattling his way up the iron fire escape. He banged on the glass window of the door.

"Hello? Hello in there?" He pressed his hands to the glass and peered in. "It's a bit of a state," he called back, "but there's no body or smell or nothing." He shifted along the fire escape, onto the horizontal iron drainpipe.

"Do be careful!" Kate called.

Moments later he scuttled back to safety again. "Unless he's shut himself in the bathroom, I don't think he's in there."

So where was he? Should she file a missing person report with the police: *I'm his girlfriend and he's always in contact?* They would laugh at her: men were always going missing for a few days. Matty had done it all the time. But Matty was Matty, and James was . . . his polar opposite. It was the most attractive thing about him.

"I wouldn't worry too much," Yusuf said, vaulting lightly back over the creaking fence. "He does go off on buying trips, and to see his mum in Wales. And of course he's always had an eye for a pretty lady. Can't blame him for that. You look a lot like his last one." And he winked at her.

Kate took a step back. "I expect that's what he's done, and forgotten to tell me." She was so agitated she walked away without thanking him and by the time she remembered she was almost at the station.

When she got home, it was to find a message on her answering phone: James, suggesting a rendezvous the next day, his message cheery, as if nothing had happened. Relief flooded in. But as she put the receiver down, she remembered what Yusuf had said, about James going off to see his mother. In Wales.

But he told me she was dead.

8

Blessings

GRANADA

1479

Prince Mohamed and I were in the Court of Myrtles after a day spent shadowing the sultan in his court duties: Momo was being groomed for power. "This is good," Qasim told me. "This suits us well." I wasn't entirely sure who the "us" referred to. "Keep your ears and eyes open and report all you see and hear. We must ensure the prince is well schooled and ready to take a step up. In case . . . anything should happen, to his father." I tried, but it was a dull job, listening to the petitioners moaning out their woes to Moulay Hasan and his *qadi*, the judge. I had almost dislocated my jaw yawning during the judicial audiences. Afterwards, Momo dragged me into the courtyard and bade me wait. "I have something for you!"

He presented it to me like a god bestowing a miracle. He was a boy no longer, and his beauty could take your breath away. All his years of training with ever more skilled sword masters had built lean muscle into him; a fine beard defined his jaw. But it was his kindness that always unmanned me. I looked down at the cloth-swathed object. Larger and longer than a book, his usual (unwanted) gift. I hoped it wasn't a sword: the best I'd be able to do with it was to use it as a crutch.

I pulled the fabric away, and stared. Considered objectively, it was a pretty thing, covered in chased gold, intricate arabesques hammered all over the metal. Whoever had made it had given it the exact likeness of a foot—toes and toenails lovingly replicated.

"Well, try it then!" he urged me. "It's made of thuya wood from the Atlas Mountains," he said eagerly. "From the root burl. That's what makes it so hard and dense. It won't rot or spoil, even in water. And see—" he pointed to a peg at the ankle "—it even articulates, just like a real foot, so with practice you should be able to walk, even run on it, without limping too badly. Here—" He helped me place the false foot over my linen-covered stump, where to my surprise it fitted well. I caught his smug expression. "I measured it while you slept. It's taken months to get it made. I was worried the stump would grow, but it doesn't seem to have. The foot was put together by a carpenter in Fez: it's where the finest craftsmen come from, you know. He worked from the drawings of a man from Florence who's made a great study of human anatomy. Leonardo something."

I wound the long leather laces in a tight criss-cross up to my knee, realizing I should be grateful for all this thought, effort and no doubt expense, but the gratitude weighed as heavily as the foot. I had been getting around perfectly well until now on a long forked stick tucked into my armpit. It seemed a great nuisance to have to bind an artificial foot as heavy as a lump of iron stuck onto the end of my leg. Leaning on Momo, I clumped around a bit, the foot clanging on the patio tiles. There would be no sneaking up on anyone in this thing.

Of course the laces did not hold for long. We both gazed at the shed leg, Momo more glum than I. Then, "I have an idea!" he cried. He grabbed the foot and ran off.

I hopped across the courtyard to retrieve my trusty stick, then stood propped against one of the slender pillars to gaze up at the Tower of the Moon looming over the Hall of the Ambassadors. The shadow of it had turned the waters of the pool a brooding umber, the colour of old blood. It was from the top of this tower that the astrologers had surveyed the night sky when Momo was born and made their grim predictions. I rather hoped they were right: I didn't want him to be sultan, for I would lose him to endless meetings and matters of state. Already I had lost so much of him.

Some of it was my own fault. I was ungracious about the constraints of my affliction, sulking when he chose hunting over a game of chess with me, sniping at his soldier's training, refusing both assistance and sympathy. My tribe, for whom *asshak*, the dignified acceptance of fate, was a prized quality, would have been ashamed of me. But my tribe was far away.

By the time he came back a chill was in the air. He looked strangely forlorn. There was no sign of the foot and for a moment I thought (hoped) he might have lost it somewhere. Dropped it in one of the deeper pools, or over a rampart.

"Apparently, I'm getting married," he said.

"Why didn't you tell me?"

Qasim did not answer for a long time but sat there paring his nails with a small knife he kept for the purpose. At last he said, "Walls have ears, Blessings," which seemed a ridiculous statement.

When I persisted, he sighed. "Come with me, then. And bring a basket so that it may at least appear we are doing something useful."

Out in the gardens, we walked from rosebush to rosebush, Qasim instructing me to cut, very carefully, only the most perfect budded roses. Each of them he inspected so that he had the excuse of placing his head close to mine so no one could hear him speak.

"Isobel de Solis has cast her net around the sultan, binding him close with every trick she can devise. For ages she refused to convert to Islam, knowing the sultan could not lie with her until she had."

It was one thing to lay claim to a captive taken in war, quite another to place an unconverted infidel in your harem. So this, he explained, was why she had originally been housed apart from the other concubines, making it harder for me to escape, impossible for him to have me released.

"If the bitch had just said the *shahada* like any sensible captive, I would still have my foot!"

"Keep your voice down, Blessings." Qasim looked around quickly. Two gardeners were leaning on their rakes, paused in their task of tidying the flower beds. As soon as they saw him watching, they swiftly went back to their work. He took me by the elbow, his fingers pinching to deliver deliberate pain, and guided me farther from them. "When she relented, it was on the promise that he put aside the Lady Aysha and make her, Isobel, his chief wife, to house her always in the greatest splendour; that she be called from now on Zoraya, Star of Morning."

This last was no news to me: it was what everyone called Isobel now.

He lowered his voice yet further. "Hasan was also supposed to declare the sons she vowed to give him his heirs and to disown princes Mohammed and Rachid."

I frowned. "But he didn't put the sultana aside or disown his sons."

"Not yet, no. When he married her, she was placed on an equal footing to the sultana. And her baby boys are still unacknowledged.

But I know her wiles. She will not rest until she has her way. So we must shore up our position."

"'Our' ?"

"The Lady Aysha and her sons. Hence this marriage."

It was a political alliance, he explained, but that didn't make it any better. The girl was the daughter of the pasha of Medina Lawsa, also called Loja, an old fortress town in the hills to the west of Granada. Her father, Ali Attar, had made his money trading spices, and his reputation fighting infidels. All this I took in with the dulled comprehension of a dying man.

I knew vaguely that the sultan's heir must marry and have children of his own to prolong the Nasrid line for the good of Granada and the defiance of the infidels. I knew that one day this would be Momo's duty and his fate, but I had managed to persuade myself it would never happen. I had come to believe that the world would somehow change shape to accommodate my love for him. But the world seemed intent on teaching me cruel lessons. I tried to learn them, and to keep my ears and eyes open, and earned extra coin, which I spent on small treasures—silver bracelets and pretty rings ("It is always good to have portable wealth," my mother always said)—by reporting back the whispers of the court staff.

It seemed that motherhood had not dulled Zoraya's powers of seduction. She spent days spent locked in the sultan's private quarters, seen by none but those bringing food and wine and taking away emptied dishes and goblets. Not even the musicians were allowed in.

"I swear she's killing him," one of the door guards told me. "To hear his moans, you'd think it."

"Oh, she will oust our beloved sultana!" the cook declared.

I did not know when the sultana had become beloved: before the ascent of the Star of Morning everyone had gone in fear of her, but now, as I reported back to Qasim, the household sided with the "wronged" woman.

In an attempt to do away with the root cause of Momo's forth-coming marriage, I made a little image of Zoraya from beeswax moulded around a thread of golden hair bought from one of the girls sent in to cook for her, and burned it in a brazier. The Star of Morning had a stomach ache for a day or two but recovered far more quickly than she should have, had the magic been working. I must have done something wrong. It must be the gold of her hair, so pale and feeble. I tried to find some way by which I might obtain a little of her blood, even going so far as pose as a washerwoman sent to take her monthly linen. Thank heaven it was not La Sabia who came out: the serving girl laughed at me. "Don't be silly. She's pregnant again!" So that was that.

Before the month was out we were on our way to Loja: Prince Mohamed, his Special Guardian, the *qadi* and a troop of men hand-picked by the vizier from among the Banu Serraj, who could, because of their blood alliance with her family, be completely loyal to the sultana (and indeed to the treasury, since it was Qasim who held the keys and paid their wages). Also with us was a curtained litter containing four maids to take care of the prince's new wife.

As we rode through the winter-sere hills, no one spoke, until at last Momo suddenly exclaimed, "I have no gift for my bride!"

My bride. So proprietorial. I felt a thread inside me pull tight and painful. The girl—whatever her name was (for no one had accorded her a name: she was nothing but an object, a pawn being moved across a board to check a king's progress)—was about to be a prince's bride. Before she had been a pasha's daughter: nothing in her own right except as defined by the man responsible for her. What would the women of my tribe make of that? I wondered. They would whistle and jeer and throw out of the tent the belongings of any man who dared to regard them as chattel; keep the children, declare themselves divorced and take a better lover to spite him.

I felt a jolt of nostalgia for my faraway home and then, taking me by surprise, a fleeting sympathy for this nameless girl who was about to be uprooted from her home and dragged back to Granada into the middle of a buzzing hornets' nest, to be an ally, a wife, a mother.

She would share Momo's bed, and his life.

And just like that sweet despair flooded me again. I was about to lose him, and nothing would ever be the same. Already I hated the very thought of her, this girl with no name. And so, when my friend cried out about the lack of a gift, I said nothing, not a word. There was nothing I could say past the lump in my throat. I just looked down at my gold-chased foot, now cleverly fitted to the top half of a tightly laced boot.

The prince saw me glance down and said at once, "No, no. I didn't mean that. Yes, all the money I had went on having your new foot made, but you mustn't feel guilt at that. I'd spend the coin again and again to do this for you. To see you riding so straight and tall like a shining *faris* fills my heart with pride. Not for what I did," he corrected himself swiftly. "Pride in you, for how you've dealt with your affliction. You've hardly complained at all."

My heart contracted at the unwarranted praise. To be called a *faris*, a chivalric knight, by this glowing young warrior was one thing; but to say I had not complained . . . Not a day—not an hour—had passed without my thinking evil thoughts about the rest of mankind. His faith in me pierced me through. "Here, give her this," I dragged at the neck of my mail shirt, lifting my tribal necklace out from under it and over my head, and held it out to him. "It was my mother's."

"I can't take such a precious thing from you." Momo's eyes shone.

"You must. You've given me so much more." Besides, I had other amulets I could adapt to make another necklace, though none so fine.

He held my gaze, then looked sharply away. His cheeks were flushed with some unreadable emotion as he placed the amulet inside his tunic. *Let it be love*, I wished at him. *Say you will love no one except me.*

But of course he was a prince and he could not.

9

The walls of Loja cast their shadow over us as the sun fell away behind them, and suddenly we felt the true chill of the air. It was a grim-looking place, rough and four-square, reflecting exactly every bad thing I felt about it on that long ride.

We were challenged at the gates: Ali Attar was vigilant, even when expecting a royal visit. I was left to stable the horses while Momo was taken, without any great ceremony, to have tea with the old warrior.

My stump ached from unaccustomed use after the long ride and I limped heavily across the yard, my sword banging against my leg. I oversaw the ostlers as they unsaddled the horses, watered and stabled them, and was shown to our accommodations to unpack Momo's things. The pasha's house was hardly any more embellished than the fierce fortress walls. Some effort had been made to cater to the comforts of a Nasrid prince, but the carpets were threadbare and of poor quality: wool, not silk, made by the Berber mountain tribes whence Ali Attar traced his heritage. A fire had been lit in the clay hearth and steam rose visibly from the floor, so that the smell of wet sheep competed with the brazier burning crystals of incense among its coals.

I opened the wooden chest and laid out Momo's wedding robe on the bed, feeling the slight lumps along the hem where I had sewn protective charms into it. I had also, with rather spiteful intent, wrapped a small knife inside his silk pantaloons to spoil his wedding night, a piece of magic learned from my mother. It had the desired effect, I am ashamed to relate, and other consequences, besides. My only excuse is that I was in despair, and not thinking straight.

I was just refolding the clothes with some squares of amber musk to perfume them overnight, when Momo returned from his duties, looking solemn. "Blessings, I have a favour to ask of you." There was a bundle of something in his arms.

"Of course, my lord."

"The maids tell me that the Lady Mariam has been weeping, saying she has nothing suitable to wear for the wedding tomorrow. I fear they laughed at her and were not kind." He held the bundle out to me.

It was a plain black robe and a white head scarf such as servants dressed in. "She can't wear this!"

"Oh, Blessings!" Suddenly he was snorting with laughter. "That's for you, not her. I thought you might take up your role of the Little Cat once more."

"You can't mean it," I said in dismay.

"The maids are worldly and cruel. I don't want her feeling inferior before we've even started. I thought you might go through the baggage and see what you can find for her. You've got a good eye for these things—you'll uncover something suitable I'm sure. Then take them to her as gift from me: help her attire herself tomorrow. Please?"

I looked at him aghast, but he made some excuse and slipped away before I could splutter out my objections.

I laboured up the narrow stairs, trying to stop my djellaba from tangling with the false leg. I would have to keep the foot hidden: no woman ever wore a gilded foot attached to a man's riding boot. The door of the bride's apartment was opened by a fierce old woman with a bent back and swollen knuckles. Behind her a fretted wooden screen blocked out any view into the room.

"God's peace be upon you. I've come from the Emir of Granada," I said, bowing low. My voice is quite light by nature: I hardly needed to modulate it. Even so the elderly serving woman gave me a suspicious look, then poked the parcel I carried.

"What's in here?" No greeting or pleasantry: she reminded me of La Sabia.

"My lord has sent a gift to the Lady Mariam, for her wedding day."

"It's very late."

"Who is it, Habiba?" called a little voice from inside the chamber.

"Some . . ." The old woman studied me up and down, her head tilted awkwardly because of her bent back, her eyes as beady as a bird's. "Some . . . woman with a wedding gift for you."

"Oh. But I'm not in a fit state to receive anyone."

From the hoarseness of her voice I could tell she had been crying. "Please tell the Lady Mariam I am just a simple body-servant, no one of any consequence," I said. Now I was overcome with curiosity to have a look at the girl who would be taking my beloved from me. I imagined her as a reverse-coin version of the *zahira*, dark where the other was pale; sloe eyed, round bosomed: every young man's fancy.

There was a rustling of clothes, then a face appeared around the edge of the fretted screen. Plump, snub nosed, round eyed; a mass of black curls escaping the hastily donned head scarf; barely more than a child. You could not imagine a creature less like Zoraya the Morning Star.

"Come in," she said in her tiny voice.

I soon saw why she had been less than willing to allow me to enter. The chamber was scattered with discarded caftans and robes, all of them the worse for wear and dowdy beyond belief. No wonder she had been weeping. I presented my bundle of offerings and she shook them out like a child discovering wonders—the white silk, the coloured scarves, the rope of amber beads and the silver amulets that had been my inheritance. By the time she had finished going through them her cheeks were red and her eyes shone: she looked almost pretty.

My heart hardening again, I prepared my escape. "I will not stay, madam, as the hour is so late, but I will come tomorrow and help you dress."

"Please, please do— Oh, I never asked your name, or gave you mine! I'm such a fool. How ever will I survive in the great palace?" Tears trembled again in her huge eyes.

"The error was all mine," I assured her. "I knew your name only too well and failed to offer my own. They call me Tudert," I said, giving her my mother's name. "And I bid you good-night."

My earliest memories were of crawling on the bright carpets in Tudert's tent with all her jewellery strewn around me, or upon me. Silver amulets and Agadez crosses around my neck, long earrings looped over my ears, too-big bangles pushed up to my armpits. "These are camels," I would tell her proudly, indicating a line of hairpins and brooches, "and these are goats—" polished beads gathered beside pieces of amber and cowrie shells traded with the travelling smith. I thought she was the richest woman in the world: certainly, she was rich in smiles and kisses, which she poured down upon me, especially when I proved my usefulness to her.

She would send me out to spy at the campfires, to listen at tents in the night. No one paid much attention to a skinny child bringing camel dung for the fire, or fetching water for the pot. No one questioned a child peeing behind a thorn bush while the men made their plans, or tracing patterns in the dirt with stones where the women were gossiping. I would commit to memory all I heard, then report back to her in gabbled whispers, and she would sort the grain from the chaff and stow the information away for future use. A day or two later she would prepare ointments and potions precisely formulated to address the problems she had learned of. "I've just discovered the perfect liniment for a strained back," she would declare, after hearing that Moussa had twisted it chasing off a jackal. Or knowing that Suleiman could not keep up with his new wife: "I hear that a poultice of crushed beetle shells can do wonders for restoring one's manhood." Sometimes her remedies worked because they had an effect on the body, but mostly they worked because of a magic effect on people's minds. It did not much matter, so long as clients paid up and came back for more.

Occasionally, her work took a darker turn. I remember a weeping woman who covered her face in a manner unusual among our people, whisking aside her veil to show my mother the ugly cuts and bruises inflicted on her by a man who had taken her against her will. I was sent out to dig up some roots. "Wait till the moon shows the whole of its face over the oasis palms," my mother told me. "Then dig in the space between the red rocks there, the ones marked with three scratches." I knew exactly where she meant. "Don't touch the plant with your bare hands but shovel it straight into this bag." I did exactly as I was told and she took the roots and spent the night boiling them inside the tent, fanning the acrid fumes away through a hole in the hide roof. Then she dipped a piece of fabric in the liquid and, using a pair of sticks, wrung out the cloth and left it to dry. The next morning the woman came back and took

the dried fabric away. It looked to me like a man's turban cloth—
tagelmust—but I might have been mistaken. And again my mother
warned, "Be careful not to touch it with your bare skin." The
woman appeared scared. Then she removed a jewelled pin from her
robe and offered it to my mother, who closed the woman's fingers
over it. "I'll accept no payment for this."

Two days later I heard the chieftain's son, an arrogant man much
given to bullying and even to hurting his camels, was carried writhing into the shadows under the palm trees because he was burning
up and raving so badly: clearly djinn had got into him and no one
wanted them in the camp. He didn't die, which surprised me; but he
crept about after that and his appetites were never the same.

But mainly her work was benign, and this was how she got by
after my father died. She was good at what she did. And so was I.
As a result of my tasks, I had learned stealth, to listen carefully, to
remember exactly. And a great deal about human frailty.

We ate well, we had status within the tribe and life was good.
Until one day my mother did not get up with the sun to fetch water
and make our morning porridge but lay there rolled in her blanket.
When she did not respond to my angry cries, I went out to help
myself to porridge from some other woman's cook pot—as a child
you have no understanding of ownership—got beaten for my trouble and wailed as if bereft.

And indeed I was bereft, and not just of breakfast. My mother
had died in the night. No one knew why or how. The djinn came
for her was the consensus.

But her name Tudert meant "life" in our language. It hardly
seemed fair.

The aunts took me in. I do not know if they were true aunts, or
in any way related to my mother, but that's how it works among
our people. They dressed me in their cast-offs, girls' robes that tangled around my legs, and shaved my head. All the other children

kept a single braid on the crown of their heads, for the angels to catch them by should they fall. But it seemed the aunts didn't care if I fell or if angels had nothing to catch me by. They didn't treat me the same way as they treated their own children at all, but beat me for looking at them askance, or for being slow, or too quick, or too noisy, for talking too much. And sometimes at the sight of me they signed against the evil eye, especially when the drought arrived and the animals died and the young men did not return from the desert.

Then one day when I was cutting up meat, with the blood all over my hands, I had a strange turn. "The baby inside you will never feed from your teat," I told one of the aunts. My voice did not sound like my own.

The aunt cried out. "It is Tudert, returned! It's a curse on what we did to her: she has come to take her revenge!"

The other women told her to shut up. It was just Blessings, being strange.

The aunt stared at me with eyes of flint. "Your mother may have named you Blessings, but you are nothing except bad luck."

"One more mouth to feed when we don't have enough to go round," agreed another woman.

"You turn the milk sour," said another. She picked up a stone and threw it at me.

"My favourite goat died."

"The well water tastes bitter."

The next stone hit me on the arm. It stung. I glared.

More stones came at me.

"Monster!" someone shouted. "We always knew you were a monster!"

The word hit me harder than did the stones. I looked to the aunts, expecting them to intervene then: but my first aunt threw another stone, shouting "Monster!" as she did so, and then all the other women, and the children, joined in. And so I was forced to run away from the only life I had ever known. It was just as well that I had foreseen something like it happen in a dream months prior, and had filched bits and pieces of jewellery and buried them some distance outside the camp in one of my mother's hidden herb gardens: if I'd had nothing to trade on my journey north into the land of the Moors, I would surely have starved.

"Now we drape this part of the fabric so, and fasten it with this fibula. And wind this scarf around your hips—"

For a moment I felt the urge to plunge the long pin of the fibula into her breast, but I caught myself thinking it, imagining the pain it would cause this awkward child, and was ashamed. It was not her fault. None of it was. I pinned the cloth with exaggerated care, then stepped back to regard my handiwork. It was a rather outlandish costume, but there had not been a great deal to choose from once the maids had been at the baggage.

"Do I look all right?" Big-eyed with doubt, Mariam appeared younger than ever.

"Beautiful," I lied. "Prince Mohamed will be lost for words when he sees you."

I arranged a scarf around her head with the tassels hanging down and the amulet pinned upon it. With the rope of heavy amber beads around her neck, some earrings I had put together from pierced silver coins threaded over her ears and a silver Berber wedding crown upon her head, the costume was complete.

By the time I had finished adjusting everything, I realized that under the veil Mariam was crying again. For a second the image of the runt kitten flickered across my mind. She was about to snatch from me the person I loved most in the world. Didn't she understand the honour this marriage bestowed upon her? I dragged the veil off her again, more roughly than was necessary. Tears had smudged the kohl I had applied: she looked terrified. With effort, I mastered my jealousy. "Don't cry," I said, wiping the kohl and tears away with the corner of my scarf. "He is kind and gentle. There's nothing to fear. And as handsome as the sun. You will be the envy of every woman in Granada." *But most of all, of me.*

Her lip trembled, then curved into the sweetest smile I had ever seen.

"How old are you?" I found myself asking.

"Fifteen."

Two years younger than Momo. A child indeed. Gently raised and sheltered from the world. And about to be parcelled off to a distant city with a group of strangers, made to bed a man she had never met. No wonder she was frightened, poor thing. Fellow feeling overtook me quite against my will, and the angry wall I had built up against her fell away, stone by stone.

With her elderly servant in attendance I led her down the stairs to be married. She was so nervous she tripped and lost a slipper along the way. It skittered end over and end in for a moment and I felt dizzy, remembering my own fall.

I will never forget the look on Momo's face when she lifted her veil with her little hennaed hand and gazed up at him. I saw his face soften like a child's. All that day, and through the celebrations that followed—the almonds and dates, the singing and drums, the dance of the town maidens, the enthronement, the candlelit feast— he ministered to her as if she were a great queen and he her obedient servant.

I felt sick to watch them, and if I had worried that she might recognize me in my male guise that night, there was no need, for she saw no one but Momo. In her gaze of astonishment and adoration I saw my own yearning reflected.

When they made to carry the bride and groom to their chamber, I could bear it no longer and eased outside for some air. There, as the moon slipped behind a cloud, I almost tripped over the Banu Serraj captain drinking from a jar of wine he had come by. We gave each other the conspiratorial look that agreed we were not very good Muslims and for a long time sat companionably together, the night silence broken only by the glug of the wine in the crock and long, slow swallows.

At last he said, "Do you believe in the prophecy?"

"About the prince?"

"That under him the kingdom will fall."

"What do astrologers know?"

"Aye, that's what I say."

"Do people talk of it often?"

I could tell by a subtle shift in the night air that he was eyeing me. "People say all sorts."

"I have heard," I said quietly, "that some think the sultan should disinherit him." Now let us see what sympathy there might be for Zoraya and her cause that I could report back to Qasim.

"What, for the *zahira*'s sons? They would prefer those brats over our Momo?"

I laughed, glad to have my friend called by this affectionate shortening. "I hear they are tiny monsters, given to screaming tantrums that go on for hours until soothed only by their father."

"I heard that too. But maybe the lady herself put it about." He winked at me. "I was on duty outside her new quarters a few weeks back, and I swear I heard her hit them." The sultan had moved Zoraya and her children into their own apartments housed inside one of the towers along the Alhambra's outer wall. Everyone was calling it the Tower of the Captive now.

"Be careful," I said. "She has spies everywhere, they say."

"Everyone has spies." It was the fact of court life, especially in one as fractured as ours.

"Do you really think the sultan would disinherit him?" I could hardly keep the forlorn hope out of my voice.

"Well, he can't now," the captain said. "Not with old Ali Attar on his side. There'd be civil war and that's the last thing anyone needs. But she's determined, the Morning Star. I wouldn't put anything past her."

10

I lay on my pallet among a dozen snoring men and tossed and turned. Momo and Mariam were safely stashed in the bridal chamber now, where I had no doubt she would be wrapping those sturdy legs and arms around him. The image clung to my consciousness, no matter how hard I tried to push it off. It was clear I would get no sleep that night. I retrieved my golden foot and pulled it on over my stump, then laced the boot high to the knee. I would, I thought, slip out into the streets of Loja. Maybe even be at the mosque as the sun rose. That would be a first.

It's hard to creep with a false leg. I was halfway down the stairs, when someone hissed, "Blessings!"

My head shot up. Momo, his gold-and-white wedding robe wrapped tight around him, his head bare. He beckoned to me and I followed him up the stairs.

"What? What is it?"

"You cannot say anything about this ever, to anyone," he said as we reached the closed door.

I gazed at him with my heart in my eyes. "You know you can trust me, always. Are you unwell? Is she?"

Momo glanced away from me, his expression indistinct in the leaping light of the corridor lantern. "She can't . . . I . . . She's so shy, Blessings. I don't know what to do. I've tried all I know, which to be honest isn't much. And I can't force her."

"You may have to," I said, rather more harshly than I'd meant. "The wedding sheet."

He looked unutterably miserable. "I know. She knows. She's terrified that people will think she's not pure. Her reputation will be destroyed. But that's just making her even more anxious. She's in tears now."

How many tears can she have left in her? I wondered uncharitably. "Leave it with me," I said. "Go back in and comfort her. I'll fetch some wine. Maybe that will relax her."

For a moment he looked appalled. Then he smiled. "Go on, then."

Down the stairs I went again, thankful for the handrail to steady me, for my knees were shaking. I'd nearly leaned in and kissed him, right there, right then. On his wedding night.

The kitchen was in darkness except for the embers glowing in the hearth. The red light picked out a tray destined for the royal pair's breakfast: a pot of honey and one of oil, some almonds to rebuild the groom's strength after his busy night. Some servant would be by soon to bake the morning bread and set a jug of sherbet on the tray. I poked around, not finding what I searched for, until I heard footsteps heading my way. I froze, trying to think of a good excuse for being there at this unearthly hour, but as the servant entered, some inner voice stopped me from calling out, something more alert than the rest of me. The figure placed a jug on the table. I could just make out the white cloth that closed its mouth. A celebratory drink for the newlyweds. Just what I had been searching for. But the movements of the servant seemed more furtive than my own. And something else too . . .

I crossed the room in three strides, caught the intruder by the arm and turned my captive toward the firelight. She wore a veil, but there was no mistaking La Sabia.

"You!" she spat, staring up at me. "When did you become a man?"

I took some pleasure in twisting her arm up behind her back. "What are you doing here?"

Such a struggle to hold her. The old woman was still strong, even after all these years. I pushed her arm higher till she squealed. Oh, the satisfaction. "What's in the jug?"

"Sherbet," she panted. "Sherbet for the happy couple." The loathing in her voice was plain.

"Sherbet and what else?"

Her eyes narrowed. "Ice. Just sherbet and ice."

"You will drink some, then," I told her. She struggled harder. I remembered how easily she had had me down on the floor, kicking me in the guts. Things had changed. We were both older, but I had gained muscle and height. Unable to escape my grip, she kicked out at me now, then yelped as her foot connected with the metal and wood of my false foot. Under other circumstances I would have laughed. Instead, I forced her toward the table. "Drink it!" I ordered. "Or I will break your neck."

She squirmed like an old goat knowing it was going to the Eid slaughter. There was a crash and somehow the jug was on the floor, smashed to pieces. In that moment I must have relaxed my grip, for suddenly she escaped me. I tried to pursue her; but, hampered by my golden foot, by the time I made it out to the corridor she had outpaced me. I patrolled the passages in both directions and failed to find the old woman. The wine was making my head swim and I was exhausted. I was cursing as I went back into the kitchen.

A small reddish cat was crouched on the floor, lapping at the spilled liquid. It did not even look up at me as I edged past it, thinking, thinking. Go beyond the wine: something more direct. A small bit of liver or heart would do. I moved crocks, pots, dishes, jars; looked on shelves, beneath clay lids. Nothing.

All the while I considered the crone and the woman who had sent her here. Was La Sabia on some sort of mission of destruction, or was she merely spying for Zoraya? Whichever it was, I must warn Momo. We should separate her from the other maids, too, I thought, before she could cause more mischief. No wonder they had had poor Mariam in tears with their taunting: no doubt it had been a small terrorizing measure to upset the child. My mind went back to the sherbet. *Why would she have brought it so early,* asked a small voice in my head. The ice would melt before breakfast—

A small choking noise interrupted my thoughts and I turned to find the cat retching, its neck stretched out, ears flat to its head, as if trying to dislodge a hairball. It was making horrible sounds . . . Oh. It was no cat. It was a fox: that was bad luck.

I grabbed it and took it to one of the water crocks, dunked it thoroughly and tried to get as much water as possible down its throat. Assuming I was trying to drown it, the fox fought for its life, and when I did not let go sank its teeth into the meat of my hand, between the forefinger and thumb. The pain was frightful and I yelled. Then it shuddered and released its grip, and died.

Poison. I sniffed the spilled sherbet. Beneath the lemony sweetness there was something acrid. Memory tickled my skull. I had smelled this somewhere before. But try as I might, I could not place it. I pushed the fox's limp body under a table and washed my wound as well as I could. Then I made my way back up the stairs. By the time I reached the bridal chamber I was sweating profusely and my heart was pounding with the effort. "Give me the sheet," I said when Momo opened the door. He brought it to me without asking why. With my belt-knife I opened the wound the fox had made and dripped my blood onto the pristine linen.

He shook his head slowly. "Why didn't I think of that?"

I propped myself against the door frame, wishing I hadn't drunk so much wine.

"Are you all right, Blessings?" He put his hand on my shoulder. I patted it. "I'll be fine. Took the stairs . . . a bit . . . quick. Don't worry about . . . me. Go tell your wife . . . to stop weeping. And get some sleep. Peace be upon you, friend."

"My dear, dear friend."

He squeezed my shoulder, then went back inside and closed the door. I stood there, relishing the memory of his touch, before realizing I had forgotten to tell him about La Sabia. Ah well, my news would keep till morning. Which was only an hour or two away. I staggered back down to the sleeping quarters, with the world spinning around me and my good leg weighing as heavily as the gold one.

I am told that I hung between life and death for almost three weeks. I lay sweating and delirious, leaking at both ends, mumbling about a witch. No one could make out what I was on about. Dr. Ibrahim bled me and gave me emetics and enemas, to add indignity to injury. I hallucinated like a madman: mandrake will do that to you. And once I woke and found the covers up around my chin and the doctor regarding me with the strangest expression. I thought they spoke my name, but I could not make out what they were saying. It was as if I had gone to a realm where djinn and demons were tormenting me.

I missed the wedding celebrations altogether, and when Momo queried why I was absent, he was told by the guard captain that I'd drunk myself stupid, which is what he'd thought on finding me in my miserable state. But when I didn't improve, they realized it was something worse, so I was loaded upon a litter and hauled back to Granada and the care of the palace doctors. That I pulled through suggests La Sabia had remained in Loja, unable to complete the wicked task she had been set. Maybe she lacked another opportunity to poison the bride and groom. Maybe she had no further reserves of poison. And maybe had that little fox not perished and bitten me in its death throes, giving me the idea to cut myself, therefore reopening the wound, I too would have died. So many maybes.

So I missed the rest of Momo's stay in Loja. I missed the royal progress back to Granada and the entrance of Mariam into the Alhambra, which occurred with little ceremony. The sultan shunned her, instead closing himself away with Zoraya, leaving the girl to the tender mercies of her mother-in-law, Aysha. Poor child, it must have been a hard transition, even coming from such a grim fortress town as Loja to the Alhambra, with its pleasure gardens and graceful fountains, its paradisal pools and heavenly cupolas. But just as a beautiful woman with no heart is uglier than the plainest woman with love in her eyes, so the palace could be a sorrowful place, binding a savagely fractured family within its lovely walls.

People all think they know the bare outlines of what happened next, or at least the consequences of those atrocious events, but this is what I heard.

La Sabia had managed to insinuate herself into the inner circle of women attending upon the prince's new bride. But this time, rather than attempting to poison her by direct means she set about her poisoning in a more insidious way. She encouraged the other women to pester Mariam about her nighttime experiences, accompanied always with much giggling and pouting innuendo. Had she been warm enough? Had she had sufficient sleep? Hadn't they heard her sigh and cry out, or had that been an owl? When they helped her dress, they made much of her breasts—how soft a pillow for her lord's head, how many babes she could suckle with such big nipples. How her wide hips would make for easy births for all the prince's many sons, and surely she would be showing any day.

Soon they had her in a complete tizzy about the marriage bed, for she had still been unable to overcome her wedding-night nerves, and Momo, too gentle to force her, had let her be, hoping that she would in time relax.

Then one afternoon a page came to him with a private message. A very private message. This part I know from his own lips. The boy waited in a niche in the Court of Myrtles until the prince was alone and they could not be overheard. Then he said, "My Lady Zoraya, peace be upon her, begs to offer her assistance to you in the matter of your wife's intimate difficulties. She is a great expert and would like to give you good counsel as to how to proceed with the lady."

"I was a fool," Momo told me later. "Such a fool."

He went. Against all common sense and his own best instincts, he went, driven to distraction by Mariam's anxieties and the very pressing need for them to consummate the marriage and produce an heir. Had I not been otherwise engaged, fighting for my life, I could have stopped him, or at least run to Qasim; but Momo was desperate, and rash.

Even given the length of the walk to the Tower of the Captive, through shaded bowers, where the winter-flowering jasmine gave out its sweet confectionary scent, Momo did not accord much thought to his enemy's true motivation, or the fact that no guard accosted him or questioned his presence. For Zoraya was the sultan's most prized possession, his most precious favourite, whom no other man was allowed near, even if he was the son of the sultan, a star in the firmament of the kingdom.

"You must seduce her," Zoraya told him once the formalities of greeting were done. "Like this—"

And then she had pulled him down upon her on the wide couch, shrugging expertly out of her flimsy robe as she did so. "Stroke her breasts, like this," she cooed at him, placing his hands on her flesh. "As gently as if they were kittens. See how the nipples stand to attention, seeking your approval."

Even when he related this to me, the memory made him colour.

"Then you put your mouth upon them. Here——" She had tried to draw his head down to her nipples, but Momo had pulled away. She'd hooked a leg around him and tumbled him into an even more intimate embrace; and this was when (of course) with a howl of fury, the sultan burst into the chamber, flanked by two of the most massive of his eunuch guards, scimitars flashing.

When they hauled the young prince off her, Zoraya just lay there, breathing heavily, apparently dazed by his unexpected assault, tears tracking down her perfect cheeks.

"I should kill you here and now!" his father raged, his fists great knots of white bone. "I swear I should!"

Spittle flecked his beard: he looked quite mad. Momo said he thought that if he had cowered or begged or pleaded his innocence, his father would have dealt him a blow, one he would not survive. He stood silent and resolute and looked the sultan steadily in the eye, thinking that if the astrologers were right, it was too soon for him to die. At last the sultan turned away.

"Take the prince and his hyena of a mother, who has no doubt engineered this vile attack, and imprison them both in the topmost room of the Tower of the Moon!"

After this, events become less focused. They say that truth and legend become so entwined in the kingdom of Granada that no one can unravel the truth. All I know is that Momo and his mother, Aysha the Pious, directly descended from the Prophet, were made prisoners in the tower. But even this did not cool the sultan's anger, and a few days later he sent out a summons to his wife's closest allies from among the Banu Serraj, giving each of them precise instructions about when and how they were to present themselves to his majesty. Slaves showed them into the sultan's private quarters, one by one. And one by one, they came in from the bright sunlight of the courtyard into the penumbrous light of that most beautiful of halls, blinking and screwing their eyes up, only to have their heads struck from their shoulders by the sultan's own blade. One by one, the heads fell and were stacked into the fountain; one by one the corpses were shrouded in sheets and smuggled out through the apartment by the sultan's body-slaves, so that the next man in line might not be forewarned of the fate of his predecessor, nor the fate that awaited him.

Thirty-six men died that day.

Their blood still stains the marble bowl of the fountain in the sultan's hall where it seeped into the stone.

Kate

NOW

"Jess? Jesus, Jess, at last!"

"*Calm down, Kate.*"

Her sister's voice on the other end of the line was tinny and indistinct, making her seem even farther away from Kate than she was. "I got your message. The coded email. What happened? My God, is Luke okay?"

"He's fine. He's with Sarah right now, down on the beach turning over stones to look for crabs. I can see them from here: I'm surprised I can't hear them, given how loud he shrieks every time anything moves. He's a complete wuss!"

Kate sat on the steps; her knees were shaking. "Tell me everything that happened. How did he find you? What did he say? Does he know you're in Cornwall now? Did I ever mention Sarah to him? I don't think I did. I can't remember. Oh God! I'll get the next flight back. Or you come to me—I'll pay for your flights, of course. There's a sofa bed in the lounge and—"

"I'm sorry, Kate. I should never have sent that email. I didn't mean to panic you. Honestly, we're okay. James didn't see Luke: he was already in bed. I shouldn't have said 'us'—I meant 'me'—he found me. He was searching for you, obviously. And look, he wasn't threatening or even unpleasant, not really—"

"I'm so sorry, so sorry, Jess. What are we going to do?" She hated the sound of her voice rising to a childish wail, as if she were expecting her twin to solve her problems for her.

The sound of Jess taking a deep breath. "Right now? I'm going to walk down to the beach, poke around in some rock pools, tickle Luke till he giggles himself sick and cook a curry for me and Sarah. That's my plan."

"You know that's not what I meant."

"Oh, Kate, he's just a man. A sad, rejected man. That's all. I shouldn't have told you, let alone come dashing down here, scaring poor Sarah half to death in the middle of the night."

"I knew something was up. I could sense it."

"Don't give me that weird twin stuff. Look, I've got to go—battery's running down. And typical Sarah, she hasn't even got an iPhone, let alone a charger. I'll have to go into town tomorrow. I wonder if they've even heard of iPhones down here . . ."

"But I need to know. What did he say? You didn't tell him where I was, did you?"

There was a pause at the other end of the line. "No, I'm not a complete idiot. Listen, I have to go—there are clouds gathering here. Bet it'll rain before I even get down to the beach. Take care, Sis, okay? I'll call you again soon."

And the connection cut out. Kate sat there, in bosky shade on a little stone bench halfway up the steep hill to the red fort, with the statue of Washington Irving standing over her and the phone pressed to her ear, listening, listening, hearing nothing. She dropped her hands into her lap, sat staring at them. They looked like the hands of a stranger, brown and narrow. She did not know who she was anymore. She had been so, so stupid. It was the best part of three years since she had left James, three years of running from pillar to post, running through her savings. She had even been thinking of going home, back to England, maybe even back to the Peak District, somewhere close to Jess, to pick up the threads of her unravelled life, putting her mistakes, and her cowardice, behind her. How had he found them? This was the question that kept running through her head. How had he tracked them down? Jess wasn't foolish enough to use social media. Could James have hired a private investigator? And had he really been looking for her, Kate, and somehow stumbled on Jess? None of it made sense. But he had sniffed her out some way or another. Which meant that he had not given up. She lowered her head onto her knees and fought for control.

All this time.

What was so special about her? She was no beauty; it was that she had capitulated. She had allowed him to control her, to feel that he had power over her; when she had fought back, it had angered him. And when at last she had escaped him, his anger had become implacable.

"Oh my God," she moaned. "What have I done?" Running away, putting Jess and Luke in danger in her place. What a dangerous fool she had been, and what a coward.

"*¿Estás bien?* Are you all right?"

Kate felt a hand on her shoulder and looked up, embarrassed. The woman had kind brown eyes and a thin, worn face. It was impossible to judge her age—she could have been anything from forty to sixty. "I'm fine," Kate lied, managing a wobbly smile.

"You don't look fine," the woman said. "You look lost and alone."

Lost and alone. The words slid through Kate's defences and all at once she was crying, crying as she hadn't in years.

The woman sat down and pulled her close, enfolding her, making soothing noises as if Kate were her child. Such generosity from a total stranger. She could not remember the last time anyone had held her like this, without wanting anything in exchange. The tears streamed down, racking her through and through. The woman said nothing, just let Kate cry, until the sorrow and disappointment and self-loathing she had held pent up all these years was undammed.

As if sensing her release, the woman sat back and regarded her. "Don't fear," she said. "God holds each one of us in his hands. He does not want you to suffer. What good does your suffering do anyone? Be at peace."

"Easier said than done," Kate sniffed. "I've ruined everything. And not just for me, but for my sister too."

"I think you're being too hard on yourself."

"I honestly don't think that's possible. I've been stupid, and cowardly. I ran away from a situation I should have stayed to face."

"Sometimes it takes strength to choose the path of weakness," the woman said cryptically. "Sometimes surrender is more courageous than resistance. But it's hard for people to see that."

Kate thought about this. She didn't feel in the least courageous, but the woman's words were like a balm.

"What's your name?" the woman asked gently.

"Kate," Kate said, then closed her mouth quickly. She had never told anyone her real name, not since she'd run away. But somehow it didn't seem dangerous to have given her name to this woman. It would have felt wrong not to do so. "What's yours?"

"I'm Khadija," the woman said, returning Kate's smile. Under the coloured head scarf, her eyes narrowed to gleaming golden-brown crescents.

Two women: strangers acknowledging a common bond across cultures and languages, countries and age. It had been a long time since Kate had experienced such a sense of fellowship.

"Are you coming up or going down?" Khadija asked.

At once a simple and a significant question. Kate didn't have the significant answer, so she just said, "Up. I'll walk in the gardens if I can't get a ticket for the palaces."

"We'll go together," Khadija said. "I work there."

"You do?" Kate was surprised, then chided herself. Of course she did: the Alhambra was the greatest tourist attraction in Spain; it must require an army of workers to keep it running smoothly. But the woman wasn't wearing the usual green uniform. "Where do you work?" she asked as they tackled the hill together.

"I'm a conservator," the woman said. "An expert in the *chahar bagr*, the tradition of formal, quartered gardens." She reached into her bag, then handed Kate her card: Dr. Khadija Boutaki, it read, followed by a long line of abbreviated qualifications, an email address and two phone numbers.

Kate read the card over and over. She had been expecting Khadija to say she worked in the café, or as a cleaner. "Goodness," she said.

Khadija's smile was forgiving, a little amused. "You'd be surprised how many of us there are in my field of study. Women, that is—and Moroccan women at that."

Kate, caught out in this moment of prejudice, felt an excoriating wave of shame. "I'm so sorry. I didn't mean . . ." But she had. She was almost as bad as Jimena. "What a wonderful subject to specialize in. I love gardens. I've always loved plants, not just flowers but weeds, the lot. As a kid I could name them all, both their common names and their Latin ones."

Khadija turned and pointed to a group of white-and-purple spikes of flower. They grew everywhere around Granada, seeming to thrive in whatever poor soil they found. "Do you know what these are?"

Kate grinned. "Bear's breeches. I've no idea why. The Latin name is *Acanthus mollis*."

"Good girl," Khadija said approvingly. "You'll find them represented in the stucco in the palace."

"I know," Kate said quietly. "I've seen them there." She spread her hands: no words would suffice. "I've never been anywhere quite like the Generalife," she finished lamely.

"There *is* nowhere quite like the Jannat al-Arif. Some translate that as the 'Gardens of the Architect,' but as the architect is in this case God, we often translate it as the 'Gardens of Paradise,'" Khadija said.

Kate nodded. It was exactly how she thought of them.

They reached the ticket pavilion and Kate started toward the queues, but Khadija took her by the arm. "You are my guest." She moved authoritatively to the counter and said something in rapid Arabic to the woman behind the glass, who opened a drawer, took out a card and fed it into a printer.

"What's your name, Kate? Your family name?"

Kate told her.

A minute later the card, slipped into a laminated cover and threaded onto a lanyard, was slid across the counter to her.

KATE FORDHAM, it said, followed by *Pase conservador*: Conservator pass.

She had her identity back.

Later, having wandered the gardens, she picked the changeover time between lunchtime tourist tickets to enter the Nasrid palaces, made her way toward the Patio de los Leones and into the Hall of the Abencerrages, a corruption—as she knew from the tours she had taken—of the Arabic *Banu Serraj*. There, in a miraculous lull in the flow of tourists, she lay down on the floor to gaze up into its extraordinary cupola, a masterwork of carved and moulded plaster, set in the form of an eight-pointed star like a great lacy honeycomb. How long she stayed there contemplating it, she did not know. Moorish ornamentation had that effect on you, the reiterated patterns sending your brain into a sort of meditative trance. She had read that a mathematical formula had been applied to every aspect of the palaces to ensure perfect symmetry and give the sense of infinite space. It was quite extraordinarily soothing and for a time she felt she was floating, gliding through time.

Then she heard voices approaching. Abruptly she was pulled back down to earth, becoming aware that the marble floor was cold against her back and bare heels. Yet when she put her hand to it to push herself upright, its smooth, worn texture felt like a sort of skin, as if the place was alive but in a state of stasis, biding its time to breathe again. She looked around into the bowl of the central fountain. The staining inside did not much resemble blood, she thought. She knew the legend that had given the hall its name: a massacre, dozens of decapitations; rivers of blood. The stained marble was supposed to be the last trace of the victims, but of course that was just superstition. And maybe a little oxidization.

As the first group of tourists drifted in, craning their necks and blinking to adjust their vision, Kate walked out into the sunlight.

Instead of taking her usual route through the palaces, she wandered toward the ramparts and towers opposite the summer palace, passing a group of noisy, bored schoolchildren pushing one another off the brick paths, paying no attention to their teachers. *But it's your history!* she wanted to say to them. *One day you'll boast of coming here but realize you remember nothing about it.*

History was rather wasted on the young, who had yet to discover that looking back could sometimes be a lot more instructive than looking forward. To the young, the future was a wide blue yonder, full of hopes and promises and possibilities. *Before their hearts and dreams were smashed,* she thought.

And what about you, Kate? What's in your future?

She had no idea. Some days it seemed too fraught to consider. As for looking back . . . She should never have married James. That much was perfectly obvious now. Even at the time, she had been beset by doubts. But everyone who met James was charmed by him: so good-looking and so easy to talk to; so polite and helpful, such a gentleman. Even Jess—usually more astute when it came to her twin's relationships than her own—had been taken in by his apparent steadiness. "He's just what you need after Matty: a man, not some hopeless, self-pitying boy. You should grab him while you can. You're not getting any younger, you know."

The bitterness had more to do with her own situation, Kate had reflected after her initial burst of anger. Jess and Evan had been trying to get pregnant for ages. They'd been married almost nine years and people had always concluded they must have decided to wait before starting a family while each pursued a career. But nothing could have been further from the truth. Jess had been desperate for children the whole time—Kate thought Jess had probably only married Evan so that she could start her brood. In the expectations of this they'd bought the perfect place to raise a large family: a rundown farmhouse on the edge of the Peak District, not far from their origins in the outskirts of Huddersfield. Jess had tried to get pregnant right from the start, but to no avail. Instead, her efforts went into the renovations, adding plastering, carpentry and electrical wiring to her already impressive skill set. The place was so beautiful—with its modern open-plan spaces and huge floor-to-ceiling windows, its massive old hearths and reconditioned Aga—that Kate had felt a sharp, but fleeting, jealousy. But sometimes she had wondered whether it was her sister's total competence in all things that had contributed to the failure of the marriage as much as the pressures of failed conception and then all the rounds of in vitro fertilization. Evan once admitted to Kate that he felt he had no useful role to play in their shared life at all. She'd tried to suggest as much to Jess, on Evan's behalf, since he was so hopeless at talking to his wife; but of course that had backfired mightily, leaving Jess furious at what she saw as Evan's treachery in confiding in Kate, and Kate's disloyalty as a sister. Her refusal to understand that Kate was trying to help had made them spiky with each other for months, despite all Kate's efforts to placate Jess, and only been when she'd apologized abjectly had Jess spoken to her again. Kate hated feeling in the wrong, hated conflict, and so, after James's disappearing act, she had fallen into that same conciliatory role, for fear of setting off a furious response. But when he offered no explanation for his absence, she found herself asking, "Did you go to see your mother?" She watched for his reaction.

He'd looked appalled. "Why would you ask that? I told you she died last year."

So Yusuf must have made a mistake about that.

"Anyway, look, I've got something to show you."

She decided not to press the point, not wanting to spark an argument.

He was full of glee and energy when he led her to his car, rolled down the soft-top and drove them west out of London onto the M40. In a pub car park in Beaconsfield he'd pulled a silk scarf out of his pocket. "Put this on."

Kate had frowned. "I don't wear head scarves."

"No, silly, like this." Quickly, expertly, he'd tied it around her forehead and pulled it down over her eyes.

"A blindfold?" she'd said in some alarm.

"Humour me."

She felt a fool buckled into the passenger seat with a scarf over her eyes, but James drove so fast down the long hill from Beaconsfield that she was comforted by the thought that it was unlikely anyone would notice her. Besides, no one she knew lived as far out as this, so she wouldn't be recognized even if seen.

James braked, then took a sharp left. She heard the note of the car's engine drop in tone as they toiled uphill, and found herself shifted left then right as they banked around several corners before at last coming to a stop. James opened her door, released the seat belt and handed her out with all the gentility of a medieval knight. "Careful now," he warned. "Lift your feet: the path's a tad uneven."

He'd guided her with a hand in the small of her back, then held her shoulders to halt her progress. With a flourish, he removed the blindfold.

"Welcome to your new home!"

Kate found herself staring at a pretty brick cottage with a tangle of winter-flowering jasmine around mullioned windows and a heart carved into the panels of its front door.

James dangled a set of keys in front of her nose. "Take them!"

She rounded on him. "What on earth's going on?"

He swept his fall of dark hair out of his eyes, looking almost boyish in his glee. "I was picking up some items for the shop from the chap who was clearing the place out after his gran died, and I knew it was perfect for us. It needs a bit of renovation, but as soon as I saw it, I was certain you'd love it. We exchanged contracts last week and Tom let me have the keys especially so I could show it to you."

"You bought a *house*?"

He beamed. "Tom and I have been clearing it out ever since. Didn't want you to see it full of earwigs and cobwebs and old lady's knickers!"

She didn't know what to say. Anything that came to mind— like, *How dare you be so high-handed?* Or, *You might at least have asked me!* Or, *What in God's name made you think I would want to live in the middle of nowhere?* —seemed so ungracious in the face of such a hugely romantic gesture. It was true that they had discussed moving in together, but the discussions had been desultory and

Kate hadn't taken them seriously. Besides, she'd thought if it ever came to that, James would be moving into her flat, after all the work they'd done on it together. It looked perfect now: she didn't want to leave.

A suspicion suddenly took hold of her. What if this had been his plan all along, and all the things he'd brought to her flat, all the artistic touches and the help renovating the damaged areas, had been a matter of getting it sale ready? But no, that couldn't be right. Her view of men had been coloured by her experiences with Matty. She shouldn't be so uncharitable.

As soon as she stepped through the front door straight into the big lounge, with its huge stone fireplace and big old beams, all negative thoughts fled. As if by some remote magic, a fire was burning in the grate, sending gusts of warm air and glowing light out into the room. Old-fashioned fire irons in the form of a pair of crouching lions, a brass coal scuttle, logs piled in a pleasing mosaic on either side of the hearth: it was all utterly timeless and completely charming. She could suddenly imagine putting a colourful Arabic rug on the polished oak boards and lying down with a glass of Rioja to watch the leaping flames, while snow floated down outside and built pretty drifts on the window ledges.

She turned to James. "It's lovely. Really lovely. But how on earth would I get to work from here?"

He grinned. "A friend of mine is selling his antiques shop in Old Amersham. We can work together: it does good trade. You could run the shop and I'll do the buying and restoration: it will be ideal. I'll sell the old shop and your flat to cover the bridging loan and we'll be quids in."

Bridging loan? What had he done?

"But I can't just leave my job!" she cried. *Or sell my flat!*

All the suspicions came roaring back. He'd made these plans without consulting her, as if they were married and living in the

1950s! She felt outraged that he thought her life was so expendable. For a moment she'd almost stormed out to walk the thirty-odd miles back to London, bloody motorways and all. But she hadn't. Instead, she'd allowed the cottage to seduce her in a way James himself had never quite managed to.

Looking back on it now, she felt appalled at her blindness, her lack of backbone. But the bridging loan hung over her head like a threat, and when the company she worked for got taken over by a larger conglomerate the following month and she found her job spec changed beyond recognition and her new manager patronizing and unpleasant, it hadn't taken her long to enjoy a glorious moment of madness by quitting, much to the admiration of her equally pissed-off, but trapped, colleagues. "Well done, Kate!" they'd crowed in the pub that night. "You were magnificent! What was it you called him, 'a pompous, pea-brained prick'? Brilliant!"

Kate had never done anything half so rebellious in her life. It felt great, until the next morning. Then the panic started. What was she going to do? A woman in her mid- thirties working in a specialist niche as a data analyst, who'd only ever held the one job with the same company, for which she now had no references, since the entire top level of managers who knew her had been cleared out in a single sweep with the takeover. A woman, moreover, with a mortgage to pay off. She put her flat on the market. Beautified by James and his expert eye, and stacked with antiques, it was indeed sale ready, and it sold in less than a week.

James asked her to marry him in the garden of the cottage, going down on one knee (carefully choosing one of the little flat stones that paced across the lawn, so as not to ruin his trousers). "I want children with you, Kate. A son to carry on my line."

Kate had felt a spike of ice in her heart. But she'd looked around at the hellebores and sedums, the *Rosa rugosa* and the tumbles of candytuft, and felt the ice melt a little. It would be a beautiful place to live. And a wonderful home to raise children in . . . Except, did she want children with James? She thought she did. So why did she feel a little sick? "It's too much to take in right now. I'm not very good at processing so much new information so quickly. Give me a week or two to think it all through."

James went all steely jawed, as if manfully holding back a sob.

"I'm not going to let you go, Kate," he'd said when they parted. "We're destined to be together. I knew it from the first moment I saw you."

At the time it had seemed such a determined, stoical thing to say: she'd even felt guilty. But now she saw it for what it really was: a threat.

12

Kate

NOW

The walk to the Tower of the Captive was spectacular, the air hanging over the gorge filled with the scent of roses . . . but when she reached it, she found cords roping off the area and a notice informing visitors to the monument that important restorations were being carried out. Still, the door was open. In the shady interior she could see two figures crouched, heads almost touching, hands working at something between them, as if they were playing chess.

"¡Hola!" she called out, and the heads jerked up. An older man in his sixties and a younger one, perhaps his son. They both had that peculiar configuration of sharp facial bones and sand-brown skin that marked them out as North African. Their dark eyes glittered at her, and suddenly she felt like an unwelcome intruder, disrupting a ritual.

Then the older man straightened up, rubbed his hands on his trousers and came toward her, one hand held out in greeting. She noticed it was covered in clay dust, and so were the knees of his overalls.

"Hello, lady."

He had a broad, pleasant face, with a close-cropped white beard and deep wrinkles around his eyes. "You're working on the renovations?" she asked.

And he grinned. "*Sí.*" Then he caught sight of the badge on her lanyard and his tone changed. "You come to inspect?"

Kate touched the badge, then laughed. "No, no: I'm just a guest."

He relaxed visibly. "You want to see?"

She did. But she felt the other man's gaze on her, wary and not exactly hostile, but not welcoming either. "No, it's all right. I don't want to interrupt your work."

"You won't be interrupting us," the younger man said. "We were about to stop for some tea. Would you like some?"

The invitation was offered in excellent English with a strange, unplaceable lilt: he might have been inviting her to join him in the Diamond Jubilee Tea Salon at Fortnum's. Which was where James had taken her to celebrate their engagement. She pushed that thought away. "I'd love some."

The younger man said something in what she thought was Arabic and the older man unhooked the rope and guided Kate through into the cool interior. For a moment she stood gazing around the hall, entranced by its serene beauty, which was nothing at all what you would expect from seeing the rough tawny walls enclosing it. Light spilled in from recessed windows on three sides, each defined by a gorgeous stucco arch. Intricately patterned enamelled tiles reached to hip height around the walls; above that, every square inch of wall was covered in carved plaster, arabesques contained by diamond grids, stretching up to the ceiling, fifteen feet or so above her head. On a dust sheet spread over the floor lay pieces of wood and tile and a pile of cement, a scatter of tools and a barrel of water. In a corner of the room a silver teapot sat on a small brazier. Beside it on a tray stood three coloured glasses, as if they had been expecting her. She felt like Alice, arrived in Wonderland.

The older man smiled. "Our custom is always to be ready for guests," he said in heavily accented Spanish. "I am Omar. This is my nephew, Abdou. He's the master, the *ma'allem*."

"I'm Kate," she said, for the second time that day.

While Abdou worked, seemingly oblivious to them, his uncle chatted away, drawing out from Kate how long she had lived in the city; what she thought of the Albayzín, of where she worked; what she thought of Spanish food. All the while Kate watched as the younger man adjusted one tiny piece of dull clay tile after another among a jumble of others in a wooden form on the floor, moving them with apparently careful intent. He picked up a sieve and scattered a fine dust over the jumble, then followed this with sprinklings of water from the barrel; then he knelt and, spreading his fingers in the resultant mud, smoothed it from side to side, his movements precise and mesmerizing. She could not look away: there was something so beautiful about his intense concentration on what seemed a simple task. It was like viewing a child immersed in some act of imagination you could not fathom. She took in the straight line of his long nose, the pleasing angle where cheekbone met the bone beneath the eye, the way his dark eyebrows and lashes contrasted with the warm brown of his skin.

When he was satisfied that the cement was spread evenly, Abdou pushed himself to his feet, washed his hands in the barrel, dried them on his overalls and sat down cross-legged in a single fluid movement beside the now-steaming teapot. Once he'd pulled his sleeve down to wrap the handle, he held the pot out to his uncle, and Kate watched as Omar added pellets of tea from a colourful square tin, then a handful of mint leaves from a plastic bag, and finally a large bar of sugar. *That's a lot of sugar*, she thought, looking away.

The younger man caught her eye. "Moroccans have a sweet tooth," he said.

"What are you doing here?" As soon as her query came out, it sounded wrong, like an accusation. She smiled uncertainly, trying to soften her words. But neither man appeared insulted.

"We're repairing the *zellij*." Abdou indicated a section of the wall to one side of the central arched window where the tiles had been cut away for restoration. Uncoiling himself, he walked to the other side of the hall. "Hold your hand out——" He rummaged on the floor and picked out a handful of bits of nondescript-looking clay. But when he turned them over on her palm, the colours were startling. Some were tiny lozenges in white enamel; some like stylized flower buds, in deep greens and blues. "Back in Fez, the tile makers place the enamelled sheets in the kiln in careful order: white at the base, then yellow, then green, then blue, then black. This particular colour——" he touched a piece less than an inch in length, and an odd shape, like a geometric bluebell flower, in a fiery burnt orange "——this is very hard to replicate." He took the piece back from her and held it up against one of the undamaged areas of the wall. "This is the only part of the palace where the tiles were glazed with magenta. We had to experiment with all sorts of minerals before we got it right. My cousin in Fez—Omar's son, Mohamed—managed to coax the magenta out of a mixture of yellow and brown at high heat."

Kate laughed. "You make it sound like alchemy!"

Abdou nodded, serious. "It is. Mohamed uses olive pits to heat his oven to eight hundred degrees. But even so, each batch comes out slightly different, according to minute variations in temperature. It can be very hard to match exactly the colours we're repairing: some of these tiles were made the best part of a thousand years ago."

Kate gave a little whistle. "Really, that old?" She frowned, trying to make her brain work. For some reason, in his presence she was finding it hard to do math she would normally find simple. "The palace dates from the 1300s—"

He looked slightly annoyed, as if she were pulling him up. "It was renovated by Yusuf the first of his name, sultan of Granada, around 1333," he said stiffly. "So, all right, seven hundred years or so."

Feeling flustered, Kate bent to pick up a fragment on the floor. It was in the form of a—she counted—twelve-pointed star; when she turned the fragment over, it was to find that it was a deep, deep blue.

"Ah, the heart-star," Abdou said. "The starting point, the centre, from which the whole pattern is born. A whole galaxy depends on that one beginning. See here—"

He took her by the arm, and she felt a sudden shock of electricity run through her as his warm fingers guided her across the hall. She had not felt anything like it since . . . She had to concede she could not remember when she had felt quite so dazed, or dazzled, or frazzled: something with *z*'s in it, anyway: hazardous, fizzing, bizarre . . . It must be the *zellij* . . .

"And then we turn it back the right way up when it's set."

Kate almost fell down: she had not been paying attention to his explanations and the thing he had picked up had looked like nothing special at all—just a form of wood about two feet square, containing rough, dried cement. But when he turned it over . . .

"Oh . . . That's . . . that's amazing." It was entirely inadequate as a response to the beauty of the *zellij* work: hundreds of tiny fragments of coloured tile fitted with exquisite precision into the mosaic so that no glimpse of the prosaic mortar that held them in place could be seen.

"There's your heart-star, where everything begins—see how the rest of the pattern rays out from it, makes embellishments based on its shape? That's what I start with when I make a section of *zellij*."

"It's like . . . like . . ." Something deeply buried in her memory came to the surface: she and Jess on a wet Sunday morning making patterns with an old Spirograph set; and at school, cutting tiny shapes out of coloured paper to fashion a kaleidoscope. She had loved the process, and the gorgeous symmetry of the results. Like fractals, she thought; like losing yourself in the heart of a many-petalled flower. The idea that it could be done out of anything so sturdy as clay and enamel was bewildering.

A noise behind them made her turn, to find Omar pouring tea from a great height into the little glasses. The stream of tea sparkled golden in a shaft of sunlight. Dust motes danced in the air like some-thing elemental—atoms at the beginning of the universe. Kate felt an otherworldly sensation shiver through her, as if she had stepped into another time. For an instant the scene spun and blurred: she thought she saw a figure in a ruby-red robe standing at the mirador, long braided hair falling down her back, as gold as the tea . . .

"Here," Omar said, offering her a glass.

She blinked, and stepped forward to take it from him, brought sharply back to the moment.

Fragrant vapour coiled up from the glass in an elegant helix. Kate took a sip. The tea was hot and sweet and quite delicious. She tried not to think about the huge bar of sugar she'd seen going into the pot.

"They say this tower is where Sultan Moulay Hasan's Christian wife lived," Abdou said. "Her name was Isobel de Solis, and if it had not been for her, the kingdom of Granada would never have fallen."

"Dangerous creatures, Christian women!"

She'd only meant it as a lighthearted remark, but Abdou's expression changed and he said something that sounded harsh and angry to Omar. She caught the name *Isobel*, or was it *Isabella*? Oh no . . . When it came to "Christian women," the worst in his eyes must surely be Isabella of Castile, who had instigated the Spanish Inquisition and purged the kingdom of Muslims and Jews with terrible determination and cruelty. Kate felt as if she had deliberately provoked him. "I'm so sorry," she said.

He turned his dark gaze upon her and she realized he was not as young as she'd thought him. There were deep lines between his nose and the outer corners of his mouth, crow's feet around his eyes.

"What do you have to apologize for?"

And suddenly he smiled and his whole face was transformed, as if filled with inner light, and she fell in love with such a ridiculous sensation of free fall that it was as if she were in a dream, plummeting to the ground.

She realized she was staring. With terrible, conscious effort she tore her eyes from him. "I must go," she said abruptly, panicking. "Sorry, sorry."

She thrust her half-empty glass back at Omar and fled.

The bodega that night was heaving with customers, but Kate felt as though she flowed between the tables, the trays and glasses balanced in her hands as if she followed the steps of some ancient dance. She was precise, efficient, graceful throughout service, and the busier it got the better she moved, as if waitressing had that night been raised to a higher art, as if she were a priestess ministering to adherents of a faith that prized wine and tapas and loud joy above all things.

Toward the end of her shift she sensed that someone was watching her, the gaze not hostile exactly, but not entirely friendly either. It was an uncanny sensation. She turned to find Jimena regarding her, head slightly tilted, black eyes glittering in the candlelight.

"So," her boss said as Kate made her way toward the kitchen with her collection of empty glasses and bottles, "what's got into you, Anna? Or should I ask *who's* got into you?"

She gave Kate a nasty smile, but for once Kate did not feel intimidated. "I've had a good day."

Jimena did not blink. "Hmm," she said. "Don't enjoy yourself too much. Life's about more than having fun."

"I meant work," Kate said coolly, holding her stare. "It's good to be busy."

At last it was Jimena who looked away. That was a first. "Well, you're not finished yet," she snapped. "You still have the outdoor tables to clear. One of the German scum vomited out there: you can clean that up." She pivoted on her heel before Kate could point out the outdoor tables were not her responsibility, and had a cigarillo already lit before she even reached the door.

Kate watched Jimena's broad back disappear into the courtyard, her earlier satisfaction evaporating as fast as beer stains in the sun. How much longer could she do this? Working hand to mouth for someone who so despised both her employees and her customers? Perhaps she would think about looking for another waitressing job. Maybe do something else entirely. Maybe even move on . . .

An image of Abdou came to her: his wary glance, the careful way he placed the fragments of tile as if each were infinitely precious, part of the jigsaw of life itself. The warm, floaty feeling she had experienced since surrendering to the geometric mysteries of the ceiling in the Hall of the Abencerrages overtook her again. A sort of shimmer of sensation, as if the world trembled with immanence, with hidden promise.

"And you can forget about tomorrow as a day off. I need Juan to come with me to the suppliers."

Jimena's voice broke so sharply into her reverie that Kate dropped the glass she had been about to set down. It shattered on

the floor between them, a perfect symbol for the joyous moment
Jimena had just destroyed. While the Spanish woman poured
invective upon her, Kate bent to gather the shards, reminded with
almost hallucinatory force of that night she had argued with James,
and broken the crystal wineglass.

James did this to me, she thought. *He made me terrified of everything
and everyone. And especially of myself. He made me into a coward.*

He had sensed her weakness and turned it upon her, as bullies
always will. Suddenly she felt rage bubble up inside her. How dared
he treat her like some medieval woman? He had tried—no, he had
succeeded—in terrorizing her: first by little manipulations, by crit-
icism and manoeuvres to cut her off from others, and from everything she had always prized about herself—her rationality, her
intelligence, her independence. He had terrorized her into following the narrow path he laid down for her, enforcing his will upon
her as effectively as any religious inquisitor. Changed her hair, her
clothes, her entire way of life. Made her learn the catechism, go
through the whole Rite of Christian Initiation, promise to raise
their children as Catholics, taken vows she didn't believe in; and
worse, far worse. The realization of all he had done, and all he had
stolen from her, made her hotly furious.

But the nagging question remained: How had he found Jess?
The two had barely spoken, and she knew he did not have her
sister's address: Kate had invited her and Evan to the wedding by
phone—they were her only guests, the few others being James's
customers or in some way linked to him. So what had caused
Jess—usually so steadfast—to flee to Cornwall in the middle of
the night with a toddler? And then, another realization: Jess must
have been protecting her by being so evasive, sure that Kate was
not strong enough to cope with the truth. Well, she would have to
be strong enough: it was time to grow up. She would not have Jess
protect her anymore, would not have her carry the burden that was

rightfully her own. She had to get the full story out of her sister one way or another. Tomorrow. Tomorrow, she would call her and demand to know.

And after that I will go back up to the Alhambra, she told herself fiercely, *and find Abdou and talk to him, make this weird feeling I have about him go away. He's just a man, after all. And perhaps I'll have a coffee with Khadija, too.*

Points of connection. Little anchors to catch her from drifting into a tide of despair. As she climbed the alleys of the Albayzín back to her apartment, she smiled. Today Granada felt a little more like home, and she felt more like the woman she had once been.

Of course it could not last.

13

Blessings

Towers. All that year and the next my life revolved about towers. I grew to hate the very sight of them, looming ugly and arrogant over the landscape, marking men's doomed attempts to possess the world. There were times when I yearned for the desert, dreamed of it, over and over. The great empty expanses under a hot bowl of blue sky. Endless and eternal and untouched by the hand of man. No one built towers there, or if they tried, the towers soon fell.

But of course I couldn't leave Momo. I was bound to him more tightly than the false foot was bound to my poor stump.

When at last I emerged from my poison fever, it was to a world gone mad. Momo had been locked in the Tower of the Moon by his own father. Word in the palace corridors was that Moulay Hasan would declare his son guilty of treason and have him beheaded: Zoraya was determined to have her own sons declared as his official heirs. Soon Aysha and her women had joined the prince as captives in the tower. But even Moulay Hasan would not slay a woman: it was Momo I was worried about.

"Can't you save him?" I beseeched Qasim, and he sucked his lip.

"I've tried to speak for him, but the sultan's in a dangerous mood. He thinks there all sorts of conspiracies to bring him down. The more his eyesight fails, the more time he spends with her. He keeps talking about the prophecy, says if he removes the prince's head, Momo will be unable to take the throne, let alone lose the kingdom, and that'll destroy the astrologers' prophecies. He's obsessed with the Christian monarchs, convinced that they're planning to kill us all—Moor and Jew, every unbeliever—in their fires. They've already burned seven *conversos* in Seville. And that's only the start, he says. I think he's right. We'll soon be at war."

I had already heard that the foreign king and queen had set up an inquisition, putting Jews, Muslims and those who had in name converted to their religion to the question to test whether they were guilty of heresy, but I had been too taken up with the matters of my own heart to be much concerned about the affairs of others far away. Yet Seville was not far away. Seville was only five days' ride from Granada.

"Perhaps he is right," I said. "But surely if we go to war, Granada will need all its warriors. Prince Mohamed is a fine swordsman, better than his father and his uncle." I had watched him showing off to Rachid, even though his brother—a boy who could not hold a sword without cutting himself, who would, given the choice, rather sit in the shadows with the women, sewing dainties—had no interest in his battle skills. I had seen Momo dance across the practice yard in the Alcazaba, his blade flashing in the sun, laying one opponent after another on his backside. I had revelled in his thrilling beauty, for it was just a game. But war was not a game.

Qasim sighed. "When did our people ever put aside their differences to fight a common foe?"

Your people are not my people, I thought. My people were always fighting one another, tribe against tribe. We had no common foe, just neighbours we hated. Perhaps, it struck me then, people of all kinds were more alike than unalike.

So Qasim, who had been my best hope, would do nothing. I would have to do something myself.

That night I crept into the Hall of the Ambassadors, that great audience room where the sultan held court. Moonlight muted the colours in the stained-glass windows high up under the cupola. The sconces burned low; the braziers had been extinguished: it was almost dark in there and the darkness weighed upon me. Above, I could feel the massive rectangular tower rising into the night sky; and below it the dark emptiness of the Darro gorge. *I would have been in there too*, I thought, *if Zoraya's poison hadn't laid me low.*

Every alcove I passed I felt sure the sultan was hiding in it. I ran into the corridor on the other side of the hall, my heart thumping, and nearly dropped my tray. The guard barely glanced at me— veil, robe, earrings, tray and all—but waved me through. Aziza, one of the sultana's maids, took the tray from me. "I must speak to the prince," I whispered urgently.

She opened her mouth to castigate me, then narrowed her eyes. "Is that you, Blessings?" I nodded and she grinned. "I will fetch him."

"I can't." He looked aghast.

"You made me do it."

"That's different."

I didn't press him on that. "But what does it matter in what manner you escape?"

"If I am caught dressed as a woman, I'll never live it down."

"But you will live."

"I can't do it. Not like that."

"You'll just meekly go to your slaughter, like a sheep at Eid?" I was angry now.

"And what will he do to you if he finds you here in my place? He dislikes you greatly, says you're a bad influence."

He does? This was news to me. "I don't care about me: I care about you. He'll have you beheaded. Even Qasim says so."

I saw his eyes go hooded as he considered. "Even so," he said at last, "this is not how I would wish to be remembered."

By now I was almost crying with frustration. I was starting to take off my veil, when the guard shouted, "Hurry up in there!"

Momo pushed me toward the door. "Go."

Two nights later I was back with a different idea.

This time he listened to me.

I waited, shivering, near the top of the gorge. Above me, the Tower of the Moon rose massive and malignant. I couldn't even see all of it from where I stood, pressed awkwardly against the cold, jagged rock on a narrow ledge. My mule whickered and I glared at it. It ignored me. Farther down in the valley the horse I had brought for the prince shuffled its feet, pulling against the picket post. I stared up again, waiting for the candle to show in the window.

Even though the dungeon windows were the lowest in the tower, they still seemed an impossibly long way above me. No one had ever bothered to bar those windows: what need when the fall would be fatal? I hoped I had left enough cloth. The guards had checked through the laundry I brought, but finding nothing except women's robes and veils, had let me through.

At last a light! The darkness of the tower made the candlelit face glow as if it were floating. I whistled—shrill and piercing: the call of a bat—and it returned to me from above. I saw the first section of knotted cloth come down and down, bobbing against the rock walls. Not long enough. Two shrill calls. The rope jerked back.

The minutes stretched. I clutched the cold rock, trying to master my fear. If I fell from here, it would not be at the loss of a foot or even a limb. I swayed, and felt the leather belt tighten. Having inched out here, I had fastened it about my waist, looped a scarf around a sapling and back through the belt; but still my situation felt precarious.

Down the rope came again, knot by knot, closer and closer, hanging farther and farther out from the cliff. I worried I would not be able to get hold of it, but the wind was kind. I caught the lowest knot. Then I gave the signal: three bat calls.

I imagined Momo squirming through that tiny window. What if he got stuck? Worse, what if he missed the rope? My heart squeezed at the awful possibilities. He would fall and die and I would lose him! Worst of all, it would be my own fault. He had entrusted his life to me. That thought had warmed me yesterday: it chilled me now.

The rope in my hands began to jerk. He was out of the window, all his weight on the knotted cloth. Fervently, I hugged the end. I must anchor it to stop him plummeting to his death. Again I felt the pull of the dark space below me, hungry for a fall, full of djinn. *He is strong*, I told myself, to push the demons away. *He is fit and young. His sword training has given him hard muscle. He will not fall.*

But if he does? the wind whispered.

If he does, he falls in an attempt to escape his father: he will not die in some gruesome spectacle over which Zoraya can gloat. His blood will not stain the Court of Lions but will seep down into the Darro River and run through the kingdom of Granada. People will wash their faces and their clothes in the water and think of him . . .

The jerking grew stronger, threatening to tumble me off my perch. When I looked up, I could see the soles of his feet, pale against the dark cloth, as flexible as a monkey's, gripping the rope. The rope twirled and I saw him shoot a foot out and push away from a jut of rock. Then he disappeared into shadow and I could not see him at all.

I looked across to the Albayzín. Were there watchers on their roofs, straining their eyes against the darkness, their attention caught by a flicker of movement where usually there was none?

"Blessings!"

Momo's urgent whisper brought me back to myself. The rope jerked like a living thing, and then he was, by necessity, in my arms. The smell of him—sweat and incense—filled my senses. We stood there on that small ledge for a long moment, bound not only by relief and excitement but also by the rope. His amber eyes were full of night as he gazed at me. "Thank you, my friend. You really are my Special Guardian."

A tremor of intent ran through me, my body knowing before my mind did that I was about to reach to kiss him, but as my lips grazed his, he turned his head aside and without a word let go of the veils that linked us and made his way carefully along the ledge toward the tethered animals.

My hands were shaking so much I could hardly undo my knots. He had broken away from my kiss. Was he angry with me? I wished I had done nothing at all, just played the faithful servant, kept my distance, behaved with decorum. Perhaps he would be cold with me now. He was, after all, a married man, and a prince: and I—I was . . .

I did not know what I was. I occupied an indefinable space in the world, in his life. More than a friend, less than a man. A Special Guardian: but a cripple.

The missing limb released a jolt of pain to remind me of my foolishness. It weighed as heavy as lead as I trudged along the ledges after him. My heart beat inside my rib cage. If I opened my mouth, it would emerge, flapping away like a small leathery bat.

We made for Guadix, a long night's ride to the east, where Momo's mother had assured us we would be welcomed. Set in a desert of jagged limestone, bare earth and scrub below the Sierra Nevada, it was not a welcoming place, but I had rarely been so happy as when we entered that dour fortress.

Momo had been silent for most of the journey, and trotting along at an ever-increasing distance behind him on my mule, I was close to tears. But once we were inside those thick ochre walls our story fired its way around the town and soon everyone was talking about it. I was treated as a hero for my part in Momo's daring escape and, after feeling very sorry for myself, was so carried away by all the flattery that I was able to put the disaster of the kiss to the back of my mind; I was in severe danger of bursting with pride. The young men of the town gathered around, chattering, praising God, slapping us on the back, delighted that Moulay Hasan and his brother had been outwitted. Some of them smiled at me and touched me lingeringly on the arm, drawing me aside to suggest a sunset walk later along the ramparts, a massage in the steam baths or that we explore the network of grottoes beyond the town walls. I was charmed to be the centre of attention, and a little light-headed from lack of sleep and food, but I suddenly became aware of Momo's slitted, disapproving glances, and gently turned these invitations aside.

At last, when we were shown to our quarters and were alone, I summoned my courage. "I'm sorry I've offended you."

He turned his beautiful, melancholy face to me. "Offended me?"

I could not look at him. "The kiss." I shuffled my feet.

"Oh, that. That was nothing."

Nothing? I lifted my eyes. "Then why are you so upset with me?"

He laughed. "Not everything revolves around you, Blessings, even though the fellows here seem to find you so fascinating."

He had noticed, then.

"I was thinking about Mariam. What will become of her, alone in the palace, without me?"

Mariam. I had forgotten Mariam. "She's been without you all these weeks," I pointed out. "And she has her women."

"She's so young, so defenceless. She'll be lonely: she doesn't know anyone. I feel responsible for her. I'm her husband and I just . . . ran away."

"Better to have run away than been beheaded," I said, already impatient.

How quickly we take our lives for granted once the right order has been restored.

When you are in love, time passes in a succession of moments: moments of anticipation, moments of possibility, moments of sweetness . . . moments of pain. Like beads on a prayer bracelet, each one focused on a small truth of your existence from which you rarely lift your eyes or your thoughts before going the rounds again. I was so caught up in my own feelings in those months that

I could not see beyond the next day, let alone to the great and terrible events that lay ahead.

Some believe that we have no free will, that all we do is determined by *qadar*, God's decree. But sometimes there may be a kink in the straight path of fate, and if that is the case in Momo's tale, that kink was me. Born to a wisewoman who was also a charlatan, I was, you might say, destined to become a trickster, a rock in the desert around which winds poured, disrupting the pattern in the sands; a disturbance in the natural world.

One day a messenger arrived to relay the news that Moulay Hasan had gathered his army and ridden out to confront the Christians menacing Granada's border. The man bore letters from Aysha and from Mariam—though I recognized the hand of the vizier in the writing of both. Momo opened Mariam's first, which surprised me. I watched with a kind of disgust as he scanned the contents—short but clearly affecting—and began to blink.

Then he unrolled the second scroll, from Aysha. There was a long, concentrated pause as he took in the words. His gaze darted from right to left, then up to the start once more. When he lifted his face, his eyes were bright. He had been so despondent in the months we had been away, a tamped-down, barely there version of the Momo I knew: but now he was back, and his gaze was incandescent.

"We're going home!"

We rode back into the Albayzín, up to the top of the old part of the city on the opposite side of the gorge to the Alhambra, in the early hours of the morning. There Qasim waited, with a group of fierce-looking men in mail and helms, the blades of their halberds catching the last of the moonlight. As we dismounted, the captain, a big man with a vast beard, sank to his knees before Momo and touched his forehead to the ground, the traditional obeisance to a king. All around, his men followed suit, even the vizier, till only Momo and I were left standing. I caught his eye. Even in the darkness I could see astonishment in his gaze, but also a burning pride; then I too bowed.

Momo bent and took the captain by his arm and bade him rise.

"I, Musa Ibn Abu'l Ghrassan, pledge to you my sword," the man said huskily, touched by the courtly gesture. "And I swear we will not rest till you are set on your rightful throne and Moulay Hasan—may God damn him for the murder of my family—is deposed—or better, dead."

So these were the surviving relatives of the slaughtered thirty-six, I realized, the Banu Serraj nobles Hasan had butchered in the domed hall all those months ago, whose blood had spilled into the fountain and stained its marble bowl. Gathered, no doubt, by Qasim, who looked proud and pleased to have brought them all together. He was risking his life, I thought, on this throw of the dice.

"If it please your majesty," Musa went on, as if Momo were already king, "we will enter the city on secret paths. I know the men posted tonight in the Tower of Water, and have ensured they will not raise the alarm. When we've secured the royal palace and released the captives, my men and I will deal with the garrison. I don't believe there will be great bloodshed: there's more sympathy for you than you might imagine."

We crept along animal tracks up the side of the Sabika Hill and entered the grounds via a little-used gate in the Gardens of the Architect and slipped into the medina. Those we encountered between there and the palace laid down without a fight whatever arms they carried: by the time we reached the Tower of the Moon our numbers had swelled so much that it seemed the entire city was with us.

But the sultan had stationed his personal bodyguards to watch the dungeon rooms and they fought like lions.

I was not much of a Special Guardian that night. Hampered by my golden foot and my inability to fight, I watched as the violence spilled out into the Courtyard of the Myrtles as the first light dawned and the muezzin's song rang out over the city; watched as spilled blood darkened the lovely mosaics and sullied the still waters of the pool. It was a brief affair. Before the call to prayer was over, it was finished. Momo held his sword aloft and cried, "For the Banu Serraj! For Aysha! For my mother!"

The captain and his men ran on toward the Alcazaba to add the garrison to their numbers, and to secure the arsenal and the city's main gates.

Freed at last from her months of captivity, the sultana swept out of her prison with all the dignity of an empress. Seeing Momo standing there, bloodied sword in hand, she fell upon him, kissing his shoulders over and over, and for the first time I saw he stood a head taller than his mother.

I swayed for a moment, my senses assailed by the scent of blood and myrtle, seeing in my mind's eye two children running in a sunlit orchard. One—smaller and darker—threw an orange at the other, who, laughing, leapt to catch it with the grace of a gazelle, and hurled it back with such force its zest misted the air. Then they were gone into a haze, to be replaced by the vision of a boy shinning down a rope of knotted veils into the arms of his shivering friend. I saw myself—distant, tiny—lean in to kiss him on the mouth, and then he stepped away, becoming larger all the while as if time and perspective were awry; and when I saw him again, he was a man, and not just a man, but a soldier, and a king.

14

On the fifth day of Jumada in the year 887, or in the Christian calendar 1482, Momo was proclaimed Sultan Abu Abdullah Moḥammed, the twenty-second Nasrid ruler of Granada. The atmosphere was wildly celebratory, a little crazed, as if everyone knew what had started so abruptly would surely end as fast, and badly. People danced in the streets and musicians played on every corner, the rhythms they rapped out entering bodies as a second heartbeat, thrumming through rib cages and breastbones. Drums, and dogs barking, and ululating women: they all bled into one. Momo sitting on his throne, clad all in white; Qasim beaming beside him, as if all his plots had come to fruition; while behind the fretted screens of the women's quarters, Mariam pressed her face to the wood and watched her young husband as if her heart would leap out through her eyes.

They had at last consummated their union. Momo had confided this to me with shy pride. I had smiled hollowly, faking delight. "You will have fine sons."

He threw his arms around me. "Thank you, Blessings. It was all down to you." When he drew back, I saw how the shadows had gone from around his eyes. She made him happy. That made me miserable.

Momo had taken his father's rooms for his own, though I knew he looked upon the chambers with distaste. "If I am to be the sultan, I must be seen to be the sultan," he said. Mariam was moved into the pretty tower rooms adjacent to his quarters that had once been the sultana's, giving her more peace and privacy than she had enjoyed in the harem, where the courtesans had been less than welcoming. For her part, Aysha had moved into the Hall of the Two Sisters, closer to the heart of the royal palace. From here, she insisted on running the household, since Mariam was "just a child" and had yet to learn the ways of the palace.

Zoraya and her boys found themselves imprisoned in the topmost room in the Tower of the Moon: poetic justice, I thought, with the roles reversed.

And I . . . I was displaced. As the sultan's Special Guardian I could have occupied an anteroom off Momo's quarters, but the small sounds of Mariam's pleasure in the night drove me to distraction and I took to walking outside in the cool air, letting the tumble of water from the lion fountain wash those noises from my head. At last I could bear it no more and asked permission to take rooms in the Alcazaba with the rest of the garrison. Momo went very still, then nodded slowly. "Of course. You are a *faris* now. You should be with the other fighting men." But when I packed my gear into a bundle and took my leave, there was hurt in his expression. I walked with my head down, trying all the way to maintain my *asshak*.

A page must have arrived ahead of me, for by the time I checked in with the captain, rooms were already being prepared. I saw servants hurriedly shifting bedding, and suspected my arrival had ousted some other officer: I would likely not be popular.

Musa himself began to train me in the bearing of arms. He seemed fascinated that someone who had lost a foot could even walk, let alone run and fight; but by the end of that summer I could do both, though awkwardly: he was a hard taskmaster.

The only time I spent in Momo's presence was when we ate together, walked the corridors and courtyards of the palace between council meetings or went hunting on the plain, where he showed off his horsemanship and his skills with bow and spear and hawk. The wild boar we killed were left in the woods—it was forbidden to eat the flesh of pigs, and no king could be seen to do so, but he gave it to be understood that a blind eye was to be turned to any others who wished to take the meat. "These are wild animals, not domestic swine: I can't see the harm."

He was equally fair-minded and unfussy in his dealings with the petitioners who queued every day for his attention in the Maswar Hall. Momo pointed out a line of calligraphy to me over the door to the hall, which read: *Enter and ask. Do not be afraid to seek justice, for here you will find it.* "I mean to be the sultan from whom my people can ask and receive the justice they deserve without fear of reprisal for speaking their mind," he said. His fervour frightened me: daily, he was becoming more of a king, and less my companion.

Word spread that their new lord was approachable and generous: the queues grew ever longer. It seemed no one had cared much for the concerns of ordinary folk for some time. They filed in, round eyed at the sight of the handsome young sultan sitting on his throne with the coloured light filtering from the stained-glass windows in the ceiling casting bright lozenges at his feet, as if he had scattered jewels there for them to take home. To each of them Momo listened attentively, waving away the vizier when he offered to take over. "These are my people," he said, "and they have been ignored for too long."

A smith had not been paid for weapons supplied to Moulay Hasan; a man's daughters had been abducted. A grain store had been raided for supplies; all of a miller's flour had been seized to make bread for the army. Young men had been pressed as soldiers.

Families starved under the burden of tax debt, their menfolk dead or sick or taken away.

"Sire, we can't pay any more of them," the vizier said at last. "I fear your majesty has been too generous. The treasury can give no more."

Momo rounded on him. "The treasury can and will recompense these people! These troubles are none of their fault: all they want is peace."

Qasim spread his hands. "There can be no peace if the Christians raid our lands."

"You're saying my father was within his rights to treat them so high-handedly?"

"As the sultan they are his subjects."

Momo's eyes flashed. "*I* am the sultan now! God knows I never asked for the burden of it, but by his will I shall do my duty. These are my people, to defend and to support."

"In moderation, sire. In moderation." Qasim permitted himself a little laugh, as if they were equals and sharing a joke. I suppose he thought that having engineered Momo's rise to the throne, he would be recognized and rewarded for it. It was a rare and uncharacteristic error. Momo rounded on him furiously. "If I must give every last coin in the treasury for them to see justice and decency, I shall!"

The next day the vizier was nowhere to be found. One of his servants said his master's old mother was sick and he had gone to attend her, but Momo shook his head angrily. "The vizier's mother died eight years ago: my father made him a gift of three sheep for the funeral feast."

The servant paled and said no more. I suspected Qasim thought to teach Momo a lesson by his absence, that he would find he could not do without him. That, or he thought he might do better by going over to Moulay Hasan. Either way, three days later a man rode in, covered in the dust of the road, and prostrated himself before the new sultan. "My lord, Moulay Hasan is returning with his army. He vows to retake the city."

From the ramparts we watched as his father's army came riding across the plain, banners flying, sun glinting off helms and armour, the soldiers' horses kicking up the dust of a long summer. Momo's father and Momo's fearsome uncle, al-Zaghal, rode at the head of their troops, their heads bent together, the two men deep in conversation. Did they know that Momo had seized the throne? I felt my stomach tighten, and my phantom limb began to throb.

I shot a look at my friend, resplendent in an ochre robe, but with the precautions of a breastplate and mailed coif. That profile! Lit by the sun, he shone. Every time it was like seeing him anew: every time he took my breath away.

Moulay Hasan's captain hailed the watchtower, calling for the gates to be opened. There was no answer. The brothers gazed upward, shading their eyes against the sun. "Who dares deny me access to my own castle?" Hasan growled. "Let us in at once or you will pay with your life—and the lives of your wives and children!"

Musa grinned through his massive beard and leaned over the rampart. "My name is Musa Ibn Abu'l Ghrassan of the Banu Serraj, whose family you slaughtered! We've declared your son rightful king of Granada, so be gone, you murdering scum!"

"Where is this 'son' you speak of?" al-Zaghal roared. "You surely cannot mean that chicken-hearted mother's boy, Abu Abdullah Mohammed!"

Momo stepped forward. "Here is the chicken-hearted mother's boy, Uncle. I am more than happy to demonstrate the skills I learned from your sword master any time you wish to test me in the field!"

He transferred his attention to Moulay Hasan. "It is just as Sidi Musa says. You've been deposed by your own people. I am sultan now."

Moulay Hasan glowered at Momo as if he could shrivel him to charcoal, and at this moment Aysha chose to make her presence known. "You miserable, fornicating, murdering, whoring worm of a man! Take your black heart away from this place!"

A look of loathing corrugated Moulay Hasan's features. "You withered old hag! That's what all this is about, isn't it? You seized your chance to take your petty revenge on Zoraya, didn't you? You just couldn't bear that I would prefer to dip my cock in her honey-pot than in your leathery old purse!"

Aysha grabbed a dagger from the belt of the nearest soldier and hurled it at the head of her husband. It fell short—but only just—and clattered on the paving stones of the ramp. Hasan's horse jumped sideways, colliding with his standard bearer. The boy dropped the banner and the horses trampled its fragile silk beneath their thunderous hoofs.

"Your standard has fallen. Your tyranny is ended!" Musa Ibn Abu'l Ghrassan yelled. "All hail Sultan Abu Abdullah Mohammed XII! Long live the king!"

The cry was taken up along the ramparts. It echoed off the rocky sides of the gorge, rang out through the streets of the Albayzín. Moulay Hasan glared as all around him people stood on the terraces of their homes, shouting defiantly, some of them even making obscene gestures.

Momo raised his hands for quiet and at last the din subsided. "Leave Granada, Father. There's no support for you here."

"I have an army with me, and if I call others to arms across the kingdom, I'll have a mighty horde!" the deposed sultan yelled back. "What do you have? Runts and rejects and disappointed old men— those who aren't strong enough to ride to war with our enemies! There are still many loyal to me within these walls—I know it!"

Momo waved a dozen tall black-skinned men forward. Al-Zaghal said something and his brother cursed. These were Hasan's royal bodyguards: if even they had gone over to the boy, all was lost.

"What do you think we were doing during these weeks away? Sunning ourselves in a pleasure garden?" Moulay Hasan rasped. "We've been fighting the infidels back from our borders! If we don't stand together, all with be lost. Would you hand our kingdom on a silver tray to our enemies, you stupid boy?"

Momo's jaw tensed. "It's time we made our kingdom stronger by giving people the chance to flourish, by treating them with respect and fairness, rather than taxing them to penury for the sake of pointless zealotry!"

His father's horse danced in a tight circle, forcing the old man to master it with difficulty. "I'll lay siege to this damned city!" he shouted. "I'll blast it to oblivion! I'll see it consumed by fire before I'll let you take my crown!"

Aysha leaned over the ramparts. "Try it and I'll catapult your whore to her death! But first I'll cut out her eyes and her tongue and cover her in tar! Then we'll see how much you desire her! I'll have her bastard children cooked in a tagine and served to the Banu Serraj!" She pulled a shrouded figure into view and ripped the veil away so that the woman's long yellow hair rippled in the wind.

"Is that . . . is that my Zoraya?"

I had forgotten how bad his eyesight had become.

"Save me, my love!" Zoraya shrieked. "Before this she-devil cuts my throat!"

Aysha laughed mirthlessly. "It's all I have dreamed of these many years."

The old sultan called down all the demons of hell on his first wife. Through it all Aysha regarded him with glee.

"Release her, Mother," Momo said softly. "He knows we hold her life in our hands. There's no need to terrify her anymore."

But the scorned woman was relishing this long-awaited moment of triumph: she dug the blade deeper, till her rival squawked like a chicken. "Get off your horse, Hasan!" Aysha howled down. "Get off your horse and grovel in the dirt! Beg my forgiveness for treating me with such disrespect. Do it, or I'll slit her pretty Christian throat!"

Hasan knew the strength of Aysha's will. He slithered from the saddle and fell to his knees, while his brother looked on in disgust and railed at him to get up and be a man, be a king. To no avail. "I'm sorry, so sorry, my dear lady, for any slight I may have done you. I was blinded by lust and stupidity. Now please let her go!"

"Not good enough." The knife bit again, and again Zoraya wailed.

"I call upon the great goodness of your heart, beloved wife, to forgive this weak and foolish man. I am unworthy of you and of the kingdom. I am an ass—nay, a worm."

Aysha smiled. "And now declare our son the rightful sultan, swear that you will ride away, disband your troops and never again take up arms against him."

His face working grotesquely, Hasan gabbled out his promises. By now al-Zaghal was purple with rage. His black eyes were trained not on Aysha but on his nephew, and the hatred in them made me go cold.

Aysha was at last persuaded to give up her captive. Zoraya was accompanied to her tower and given some minutes to collect her children, and to select clothing and jewellery to take with her, despite Aysha's demand that she should be sent out of the gate naked and shameless on a mule so that all might see her for the whore she was.

The gates opened and out Zoraya rode with her small boys, dressed in her most splendid robes, accompanied by her faithful servant, La Sabia. I saw Momo's shoulders relax the moment the gate closed behind them. I knew exactly how he felt.

We watched the army of Granada wend its way back out onto the plain, the dust raised by its horses making it look like a desert mirage, something out of legend. Was it my imagination, or were there considerably fewer soldiers leaving than had ridden in? I wondered if deserters were even now throwing off the colours of the old sultan in dark alleyways in the Albayzín and slipping into the arms of their wives and mothers.

And somehow, the vizier was back, old Qasim Abdelmalik, who returned as if nothing had ever happened. He brought rich gifts—silks and perfumes—for Mariam, knowing Momo would not accept anything for himself, and the young sultan received them graciously, though the way he looked upon the vizier's prostrate form with narrowed eyes told me he suspected Qasim had tried his luck with Moulay Hasan and been turned away; And while I realized that although Momo would love to punish the vizier for stealing from the treasury and for his disloyalty, he needed someone by his side who knew how to run a kingdom. Then he told Qasim to get up, and sent him off with a dozen tasks to arrange the shoring up of the defences. "And we will see if my father keeps his promises."

Months passed. Fittingly enough, it was pomegranate season—that time of symbolic fertility—when Momo told me his news. We were walking in the orchards so he could inspect the persimmon, mulberry, fig and pomegranate trees. The sun was bakingly hot and I could almost taste the fruit in the air.

"I'm going to have a son."

Sweetness turned to wormwood in my mouth.

"Mariam is pregnant. The baby will be due before year's end, *alhamdulillah*."

"Praise be to God," I echoed weakly.

A son. Momo a father. I remembered the wedding night, the fiasco with the fox's blood. Mariam's blushes—deeper than the ripest pomegranate . . . "Congratulations." My heart felt the size of a walnut, as hard and as bitter. I should be glad for him: it was what any man wished for, what every king required. But my vile envy lasted only for a moment: the way his amber eyes scanned my face, seeking my approval, made me ashamed. I grasped his shoulder. "I'm so happy for you . . . both."

He embraced me then with such relief that I felt all the more unworthy.

Of course it was inevitable that Hasan would not give up his throne so easily, or that his brother would allow the damage done to their pride to go unavenged. We were asleep in our beds one night a few weeks later, when there was a scream from the ramparts, followed by the screech of clashing steel.

I was up and out of my covers in an instant, my heart beating abnormally fast, as when you wake from a nightmare, rather than in one. It took a minute or two more to strap the false foot on, for I never could sleep comfortably with the thing attached, and by then all was chaos. I hobble-ran out into the training square. All along the western rampart there was fighting. Hundreds of men skirmished on the ramps and steps, more flooding down into Alcazaba. I had to get to Momo.

In the darkness and confusion it was impossible to tell who was who: people were shouting out their allegiances in order to tell friend from foe. A huge man in black robes came flying at me, swinging a sword and roaring, "For the sultan!" This did not help me identify for which side he fought, and "For the sultan!" I cried in response, dodging him and leaving him equally bemused.

As I neared the palace, the fighting was at its thickest, tangles of men battling fiercely for entry, fought back by erstwhile comrades. I hoed my blade into the hamstrings of a man in front of me—an agricultural stroke. With the dagger in my left hand I disabled another raider, allowing the palace guard who was engaging him to finish him off. In this way I finally made it inside the inner circle of defenders, where I found Momo battling several men at once, his blade flashing in the gloom.

When practising his swordplay Momo had flowed across the training square like a poem, graceful and elegant. But this was no poem. This was brutal. No space for sweeping sword strokes: he was reduced to hacking, chopping, stabbing. Even so I was transfixed. There was a ruthless economy to his movements, an intense focus. I saw him kill four men in the space of a minute. It was nasty work, but brilliantly done. I felt a sort of awe and hoped Al-Zaghal had witnessed his nephew displaying the butcher skills he'd been so keen to teach him. I hoped he'd been on the other end of them.

I dodged and stabbed my way toward him. The force of one of Momo's blows made his opponent drop his sword. As he reached for it, I stamped on his hand with my golden foot and heard him scream, and in that second, Momo finished him. Much to my relief the fight was effectively over. But Momo embraced me as if I were the hero of the hour, tenderly wiping a splash of blood from my face as soon as he had ascertained that it was not my own. Then he sent Musa and his captains radiating out through the medina and the Alcazaba and down into the city, to kill or take prisoner any invaders who remained.

Reports gave no sighting of Moulay Hasan, though his brother had been in the forefront of the assault, one of the first to scale fortress walls long thought impregnable. But his corpse did not lie among the many that littered the grounds, or the streets of the medina: he must have escaped through one of the city's thirty gates.

First thing the next day, Momo sent master masons over the top of the ramparts to mortar up any hand- or footholds the invaders had used in that bold ascent: then he doubled the watch.

Shortly after the attack, we celebrated the birth of his first son, Ahmed. Mariam laboured long, leaving Momo pale and desperate, striding up and down the corridors outside the chamber with the pent-up energy of a trapped wolf. When at last the baby was presented, the wonder in his father's face took my knees from under me. Unremarked amid the rejoicing, I sat on the cold stone floor, watching and hurting. Such tenderness in his expression, such a softening of the pure, hard lines of his face.

He had never looked at me like that. And I knew he never would.

A bitter, black wave of jealousy washed over me, leaving me shaking and nauseous. It was disgraceful to feel this way about such a joyful event. To be jealous of a tiny scrap of humanity, who had never done anything to me, who was innocent and defenceless, was a wicked thing. I knew this. But it changed nothing.

Word reached us in the spring that the enemy monarchs of Aragón and Castile, Ferdinand and Isabella, had pledged to devote their effort to driving out every unbeliever from the peninsula, calling it a holy war. Nobles keen to win favours rallied to them. There was a responding call to arms among the Muslims, initiated by al-Zaghal; but Momo did not answer it. "Only a few weeks ago the Christians asked us to pay the usual tribute monies. We're still negotiating. And if Granada's treasury can't afford to pay the tribute, how can it finance a war?"

At the time it seemed a reasonable question. But there was dissent, not only in the council but out in the city, where a blind old hermit who lived in a cave on the Sacromonte, the great hill to the east of the Albayzín, stirred up the populace by reminding them of the old prophecies surrounding the young sultan's birth.

Insulting words were daubed on walls. Pronouncements of loyalty to the old sultan, even to al-Zaghal: the people were as changeable as the weather.

One day Momo and I were sitting together on a bench in the shade of the Gate of Justice. "I swear he said 'Baba'! Imagine that—his very first word, *father*." Momo's eyes shone with sentimental pride. I stifled a yawn.

"Babies make all sorts of nonsense sounds."

"No, really, it was very clear. And he was looking right at me when he said it. He's a prodigy, Blessings. I can't believe I've produced such a thing of beauty." He gave me the sweetest smile. "It's because he was conceived here, in this beautiful place, rather than back in grim old Loja. The Alhambra gets into your blood and bones. It's like a spell, like God's grace—"

At this moment a messenger charged up the road to the palace on a sweating horse. Seeing Momo, he hurled himself from his mount and prostrated himself at the sultan's feet. "News, my lord!" he cried.

Momo drew him up. "There's no need for that. What's your name?"

The messenger looked so startled he seemed to have forgotten. "Uh, Latif, sire."

"Come, Latif. Take some refreshment and then I'll hear your news." He led him away as if he were a nobleman of equal rank, leaving me holding the horse's bridle.

I shouted, and someone came for the horse. I had to run to catch them up, by which time they were entering the Maswar and the messenger's eyes were darting left and right, taking in the exquisite stucco and tilework.

In a small chamber off the hall Momo bade him sit down. Then he turned to me. "Blessings, go bring hot water and towels, and some refreshments."

I dragged my feet.

"Go!" This time his tone was sharp.

By the time I got back with sherbet and almond biscuits, it was to find Momo dipping a towel in bowl of scented water brought by a page, cleaning the messenger's face himself. I almost dropped the tray.

He heard me approach, waved for me to set the tray down. His eyes gleamed. He seemed rather pleased about something. "My father-in-law is a remarkable old man."

I remembered Mariam's father at Loja—formidable and frightening. "He's still alive then?"

Momo chuckled. "Oh yes, very much so."

It was all he would say: it seemed I had missed the relaying of the important news, whatever it was. I did not have long to wait to find out. Momo had his council assembled.

"The Christian army has been defeated," he announced to shocked silence. "Led by King Ferdinand, it foolishly attacked Loja, thinking to take the town to gain access to the plain and then to march on our city. But they reckoned without Sidi Ali! My valiant ninety-year-old father-in-law lured them into an ambush and, as he says in his message, 'We gave those strutting *caballeros* something to remember us by!'"

There was much amazed laughter.

"As well as many of their knights, the enemy also lost their baggage train. Sidi Ali sends this cup, marked with the yoke and arrows of Ferdinand and Isabella, as a gift to his grandson Ahmed." Momo waved a handsome golden goblet in the air. "The remains of the Christian army were driven down the gorge. My father and uncle fell upon them as they retreated into the lowlands. Sidi Ali reports that although King Ferdinand escaped, eight hundred of his knights were killed and fifteen hundred were taken captive. This is a great day for Granada!"

An enormous cheer echoed around the hall. Then someone cried, "*Y'Allah*, Moulay Hasan and Moulay Zaghal!" and the cry was taken up.

The young sultan looked crestfallen. Then he held his hand up and the hall quietened. "We must indeed give thanks to the brave men who have defended our borders—my father-in-law, Sidi Ali, foremost among them. But we must also say a prayer for the souls of those lost in battle."

The hush dropped over the council chamber and the prayer was chanted.

"I heard them." The sultana's face was as hard as an axehead. "Shouting out '*Hasan*,' may God curse them for calling praise on his name." We had barely been back in the Palace of Lions for a minute, but it seemed the sultana had ears everywhere. "Give me the goblet!" she demanded.

Momo passed her the golden cup and she examined it gloatingly, running her fingers over the entwined letters of the monarchs of Castile and Aragón. "One day it will be filled with the blood of our foes and Ahmed will drink from it!"

Mariam cradled the boy to her chest.

"Mother! I will not have our small son turned into some sort of *ghûl*. Mariam and I wish for him to have a proper childhood, growing up in peace in this beautiful place. He's not going to be a game piece in your war against my father!"

"Ferdinand's pride will have been stung by this defeat. He'll be back with five times the army he took against Loja, and if you don't defend your kingdom and show the people you're a true leader, they'll turn on you. They're as fickle as cats, the Granadans, and as easily swayed as peasants everywhere."

"Don't call them peasants, Mother. They are my subjects. Without them you are nothing. I am nothing." He flung his arms wide. "Granada is nothing. I do not want my son raised in a war zone, and I do not want my people taken from their fields and pressed into battle, or run ragged with taxes. I will not enter this war." He beckoned Mariam to follow him, and together they retreated into their private quarters, where even Aysha was forbidden to enter.

She stared after them, her eyes narrow. "Remember my words, Blessings," she said without looking at me. "We'll be at war before the almonds flower."

15

Kate

THREE YEARS EARLIER

The preparations for her wedding went by in a kind of speed-blur. Kate felt at one remove, but James had taken it upon himself to organize everything. He had met with the bishop, bringing with him Ingrid's death certificate; booked a local church (after charming the vicar with his knowledge of ecclesiastic architecture and mention of his long line of local ancestors); secured a country house for the reception; whittled down the invitation list to a chosen few; booked caterers and a florist; ordered the rings. He was a whirlwind, charged with ever-increasing energy. Whenever she was in his presence, Kate felt oddly docile, powerless and exhausted.

"I need time to think, and there is no time," she told Jess. "I spend my whole life assimilating information then coding it, but everything in my life is moving so fast I'm not getting the chance to take it in, and when I ask him to slow down so I can think about it, he gets angry with me."

That very morning she had queried some small detail—she couldn't even remember what it was—only to have him glare at her. Was that rage in his eyes? It was gone as swiftly as it had appeared it, like a smothered fire. "Why don't you organize it, then? I'm more than happy to hand the whole thing over to you: the menu, the wine, the flowers, the cake, the string quartet, the photographer, the lot." He ticked them off, one by one. "Because I'd love to be able to get some work done, you know. Believe me, I'd love that. I do have a bloody business to run."

Kate had felt her eyes fill with tears. But instead of apologizing for his shortness, James had stormed off, leaving her to pour her complaints down the line to her sister.

"At least James really seems to *want* to marry you," Jess snorted. "I got the sense with Evan I was trapping him in a corner and pinning him in place with marquee tent pegs and buttonholes."

"Can you come down here? Just for a day? I need you." Even Kate could hear the whine in her own voice, and hated herself for it.

Two days later, the sisters stood in the changing rooms of a Beaconsfield bridal shop. Hangers sagged under the weight of discarded dresses in every style, from simple satin sheaths to Bardot necklines, fishtails and flounces. Nothing looked right, according to Kate, and now she was in tears. "I feel as if I'm playing dress-up."

Jess, tired from the drive, rolled her eyes. "Well, you are. It's not as though you're looking for something to show off the everyday you, is it? This is supposed to be your princess moment. You might as well embrace it, no matter how ridiculous it seems."

Kate's chin corrugated.

"Oh don't. Please," Jess said, recognizing the symptoms of yet another crying jag. "Come on, Sis, chin up. What's with you?"

Kate lifted miserable eyes to her twin. "I don't . . . I don't . . ."

"Don't what? Don't want to get married? Don't want to marry James? What? Tell me."

Kate nodded dumbly. It was a relief to have it articulated, especially by her twin, who knew her so well.

"Oh, Kate."

"I know. I'm so stupid. I shouldn't have let it get this far." She gazed hopefully, expecting a hug, some sort of reassurance that she could escape all this and everything would be fine. But instead all she got was "For God's sake, Kate, you're a bloody mess. What's got into you? You said after Matty you wanted to have a relationship with a proper grown-up, and now you've got one and you want to run away? Honestly!"

"Is everything all right in there?" The faux-chirpy voice of the shop manager, used to tears and tantrums and chivvying the unwilling into spending more money than they'd planned.

"Fine," they called in unison, and waited for her footsteps to recede.

"It's just pre-wedding jitters—everyone gets them," Jess said in a low voice. "You're just not used to the idea of getting married. Well, you'd better wrap your head round it sharpish. It's high time you settled down and got a life of your own. Evan and I have our own problems—we don't need you compounding them. I'm fed up with finding you giving Evan a sympathetic shoulder to cry on all the time."

Kate stared at her twin, appalled. "I thought I was helping."

"Helping? You're kidding! Kate, for God's sake, just marry James and grow up! And leave me and Evan alone!"

It was as if all this time Jess had pretended to be her sister but had suddenly allowed a glimpse of her true reptile skin and nicitating eyelids. Kate took a step back. "I thought you'd understand," she said quietly. "Of all people, you're the one who knew what a nightmare I had with Matty. I thought you'd understand I didn't want to make another stupid mistake."

Jess firmed her lips into a hard, thin line. Kate recognized that look: that mulish look her sister had when she was in the wrong and knew it but would never back down. In a sudden fury Kate grabbed the first dress that came to hand and marched out into the shop. "I'll take this one," she said, thrusting it at the surprised manager.

The woman reached for it with alacrity and started ringing the price into the till. "Are you quite sure? Does it need any alterations?"

"No," Kate said through gritted teeth. "It's absolutely fucking perfect."

Jess drove straight home and they didn't speak for a fortnight. Then one day an envelope arrived at the cottage. Out fell a lovely notecard bearing an image by one of her favourite artists. She opened it to find two lines of *Hobbit* runes:

Can you forgive me?
Two hearts beat as one.

She pressed the card to her chest, feeling choked up. Then she called Jess. There was a long moment of laden silence on the line, and then they both said "I'm so sorry" at exactly the same time.

"You bloody well should be," said Kate.

"I know," said Jess.

The dress, of course, was awful. Kate stared at her reflection in the mirror and despaired. Her new haircut, a sharp asymmetric bob with chestnut highlights, looked wrong on her: too tailored, too harsh, more like a wig than her own hair. The dress was the opposite: too loose, too soft. She had steadfastly refused to try it on again since buying it, and now she was paying the price. Plus, she had lost weight in the past month; she smoothed the satin over her hips but still it hung like a sack, and one false move would have the bodice sliding down around her waist. It was no surprise, she thought. She'd been working flat out on the cottage and down at the new shop, in an attempt to hold back thoughts of an existential nature. Not eating enough either, since that meant sitting down with James at a table and talking (he refused to eat with a tray on his knees in front of the TV, as she was used to doing: in fact, having a television at all had provoked a major fight between them). In just two hours she'd be walking down the aisle.

For one mad, fleeting moment, she glanced out the window at where her car sat parked on the road and considered running downstairs and jumping into it. Her car, the boot packed with all the things that didn't fit into the cottage—modern paintings, knick-knacks and her coffee machine, which James refused to use, deeming coffee a filthy foreign drink. She could drive to an airport and run away. Anywhere would do. She imagined herself turbaned against the sand-laden winds of the Gobi Desert, swaying between the humps of a camel. Living in a treehouse in a Scandinavian forest; sunglassed and incognito at a café table in the sunlit plaza of some southern Spanish town . . . The last idea was so alluring she could almost taste the coffee.

"Kate!"

Jess's voice downstairs. It was too late now. She'd allowed herself be carried along by James's strength of will, and as Jess had said, it was time for her to grow up. She did not know how she had ever become such a passenger in her own life. Besides, he loved her so much—he kept saying it over and over. "I don't know what I'd do if I lost you: you are everything in the world to me, Kate." How could she be so ungrateful, and so stupid, to cast such love away? James was a clever, courtly, handsome man with a successful business. He'd bought her a beautiful cottage in a lovely village. He had a vision for their shared future that was truly seductive. Of course she loved him. Of course she wanted to marry him.

"Up here!" she called back, as brightly as she could manage.

Jess, with her special combination of flair and practicality, had saved the day, ruthlessly chopping the hem off the veil to make a halter strap to pass around Kate's neck and fasten to the bodice at the front with pinned silk roses. For good measure, she pinned another silk rose at the waist so it seemed a deliberate part of the design.

"There."

Evan turned when she entered the front garden, as Jess, bossy as ever, gave instructions to the limo driver. His eyes went wide. "You look gorgeous, Kate. James is a lucky man."

Kate's eyes welled up at the compliment, and Evan was alarmed. "God, don't cry—Jess'll blame me!" He handed her his handkerchief. "Quick, blow your nose."

At that instant the other car arrived and from that moment Kate had no time to think about anything other than avoiding tripping over the hem of her dress or dropping her bouquet.

In what seemed mere minutes she emerged a married woman. She appeared—and felt—dazed. The photographer caught her perfectly: large eyed and nervy, smiling uncertainly, once looking entirely forlorn. In every photo James had the same expression: one of jovial victory, his hand always on his bride's waist or elbow, as if to guide her across stepping stones over a fast-flowing stream.

There was champagne and bellinis, a string quartet playing French Baroque music, a buffet table with roasted guinea fowl, beef and Yorkshire puddings, coleslaws and salads and jewel-like vegetables. And as a centrepiece, a cherry-red suckling pig with mournfully clouded eyes and an apple in its jaws.

Kate stared at it, appalled. It seemed a throwback to a medieval age. She went back to the top table empty handed. "Lost your appetite?" James chuckled. "We can't have that. You'll have no energy for later." He gave her a knowing look.

She smiled at him, a little too brightly. "Too much excitement," she said. "I didn't sleep well last night. Sorry, I'm being a bit feeble."

James leaned in and put his arm around her. "It's a big day for both of us." He paused. "A big night too . . ." He pushed a large glass of red wine her way. "Here, drink this. It'll relax you."

Kate blinked and stared upward at the canopy of the four-poster bed in the bridal suite. She couldn't remember how she'd got to their room, let alone onto the bed without—she realized now, feeling a flicker of air brush the skin of her naked belly—a stitch on. Had she passed out and been carried here? She cast a glance around. There were candles everywhere, giving off a heavy scent, causing the room dance and spin. She made to move her hand to rub her eyes and found that it would not reach. Something was stopping it. Panicking now, she turned her head, to find her wrist tied with gold-and-violet velvet. What?

She pulled against it, and the knot tightened. The same on the other side. She was bound to the headposts of the bed.

Sex is all about strange kinks—wasn't that what Jess had said? But James had never shown any interest in bondage before. She began to feel unnerved, the more so as she realized there was a muttering in the room, chanting in a foreign language. Kate's skin rose in gooseflesh. She craned her neck. At the foot of the bed, gilded by candlelight, his hands clasped upon the extravagant counterpane,

James was praying: "'*Salve, Regina, Mater misericordiae. Vita, dulcedo, et spes nostra, salve. Ad te clamamus exsules filii Hevae. Ad te suspiramus gementes et flentes in hac lacrimarum valle . . .*'"

Was that Latin? "What the hell are you doing?" She could hear her words slurring. How had she got so drunk?

At the sound of her voice he raised his head and smiled beatifically at her. "We are about to consummate our union. I am praising the Blessed Virgin before I do what I must do. It's the least I can do after not entering the priesthood as I promised her. You are the holy receptacle for my seed."

Kate tried to sit up onto her elbows and force the fumes from her head. "What do you mean? Why am I tied up?" She kept pushing against the restraints. This all felt so wrong.

There was a fervent light in his eyes as James got to his feet, revealing a long white shirt she had never seen before. It reached his knees and looked as if it should be in a museum. "We have been brought together as man and wife in the eyes of God: and now it is my holy mission to bring our union to true fruition. Tonight we shall make a son."

He shrugged his way out of the shirt and stood before her with his erection protruding proudly. She had never seen him so aroused. Kate felt repulsed. "Untie me, James. I'm not having sex with you tied up like this!"

By way of response, he climbed on top of her, his breath against her neck. She wriggled and tried to bring her legs together, but his knee was between them; then both knees, forcing her wide. "No!" she cried, and his hand closed over her mouth.

"You're mine forever now. Marriage is a sacred bond and nothing shall ever break us apart. Mine, mine, mine!"

He fell asleep immediately afterwards, leaving her sobbing and sore, staring into the darkness in a sort of terror.

She should have left him the next day, told her friends and her sister; gone to the police, pressed rape charges and walked away. But she didn't. Partly because she realized with an awful sinking feeling that she didn't really have any friends she could go to: over the past months she had become detached from them both emotionally and geographically. And Jess and Evan were out of the country, on a second honeymoon, trying to mend their marriage. But she stayed mainly because when she had demanded of James why he had raped her, he had simply punched her in the face, so hard that she thought he might have broken her jaw. He hadn't, it turned out, but she couldn't speak or even eat for a week without excruciating pain.

She felt so . . . stupid. Stupid to have married such a man; stupid for having allowed him to isolate her so successfully from every aspect of her previous life; stupid for not seeing him for the monster he was. Stupid because—well, just look at her, all bloat faced and bruised, with a bloodshot eye and stringy hair because she couldn't even bear the touch of water on her head. They would all laugh at her—she could imagine it with hallucinatory clarity—and she knew she deserved their derision. And so the moment passed and the abuse continued, with James glorying in Kate's increasingly meek, if stony, acceptance of the treatment he meted out to her, as he ceremonially emptied himself into her night after night, as the bruises flowered and faded and she became all but mute.

So warped did her view of this new reality become that every time she thought of picking up her phone to call her sister she could conjure Jess's voice telling her to "get over it," that marriage was a series of trials and that she would have to "woman up" and deal with her new life. When she did speak to Jess, it was always in James's presence on those rare occasions after she had earned enough indulgences, as he termed the system by which she could tot up such special treats as speaking to her twin, and with the hands-free function enabled so that he could hear every word. James removed the landline from the cottage, impounded Kate's laptop and iPad, took her mobile phone away, monitored the few emails she was permitted to send, put her car up for sale and locked the keys in his safe (though it seemed no one appeared to want a third-hand Fiat). She learned from Jess that her trip away had failed to paper over the cracks of her relationship: Evan had moved out. When Jess had wailed down the phone, Kate had felt nothing: she had descended into an ever more moribund state.

A profound shame had enveloped her, a desperate, excoriating shame. Shame at her own gullibility, shame that she was so weak as to allow herself to become a victim, shame that she had become complicit in this new life. Shame, also, at the perverse nature of the man she now had to call "husband." She just couldn't face speaking to anyone about what he did to her, the ceremonial nature of the sex, the sheer bloody weirdness of it all.

Four months after the wedding Kate realized with a slow, dull burn of understanding that she had missed her period. And all of a sudden she felt as though she had woken up. The idea of bringing a child into this hell galvanized her as her own fate never had.

It took her a month longer to escape. She planned it like a military campaign, like a world-class spy, meticulous to the last detail, her analytical brain finally kicking back into gear. One night with shaking hands she added five nightshade berries—*Atropa bella-donna*—picked from the woods behind the cottage into the black-berry-and-apple crumble she made for James (his favourite) and then waited for the vomiting and drowsiness to set in. This number would not kill him, she was pretty sure, because as a child she and Jess had eaten a few of the berries, and though they had been horribly ill for a day, they had survived. After putting James to bed with a bottle of water, a bucket and the number of the out-of-hours doctor by his side, she took the key to the safe out of his trousers pocket, removed her car keys and a bundle of cash. When they had sold her flat, James had transferred the proceeds out of their joint account into his own, leaving only enough money for her weekly shop, and inspecting every bill and outgoing payment with forensic scrutiny. She left her phone, iPad and laptop: all three would, she knew, contain tracking software that could lead James right to her.

She called Jess from a motorway service station.

"You left him?" Her sister seemed astounded, which was only to be expected, given how thoroughly Kate had withheld the truth of her existence from her.

"I'll explain when I see you."

"Are you sure he won't follow you?" Jess asked.

Kate thought of how she'd left him, white lipped and retching. "No," she said. She started to tremble, a tremor that threatened to turn into a full-blown shaking fit. "And he has no idea where you live." The one secret she had managed to hug to herself in all this time. Perhaps deep down she had always known she would need this escape hatch. When she put down the phone, her knees buckled and the tears started. It was late at night, almost midnight. Customers in the service station were sparse, almost all of them single males. She shut herself in one of the ladies' loos and wept and wept until an attendant knocked on the door and asked if she was all right. Of course she wasn't all right. She'd been raped every day for five months, kept a virtual prisoner, beaten and belittled. She mumbled something about a tummy bug and managed to muster enough wherewithal to drive the rest of the way to the Peak District.

Once at Jess's remote farmhouse, she collapsed as if she had been hanging on to a long rope over a deep drop with the last of her strength. Down she fell, down and down and down, into misery, self-loathing, self-blame.

Luke was born in hospital in Sheffield. Against all predictions, it was an easy birth, as if her body had been intent on expelling the last trace of James, but that was the last easy thing Kate would experience in a long, long time.

"Usually it's a traumatic birth that causes post-traumatic stress disorder," said the psychiatrist Jess had bullied her into seeing, frowning over his notes. He looked up just as Kate tugged her sleeves down over her hands. "What are you hiding, Kate?" he asked gently, but with the tiniest hint of the intonation James had employed before one of his crueller forms of temporal punishment, having maybe caught her filching a biscuit during one of his imposed fasts.

The psychiatrist had much quicker reactions than you'd expect in a sixty-three-year-old man with a hip replacement: the paper-weight smashed the glass bookcase behind him, and before Kate could turn his paper knife on herself, he caught her arms and restrained her. She was sectioned under the Mental Health Act. Social Services allowed Luke to remain with Jess.

By the time she was released it was clear that her sister and her baby had bonded, and Kate felt excluded and yet again worthless. Every occasion she held Luke, he wailed. Nothing she could do was right. After enduring two months of this—a terrible, traumatic time—by mutual agreement she had handed her baby over to Jess, and fled to Spain.

16

Blessings

GRANADA

1483

Some battles you can't win. Some should never be fought at all. When it came to pitting himself against his mother's will, Momo was always going to come off second best.

"I have no experience in battle."

"High time you acquired some, then."

"Our forces are divided."

Aysha jabbed a finger into her son's chest. "I keep telling you: you're the one who should be riding out to do battle with our enemies, claiming the glory, not that bastard and his brute of a brother."

"Mariam is pregnant again. She needs me by her side."

Aysha threw back her head and laughed. "Men! Your place is not in the birthing room but on the battlefield!"

"But no one's attacking us," Momo said unhappily. "The defeat at Loja stopped them."

"All the more reason for you to strike the first blow. What will your people say if you let your ninety-year-old father-in-law take all the glory while you sit on your hands with the harem women, waiting for your wife to deliver? They've already risen up once to place you the throne. Do you think they'll do so again if they're disappointed in you?"

Momo clenched his jaw. "War does not benefit our people: they starve and suffer or are pressed to be soldiers and die for want of training or care, when all they want is to tend their animals and their land, their shops and their families. They need peace in which to thrive. We should renew the treaty with the Castilians and negotiate for a lasting peace."

Her hand shot out and clouted him around the head. "You're a coward!" she screeched. "I'm ashamed of you!"

Her hand had raised a wide red welt. I wanted to sink my teeth into her throat and rip bloody chunks out of her. I wanted to drag her heart from her chest.

But Momo was deadly calm. "Call me a coward, then. Call me whatever you want. But know that when I ride to war as you demand, I go unwillingly."

Some short weeks later we rode out to war. Unwilling though he was, Momo put a brave face on it. When he walked into the courtyard, my breath caught inside me like a knife he was so beautiful. His marlota was of brocaded crimson velvet, the colour of the Banu Ahmar, with wide skirts and belled sleeves. A white cloak swirled around his shoulders and there was gold in his turban and on the breastplate he wore over the robe. At his side hung a gold-hilted sword in an extravagantly decorated scabbard. I knew it well: I had polished it for him many times. Among the twining arabesques that decorated it was engraved the motto of the Nasrid dynasty: *Only God is victorious.* I had always thought it an unfortunate reminder of man's frailty. Surely if you were riding to war, you should carry a more bombastic weapon.

Careless of the proprieties, Mariam came running out into the courtyard, her feet bare, her hair loose and wild. "You can't leave me here alone with her! You will die and I will be a widow!" She caught Momo by the cloak, her fingers like talons.

Patiently Momo unpicked them and held her hands between his. "My love, you know this isn't my free choice. I would never willingly leave you and our son."

She pulled his hands down to her belly. "Our sons."

I watched his face contort as he fought his emotions. Enfolding her in his arms, the great white cloak making a single creature of them, he sobbed into her hair.

I turned away, ashamed of him. This was not *asshak*. I limped across the marble, between the flowering jasmine and slender pillars, away from the sounds of sparrows and tumbling water and the cries of a terrified woman, and made my way out to the Alcazaba.

The barracks had emptied themselves like a holed cistern. Soldiers flowed out into the square below the great towers, milling about in cheerful array. Sunlight sparked off polished helms and lances, off harness and mail: and everywhere a sense of carnival, as if we were off to stage a great parade rather than to fight barbaric men who hated us and everything we stood for and wanted nothing more than to murder us. Months of inaction will do that to soldiers: boredom inures them to the very idea of death, as if their imaginations—running after the seductive dream of glory—stop wilfully short of the sword-blow that shears off a limb, the lance-point that slides beneath a helm, the arrow that pierces the chest.

I had never been to war, but seeing Mariam and Momo wrapped together was more than enough to make me want to saddle up and ride out. He would be mine again, in a world in which women had no place. I relished the prospect.

But as we rode out through the city's gate, Momo's shining lance, held high as he led his troops to war, hit the arch stone. The gleaming shards of the blade shattered, making his great white stallion dance in panic. He caught the cantle of his saddle just in time to prevent an ignominious fall; but even so I could hear the muttering all around us: "A bad omen . . ." "The djinn . . ." "Just like the prophecy . . ." "He is cursed . . ." I felt the impact as if it were a part of me that broke, and knew in that instant that we rode to our doom.

It had been a dry winter and the plain beneath the city was as dry as the desert. Stirred by our horses' hoofs, it rose around us in clouds.

At Momo's instigation, I sat backward on my horse, to be his eyes.

"I mustn't look back. Tell me, can you see her?"

"She's still watching. You make it sound like one of the old tales, as if you'll be cursed," I teased him, glancing at him over my shoulder. "Turned to stone?"

"My heart is like a stone. It must be: I am the commander of the faithful now, and a commander must never look back or he will be lost."

I had never heard him talk like this. Never heard him call himself "commander." Here was a change.

We rode on.

"Can you still see her?"

I could see nothing but dust and sunlight and men and horses now. Even the great promontory on which the Alhambra sprawled was gone from view, erased by our miasma, as if—peaceful and serene—it occupied another world to the one we now entered, one of violence and horror, in which its tranquil courtyards and sky-reflecting pools, its cool pillars and sacred geometries, had no place.

"She is still watching," I lied.

A little way into the hills on the following day, a stab of orange amid the scrub hooked my eye. I peered at it warily, thinking thoughts of ambush, but a few moments later when I caught sight of it again, I was sure it was an animal, and a small one at that. I watched it disappear into the dark vegetation between the boulders in the barranca; then suddenly it was running right in front of us and I saw it was a fox, lithe and fleet, with a sharp muzzle and beady black eyes. Someone made the sign of the evil eye against it, and my heart chilled as I remembered the fox in the kitchens at Loja, expiring painfully from the poison La Sabia had put in the jug of sherbet meant for Momo and his bride.

"We should turn back," I said to Momo. "That's two warnings now, and I doubt we'll be blessed with a third."

He gave me a sharp look. "You're such a heathen, Blessings." His dark eyes scanned my face and I saw his expression soften. "You're afraid. I understand that. But there's no shame in being afraid of your first foray to war."

"I am afraid," I admitted. "But for you, not myself."

"Don't fear for me: my fate is written."

And still we rode on, to his fate.

Some battles you can never win. Some should never be fought at all. Lucena was one such.

Did they know we were coming, the Christians? Had their scouts spied our army from afar? Had Ali Attar's column, joining us from Loja, alerted them to our presence? We saw fires in the hills as we crossed the border: I know now they had been set to pass the message. At dawn, with fog covering the hills and ravines, they caught us in a marshy river valley where our horses got bogged down in the soft ground, churning up the mud so badly the foot soldiers could barely make progress. The enemy came out of the mist like phantoms, so many they were uncountable. "All Andalusia is against us!" cried Momo's father-in-law. The old man looked frightened, and he was never frightened. "Flee now, my lord—there are too many of them!"

But Momo would not run. We would stand and fight, and we did, bravely. All might have been well had my mount not got tangled with an oleander. I was dumped in the river, where, unable to stand, my false foot caught up in roots and stones, cold water up over my shoulders, threatening to take me under, I cried out. If I hadn't, he might have saved himself. But I couldn't stop myself. "Help me, Momo!"

Some Special Guardian I was. Bound to protect him, I was the one who placed him in harm's way. Because, instead of being the commander of the faithful, acting for the good of his army and realm, he came for me.

"Blessings, stay there—don't move!"

He rode his white stallion through the muddy river. It loomed bright against the dark waters, as bright as a star, making the clearest target any infidel could ever wish for. And just as he dismounted to rescue me, a pair of enemy knights appeared, their vast chargers wading through the shallows. One grabbed the stallion's reins; the other leapt from his saddle and set about Momo. For a brief, heart-stopping time the two of them traded blows. His opponent was a head taller, a giant. He pressed forward, taking advantage of Momo being unable to turn. Momo took a step backward and disappeared suddenly from view where the riverbed shelved. Sword in hand, he came back up spluttering, helmet askew, blade swinging, water arcing off his cloak. The knights laughed at him. The one not holding the horse ran under his sword arm and shoved him backward and he fell again, and this time they were both on him, and I could do nothing but watch helplessly as they pinned him between them and twisted the decorated sword out of his hands.

Then one of them dealt him a blow with the hilt that knocked him unconscious. I shrank into the embrace of the oleander, smelling its deadly flowers, as they unceremoniously threw him over the saddle of his useless warhorse and led their prizes away.

Twenty-two Muslim battle flags fell into Christian hands that day. And our sultan, my beloved, was taken to the Torre del Moral in Lucena, in chains.

Only God is victorious.

17

Kate

"Luke! Luke, is that you? It's Mummy."

There was a moment of puzzled silence that made the breath catch in her chest as she waited for him to speak. Did he even remember her? Time moved so slowly when you were a child, so fast as you aged. If he *had* forgotten her, it was no more than she deserved, abandoning him as she had. No, she corrected herself, not abandoned. Left safely with Jess, her sister; her twin, who loved him dearly.

Perhaps he was confused. She and Jess were not identical, but they were very similar. Medium height, slim build, dark haired, dark eyed. Perhaps he thought of Jess as his mother now, and her as some distant relation, barely recalled. So long as he felt secure and loved, that was really all that mattered; but, oh, how she missed him! Too many conflicting emotions threatened to choke her as tears began to gather. She swallowed them down, reached for calmness.

"Mummy?" Luke's voice was querulous.

"Are you all right, darling? Where are you?"

"In the car." He sounded much surer of this. "Going fast!"

"Oh." She had called Jess, so Luke must have picked up her phone. How did a toddler know how to swipe screens and press buttons? "Well, that's fun. I hope not too fast. Can you ask Auntie Jess to call me when she can? When you get out of the car?"

"Okay. I saw a—"

He had moved away from the phone: all she could hear now was the distant rumble of tires on tarmac, and the muted voice of her sister. Then Luke bellowed, "A seal! I seen a seal! In the sea."

Kate's grin stretched wide. "Did you? See a seal? How brilliant."

"He was wimmin."

"Swimming?"

"Wimmin."

Solemn and pedantically corrective even when he was in the wrong, just like his father, even the disapproving intonation. It was such a tiny thing, but it struck her hard.

For a second she remembered her child's violent conception: then the painful memory was obliterated by a ray of golden light, and in her mind's eye she saw Abdou, intent on the intricate *zellij* tiling, as beatific and mystical as an angel in a medieval painting.

Luke's excited gabble chased her thoughts away. "Then we went to a plees station."

She frowned. "What was that?"

"Plees. *Pleees station.*"

"Police? A police station? Why did you go to the police station? Jess! Can you hear me? Has something happened?"

No reply. She heard the crunching of tires on gravel. Then Jess's voice came on the line. "It's okay—don't worry—just something I wanted to follow up. Look, I'll call you when we get back to the cottage, all right? There's too much to say, and it's not for small ears."

For the next twenty minutes Kate paced the apartment, unable to still her rising panic, unable to do anything useful. She hated herself.

When her phone rang at last, it seemed startlingly loud, the minimal furnishings of her rented flat doing nothing to dampen the strident ring tone.

"It was the foot," Jess said without preamble, throwing Kate completely.

"What?"

"I don't know how he found the farmhouse, but he did, and when I opened the door, he saw it —I was using it, the foot, the one you gave me, as a doorstop."

Kate went cold. The wretched Moroccan foot that had come from James's antiques shop. She had never been able to find a place for it in the cottage, so it had been relegated to the boot of her car, whence Jess had claimed it with gusto. "What a weird and brilliant thing! I love it." She'd even had Sarah restore it, cleaning it up, painting gold leaf into the carved arabesques that decorated it, till it looked resplendently weird, more vase than prosthetic.

"He thought I was you, tried to push his way in—"

"What?" Kate's voice rose to a shriek.

"Calm down—let me finish, okay?"

Kate took several deep breaths. "Okay. Sorry."

"I pretended Evan was still with me. I shouted for him and James backed off, but said he'd return."

"My God, my God!"

"It was pretty unnerving, I'll admit it, especially when I remembered what he did to you. So I put Luke in the car and drove down to Sarah's. Kate, you know what you said about his wife, about how she fell off the cliff? I've been thinking—what if he pushed her?"

"You don't think that didn't occur to me? I searched online and came up with nothing."

"I know, but I wanted to check for myself. So I thought I'd visit the local police here in Cornwall, see if they had anything on record."

Kate felt her stomach muscles tighten. "And did they?"

"Not a thing. That's quite strange, isn't it? No missing person report for a woman of her age or description. Not for that whole summer, or the one before or after, in case the dates were fuzzy."

"He said the body washed up down the coast and he identified it."

"I checked with the local coroner too. No mention anywhere of an Ingrid Foxley. And nothing about a woman falling off a cliff, except for a sixteen-year-old tanked up on cider who fell off rocks near Mousehole and got helicoptered to hospital. That was it."

Kate mulled this over. "Okay," she said at last. "Well, I saw the death certificate he took to the bishop." She paused. Had she? She remembered the official-looking envelope, but had she seen the actual document? She thought she had, but everything had been a bit of a blur. "I'm just glad you got Luke away," she said finally. "But Jess, what are you going to do? He knows where you are now—and he said he'd be back."

"Leave it with me. I'm going to do some more digging."

It was a slow shift at the bar that night. The few tourists who wandered in occupied their tables quietly and left as soon as they'd eaten. Jimena, bored and bad tempered because of the low turnover yet unable to pick holes in her staff's performance, said something about going to see her cousin and, armed with two packets of cigarettes and her rose-embroidered shawl, stomped out, banging the door behind her.

Immediately the atmosphere lightened, as if a stiff wind had pushed a storm front out of range. Juan winked at Kate. "Fancy a beer?" He flicked the top expertly off an Alhambra and held the bottle out to her.

Kate shook her head. "If she catches you, she'll kill you."

Juan grinned. "She'd have to catch me first."

"Oh, go on then," she said. "Just a swig."

Juan quirked an eyebrow and handed the half-drunk bottle over. "Living dangerously?"

"Just living."

She watched the door nervously, till Juan burst out laughing. "For God's sake, Anna, get it down you. She's not a monster. She can't be in two places at once."

"Of course she is, and she can."

"She is—you're right."

They laughed nervously. Then Kate took a long swallow, savouring the bitterness as it cold-scalded the back of her throat.

"Kate?"

She choked. The light was behind the speaker's head, casting his face into shadow, but she knew who it was right away. She coughed and caught hold of the bar to steady herself.

Juan took the bottle from her. "I'll be out back if you need me . . . *Kate*." He gave her a long, quizzical look, then was gone.

"What are you doing here?" Kate felt her heart beating and the blood rising in her face. He was taller than she'd remembered. Candlelight sparked in his dark eyes.

"I came to find you. To ask you a question."

She swallowed. "So ask."

Abdou dipped his head for a moment, then held out his hand. "Hicham, at the Internet café, told me you had something like this."

Kate stared at the fragment of paper in his palm. Spiky symbols in faded ink, arranged as in short lines of poetry. At once she recognized the similarity to the slip of paper she had removed from the wall in the gardens. "My God," she whispered. "How strange."

"I found it in the wall we were repairing in the Tower of the Captive. It was not the first one Omar and I came across. But that first one was too water damaged to make anything out on it. So I would very much like to see the one you have. Hicham described it to me, though he said you said it was just a bit of rubbish."

"You're a friend of Hicham's?" Kate asked hesitantly, remembering how curt he had been with her—rude, even.

Abdou cocked his head and light fell across his fine features. "Not really, no. More like an acquaintance. His cousin Saïd is my friend."

Kate smiled. "I like Saïd."

Abdou grinned. "Hicham has . . . an awkward manner. He doesn't know how to behave to women." His eyes lingered on her.

Kate felt a slow, warm tide swirling in her abdomen and tried to ignore it. She found she could not look away from him, no matter how uncomfortable. She tried to think of something to say, but her mind was empty of everything but sensation.

"Do you have it with you?"

"Sorry?"

"The fragment like this?"

She put a hand to her forehead as if to master her thoughts. "In my bag, I think," she said at last. "Let me go and check." It seemed rude to run away, leaving him there. "Would you like a beer? On me?"

His eyes widened. "I can't let you pay."

"Because I'm a woman?"

"Because I'm a customer in your bar, and we hardly know each other."

"Well, okay. Would you like to buy a beer?"

His eyes darted to the price board then back to her. "Maybe not. A glass of water?"

She fetched him one and set it down, then turned on her heel, feeling embarrassed that she might have appeared to have been flogging him a beer.

The back room was cooler than the bar. She retrieved her handbag from under the bench and went straight into the cloakroom, where she locked the door. She ran her hands under the tap and patted her hot face. In the mottled mercury of the old mirror her eyes struck her as hectic, too bright, a little mad. She hadn't felt this way, gauche and girlish, filled with stupid desire, since she first met Matty—and look how well that had turned out. *Don't be ridiculous*, she told herself. *You know nothing about him, and anyway, he doesn't seem interested in you, just the scrap of paper. Get a grip!*

She put the toilet seat down and sat on the cold plastic lid. The fragment of paper was in the zippered compartment where she'd put it for safekeeping. She fished it out and examined it under the bare electric bulb (no little luxuries like lampshades out here for the staff: typical Jimena). A thrill went through her. It really was similar to the one Abdou had just shown her, even at a glance: four lines of spiky, runic, symbols. Maybe it was a short poem, or a prayer.

Filled with purpose now, and slightly calmer, she returned to the bar. She was about to cross the threshold, when she heard raised voices. Or rather, one raised voice, and a familiar one at that.

"What are you doing in here—drinking free water? I don't serve Moors in here, let alone offer them charity. This is a respectable *Spanish* establishment."

Jimena had her hands on her hips and her jaw thrust out. Abdou set the glass of water carefully down on the bar. But he did not look cowed in the way she might have expected, the way she had seen other Arabs react to Jimena's aggressive tirades: he had drawn himself up and held his head high. Hundreds of years of prejudice sparked between the two of them like an arc of electricity.

"I came to see Kate."

"There is no Kate here."

Abdou frowned and looked past Jimena's shoulder, and Kate felt her stomach flip inside as her boss turned.

"There must be some kind of mistake. My name is Anna Maria," she said, and watched as his gaze became hooded and wary.

"My error. I apologize."

Jimena gave Kate a hard stare. "You know my policy," she said stonily. She turned back to Abdou. "Now, fuck off, *bastardo de mierda*."

He regarded her coolly, letting the vile words flow over him. Then, dismissing Jimena, he looked over her shoulder at Kate: "If you are interested in the matter we were discussing, you will find me at the Nest of Storks."

Before she could ask where this was, he was gone, leaving a sudden vacuum of highly charged air. Kate could feel the eyes of the tourists upon her and Jimena, disapproving, disquieted.

"Fucking Arab scum," Jimena said loudly. She rounded on Kate. "What the hell were you thinking of, letting him in as soon as my back was turned and giving him a glass of fucking water, like we're some sort of refugee camp? Besides, I've seen that one before—he's a terrorist."

Kate stared at her boss, her throat tightening as if she might vomit. It was not bile that came up, though, but words. "You know what?" she found herself saying, even as her fingers fumbled with the knot of her bar apron. "You can stick your job, Jimena. I'm fed up with working for such a foul-mouthed, bigoted old bitch." She unlooped the apron strap from around her neck and threw it on the ground between them with a flourish, as if it were a toreador's cape.

From the table of tourists sitting by the mirrored wall there came a single quiet cheer, a couple of whistles and a round of applause. Jimena swivelled her head to regard them with a basilisk stare and they hunched over their beers again, grinning and whispering.

Kate took her opportunity to retrieve her handbag from the back room, but as she re-emerged, Jimena stood in her path, her face dark with blood. "Not so fast, Anna Maria . . . or whatever your name really is." As Kate tried to sidestep her, Jimena caught her by the arm, her nails digging in like talons. "You work out your notice, or I'll be talking to the *poli*."

"Fine. You go talk to the police. I'm sure there's plenty they'd like to know . . . about your employment practices. For a start I've regularly been made to work for more than the forty-hour maximum, without extra pay. I've been employed here for almost two years and not been given my statutory vacation leave, and when you fired Gustav, you never paid him the *finiquito* he was due. I'm sure there's plenty more I could come up with."

"*¡Hija de puta!*"

Kate peeled Jimena's fingers off her arm and pushed her aside. "Leave what's owed to me with Juan or I'll be back with a lawyer."

By the time she reached the corner of the street she was shaking. Not just a mild tremble of excitement but a full-on adrenaline-rushing, teeth-chattering spasm that made her clutch the wall before she fell. What had she done? Jacked in her job, her only means of support. Just because Jimena was being Jimena. She felt as though she was teetering on the edge of an abyss—then she remembered Abdou's dignity as the Spanish woman insulted him and her panic evaporated into the night. For the first time in ages she felt proud of herself. She had taken a stand: she had done the right thing, the sort of thing the Kate of old would have said and done, before James had reduced her to human rubble.

Where was it Abdou had said to meet him? For a moment her mind was a perfect blank, then she remembered the name: the Nest of Storks. But the Albayzín was a labyrinth of little alleyways containing hundreds of cafés and bars. She should go to the Internet café and Google it; better still, ask Saïd, who would surely know.

But when she got there, she saw with a sinking heart that Hicham was behind the counter, and she hesitated, remembering how unpleasant he had been. Then before she could lose her nerve, she firmed her jaw and marched in. "Hello, Hicham. I'm looking for a place called the Nest of Storks. Do you know where it is?"

He seemed taken aback. "Is not a place for people like you."

Was that contempt she read in his expression? She was still fired up by her encounter with Jimena. "What the hell do you mean by that?"

His eyebrows lifted. "Is for men. Women can't go there."

"Well, this woman's going there. So please tell me where it is."

"Why you go there?"

"I'm meeting someone."

"I not tell you unless you tell me who."

Kate stared at him. "Why do you want to know?"

Hicham stared silently at her in reply.

The impasse stretched between them for a long, uncomfortable moment.

"A *zellij* expert who works at the Alhambra, doing restoration."

An unreadable flicker in his expression. "Is not a bit late to discuss tiling?" He was playing with her now, his dark eyes insolent.

"That's really none of your business."

He jerked his head to the left. "Down the alley out back, left, then right."

"Thank you." She turned to leave.

"*Puta.*"

Kate whirled. "I beg your pardon?"

"Only whores go there."

Before she could make a rejoinder, he was moving away, his mobile phone to his ear. She hurried outside.

The Nest of Storks was identifiable by what looked like a child's painting of a stork landing on a pile of sticks, to the left of an inset door. Above the door was an odd symbol, like a figure with bowed legs and uplifted arms. Kate frowned: it felt familiar.

As if he had seen her staring, a man suddenly stuck his head out the door.

"*Hola*," said Kate, having meant to say *Salaam*.

He eyed her up and down. Kate wished she'd worn a coat: his gaze felt penetrating. Doubts assailed her. Did she really want to see Abdou in this place? Wouldn't it be easier just to go up to the Alhambra the next day and talk to him while he was working with Omar? But perhaps Omar didn't know about the fragments. Perhaps there was a reason Abdou wanted to keep it quiet. That in itself was also alarming: she'd had enough of secrets.

She steeled herself. "I'm looking for a man named Abdou," she said quickly.

"Ab-doooo . . ."

The way he elongated the syllable was suggestive. In the darkness, Kate felt herself flush, remembering what Hicham had said.

He took a draw on his cigarette and it flared to life in the gloom; then he tossed the butt down and stepped aside for her. Even so, she had to brush past him to enter the bar: she felt his hand touch her buttocks as she passed.

"Hey, Abdelkarim!"

The man called the name loudly over her shoulder and added something in what she presumed to be Arabic, and the whole place fell quiet. She felt like an unwanted intruder.

It took a while for her eyes to adjust to the low illumination of the single hanging lantern. Scatters of jewelled light leaked from its leaded panes of coloured glass into the clouds of smoke but did little to help her pick out the man she knew as Abdou, whose real name appeared to be Abdelkarim. She remembered his closed expression as he registered her own assumed name and wondered just what *he* was hiding. The bar had an edgy feel to it that made her uncomfortable: was that because there were conspiracies in the making all around her; or because she was the only woman in here and everyone was staring at her?

And then Abdou was in front of her and his smile dissipated her doubts. "Come," he said, and guided her through the crowded bar. At a corner table a younger man rose, bobbing his head at Kate in greeting. He and Abdou exchanged a few words and he was gone, weaving his way through tables and chairs like a feral cat.

Abdou pulled out the chair the young man had vacated for Kate, then sat down opposite her with his back to the wall. It was only when she sat down that she realized the clouds of smoke were not from cigarettes—at least, not just from cigarettes—but from little censers on the tables. She leaned in, inhaling—roses, something woody, something that caught at the back of her throat.

"Incense," Abdou said. "From the souks of Marrakech. Rose petals, agarwood and sandarac gum—a mixture that's been used for centuries. The chambers of the sultans of Granada probably smelled just like this."

"Apart from the beer." Kate grinned.

Abdou tipped his head in acknowledgement. "I'm afraid I ordered us tea." At that moment the young man reappeared, carrying a small brass tray. "Thank you, Aziz." He looked back to Kate. "My friend."

Aziz had a huge smile and a neat Afro: he was extravagantly handsome. He set down the tray, then turned to Abdou and flicked his thumb under his chin. Abdou laughed. It was not a gesture Kate recognized. "What did that mean?" she asked as Aziz left, mobile phone pressed to his ear. For a moment, just a moment, she wondered if Abdou was gay and Aziz his lover. It wasn't impossible, was it? She felt a little sick for allowing herself to harbour absurd thoughts of romance.

Abdou applied himself to swirling the tea in its little silver pot, then to pouring it into a small, gold-topped glass, but a light in his eyes danced with mischief. "I wasn't expecting to see you so soon."

"Yes, well, I quit my job." Her words were clipped, determined as she was not to make even more of a fool of herself than she already had.

A small stream of golden tea spilled onto the tray. "Really?"

"Jimena's a cow. I've been meaning to leave for a long time."

"Hard on cows. I'm sorry. It was probably my fault."

"She's always like that. It was time I stood my ground. Anyway . . ." The intensity of his gaze was disconcerting. She tried to change the subject. "I brought the bit of paper I found." She placed it carefully out of the way of the tea.

Abdou set the teapot aside and craned over the fragment, his head almost touching hers. "Incredible."

He raised his eyes and Kate found she was holding her breath, as if he might kiss her—ridiculous, in this place, in front of all these people, and anyway, he might not even like women, let alone her . . .

He straightened up and the spell was broken, until he brought a folded card out of the pocket of his leather jacket and from it extracted his own fragment. Laid side by side, there was no question the writing was in the same form, and the same hand. Kate's heart began to thud. "What do they say?"

"A good question. I don't know."

Disappointment was a stone in her chest.

"I recognize the language," he went on. "It's the language of my people."

"Your people?"

"The Imazighen—'Free People,' which is a joke." His lips twisted.

"I've never heard of the Immer—Ima— Sorry." She gave up.

"Most people call us Berbers, though that's an insult. It's what the Romans considered us—from *barbari*, meaning barbarian. Just like the Spanish, though we were the ones civilizing them! We brought them baths and irrigation and beautiful buildings built around pools that reflected the sky, and now they treat us like shit! They will always hate us. But if their King Fernando had had his way, the Alhambra would have been blown to ruins and the tourist industry—the only thing that makes Granada any fucking money—wouldn't exist."

He looked so angry. She thought of how insulting Jimena had been. She and James would get on like a house on fire, she thought, then wished she hadn't thought about him at all. She bowed her head over the fragments of paper, not knowing what to say.

"Where did you find this?" he asked.

"In a wall in the gardens."

"I know that. Where, exactly? It matters, I th—"

Whatever he was going to say was interrupted by a ruckus at the entrance to the bar and as Kate turned to see what was going on, Abdou shot to his feet. Someone shouted "*Poli!*" and a there was a sudden rush for the back door.

Abdou reached down and swiped the two fragments of paper. "Sorry!" he called over his shoulder. "Got to run." And then he was gone.

Kate sat there, disbelieving, anger rising at being abandoned in this hostile place. But she was just as angry that he had taken the fragment with him. How dare he? But before she had time to stand up and go after him, four armed officers stormed into the bar.

"ID cards and passports!" one cried. "Everyone line up by the wall, hands on heads, papers in hand!" Another officer repeated this in Arabic.

Kate blinked. She was a European national and had every right to be in the country. Nevertheless, she felt afraid. Perhaps she was picking up on the anxieties of the men around her. Or that bit of graffito she passed every time she walked to the top of the Albayzín—*Don't trust the cops!* How many of the men here were in Spain illegally? she wondered. Or engaged in activities on the black market. Or, and she felt a chill, in terrorism?

She chided herself for falling into Jimena's way of thinking. The Muslim population had been rising steadily in the city, especially since the mosque had been built in 2003. The Nest of Storks was just a bar in which North African men liked to gather to drink tea or coffee or beer; to smoke and play cards and talk in their own language. What was wrong with that? She got to her feet and bent to retrieve her handbag.

"Leave that!"

Kate looked up, to find a pistol pointing at her. Trembling, she raised her hands.

"Passport?"

She didn't have her passport with her. It was in a drawer in her rented apartment: she never carried it for fear of losing it. She tried to explain this, but her terrified brain suddenly forgot every word of Spanish it had ever known. Pathetically, she felt her eyes sting with tears. "I'm sorry," she said in English. "I don't have it with me."

The officer's face was stony. He exchanged some machine-gun-fast words with one of his colleagues who was patting down the ranged men and checking their papers.

Kate caught the name Moreno and her heart faltered.

The officer turned back to her, looked her slowly up and down. "Anna Maria Moreno?" he asked.

Kate wanted, with terrible urgency, to piss, then feared she might do it where she stood, just as she had once in infant school, standing on a chair in front of the class, a punishment for talking. She fought the urge. "No. I'm a British national w— Uh, visiting Granada." She'd nearly said *working*, and realized with sudden certainty that Jimena had been the one to send the police here, with some trumped-up story about terrorists. She'd heard Abdou mention the Nest of Storks and probably already knew of the bar. It was a sort of revenge—on him, for entering Jimena's Arab-free zone; on Kate, for allowing him to do so, and for calling her a bitch and then exerting the only power she had by having the last word and walking out. But she couldn't mention Jimena or the bar, or she'd have to explain why she was working under a false name.

"You'll have to come with us so we can check the system," the officer said.

Which was how she ended up riding in the back of a police van with half a dozen furtive-looking men who stole puzzled glances at her and whispered among themselves in their impenetrable tongue. She turned her head away from them, watching the lights of the city blur past into the darkness. She had done nothing wrong. So why did she feel so guilty?

18

She had to wait her turn as one by one her fellow passengers were taken off into interview rooms and without exception some time later led off to the cells, no doubt to be handed over to the border force to be deported back to wherever they'd come from.

When the officers arrived for her, they were stiffly courteous, apologizing for the wait. They had found her in the system, they said as they seated her in the interview room and took their places at the opposite side of the table there, one manning the computer, the other with a pen hovering over his notebook, but they wanted to know what she'd been doing in Spain for two years, since there was no record of her paying taxes or claiming benefits.

In the bus, Kate had prepared her story. She was researching a book about the Alhambra, she told them. She'd received an advance for the book and was living off it while she completed the commission. Writing didn't pay much, she said with a laugh, but she lived very simply, renting a small apartment on the Calle Guinea. They asked for the address and she gave it to them. The book was why she'd been in the Nest of Storks talking to a *zellij* specialist about the traditional methods used for the restoration of the old tiles.

They looked openly skeptical. "A bit late to be discussing tiles, wasn't it?"

It was exactly what Hicham had said, and stifled the nervous urge to giggle. It was the only time the specialist could meet when he wasn't working, she told them. What was his name and where did he work? She spread her hands—she didn't know: she'd only met him briefly once before and thought he was an academic of some sort, not wanting to lead them too easily to Abdou. Or Abdelkarim, or whatever his name was. The way he'd run suggested something shady was going on: she wondered what.

The next question took her aback.

"Is there someone here who can vouch for you? Who can confirm you are who you say you are?"

The name of her landlord was almost out of her mouth before she bit it back. Sergio might easily mention that she was working at the bar. And he knew Jimena. Panic scrabbled inside her. She couldn't think of a single person she knew in this city who didn't have something to do with the bar.

But there was one. "Khadija," she blurted out, then realized she could not remember the Moroccan woman's surname.

"Khadija who?" There was a sneer in the first officer's intonation, though his face remained impassive. But the implication was clear: *First we find you hanging out with Arab men in a bar and now you give us an Arab woman's name. You must be some sort of conspirator.*

This was getting worse and worse. "It's late—she'll be asleep now," Kate said awkwardly, wishing she'd said nothing at all.

The second officer shrugged. "She'll either vouch for you or it's a night in the cells for you. Give us her number."

Kate felt a fool. "Hold on." She fished in her bag. Had she put the card Khadija had given her in here? There was such a jumble of rubbish to go through and the more she searched for it the worse it got. "Sorry, sorry . . ." She tipped the contents of her bag out onto the tabletop—tissues and receipts, pen tops, a half-used packet of paracetamol, cosmetics tubes and compacts, loose change she hadn't bothered to put into her purse. A boiled sweet that had somehow lost its wrapper and replaced it with a coating of dust and filth . . .

A plastic-wrapped tampon rolled across the table toward the officers, one of whom smirked. She retrieved it, but he was still smirking. That was when she realized, oh God, that he must have spotted the strip of brightly foiled condoms. She'd had them for donkey's years, probably even before she'd met James, but the officer wouldn't know that, and there was no way she was going to explain. Blushing, she swiped them back into the dark confines of the leather handbag, and rooted around till she found her phone, then her battered old wallet. And there, in her wallet, was Khadija's card, listing a mobile number as well as a landline. But would Khadija even remember her? They'd spent only a couple of hours in each other's company and now Kate was dragging her into police business—a shameful, unforgivable imposition on someone who was barely even an acquaintance. And even if Khadija did recall their meeting, there was no reason she would have retained her name, or be willing to go out of her way to help a foreigner. Kate looked up, hoping the pass might be sufficient evidence, but the first officer handed it back to her.

"The number?"

She sat frozen and unhappy as the officers took Khadija's number and called her from the big old-fashioned desk phone. It seemed to ring forever and Kate was almost relieved, thinking that maybe a night in the cells was not such a bad thing after all. Then someone answered—a male. There was a lot of back and forth in rapid Spanish, a pause, and then the officer asked, "Would you mind coming down to the central police station to vouch for her?"

Kate hung her head in shame.

The wait was interminable. One of the officers went out to talk to a colleague; the other sat at the computer, his fingers moving over the keys. Kate couldn't see the screen. Was he searching for more information about her? Googling her? Or was he simply playing Solitaire? The reflection in the night-dark window gave nothing away. Twenty minutes later a smartly dressed, head-scarfed woman in her sixties walked into the office, followed by the other policeman.

Kate met her eyes. "I'm so, so sorry. You were the only person I could think of."

She'd expected impatience at the least, or even a flash of anger, but there was only compassion in Khadija's gaze. "I am more than happy to help you."

She showed the policemen her national identity card and her work permit. When they took note of her title and where she worked, their expressions changed, in just the way Kate's had when she'd read Khadija's card.

"We apologize for getting you out at such a late hour, Professor Boutaki," one of them said.

"This young woman tells us she's doing research for a book on the Alhambra," the other said brusquely, determined not to show he was impressed.

Kate saw Khadija's lips twitch. "Yes, indeed, Officer. She's become quite an expert, especially on the plants." Her gaze slid toward Kate, gleefully conspiratorial.

Ten minutes later, once a lot of forms had been signed and rubber-stamped, Kate was released on the promise that she would return with her passport the next day—"For our records, you understand."

Neither woman said anything as they exited the huge official building, dwarfed and cowed by its vast officialdom. On the corner of the plaza Khadija said, "Tell me why you were in the Nest of Storks."

A cloud passed across the moon. Kate was glad: it hid her embarrassment. "I went to meet one of the men working on the *zellij* restoration."

Khadija laughed, a peal that rang out across the square. "I can't quite imagine Omar inviting you to such a place so I'm sure that must have been Abdou."

Of course she would know them well. Kate's embarrassment deepened. "Yes."

"It's really not the most respectable place to be meeting late at night."

"I realized that when I went in."

Khadija tutted. "He shouldn't have invited you there. What was he thinking? The Nest of Storks? More like the nest of thieves."

Kate didn't know what to say to that, so she said nothing.

"Come to the house on Thursday," the other woman said. "Around eight or nine, unless you're working, of course. Have dinner with us—my husband will cook."

Kate grinned. "I'd love to, and no, I'm not working."

"Here's the address." Khadija scribbled in a notebook, tore out the page and handed it to her. "Better get home. Brahim will be worried." She enfolded Kate in a sudden embrace, and marched away, her cellphone pressed to her ear. Kate caught the words "*habibi*" and "okay, *wachha*," and then she was gone.

The next morning Kate woke at her usual early hour and lay there, luxuriating in the miasma of a dream that she couldn't quite re-enter but that had left its touch on her in the small hours of the night, hot with yearning. It had something to do with baths and oil, and a man. Then with sudden clarity she recalled the stirring sensation of a man's hand between her thighs, the perfection of the pattern of tiny tiles on the wall of the bathhouse. Oh . . .

For God's sake, Kate, she told herself sharply. *Not only do you hardly know him, but he ran out on you during a police raid.* She pushed the dream away and considered the unfamiliar idea of a day that lay before her as blank and clear as a fresh sheet of paper.

Despite the unhelpful dream and only five hours' sleep she felt alert and energized, and lighter somehow, unburdened. She hadn't realized how crushed she had been by working in the bodega, or more specifically, by working for Jimena. She swung her legs out of bed, went to the window and pushed back the curtains. The imposing walls of the Alhambra rose to meet the sky and her spirits rose with them. She was free to go there whenever she wished. She had her pass and acres of time, and in two days a dinner date with a new friend who was a great expert on the beautiful gardens: she felt like the luckiest woman in the world.

Of course, the feeling lasted only briefly. Turning on her phone, she remembered it was Luke's birthday. Which she had completely forgotten in the heat of her intrigue with the tile maker and her run-in with the law. What a terrible mother she was. A pang of loss and a love as sharp as a shard pierced her through. *Oh, Luke,* she lamented, punching Jess's number into the phone. *My boy, my lovely boy.* When she thought of him, it was as a baby enfolded in a chick-yellow blanket; yet there he had been, answering Jess's smart phone and running around on the beach. She had no image of him as the toddler he was now; wouldn't even be able to pick him out of a group of children at a play group. The phone rang and rang and at last went to voice mail. She tried to muster as much energy as she could, sang a horribly tuneless "Happy Birthday" and finished with a plaintive "Ask Auntie Jess to call me back!"

Guilt enveloped her. Perhaps it was time for her to return to England. But the very idea made something inside her shrivel. Fear of James lay deep within her, dormant but not dead, like a microscopic cancer ready to blossom back into life. She might have stood up to Jimena, but she still wasn't ready to take on her husband.

And, she reminded herself, she still had to go back into the police headquarters and present her passport. A frisson of anxiety drove her to the espresso machine to bolster herself before she went to take care of that onerous task.

On the way back, having circumnavigated the complex matter of Christian names and surnames and had her passport verified then copied by a perfectly nice policewoman, she found, by sheer chance, another Internet café.

As she waited for the ancient computer to boot up, she found her mind wandering yet again to Abdou—or Abdelkarim, though it was hard to associate him with this unfamiliar name. She tried not to think of the candlelight on his cheekbones, making golden crescents in his dark eyes, and failed. She thought of how he had touched her in her dream, and felt a dark flush of blood deep inside her. Then once again she reminded herself of how he had abandoned her, taken her little paper treasure with him. She was, she told herself fiercely, as the hard disk cranked to life, a hopeless case when it came to men, always managing to choose the liars and deceivers, the unreliable and the downright dangerous. Just for once, couldn't she find herself a nice man who would treat her kindly and honestly? She sighed and entered the code she had been given at the counter to get on Google.

INGRID FOXLEY, she typed in. The search brought up absolutely nothing relevant. Damn. She wished she'd been nosier about her predecessor, at least found out her maiden name. She typed in JAMES FOXLEY INGRID, but this also rendered nothing useful. It did, however, bring up two photos of her husband, both of which looked pretty recent. Her skin prickled. There he was smiling at the camera as though he was the perfectly normal, charming, slightly old-fashioned middle-aged gentleman antique dealer he liked to project, with his floppy dark fringe, greying at the temples, his eyes narrowed so you could not read their expression. In a tweed jacket and an open-necked shirt that she didn't recognize he appeared the complete antithesis of a *rapist*.

With some venom, she obliterated that search page by entering INGRID ACCIDENT CORNWALL.

Nothing.

WOMAN CORNWALL CLIFF FALL brought up hundreds of stories, some about rock climbers being rescued by local emergency services, two about women trying to save their respective dogs that had fallen onto ledges, a suicide, and a drunken tumble by a teenager. There seemed to be no mention of a James or Ingrid Foxley, at least in the first seventy-five articles or so. She moved on.

JAMES FOXLEY ANTIQUES INGRID brought up references to the shop in East Molesey with INGRID crossed through in the search criteria and nothing of interest.

What now? INGRID UK: 27,500,000 search results. So much for thinking the name was unusual.

Bracing herself, she went back to using her husband as her starting point. JAMES FOXLEY EAST MOLESEY, she typed. Again, dozens of references to the antiques shop in local listings sites and two mentions in blogs by antiques dealers who had done business with him. "Always a pleasure buying something from James," one of them claimed, accompanying a photo of a frankly hideous vase. "He is a man of exquisite taste in *objets d'art* and *fin de siècle* furniture. Oh, and women as well. Here I am with James and a really beautiful piece."

Beneath this oily pronouncement was a photograph. Kate felt her innards turn to ice. There was James, with the strong sunlight carving his face into striking planes, beside an older man in a smart shirt marred by darkened patches beneath the arms, and . . . her,

Kate. Except, of course, it wasn't. Not quite. The woman had a heart-shaped face framed by a neat dark bob with chestnut highlights that was shorter than Kate's usual style. But it was almost exactly the cut James had urged her to have—just before the wedding. And then, when she had run away, a bit out of her mind, wanting to destroy the woman she had been, she'd shorn her head and sliced her arms. It had taken ages to grow her hair back to the length it was now.

Trembling, she scrolled down, sure of what she would see. That the woman's name was Ingrid. Ingrid Foxley.

But it wasn't. According to the blog, her name was Michelle—or as the blogger insisted, "*Michelle, ma belle.*" Kate read on, looking for further information, but there was nothing at all. Frustrated, she skimmed through the rest of the man's blogs, but there were no more references to James or this Michelle, though tons of boring details about classic cars and boozy trips to the Continent, as if he were some archaic tourist undertaking the Grand Tour.

MICHELLE FOXLEY. Over a hundred thousand references. Great. Kate clicked on Images, but even though she pored over the first few pages this brought up, there was no sign of the woman. Kate rubbed her eyes. She needed a break.

Two coffees later and reduced to almost random Googling, she was about to give up, when an idea struck her. Logging into her old Facebook account—left un-updated ever since she'd married James—she typed in the name of the boring blogger: Mike Weston. Facebook offered her several choices: a man in a Chelsea shirt, another with hipster facial hair, one in Swansea, another in Cornwall, a third in drag. None resembled the man in the blog, whom she had seen lounging in a pre-war racing car, in Cannes, in Barcelona, at Ascot . . .

She asked for more, and more she was given. She spotted him at once—slightly overweight, rather red in the face, in an England rugby shirt. She clicked on his profile and was gratified to discover he did not appear to care overmuch about his privacy settings. Among his list of friends she came across a Michelle Englefield. Clicking on the profile photo, which showed a tabby cat licking its paw, she found the mysterious woman she had been seeking: in a short, slinky dress as she raised a glass; amid a group of girlfriends with the sun setting behind them; with the tabby cat in her arms; posing in a smart black shirtdress under a sign for a company, as if for a corporate brochure. But in none of these images did James appear; neither was he among her list of friends. Which was no surprise, given James's views on social media.

Kate spent half an hour snooping through Michelle Englefield's Facebook timeline and came away feeling guilty and depressed. The woman seemed preternaturally cheerful and popular, posting little mantras of positivity that made Kate feel rather nauseous ("Enjoy your life: every second is a precious gift!"; "Every experience, no matter how bad, holds within it a blessing of some kind: the goal is to find it"; "Diamonds are just little bits of charcoal that handle pressure extremely well"; "Don't carry your mistakes around with you: use them as stepping stones to rise above them").

She mused over the last one, draining the dregs of her third coffee. Then she left three messages on her sister's voice mail, spelling out names and places, closed out of the computer, took her tray to the counter and marched purposefully up to the Alhambra. Her conservator pass saw her quickly through the crowds of tourists: she felt guilty about that too. The sun beat on her back as she made her way to the Tower of the Captive. The cords were still in place, but Kate ducked under them and marched right in. There they were, Omar and Abdou, bent over a section of tiling in the far corner, their heads almost touching: one man's hair grizzled almost to white, the other's close-cropped and as black as a crow's wing.

"*Salaam!*" she called out, and they both turned. Her disappointment felt physical. "Oh. I was looking for Abdou."

Omar came hurrying over, wiping his hands on his overalls. "Sorry. Is not here today. Can I help you?" The lad who was not Abdou sat back on his haunches, watching them curiously, his feet splayed, his spine straight: the posture patient men of this culture had adopted since ancient times, which modern people could never comfortably achieve even after years of earnest yoga and Pilates.

Kate managed a smile. "No, it's fine, Omar. It can wait. Will he be working tomorrow?"

He shook his head.

"The next day?"

"The next day Friday."

Omar laughed. He said something to the lad, and he started to laugh too. Kate looked from one to the other. Were they joking about her desperation to see a man she'd only met twice? She waited, her smile becoming a rictus. At last the older man took pity on her.

"Friday's when Abdou make couscous. It's a ritual. Some for us, some for the djinn, eh, Mohamed?"

Mohamed grinned and got to his feet. "Nice to meet you—" he walked over to read her badge "—Señora Fordham." They shook hands.

"Señorita," Kate corrected. "*Miss* Fordham." How she wished she could wind back time to a place when that was true, when she hadn't become Mrs. Foxley. Why had she taken James's name?

"Miss . . . Ford-ham?"

She blinked. "Sorry. Miles away. What did you say your name was?"

"Mohamed—I am Omar's son."

Memory connected with a flash of insight. "Oh, the *zellij* expert from Fez?"

His grin widened even more and he gave her a courtly bow, his hand on his heart. "Yes, madam. I am flattered that my reputation has travelled so far," he said in excellent English.

"Abdou told me about you. Or was it Abdelkarim?" She watched his reaction to the name that had been used at the Nest of Storks, but he just looked slightly puzzled.

"Come back here on Friday, Miss Fordham. You will see why my cousin's couscous is famous."

"I . . . uh . . . okay. Is Abdou a shortening of Abdelkarim?"

Mohamed again looked puzzled, perhaps by her choice of words. "Everyone has more than one name, no? People often call me 'Momo.'"

Different names for different facets. Even plants had their common names and their Latin names. It was the same with people. Then it struck her: maybe Michelle Englefield had not become "Mrs. Foxley" after all; maybe she had kept her maiden name all along. Why hadn't she thought of that? Because James had been so insistent that Kate take his name when they'd married, that was why: perhaps because his first wife had refused to do so.

But if this was the case, and Michelle Englefield was still alive and well and maintaining her cheery Facebook page, what on earth was going on?

Kate hurried away, with a promise to return to try the famous couscous. On the way back down through the Pomegranate Gate she punched Jess's number into her mobile phone and waited impatiently as the international code took its time to connect—and went to voice mail yet again. Kate felt like screaming but left a long message.

The next day she received a text message, in the usual code:

YOU WERE RIGHT. AND THAT'S NOT ALL.

Her heart felt light and fiery, ablaze with sudden hope and fear in equal measure.

19

K ate crossed a small paved square studded with pollarded
trees, where children played on scooters and bicycles
and two old men sat on a concrete bench, the smoke
from their cigarillos spiralling into the greying twilight, and
turned into one of the narrow streets leading off it. From the outside the house looked like nothing special at all: plain whitewash
peeling away from old stucco; blue paint flaked off the wood of a
wide door set with big flathead nails. On the wall across the alleyway someone had daubed a large graffiti tag, followed by the
same odd little stick figure she'd seen outside the Nest of Storks.
Kate had no idea what it meant, or indeed if it meant anything at
all. A little nervous, she banged the round iron knocker against
its striking plate and waited, feeling a chill in the air. A moment
later the door cracked open a fraction and a long-lashed eye
peered out at her.

Kate smiled uncertainly. "I'm Kate Fordham," she said in careful Spanish. "Khadija invited me to supper."

"*Marhaban.*"

It seemed to be some sort of greeting: the intonation of the
speaker—a woman, young and definitely not the professor—did
not rise. The door moved back to allow her inside.

"Come with me," the speaker said, and led her around a bend in the corridor. Quite unexpectedly, the house offered up its secret heart. In front of her lay a small, arcaded courtyard, its balconied upper storey draped in tumbles of bright bougainvillea. In the centre a fountain gently dropped water into the crossing of four tiled channels. Fretted iron lanterns scattered golden light across the paving stones and gilded the water so that it seemed the court-yard ran with rills of liquid fire.

In the farthest corner a low round table surrounded by cush-ions had been spread with an embroidered cloth upon which glasses gleamed, their bowls catching and reflecting the light from half a dozen candles on silver-etched stands.

"Oh," sighed Kate. It was like walking back in time, like enter-ing a tiny private palace in which a feast lay prepared for a visiting princess.

"Beautiful, no?" asked the girl who had led her here.

"Beautiful." Kate agreed, though the word could not do justice to the enchantment of the scene.

"I am Fatima," said the girl, and held out her hand. It was small and smooth, covered with a complex orange-brown pattern of curlicues and flowers.

"Is that henna?" Kate asked.

The girl smiled shyly. "I am betrothed."

Charmed by this old-fashioned word, Kate was about to ask more, when Khadija swept into view, carrying a large water jug in one hand and an open bottle of wine in the other. She bore down upon the guest and embraced her, the jug and bottle chinking as they met behind Kate's back. "Welcome, Kate. I'm so glad you could be here. Take a seat— no, first come and meet Brahim and Salka, see what happens in a Berber kitchen out of sight of the guests!" She deposited the water and wine on the table, caught Kate by the hand and towed her through the courtyard and between the pillars of the far arcade, into a long kitchen wreathed in perfumed vapour. In the midst of this, a large man in a brown cotton robe bent over a huge clay pot on a roaring gas ring, prodding its contents and muttering. Beyond him a young woman in a red-and-gold head scarf and dangling earrings shelled boiled eggs with an expert crack and flick, all the while chattering away in what Kate took to be the language of the Free People.

At her appearance, Brahim stepped away from the gas ring and unceremoniously kissed her on one cheek, then the other, then the first cheek, until Kate, confused, moved the wrong way and they banged heads. They both burst out laughing, and any nervous tension Kate had felt about entering this unfamiliar environment evaporated.

"And this is Salka."

The red-scarfed woman looked at Kate and a secretive expression passed across her face.

"Hello," Kate said, holding out a hand as Fatima had done. But instead of replying in Spanish and taking her hand as the other young woman had done, Salka just bobbed her head and said quietly, "*La bes.*" Then she glided past Kate with a toss of the head that set her extravagant earrings tinkling, giving the Englishwoman the sense that she was an interloper into this private world and that one person at least resented her presence.

Khadija's brow furrowed as she watched Salka leave the kitchen, but when she turned back to Kate, she appeared quite serene. "Come, help me with the bread."

At the table, Kate found herself flanked by Salka and Fatima. Brahim, his big face wreathed in smiles, removed the lid from the clay pot with a flourish, like a magician performing his pièce de resistance. Steam billowed out, engulfing Kate in a wonderful scent. She leaned in under the spice cloud to gaze at the dish that had been revealed in all its scarlet-and-ochre wonder.

"Lamb tagine," Khadija pronounced. "A classic Berber dish, but with a few Andalusian additions."

She handed Kate a plate and cutlery, then dealt out heaped spoonfuls till Kate had to protest about the limits of her appetite. She was, she noticed, the only one thus honoured: all the others used their flatbreads and fingers to delve into the tagine, selecting their mouthfuls deftly and without spilling a morsel. A neat trick if you could manage it, but she was glad to have her spoon and fork. Among the tomatoes, peppers and onions and the browned chunks of lamb, Kate found garbanzo beans, apricots, almonds, and the hardboiled eggs Salka had been shelling. The spices were less easy to identify. Chili seared along her tongue, but its edge had been gentled with cumin and something sweeter—not cinnamon, but something similar that held a faint taste of flowers and honey. And was that saffron that gave the onions their golden glow? After the third mouthful, she found she was no longer assessing the food but merely scooping it up and savouring it in a sort of dream. Opposite her, the man of the house lazed on his cushions like an Ottoman sultan, beaming at his harem as they enjoyed the exotic stew, which hardly seemed to diminish despite their best efforts.

"Sorry I'm late."

Shocked out of her haze of pleasure, Kate swallowed too fast the mouthful she had been contemplatively chewing and burst into a mortifying, eye-watering round of spluttering. Several solicitous back pats and a glass of water later, she wiped her eyes and through teary vision made out the face of the late arrival: the *zellij* worker, stealer of fragments and hearts, grinning as he held out a paper napkin to her.

By the time Kate had dabbed her eyes dry and drunk the rest of the water to control her coughing fit, Abdou had seated himself beside Brahim and was digging into the clay pot with gusto, between mouthfuls throwing into the conversation noisy bursts of foreign words that had both Fatima and Salka shrieking with laughter. He looked mightily at home, she thought, caught somewhere between admiration and jealousy. Whatever was he doing here, appearing unannounced and apparently uninvited and helping himself to dinner without a care in the world? It was only when his gold-lit eyes met hers with the lambent insouciance of a cat that she realized she had been staring at him the whole time.

"Hello again, Kate," he said, in English.

"Hello." She tried for calm aloofness and poise, and failed, as something inside her had swelled hot and unhelpful. "You disappeared rather rapidly the other night."

"I'm sorry. The police . . ."

He gave a small shrug that could have meant any number of things: *it's not important; you know how it is; who wants to stay to talk to the cops?*

"Yes," Kate said, still in English, "the police. They arrested me, you know."

"Arrested you?" That cut through his charming ease. "What did they charge you with?"

"Well, okay, they detained me. For hours. I had to call Khadija in the end, to come and vouch for me."

Abdou winced. He shot a look at the professor, who all this time had been watching the pair of them with interest. "Sorry, Mother," he said, in Spanish.

Mother? Kate glanced from Abdou to Khadija and back again. There was no mistaking the resemblance, she saw now, if you sought it. Khadija's face was thinner and more lined, but the pair shared the same straight nose and high cheekbones, the same set to the mouth. Why hadn't she seen it before?

"You never should have invited Kate to the Nest of Storks. What must she think of us?" Khadija shook her head.

Salka gave Kate a narrow look. Then she said something to Abdou in their shared language that made him hit the table with an open hand so that the water shook in the glasses. There followed what appeared to be an angry exchange between the two: but perhaps it wasn't, for a moment later the pair broke into a gale of laughter. Kate watched, appalled, confused, fascinated, shut out. She tried to detect similarities in Salka's appearance that might denote kinship, but really, Abdou and Salka didn't resemble each other much at all, which was disturbing. Did he wear a ring? She had not noticed one, but she stole a glance at his hands now. No ring. But that didn't necessarily mean he was not married: a lot of men didn't wear a wedding ring. Then, with a sinking feeling, she found herself checking Fatima's hennaed hands. When she looked up again, it was to meet the girl's dark, kohl-edged eyes. "When are you getting married?" she asked, forcing a smile.

"Oh, not for a long time," Fatima said, blushing. "We are saving for a house."

"What does your fiancé do?" Kate inquired, dreading the answer.

"He's working in Marrakech as a tour guide. I haven't seen him since March," she replied mournfully.

Kate's heart lifted. "That must be hard for both of you," she said more gaily than the response required.

"It is, but he will visit soon, *alhamdulillah*."

"And you, Kate," Salka interjected. "Are you married or engaged?"

Was that a spiteful light Kate detected in her eye? "Are you?"

"Not yet." A smug smile.

Avoiding an answer to Salka's question, Kate turned a shoulder to her. "So, Abdou, tell me why you ran off and left me in that place. It wasn't very gallant."

He had the grace to appear sheepish. "Force of habit. In our community you don't welcome police attention. Give them half a chance to accuse you of something and they'll find a way to make out you're some sort of drug dealer or terrorist—or both."

"I hope you're neither."

He grinned. "I may be many things, but neither of those."

"Just a thief, then."

"What?"

They all looked at Kate, but she ignored them, enjoying the flicker of shock in Abdou's widened eyes. "Oh, that," he said at last.

"And what would 'that' be, my lad?" asked Brahim, straightening up on his cushions.

"Nothing important," Abdou assured him. "Really."

There was a subtext here, Kate realized. Secrecy and things unsaid drew a tight line between her and the *zellij* worker. It should have been thrilling, but it made her uncomfortable. "It might be important," she persisted.

"We'll talk about it later," Abdou said in a tone that brooked no discussion.

It was past eleven by the time the meal came to a lazy end with an assortment of fresh fruit from the market, and creamy homemade yogourt, and glass upon glass of mint tea accompanied by little pastries that tasted of almond and orange and honey. These were arrayed on the plate in such an intricate way that Kate was suddenly struck by their likeness to Moroccan tiles. There were crescents and stars, tiny squares and hexagons. "Oh!" she exclaimed. "They're exquisite! Just like *zellij*!"

"You are kind." Brahim beamed. "Even now that I am retired I cannot help but return to my old trade."

"You made these?" Kate was amazed. She thought of her own father, shooing away the acrid smoke caused by setting light to the sausages he had left too long under the grill in an ill-fated attempt to feed his family.

"Once a tile maker always a tile maker, eh, Papa?"

"As a master *zellij* worker, Abdou has not yet felt the need to turn his hand to pastries," Brahim said, giving his son's head a gentle push with the flat of his hand.

It was such a gesture of affection that Kate felt her heart clench. She should be with Luke, giving him the warmth and stability of a loving home, not leaving him in the hands of her sister, no matter how much Jess cared for the boy. One guilt slid into another as Kate realized that in all these hours—this lacuna of joyful hedonism—she had not even thought to check her phone. While father and son joked together about Abdou's failings in the kitchen, she snuck a look at her mobile. No message, no emails, no missed calls. Nothing. The absence left a hole inside her, a small pit of anxiety. Well, it was too late to call her sister now. She'd try again in the morning.

When the table was cleared and Khadija and her daughters were in the kitchen with Brahim, washing and drying the glasses (Kate having been firmly told her help was not required), she found herself alone with Abdou, who leaned suddenly across the table and ran a finger across her forearm. A shock of electricity thrilled through her at his touch, making her head so woozy that he was forced to repeat his question.

"What gave you these scars, Kate?"

Mortified, she pulled her sleeve down to cover the marks of her self-harm. "Oh, it was nothing."

"'Nothing' like the scraps of paper?"

"Touché. Why wouldn't you talk about them in front of your family?" She paused. "Are they all your family?"

The dark eyes became golden crescents of mischief. "Maybe."

Kate pressed her lips together to prevent a more direct question escaping. "Fatima seems lovely," she said at last.

"She is indeed lovely." He watched her mercilessly. "But by omission, Salka is not?"

You're digging yourself a hole. "Salka is lovely, too," Kate lied.

"You know she is not. My cousin is *descarada*."

Between them they worked out that this equated to *minx* in English, and Kate felt an absurd rush of relief, but it was short-lived. Didn't cousins marry in many other cultures? Anyway, why did it matter? This man was nothing to her: she'd only just met him. But he inhabited her dreams by day and by night. And she felt the aftershock of his electric touch still.

"She lives here, your cousin?"

A lazy smile. "She lives here. The whole family lives here." He let the moments stretch annoyingly. "Except me, of course."

Kate felt her shoulders drop. "Oh. You live somewhere else?"

He lounged back on the cushions, so that the candlelight gilded his cheek and the tendons of his neck. The gesture was brazenly sexual: it offered his body up to her view, and he knew it—she knew he knew it. Then he tilted his head toward her. "Would you like to see where I live?"

If Kate's groin could talk, it would have shouted *yes*. But her mouth said quietly, "I hardly know you."

She was saved by the reappearance of Khadija. "You two look deep in conversation," she said. "I hope I'm not interrupting."

Abdou gathered his knees to his chest and sat up. "Not at all, Mother. In fact, we've been meaning to share something with you. I just didn't want to do it with curious eyes around."

Kate stared at him nervously, but when he drew out the wallet and extracted from it the folded card the same way he had the night before in the Nest of Storks, she understood. He laid the two fragments side by side on the white cloth and looked at his mother. "I found one of these in the wall we were repairing in the Tower of the Captive, and Kate found the other."

"You should have brought them to me immediately!" Khadija said, shocked. "Or to one of the other conservators. They could be important!"

"I know," Abdou said. "But when I found the first one, it looked like nothing at all, just a scrap of paper with faint markings on it. On the day we found the second, in the Tower of the Captive, I was . . . distracted." He slid a look at Kate that made her heart stutter. "It was only when Kate showed me the one she'd found that I realized they must be linked. I took them to Córdoba to show them to Dr. Hamza."

"Without telling me?"

He shrugged. "I didn't want to tell you in case they were nothing. But look, here they are."

Khadija bent her head over the scraps of paper. Silence fell as she studied the inscribed lines.

"They resemble Viking runes," Kate said. "Or even Greek."

Khadija looked up at her son, astonished. "It's Tamazight!"

"That's what he said. No one's ever found anything like it before in Granada."

For a minute or more the two of them chattered like magpies, till Kate felt like screaming.

At last—very patiently, she thought—she said, "Would you mind speaking English?"

They both turned and stared at her. Khadija apologized. "It's just that this is an extraordinary find. These fragments are written in a dialect of Berber, or rather, a very old form of it, from the south, out of the desert. There are scholars who claim that Tamazight is one of the most ancient languages in the world, that it has links to Punic and Old Phoenician, and so was at the root of Greek, and thus all Western languages, so you weren't too wide of the mark." Her eyes were gleaming. "It started as an inscribed language. Carved into stone. That's why it has so many straight lines."

"Can you read them?" her son asked. "Dr. Hamza could make out only a word here and there. But he says it's definitely the Tifinagh, probably a Saharan form."

"Tifinagh?" Kate asked.

"That's our alphabet," Abdou said. "I recognize some of the symbols. Here—" he traced the shape of what resembled a sideways *W* "—and this—" a backward *E*. "But—" he looked up at Kate again "—I can't even write my own name in my own language."

Khadija picked up the first fragment and frowned over it. "Our language was suppressed for centuries, first by the Romans, then when the Arabs first conquered North Africa in the eighth century. Even as recently as the 1990s people were getting imprisoned for using it in Morocco, including my own father. It was thought that by making our language illegal they could force our people to their way of thinking, destroy our identity, render us subservient. It had quite the opposite effect."

"The Imazighen fought them hard," Abdou said. "We have a long history of rebellion, whether we were in the mountains, in the desert margins or the alleys of the Albayzín. And all that time we kept our language alive by speaking it in secret. Even now, two thousand years later, we carry it with us wherever we go, this pride in our identity, this resistant spirit, no matter how others treat us. We carry it in our hearts. Not that it does us much good. See this here? This is the sign of the Free People." On the paper he pointed to a symbol like opposed brackets, the lower one facing down, the upper one with arms raised, a vertical line making the body.

"I've seen that graffitied on walls," Kate said thoughtfully. She had also seen it at the Nest of Storks. Did that mean it was a place where rebellion brewed? Wasn't there one right outside the house? She wondered what that might mean. "So there are people around who can write in Tamazight then?"

Khadija smiled. "There are some academics studying it now. And a simplified form of it was reintroduced to schools in Morocco in 2003. But for the truly old version of the language you'll need a Kel Tamasheq woman from the Sahara Desert."

"Kel Tamasheq?" Kate queried; those were not words with which she was familiar.

"Westerners call them the Tuareg."

Kate frowned.

"The nomadic peoples of the Sahara."

A vague image emerged from Kate's memory. "Really? The women in blue, with the veils, on camels?"

"Those are the men—they're even called the Blue Men, because of the staining of the indigo dye from the veils on their skin." Khadija laughed. "The women of the tribes don't veil. But they're the ones who carry the tradition, passing it down to their daughters. It's said they use the Tifinagh for spells and love charms."

20

Blessings

1 4 8 3

I learned the Tifinagh at my mother's knee, in the privacy of her
tent. Among the tribes everything belongs to the women—
the tents, the rugs, the silver, the lineage, the language. The
men have their camels, their salt and their trade money. They come
and they go, the men. Mainly go, leaving the women to run things,
and to raise the children and teach us their secrets.

I don't know why there was only me in the tent, no brothers or
sisters. Maybe something happened during my birth that meant that
my mother couldn't have other children. Or perhaps she chose not
to: after all, she was a wisewoman; she knew about such things—
what herbs to use, what spells to cast, which djinni to summon. It
wasn't as if she didn't have lovers—men were always coming by
her tent, bringing her gifts of food and cloth and coin, and I would
be shooed away with a laugh and a bauble to play with. Then, I
thought how nice it was that she was loved. Now I know it was how
we got by after my father left.

"See this set of symbols?" she asked me one day, not long before she died. "This will bind a man's soul to you."

I was puzzled. "Why would you want to do that?" I asked her. "Is it like binding a djinni to do your bidding?"

She laughed at that, but in a strange, solemn manner. "It's really very like that," she said. "In many ways it's just the same thing. Love has its dark side."

I didn't know what she meant by that. Then.

"Memorize the symbols, their shape and their relationship to one another. How they flow from line to line."

There were three lines—the top one long, the middle one shorter, the third just two words long: "to me" by name. This much I knew. When she erased the writing with a sweep of the hand and then patted the sand flat and smooth for me to prove the lesson, I wrote it out, quick sharp. Three lines, from left to right in the normal way, blunt symbols and unfussy strokes, not like the writing of the Arabs, with its curls and flourishes and its strange rightward start. The Arabs came sometimes, alone on horseback to do business at the camp, to buy sheeny indigo cloth from the south, cones of salt from Taodenni; sometimes with slaves. Their horses were neat hoofed and shiny, quieter, smaller and more elegant than the camels. But their shit smelled much the same. Thinking this, I had inscribed the word for *shit* in the sand and then sniggered at my own boldness. My mother rewarded this levity with a painful flick of my ear. "Never mock writing, child," my mother told me severely. "Letters are sacred things, full of power."

At that age I couldn't understand how scribblings could possibly contain anything much, but I don't claim to have been the brightest student.

Now I framed the words with a cartouche, to prevent their power from leaking. Often we would write such spells on a bit of thin parchment and confine the parchment within a silver amulet, for the same reason: to contain its power and keep it secret. I wore several such pinned to my clothes. "To protect you," my mother said. Even our goats wore them, on their collars. But it didn't do them much good when my mother died. Or me either.

Even so, I wore them now. Superstition is strong, especially in dire circumstances, and these were the direst of circumstances. I had charms sewn into the hem of my robe, in an amulet beneath my shirt; on the lining of my cap. From head to toe I was wreathed with enchantments, invoking every wild spirit of the desert of my youth, every djinni and minor goddess whose name I could summon. I was taking no chances, for I was about to enter the lair of the enemy. I was about to place myself, voluntarily, in the hands of the very infidel. Love can make you do mad things.

After the knights had captured Momo I had waited there in the stream, frozen in misery and fear. It had taken some time to disentangle myself from the oleander, mainly as I couldn't see for tears. I had followed my lord as the enemy moved him from town to town and tower to tower, until at last we came to the place I knew as Bulkuna, which the Castilians called Porcuna. Here, on a promontory overlooking the Guadalquivir valley, lay an old fortress. And in its greatest tower Momo was held prisoner. It loomed above me, its massive walls broken only by arrow-slits and small arched, lobed windows high, high up. The stonework was new and solidly mortared, leaving little in the way of holds: I could not climb so high; nor was this a prison from which Momo could escape by tying a few veils together. So, cunning it would have to be.

Listening to the chatter in the market, where I read palms for a few days, I found out that the men charged with the care of my lord were the Count of Cabra, DonDiego Fernández of Córdoba, and a man called "the Great Captain." After gleaning as much information as I could in the town beneath the fortress, I changed out of the fortune-telling garb I'd purloined from various washing lines back into the fine costume in which I had so foolishly gone to battle, long since washed of blood and the slime of the river below Lucena, and made myself known to the guards at the postern gate as a scribe, recruited into the service of the Count of Cabra.

They searched me roughly for weapons before passing me into the hands of the men who stood guard at the castle proper. These guards took greater liberties, as if knowing themselves more powerful than those farther from the castle's heart. They were free with their words, freer still with their hands. I hoped my spells would protect me and steeled myself not to react.

"Hey, what's this?"

The guard with a wart on his nose had reached my false foot. He tapped it with a finger, puzzled, then with the butt of his dagger, and it gave back a solid *thonk*, nothing like the sound of live flesh encased in leather. He tried the same with my other leg, causing me to yelp, which made him grin.

"See him dance. He's a lively one, eh?" He grinned up at me, his teeth showing through the stained hair of his moustache.

I gave him back a look that should have seen him dead many times over.

"Oho," chuckled Wart-nose. "I don't think he likes me."

"Who does?" said his companion quietly.

But Wart-nose was now too busy prying the gold leaf off my false foot to pay attention to the insult. I watched with some annoyance as a good-sized piece was peeled away: the guards at the gate had taken the few coins I possessed and the gold leaf was all I had of any value for bribes or paying for horses.

"It's cursed, that gold," I said in decent Castilian.

Wart-nose fell back on his arse, the gold falling from his fingers as if it burned.

The other guard laughed. "Perhaps the lad isn't a Moor after all."

"Quite right, I am not," I said, which was true.

Wart-nose swore again. "Well, what in God's name he doing sneaking into Porcuna with a gold-plated leg and such outlandish gear?" He heaved himself to his feet.

"I've come to render service to the Count of Cabra," I told him.

"What service?" Wart-nose sneered.

"I am a scribe and a scholar," I said, which clearly didn't impress them. "And I can tell fortunes from the lines God has inscribed on every man's palm."

"Fortunes? The count doesn't need his fortune told. Not while he's working for the blessed Isabella."

"Tell mine," said the other, thrusting a gnarly hand at me. "And make sure it includes owning a vineyard and a brothel."

I made a deal of scanning the lines between the dirt and calluses. "A vineyard, a brothel and the *auto da fe*," I said, and watched as he paled. "Shall I tell yours?" I asked Wart-nose. "Perhaps it will end better than your colleague's."

"Perhaps I should lob you over the wall."

"Lob who over the wall?" asked a man with a lion's mane of yellow-brown hair, who was suddenly rounding the far corner of the corridor. His voice held authority.

I took in the details of person I had learned to note of during my begging days. Plain clothing, but of good quality: not much embroidery, but what was there was expensive and laced with silver thread. Not gold, then: second son? Scuffed boots bespoke a contempt both for fashion and any court pecking order, which probably meant he was further up it than he might appear: hence the sudden nervous attention of the guards. As he came closer, I also noted he was trim, wore no perfume and could be no older than thirty. Not the Count of Cabra either: I knew from my eavesdropping that that gentleman was portly and middle-aged.

"Captain." The second guard walked on ahead and saluted him smartly.

Shielded by his companion, Wart-nose handed the bit of gold back to me. "Not a word about this," he said quietly, and grabbed me painfully by the upper arm to drag me before the newcomer. "Don Gonzalo." He bowed. "We've checked this fellow thoroughly for weapons. He's come here to, er, 'render service.'"

"As a scholar," I said. "And a translator. I know you hold an important prisoner."

Don Gonzalo turned his attention to me and for a long moment we regarded each other. His broad face had lines radiating from his mouth and the corners of his eyes and spoke of decency and humour. He looked as if he'd spent considerable time outdoors, for when his face fell into repose, as it did now, those lines showed white against the darker sunburn. What he saw I could not tell: except that I was small and dark, slight and maybe a bit puzzling. Then he took the fabric of my sleeve between his finger and thumb. "No pauper," he said, as if to himself. Assessing me just as I had assessed him. Raising his voice, he asked my name.

"Baraka," I said, giving the Arabic form of my name. "And indeed I am no pauper. Among my own people I'm a type of prince."

"A type of prince, eh?" He grinned, showing sharp incisors. "And who might your people be?" he asked in a tone of teasing disbelief.

"There are many names for us. But I doubt you'll know them."

"Try me. I'm quite well travelled. Soldiering will do that for you, scholar."

"The name we give ourselves is Kel Tamasheq: Those Who Speak Tamasheq."

He raised an eyebrow. "That, I admit, is not a name, or a language, I know."

"Some call us the Blue Men."

"The desert dwellers who conceal their faces behind blue veils?"

"Indigo," I corrected him. "And we call our veil a *tagelmust*. The mineral that gives the blue colour protects us from djinn and dyes our skins as we cross the desert."

"And yet, you do not have a blue skin."

I inclined my head. "I left my people at an early age."

"Sounds like a tall tale, but one I'd like to hear. Doing guard duty in a castle is dull work. Come." He beckoned me to follow him. As we passed the guards, they snapped to attention. "Are there other names by which your people are known?" Don Gonzalo asked as we started up some stone stairs. He took them two at a time with his long stride; I could barely keep up with him.

"Our enemies call us the Tuareg, Those Abandoned by God," I said a little breathlessly as I hobbled after him.

The stairs circled upon themselves like a sleeping snake. He was so far ahead of me now he hardly had to turn his head to regard me. "Don't let the Inquisition hear that or you'll be put to the question."

His tone was solemn; my heart knocked against my ribs. On the road between Lucena and Porcuna I had heard stories of the Inquisition—the religious zealots appointed by Queen Isabella to drive the kingdom back to her God. Mostly they were spoken of with fear; but there were a few voices that claimed the Inquisition courts were fairer than those that had preceded them, for they accepted no bribes. I had even seen two of their men striding through the streets here—black robed with gaunt faces, whose dark-ringed eyes suggested they did not sleep well after witnessing the rackings, the red-hot pincers, the extraction of teeth and nails, the breaking of fingers and limbs; as if the stench of the *auto da fe* haunted their unpillowed, lonely beds.

I hoped, with a sudden cold sensation, that they were not here for Momo.

"I've heard you hold the sultan of Granada prisoner here," I said as evenly as I could manage.

"Did you come to rescue him, all alone?" he asked lightly.

I lifted my chin. "Hardly. I'm told he is guarded by the queen's bravest soldier."

He gave a short laugh. "My instructions are to prevent his escape at all cost, even of his life, so it would be a foolish man who'd attempt to spring him from his prison."

"He's not much use to your queen dead."

"Not many dead men are useful."

"But then again, he's not much use to her alive and in this place." That halted him in his stride. We had reached the top of a stair giving onto a broad thoroughfare along which castle servants bustled, carrying jugs and trays of food. The smell of fresh-roasted meat drifted to my nostrils and suddenly my stomach grumbled like a riled dog and I remembered I'd eaten nothing for two days. It was all I could do not to leap upon the next passing tray and wolf down the contents of every dish upon it.

Gonzalo gave me his yellow stare. "What do you mean?"

"His subjects will rally to the cause of Sultan Abu Abdullah—"

"Do call him Boabdil: it's so much easier. Or el Rey Chico."

The Boy King: was that what they were calling him? Poor Momo. "Boabdil, then," I said, mangling the Arabic as the Great Captain had done. "If you hold Boabdil, it leaves the door open for far worse men to seize the throne. And then you will have a far worse problem. Men like al-Zaghal. Even now he's mustering his forces and support."

He looked thoughtful. "Perhaps you'd prefer a different scenario to be played out?"

"Perhaps I would."

"Might you share it with me?"

I paused. "I might."

His smile was catlike.

"But not until I've seen the sultan and had a chance to talk to him."

"I don't have the authority to allow you to do that," he said levelly.

Now that we were standing still, with the busy folk of the castle flowing around us, he really did look like a caged beast, this Great Captain: a man completely out of place, unfitted to such surroundings. "I can't imagine you relish spending long months—even years—stuck here in Porcuna," I hazarded, remembering his mention of "dull duty."

"I can't imagine any of us much want that," the Great Captain said.

"So take me to the sultan."

He gave me a long, considering look. "How do I know you're not an assassin sent to remove him from the chessboard?"

I appeared stricken. "What, with my bare hands? They've taken all else from me."

He glanced down. "You might brain him with that."

He really was very observant. "What, I could hop at him with my false leg as my only weapon? That's certainly a picture to conjure with." We both laughed.

"All right," he said. "Stand still. I'm sure they've done their job perfectly well, but I've learned never to take anything for granted."

I stood there while his hands moved expertly about my body, checking all those places in which a trained assassin might secrete the smallest weapon. But while others had been prurient, he was briskly professional. Even so, my heart beat out a hard tattoo.

At last he stood back, his expression unreadable. "I'll take you to see the count."

Up through the castle we went, past flickering sconces and walls hung with tapestries showing scenes of men at war or hunting. At various points guards leapt to attention, shouldering their halberds. I saw respect and admiration for the man who led me, even though he was young enough to be a son to many of them. He had clearly earned the name by which they knew him. But the Count of Cabra might be a different man entirely, one who might yet consign me to the Inquisition. I began to sweat again.

I need not have worried. We found the Count of Cabra in his cups, even though it was barely past midday. He sprawled on a couch with a great mass of papers strewn over the floor before him, his big hand wrapped around the stem of a sturdy silver goblet. The Great Captain explained my presence, saying I was a young noble-man of African extraction, that I was an accredited translator, had served time in the Granadan court and would be helpful in per-suading the captive to speak more freely than he had thus far. He would like to take me on as his aide, he said, while he further ques-tioned the young sultan. With my help, he hoped he might find a way through the political web surrounding the sultan and his ties to his kingdom that might serve Queen Isabella and King Ferdinand well, and thus, reflecting his contribution in this difficult process, bring gratitude and acclaim to the count himself.

During all this, the count did not appear to be paying much attention but instead applied himself to the contents of the goblet, which he refilled twice from a gigantic engraved flask set on the table in front of him. He was in his middle years, of solid build, shorter than me, with a curling brown beard and a meaty arm that showed no strain when he lifted the jug. A soldier run to fat, drinking himself half to death while others did his work for him, I judged. Thus, I was taken by surprise when he leaned forward and his brown eyes bored into me, and they were as sharp as an eagle's. "So, Don Baraka," he said. "You know the workings of the Granadan court well, do you?"

I bowed in the Castilian style. "As well as any, sir."

"Are the rumours that Moulay Hasan has the falling sickness true?"

Did the enemy have spies in Granada? "He does lose consciousness on occasion, sir, and fall twitching to the ground."

"I've heard he's gone blind."

"His eyesight has been failing gradually for the past year. The
doctors have examined him for the signs of cataracts, which they
can cure with delicate surgery, but cataracts don't appear to be the
cause of Moulay Hasan's affliction."

The count banged the goblet down on the table, so that the
liquid within dashed over the edge onto the decorated surface, and
I saw that it was water. "I knew it! So with Moulay Hasan incapaci-
tated and his son in our hands, the infidel must be in some degree of
disarray." His eyes gleamed.

"That would certainly be the case, sir, if it were not for the emir
of Málaga."

"Al-Zaghal," DonGonzalo said grimly.

"Yes, al-Zaghal. Moulay Hasan proved himself a great warrior
over the years—indeed he killed thirty-odd men singlehandedly—"

The Count of Cabra interrupted me. "That was by treachery
and within the walls of his own palace, though, no?"

So word of the Banu Serraj massacre had reached far and wide.
"True, my lord; but in his prime he was also a great warrior on the
battlefield. But al-Zaghal is more formidable by far. If you keep
Sultan Abu Abdullah—or as you call him, Boabdil—here as your
prisoner, rather than falling into disarray the Granadans will rally
behind al-Zaghal, and he'll seize the throne. He won't sit peace-
ably within Granada's borders. He'll use the imprisonment of the
young sultan as a rallying point for all good Muslims and carry
holy war to you."

The count and captain exchanged glances. Neither looked
entirely surprised. I plowed on. "But if you're thinking to battle
him with superior numbers, you should know you'll have no open
battles if al-Zaghal is the commander. He'll use the ground and the

people against you, and he'll use them mercilessly. Once he has the whole army at his disposal he'll devote himself to the fight and demand reinforcements from across the Muslim world. From across the sea in Morocco and the desert. From the Orient too: thousands of Turks fuelled by the zeal of their faith and all the money the Ottomans can put behind them. Rather than bringing the last remaining Islamic kingdom of Granada under her control, your queen will be fighting for her life."

I'd heard such declarations voiced many times within the walls of the Alhambra and had dismissed them first as dull and second as fantasy. But now I marshalled them authoritatively, and by the way the two men listened, they believed me.

"Al-Zaghal is wily and dangerous, a clever soldier," I went on. "He is fanatical, and in the pursuit of his fanaticism he is ruthless and cruel. All he cares about is war: he loves it more than other men love their wives and children. Indeed, he has no interest in women, or in men either. When he's not fighting, he's praying; when he's not praying, he's fighting."

"He sounds a monster," the Count of Cabra said. "And what about our captive, Boabdil?"

"He is quite different to his uncle. There is nothing Abu Abdullah Mohammed loves more than his wife and child—apart maybe from the Alhambra itself, for he loves beauty above all things. Beauty and harmony and peace. I think if you were to allow me to talk with him, I could explain the benefits of paying tribute to your crown as his grandfather and ancestors once did." *You see, Momo, I was listening during those interminable lessons!* "Then your army can devote its efforts to the business of dealing with his uncle."

This was treason, and I knew it. But I gave not a fig for religion, for strategy or holy war; for Granada's independence or the furtherance of the Muslim cause. It might mean that Momo would be king in name only, but it would stop him going to war, remove his uncle as a threat and leave his mother with no grounds for argument. I would make him safe at all costs and return with him to the Alhambra, to live out our days in peace and sunshine.

The Count of Cabra said something in rapid Castilian of which I could make out only a word here and there. At last the Great Captain turned to me. "Come, Baraka. We'll go to see your little king."

21

It had been months since I'd seen Momo, knocked unconscious by the giant enemy knight and led away on his captured warhorse. He was sitting by the tiny window, his nose practically pressed to the mullioned panes as if he yearned with every drop of blood to be out among those olive grove–scattered hills, under the wide blue bowl of the sky. He turned, and for a moment his face was in shadow, and it seemed to me that there was just the shell of a man sitting there: that the robes—more gorgeous than any I had seen him wear even in his own home—contained nothing but a dark phantom; that the Christians had stolen away his soul.

Then he stood and came toward me, showing no sign of shackles or wound, and with no care for the presence of the foreign captain, wrapped his arms around me and kissed me over and over—on the cheek, the forehead, the eyelids, the neck. In a sort of terrified rapture I accepted his embrace, trembling with the effort not to reciprocate with even greater passion, while at the same time trying to consign each touch of his lips to memory so that I might replay each over and over in times of need.

At last he broke contact and we stood apart, gazing at each other. "I've never been so happy to see anyone in my life," he said, just as I said, "You look well, my lord," trying to set our meeting back on a less intimate path. But I could see from the expression on the Great Captain's face that he had missed none of the signs of affection and was carefully noting every word and gesture we exchanged.

"I've come to act as DonGonzalo's aide," I told him, holding his gaze so that he knew to hear me carefully. "To be a translator between the two of you and to help in the negotiation of your release."

Momo seemed surprised. "My release?" He looked to the Great Captain, who said in passable Arabic, "We not there yet, *sidi*. But hope, God willing, with help DonBaraka, we find way."

"Don Baraka." Momo tipped his head toward me and gave me, out of the Great Captain's sight, the minutest wink. "It will be my pleasure."

The chamber was comfortable and well-appointed. Thick Turkish carpets lay over the flagged floor, and the walls had been lined with falls of tabby silk from the markets of Persia. Upon the tables and in the angles of the tower stood tall silver candlesticks topped by fat yellow candles of good quality beeswax, by whose light Momo might read the handsome leather-bound Quran that lay open on a page upon which the calligrapher had been liberal with the inking of gold medallions. Someone had gone to inordinate effort to make Momo feel at home. All he lacked was his throne, his palace, with its gardens and pools, the loving arms of his wife, and his little boy. And his freedom.

Well, I would do my best to restore as many of them as possible to him.

The trouble was, I could come up with no permutation by which he could have them all.

The ride between Porcuna and Granada was long and hard and beset with danger. The Great Captain offered two guards to accompany me, but I refused them. The business I was on could see me killed by all manner of folk with differing vested interests in the deal I was trying to broker. Some on both sides would prefer to see Momo dead, including his father and those Christian zealots for whom the only good Muslim was a dead Muslim. "I'd rather not draw attention to myself," I told him, and went to arrange my disguises: as a Catholic priest for the first part of the journey and as a travelling wisewoman in the emirate. Superstition can play a handy role when you're travelling alone: no one wants to risk their immortal soul or draw djinn down on themselves. And it's remarkable how many people will offer confession in return for indulgences or charms. A black robe did for both, with the visual additions of a Bible and a crucifix for the first, and kohl, earrings and plant stains on the lips and hands for the second. A bag of rat bones, some coloured pebbles and some dried bees I took with me for my wisewoman act: the plants I would pass off as my remedies I could gather along the route. This play-acting would have been fun had it not been in deadly earnest. I carried a sword beneath the robe, and a dagger in the top of my false limb.

Moulay Hasan had offered a significant ransom for the return of his son. "The queen is considering it," DonGonzalo told me. "It's a handsome offer."

"You can't let them give Momo up to his father—he'll kill him!" The way Moulay Hasan had phrased the offer—*on his feet or on his back, it makes no odds to me* —told me the whole tale. He would prefer his inconvenient son to be dead: all he wanted was to remain sultan within the walls of the Alhambra in the arms of the witch Zoraya, safe from attack from the enemy and from any insurrection of the people, who had no love for him. His power was waning as fast as his health, and he knew it.

"You had best persuade the Lady Aysha to come up with a better proposal, then," he said solemnly, helping me onto my mule.

Of course I did not go directly to Aysha on my arrival at the city gates of Granada. Instead I found a ragged boy and paid him a silver dirham to fetch Qasim Abdelmalik to meet me down by the river near the city gate at the bottom of the hill.

I sat with my one good foot cooling in the chilly waters of the Darro, wishing I could as easily quell the angry buzzing-bee sensation in the other, missing, limb.

"*Las bes, lalla.*" Good day, lady. Keeping a respectful distance, the vizier sat down beside me. "I see your funds are running low, Blessings. Is that why you're back?" His eyes were on my gold-denuded false leg as it protruded from the hiked-up robe.

"Times are hard," I said. Then I told him of my errand, and of what I had learned in snippets from listening at the Count of Cabra's door and from talking to people on my way south. It appeared that many councillors at the royal court in Córdoba argued that releasing Momo—a virile young king—back into Granada would be foolish while Hasan sat the throne, given that the old sultan was too ill to ride to war; but others argued that his release would be "like a fire eating away the entrails of the enemy" and that they could take advantage of any civil war that might erupt among the Muslims.

Qasim nodded to all this, as if my words accorded with his own reports from Córdoba. I was sure I was not his only ears and eyes in the royal court, but he said nothing, as if salting it all away. He knew, of course, exactly how much Hasan had offered. "We can't match it."

"But we have to!"

"Hasan holds the keys to the palace treasury. The infidel need gold for their wars, to fulfill their promises to the pope in Rome.

We don't have any leverage." He sucked his teeth. "I suppose we could let Hasan make the deal and then bribe their guards to release Momo into the hands of our men, not his. We're all just Moors to them—it would be relatively easy to sow confusion. Then the Castilians get their gold and we get the prince."

"The sultan," I corrected him angrily. "Anyway, that won't work: they are very punctilious." *And I can't risk losing him.* "Perhaps the sultana could call upon the people of Loja: it is a rich town."

"Sultana?" He laughed. "Momo is no longer sultan, so Mariam is no sultana. And I don't think Loja will offer a tin piece for young Mohamed's release, not after losing their beloved pasha. Old Ali Attar, his head split down to the neck, died a martyr to the cause in the battle at Lucena." He watched as I took this in. "Poor Mariam. She's come apart, losing her father, her husband and her home at a stroke. I would like to see the poor girl smile again, but I can't see a way through this puzzle. Our coffers are empty."

I didn't believe him. "Let's see what Aysha says," I told him, meaning: *If you don't come up with a way to save him, I will tell her everything.* We locked eyes and he held my gaze coolly, but I could almost hear his thoughts buzzing as furiously as the phantom bees in my missing leg.

"There may be another weight we can add to the scales," he said at last. "Though it may be more than anyone involved in the bargain wishes to pay."

When he told me, I could hardly take the words in for shock. "She won't agree to that."

"She must. Besides, Aysha is the ultimate pragmatist when it comes to getting her way. She means to wreak vengeance on her husband, which means freeing Momo to spearhead her war against him—on whatever terms that takes."

"Momo will never agree to it."

"Ah, Blessings, that is where you come in."

With her husband and his whore re-established behind the high red walls of the Alhambra, Lalla Aysha had moved her retinue, including Mariam and little Ahmed, across the River Darro into a fortified house on the top of the Albayzín that had a little tower from which there was a clear view across to the Nasrid palaces, so that she could send curses winging their way to her reviled husband. She agreed to the proposal after only a brief explosion

As I left Granada for the ride back to Porcuna, Qasim placed a hand on my shoulder. Muslims believe that we all carry an angel on each shoulder: a good one on our right, to guide us through the mire of life; a bad one on the left, to tempt us into wickedness. The vizier's hand weighed heavily upon my left shoulder. "Work your wiles, Blessings" was all he said as he sent me away to break my beloved's heart.

I went straight to the Count of Cabra with the sultana's offer. He bade me remain in the corridor outside while he discussed it with his nephew and cousin. (Of course I listened.) They would not let me see Momo. At last the Great Captain came out and told me to prepare myself for a ride to Córdoba.

In a dark antechamber in the enemy's palace I kicked my heels, waiting for the call to aid in the presentation of Aysha's offer. I half dreaded the audience, half wished for it. The sooner it could be done, the sooner I would be out of this place, and the sooner I would see Momo after all these weeks. But if our proposal won approval, I would have to break the awful terms to him. For a moment I could not help but hope it would be rejected. But that would condemn him to certain death . . .

"Cheer up, youngster. The heavens have not yet fallen!"

I turned the best glare I could muster upon this speaker, giving him the evil eye. He seemed entirely oblivious to my ill-will but clapped me upon the shoulder. You'd have thought from his exclamation that he would be advanced in years, but I judged him to be around thirty, with his bluff, smiling face and unruly bush of curly dark hair. His shirt was stained, a cuff ragged; his shoes scuffed; and he held a bundle of ungovernable, ever-unspringing scrolls under his arm: a beggar-ruffian down on his luck, come to beg money for some mad scheme. I dismissed him and turned away to wallow in my miserable thoughts.

"My name's Cristóbal, what's yours?"

I ignored him.

"Of course, that's not what I was christened, but you know these people, they hate foreigners, so I always use the local version. Cristoforo is what they call me back in Genoa. I'm here to see the king and queen."

Given that we were in the antechamber to the royal audience room, this hardly needed saying. I sighed and wished him elsewhere. I needed to summon every iota of my eloquence and calm if I was to save my friend.

"That's an interesting necklace," he said, determined to worm his way into my attention.

"It's an amulet," I replied curtly; but my tone did not stop him.

"I've never seen anything quite like it, and I've travelled widely."

"Not as far as the Sahara, then."

He conceded this. "I hear the Great Desert is a sea of sand. Perhaps I should visit it—seas are my speciality."

I hated it when people said this of the desert. The dunes were hot and full of life, their curves and angles resembling those of a human body, while the sea was cold and grey and hideous. "My people use such amulets to navigate themselves by the stars across the great emptiness." I thought that might shut him up.

I could not have chosen words more likely to invigorate him if I'd tried. He prattled on and on about different forms of navigation—about sunstones and lodestones and some Arab instrument called the *qarib*, which he wanted to learn more about. "The stars are the navigator's friend," he said, and then recited by heart an excerpt of a long poem by a Greek in which some woman called Calypso told a man whose name I failed to grasp that he must sail keeping the Great Bear on his left while at the same time observing the position of the seven-starred constellation known as the Pleiades.

Against my best instincts, I found myself drawn in by this. "The Great Bear? That must be Dubhe. And we call the constellation the Seven Daughters."

Soon he had his charts down on the floor and I was showing him how the sharpest angle of the amulet was lined up on the North Star, with the circle that represented the Earth pointing down, and the painful wait evaporated into a magical mist of travellers' tales and grand schemes. When the Great Captain appeared, he had to call my name twice before he could get my attention, so thoroughly were the navigator and I engrossed.

I had been looking forward, with a macabre curiosity, to laying eyes on the foreign monarchs, but it seemed I was not to be accorded that honour. The deal for Momo's freedom—such as it was—was done over a candlelit table with dark-robed men with the pale faces and pinched eyes of court scribes who rarely saw daylight. It involved an immense sum of money, the release of all the Christian captives held by the Banu Serraj and the special seal to the bargain of which I could not bear to speak. Don Gonzalo took over when my voice dried to a whisper, and the scribes bent their heads over the table, dipped their quills in their ink and scratched out the terrible words.

Back at Porcuna, after an absence of two months, I raced up the stairs as fast someone with one good leg could manage. Although I was caught between yearning to see Momo and the exquisite dread of telling him of the terrible proposition, I knew I had to get to him before his captors. "I'm back!" I flung open the door, panting.

Momo sprang up from his chair, in its usual position by the window that showed him the world but would not open, nor even allow him to breathe the air beyond its diamond panes. His embrace was fierce, and how I savoured it. Then he held me away from him and I felt my heart unravel like a fast-blossoming flower under his regard. How pale he looked, I thought. And thin too. "Are you not eating?" I asked, at the same time as he said, "And how is my Mariam?"

My heart fell into my stump.

"Was she well? Is her pregnancy weighing her down? Is my mother taking proper care of her?"

"Her father died in the battle and she's finding it hard to endure living under Lalla Aysha's rule in the family house, now that your father has taken back the Alhambra. So she's sad, and missing you. Though she's eating a lot to comfort herself and her unborn child: she's got quite fat." Such unnecessary spite. To make small amends I added quickly, "My sultan."

Momo sighed. "I miss her so." He rested his head against the stone window frame. "Sultans come and go as they please. They ride and hunt and walk in their gardens. They fly their hawks and go among their people. They play with their children and lie with their wives. They aren't locked in a tiny room, denied their freedom."

For a prison cell the room was huge, but I knew better than to quibble. Beyond him the view showed sun-seared grass browning on the hilltops. There had been no rain since we'd lost the battle at Lucena. In the Moorish villages I'd heard them speak of "the little king" as a talismanic figure: they believed that their crops were failing because of his imprisonment, and that only when he was released would the world right itself once more.

Momo turned back to me, his eyes burning. "Does my son flourish? I can't bear that Ahmed can't play in the Alhambra gardens and watch the sun shimmering in the pools; or run through the orchards, gathering fruit, as you and I did at his age."

I didn't correct him. Ahmed was barely three; I hadn't arrived at the palace till I was gone ten. Inside me, my heart shrivelled like the sere grass.

"Does he speak of me? Does he miss me as much as I miss him?"

Like a dog he had unerringly gone to the meat. Stupid Blessings, get on with it: tell him what you must tell him. I had just opened my mouth to frame the awful words, when the door flew open to admit the Count of Cabra's nephew (also Diego) and DonGonzalo, the Great Captain. I recognized the nephew as one of the two huge knights who had battled Momo in the river at Lucena, but Momo greeted him warmly, and the young man responded in halting Arabic. It seemed while I had been gone he'd acquired a new friend.

"Am I to be released?" Momo asked eagerly.

"Things are moving in that direction," DonGonzalo replied. "The sultana's offer appears to have swayed our queen's judgment toward that end."

I mumbled my way through the translation and watched Momo's face soften. "My wife's letter must have touched her heart."

So he really did think he was still the sultan and Mariam his sultana.

"The offer came from your mother," I corrected gently. "But you must acquiesce to the terms and sign the contract before matters can move on."

"Thank you, thank you," Momo said over and over in Castilian. "Just bring me the contract and I'll sign it straight away."

"Be calm, my lord," I begged him. "Please. You must listen to the terms."

"I am to be released!" He was almost dancing with delight, there was so much restless energy coursing through his pent-up frame. "I'll be with Mariam before the birth of our new son."

"*Amghrar*," I said quickly in Tamasheq. My chief. I had spent these last months teaching him to speak and to read the language, for times when we needed to communicate in a way that no other could understand. I watched his face go still.

"What you mean?" He didn't speak it well.

"Don't betray in any way that I'm telling you something shocking."

He was staring at me now. "My God, tell me now or I die."

"Smile," I told him.

The smile he gave me was ghastly with anxiety.

"Your mother has offered your son as part of the agreement. As a hostage. To be held by the foreign monarchs against your good behaviour."

The smile became a rictus. Tears welled, and I was embarrassed for him, that he should so lose his *asshak* as to show his emotions in front of these strangers. "Smile!" I ordered him ruthlessly. "You mustn't show them your weakness: don't hand them more power over you than they already have."

"Stop this! I pay you to translate, not to chatter." The count's brown gaze had become as hard as glass. "As for you, sir," he said, addressing Momo, "I expect you to behave as befits a noble captive and not to conspire in front of my eyes."

The Great Captain intervened now, his golden gaze curious. "What's this secret language you speak together? I don't recognize it."

I braced myself, but it was Momo who replied, channelling his sorrow into cold anger. "It is the language spoken by the original conqueror of this land, Tariq bin Ziyad, the tongue of the mountains and the deserts, of those who stand against oppression, of those who came this place with philosophers and poets, men who make engines and men who read stars, who bring bathhouses and running water when your kings smelled like rats and could not even write own names."

I translated this into Castilian as fast as I could and watched as the lords' expressions changed. They had thought Momo weak and pliable, a pawn on the chessboard they could move where they wished to gain the best advantage. They'd come to bring him the terms of a truce that suited them well, and had expected him to roll over like a dog for it.

"Don't think me a child you can make plots around! Don't smile and pretend to be my friend, then treat me like a slave! I come from a long, proud line of kings, and I am no fool. If you want to talk cold, hard business, you had best present your terms."

When I translated this, the Count of Cabra nodded. "In that case, sire, we'll sit down like civilized men and I'll lead you through the treaty that has been drafted."

They assumed their places at the octagonal table, with the Great Captain and young Diego standing behind the count, and me at Momo's left shoulder. The Count of Cabra explained the proposition Aysha had made, taking his time to spell out the sums of money involved in both the gold *doblas* of al-Andalus and the *maravedis* of Castile. Tribute would be paid annually, as it had in the time of Momo's father (till he stopped) and grandfather. All this Momo agreed to: there were no surprises here, although the sums were huge. "War is more expensive than peace," he said, "and if I must sell the sovereignty of the last Muslim kingdom in the peninsula to gain the safety of my people, I will. I do not wish to see my towns besieged and my people starved into submission while their wells are poisoned and their crops burned, or preside over a land full of weeping women and fatherless children. If I must humble myself by presenting myself as a vassal to your king, then so be it."

As I translated, the count nodded, and made a note in the margin. "You will be a vassal to both our monarchs, not just to King Ferdinand," he said mildly. "Queen Isabella has had as much to do with this agreement as her husband and holds at least equal power in the conjoined kingdoms. And so we pass to the matter of those Christian prisoners your allies hold captive."

Momo inclined his head. "We will give her plenty of souls back, which will no doubt assuage the lady's tender heart."

The Great Captain smothered a smile.

"I don't think the Castilian queen is that sort of woman," I said quietly.

For a long time Momo and the count dickered over the exact number of prisoners to be released, and at last fixed upon four hundred captives up front to be followed by seventy each year. I was surprised at how hard Momo bargained over these terms. I supposed he was showing his mettle, knowing what was to come.

"In addition, the emira has offered one more provision, which Queen Isabella is particularly happy to accept." The count had the grace to flush as he read out the hard words, and I felt rather than saw the way Momo gritted his teeth as his son's fate was spelled out to him.

"This is a bitter draught to swallow," he said at last, and I was proud at how he mastered himself. "He is my firstborn, my one and only child."

"The queen recognizes the generosity of the offer and makes an offer in her turn: young Ahmed will be raised in the royal court as if he were her own son, alongside her own children, who are of much the same age. He will want for nothing."

When I translated this, Momo turned his face to me, and his eyes blazed. "Want for nothing? What about the love of a mother and father? What about the most beautiful home in this world? What about his birthright and the faith of his ancestors?"

I relayed this to the count.

"I understand your qualms, sire: it is surely a hard clause to accept. But it's key to the whole agreement. Our queen adores children: your son will be greatly cosseted."

"But he's a son of the Nasrid line: how can he be raised by Christians? How will he know the word of Allah in a court of heathens?"

I must admit I did in some small ways reword this furious question.

"Be reassured he'll be well taught," the count reassured. "He'll learn all he must of statecraft and kingship."

"And when he's of an age, will she turn him over to the Inquisition?"

He was being mulish now: he knew there was no way around it. "Be calm, my lord," I said softly. 'You can have other sons."

"I can't believe Mariam agreed to this."

I knew she had not. I said nothing, imagining how this new blow would fall upon his poor young wife, who was already so distressed.

The look he gave me was so agonized that I felt as if he had stuck me with a lance. I deserved his anger, and more.

At last he nodded. "I agree," he said hoarsely, then laid his head on his arms and refused to speak again.

22

In the dog days of summer we were summoned to Córdoba.

I went racing up the tower steps with a smart new robe for Momo to wear, but he seemed uninterested in either the news or the finery. "Please, my lord, take cheer! Just think, soon you will see Mariam again." It hurt me to say it, but his expression hurt even more: he dreaded going back to Granada as much as he wished for it.

Qasim had arrived with a battalion of armed guards from Granada, along with the first payment of tribute. The soldiers were equipped in full Moorish fashion, with pointed helms and shining weaponry, their Barbary horses brightly tricked out with colourful caparisons and tasselled harness. They were a brave sight, but after greeting the vizier quietly Momo barely registered them.

Córdoba held little mystery for me: it brought back memories of interminable waiting in rooms stuffed with heavy dark furniture and ugly wall hangings that devoured the light, as if the business of the royal court was best done in semi-darkness. But Momo had never seen the city that had once been the seat of learning through-out the world in the golden heyday of al-Andalus, the centre of the Moorish empire, and as we crossed the magnificent Roman bridge spanning the Guadalquivir River, he could not help but look around in interest.

"Do you know, Blessings, that before the Christians reconquered Córdoba two hundred fifty years ago there were three thousand mosques here, eight hundred bathhouses and a library containing more than four hundred thousand books?"

These were unimaginable numbers, and of things of no great meaning to me, but I tried to look interested if only to keep him talking in this animated way, showing a flash of the old Momo I so loved.

"This was once the greatest city in all the world, greater even than Fez. Oh, how I wish I could have seen it then, with its observatories and palaces, its souks and its great university. Scholars from every country and the three great faiths—Jewish, Muslim and Christian—all came here to share their knowledge for the betterment of mankind. It was the fount of science and the heart of faith. Philosophers and poets, alchemists and mathematicians, musicians and doctors—they all brought their bright minds and ideas. There were even women poets, luteists, calligraphers and teachers, can you imagine?"

"Were there really?" I gave him a wry smile. "Remarkable."

"And merchants came, bearing goods from the farthest reaches of the world, and a hundred thousand of the finest artisans and architects, to create wonders in *pisé* and *tadelakt*, copper, brass and silk; wood carvers and stucco carvers, ζellij workers, leather crafters and silk weavers." He stopped to draw breath as we passed into the city streets, and his face fell. "Oh."

The smell of excrement and urine was stifling in the heat: clouds of bluebottles drew away from the bloated corpse of a donkey and buzzed about us. We rounded a corner and had to detour around the side of a fallen building. There was a brawl ahead that had to be broken up by the guards so we could pass: the brawlers, bloodied and bruised, stared at us as if we'd just fallen from the moon. I suppose we made quite a sight—fifty Moorish cavalry in full battle dress and an even greater number of Castilian nobles and *jineta* shouldering silver-headed halberds, guarding a foreign prince wearing a vast white turban pinned with a big ruby, and with jewels glittering in the hilt of his sword.

In front of the great tawny walls of the Alcázar there was another disturbance. A crowd had gathered and someone in its midst was shouting, raising a chorus of cheers and boos. When the crowd parted for us, it revealed a scrawny old greybeard yelling in some language I could not understand. It seemed I was not the only one. A man shouted, "Speak Castilian, you lunatic!" The old man looked our way. His eyes were sunk so deep under his eyebrows it seemed as if the sockets were filled only with shadows. I felt a shiver run down my spine.

Coming to within a few paces of Momo, he described an elaborate bow. "Woe to the world!" he cried out in a form of Castilian this time. "The Lord has spoken: Iberia, the nursemaid of Mahometan depravity, will be torn apart. Each kingdom will battle against another."

"Out of the way!" shouted the Great Captain, riding forward.

But the old man stood his ground. "When the young ox has lived three times seven years, the consuming fire will be multiplied until the Great Bat, who is our saviour, will devour the mosquitoes of Africa and, trampling on the head of the beast, bring the world under his rule!"

"He's like the mad old hermit who lived on the Sacromonte." Momo turned to me, his face ashen. "Is it the same man? Has he come all the way from Granada to torment me?"

Qasim and the Great Captain had ridden up beside us. "Madmen abound, majesty. Pay him no attention," said the vizier.

"This is no simple madman," DonGonzalo said, "no matter how odd his appearance or how curious his words. I've heard this prophecy among the Catalans, whose word for mosque is much the same as for mosquito—*mezquita*—a silly wordplay, but people like that sort of thing. They say the Great Bat is Ferdinand, and Ferdinand's almost come to believe the prophecy himself: he strides around like a conqueror in all but name."

It seemed the Great Captain was less enamoured of his king than of his queen. But who wanted to be likened to a bat? Lions, yes—even bulls or cats—were suitably heroic creatures, but bats? They were ugly black things, flittery and repulsive. With an inward grimace, I translated this for Momo, who nodded. "So we're to be eaten up by this Aragonese king and his son-stealing queen. We're just flies to them, buzzing around a dead donkey." He closed his eyes. "I don't think I can sign this treaty."

My innards became cold and heavy. "If you don't, they'll keep you prisoner forever. Or kill you. And how will that help Granada? You'll leave the kingdom in the hands of your uncle and he'll drive the population to war till there's no one left standing. And what of Mariam, and your unborn child? What use is a lost husband, a lost father?" I could see him wavering. "What use to me?" I whispered.

After a very long time he sighed. "Very well. I'll play my part. But I feel that whatever I do, I am damned."

As we passed inside the palace walls, Qasim leaned over his horse to say quietly, "That was well done, Blessings."

We were received in the cavernous main hall, its elegant Moorish pillars, arched windows and scrolling ribbons of Arabic calligraphy incongruous above the heads of the crowd of overdressed Christian nobles, who stared at us no less avidly than the plain folk outside the palace walls.

"I feel their eyes on me like a touch," Momo complained quietly as we passed through their ranks.

"It's as if they expect us to have extra limbs or a second head," I said.

"And yet we are all men." I glanced across at him as he said this and saw on his face a wistful expression I did not recognize. He had aged, I thought. It was as if he had gone from twenty to middle age in the space of these past few months. I did not know him anymore. He had changed, and I was losing him.

Abruptly, the crowd parted and we found ourselves before two great thrones set upon a dais. The light fell from behind, forming sinister silhouettes of the seated figures: I could make out no more than the glint of golden crowns and the gleam of chains and jewels, as if two shadow-creatures sat the thrones and gazed down upon the mortal world with a scant interest bordering on scorn.

"Pray silence for their royal selves, the Catholic monarchs of the conjoined realm of Castile and Aragón!" cried a master of ceremonies, and at once a dozen trumpets sounded, their notes harshly grating to our ears.

"Tell your lord to fall to his knees," the Great Captain whispered to me.

I turned to him, shocked. "Kings don't kneel before other kings."

"Your sovereign is a prisoner and mine are his captors," he said dryly. "It will go better for him if he plays his part."

I relayed this to Momo, my voice shaking as I did so, but he was unperturbed. "What must be done must be done." And he cast himself to the ground in the full body-to-the-ground obeisance the peasants gave him when they came to make petition.

At this, one of the shadow-figures sprang to life, leaping from his throne and jumping down from the dais to raise him up. "We are kings, my good Boabdil: kings do not bow to kings. Pray rise, and welcome to our city of Córdoba."

The speaker had stepped into the illumination of a great tree of candles: I scrutinized him with as much curiosity as we had been accorded by his nobles, searching for signs of his batness. A jowled face with a sharp nose and shining dark eyes. A neck corded with the muscle gained, I guessed, from wielding a broadsword, for his reputation as a soldier went before him. Of middle height and sturdy leg; giving a general impression of vast energy packed into a small space. So this was Ferdinand of Aragón. I had heard he was handsome, and perhaps he was to the infidels' taste, but to me he seemed stocky and unremarkable, though some of that might have been the cut of his brocaded doublet, with its bumptious great collar of fur, and some that he was so different to the aquiline beauty of my own king. He looked not much like a Great Bat.

Momo took his hand and rose gracefully. He was a good head taller than the Aragonese: and perhaps that was why the latter retook his seat on the high dais.

"I am honoured to be welcomed into this fine city, the city that once gleamed like a jewel, that drew all the brightest and the best, where the greatest scholars and scribes once gathered to record and share the wisdom of the ages—"

I translated as Momo began to speak, but King Ferdinand waved his hands to cut my words short. "Enough of these pleasantries! There's one further proviso I have added to the document before we all can sign it, which is that my soldiers must be granted safe and free passage through his territories during the time of this truce."

I relayed this to Momo and watched as he took this new demand in and mulled it over. There was only one good reason for such a clause: to grant tacit permission for an attack on his uncle in Málaga. Al-Zaghal wanted the entire kingdom for himself and would stop at nothing to have it: but if Momo signed this treaty, his uncle's hands would be kept full defending his city, which was said to be impregnable. At last Momo nodded. "I accept."

King Ferdinand smiled and leaned back in his throne, his job done. Now the other figure leaned forward so that she was illuminated by the candlelight and I sucked in my breath. Surely this was not the fearsome queen who had established the Inquisition, who was so famously pious that she spent most days on her knees in prayer. This woman looked barely thirty; her pale skin and reddish hair glowed with good health, and there was a lively light of what might under other circumstances be mischief in her brown eyes.

"The wording of the treaty has been witnessed by our good servants DonDiego Fernández, the Count of Cabra, and DonGonzalo Fernández, our most loyal captain." She nodded to them in turn, then tilted her head and regarded Momo warmly. "I thank you for coming to terms with us in such a generous and reasonable manner. I understand, as a mother, how very hard it must have been for you and your good wife to make such a great sacrifice. But be assured, your young son Ahmed—" she pronounced the child's name in such a fashion that Momo did not appear to have discerned in it her foreign discourse, for he betrayed by no flicker of movement or expression "—shall be raised by us as if he were one of our own, here in this court, beside our own children."

There was more of this—much more—but I curtailed in my translation. In the end, all he could do was nod and lay the palm of his right hand to his breast and bow his head over it. I watched as he fought his emotions, but a single tear rolled off the end of his nose and fell, lit by the dancing candles, like a drop of molten gold onto the flagstones.

Queen Isabella was speaking again, her voice sharper now. "Of course, we cannot raise him as an unbeliever in this most Christian of royal courts. He shall be blessed and baptized by the hand of Father Torquemada himself and be welcomed forever into the embrace of Holy Mother Church. We shall grant him the name of Alfonso, after my beloved brother whom the Lord has seen fit to take before his time."

Only now, as I took in this terrible pronouncement and wondered how on earth I could soften it, did I see the signs of her austere fervour. A pucker between the hawk's-wing eyebrows, a pinch to the nostrils, an upper lip that was a mere line, a jut to the chin that told of iron will and fierce pride . . .

For fear that Momo might lose his composure entirely, I'm afraid I mistranslated somewhat, telling him that the boy would receive tutoring on all subjects from geometry to poetry from the finest teachers in the civilized world. But I could tell he wasn't taken in: over the months he too had picked up a little Castilian.

"Ask the queen the name of the imam she will appoint to teach my boy to read and recite the Quran and each hadith. Ask her where she will find such a paragon in a kingdom in which Jews and Moors who have been raised in al-Andalus all their lives, who come from families who have dwelt here peacefully for generations, are being burned alive for the sins of washing the bodies of their dead in hot water or swaddling them in new shrouds; for refusing to eat the flesh of pigs or dressing their food with olive oil instead of lard."

I hesitated.

"Go on, ask her!" He spoke softly, but his eyes burned.

"My lord, you know I can't ask her this, for she will have no answer."

The ferocious light faded. "I know you can't, Blessings. I know. Tell the king and queen to show me the treaty, then, and I will sign it." His shoulders slumped.

"There was just one other thing, sire . . ." I hadn't told him it was not only Ahmed who was to be a hostage but eleven other boys, the sons of his closest allies. Ah well: it was a shared sacrifice; and what could make him sadder than he already was?

He waved my words away. "No more now. Just hand me the pen."

The monarchs all signed the parchment and there was a great deal of business over hot wax and the royal seal; then the queen made a signal and a fanfare sounded. To the left of the royal dais the court-iers parted to allow a small procession to enter the hall, a procession headed by a girl of thirteen or fourteen in a white gown, with long red hair and features very like the queen's. Behind her trailed other children, maybe twenty or so, of varying age and height. The girl at the front led by the hand on one side another red-haired girl, attired like her in all details; and on the other side, a toddler of two or three, wearing a miniature version of the Castilian nobles' cos-tume: a cap, a fur-trimmed velvet tunic and a silver amulet.

I stared at the amulet. It was of Tuareg design and achingly familiar. In a rush, I realized it must be taken from my mother's pendant, the necklace I had given to Mariam on the eve of her wed-ding, on that fateful night in Loja. Then I stared at the boy. So this was why they had kept us waiting so long at Porcuna after Momo had agreed to the terms: so that they could take Ahmed into their hands for this small moment of cruel drama and triumph, and confirm the utter emotional capitulation of our king. I glared at Qasim—for surely it was he who had done this—but he would not meet my eye.

Momo sobbed out a single word. "Ahmed!"

The child startled. I saw him scan the richly garbed figures and fix upon the tallest. He pulled away, but the girl in white held on tight. "*Baba!*" he cried. "*Baba! Baba!*"

Even I felt a lump rise in my throat.

"Let him go," Isabella told her daughter, and Ahmed ran with a toddler's wild drunkard's stagger into the arms of his father.

I couldn't bear to watch their farewell: instead, I turned my eyes to the queen. With her plump cheeks and small, satisfied smile she looked like a cat that held her prey between her paws.

As if to prolong the agony, or perhaps to make sure we left, King Ferdinand accompanied us to the city limits, extolling the beauties of Córdoba as we moved through cheering crowds, as if nothing world shattering had just occurred. Momo did his best to respond, but I could see the dark thoughts churning in his head behind those bare, polite answers. It was a relief when we reached the Roman bridge and the Aragonese and his retinue turned back.

"Are you all right, my lord?" It was a foolish question and deserved an angry reply, but he managed a wan smile.

"Always you think only of me, Blessings. I don't deserve you as a friend. Best you go talk to someone else for a while. You shouldn't have to suffer my black mood."

I went quiet. There was no pleasure to be had among the company of guards. Some of them I knew from the Alhambra, but most I did not. Some were likely to be remnants of the Banu Serraj, men who thought they could suffer no more loss than they already had. Now, if their sons had been taken along with Ahmed, they were discovering that was not the case.

Instead, I regarded the people we passed, noting a preponderance of darker skins the farther from the centre of Córdoba we went: or perhaps those folk knew they would catch sight of the young sultan and had stayed out on the streets to watch us leave, for there were some who dared call out greetings and *baraka* upon him. I wondered how they managed their lives under the increasing intolerant Catholic rule and if they lived in a state of permanent anxiety, practising their beliefs covertly and in fear of being turned in to the authorities by their neighbours, or even members of their own family.

"I never got the chance to see the Great Mosque," Momo said wistfully, breaking the long silence. "They say it had eight hundred pillars and in the right light the trees in its courtyard are a perfect reflection of the pillars within. If you stand in the precise centre between the two, they say a broken heart will be healed. I would have been able to test that belief."

It took me a long moment to master my emotions. "It's a place of Christian worship now," I told him at last. "I heard that they installed bells in the minaret and the prayer hall."

He shook his head sadly. "Such disrespect. I pray such sacrilege is never enacted upon Granada. *Insha'allah.*" God willing.

But his god did not seem to care overmuch for the protection of his people. This was no wonder to me, who had travelled farther than my lord and seen how large the world was. How could any one god oversee so much? Better to pray, I thought, to the small deities—the ones who kept the wind in check and brought rain to fill the oases; the ones who made babies ripen and the tribe healthy; the ones who stopped camels straying and brought mountain hares out for the hunters' hawks. To try to force an entire populace, with all manner of conflicting backgrounds and loyalties, to worship in precisely the same way on pain of torture and death seemed to me violently wrong, perversely cruel. But I knew if I said any of this to Momo, he would frown and call me a heathen. Which I supposed I was.

We rode on through the dusty squares and thinning crowds till we came to the edge of the outer city, and it was here that the Great Captain who had led us thus far at the head of his contingent of guards rode back to us and clasped Momo's outstretched hand. "Go with God, my friend," he said in good Arabic

Without missing a beat, "*Vaya con Dios, amigo,*" Momo replied.

For a moment Don Gonzalo's face went very still. "I see you've learned a little Castilian in your time with us, sire."

"A little, but it seems not enough," Momo said stiffly, holding his gaze.

The Great Captain nodded slowly. "I'm sorry to have been a part of this hard bargain," he said. "But you must understand the necessity."

"Children have no part to play in the wars of men."

The Great Captain grimaced. "I fear children play a part in all wars."

"And then grow up to be angry young men."

Gonzalo inclined his head. "I fear so. I pray I may never meet you or yours in any future battle. When we meet again, may it be in peace. That's the best either of us can hope for."

And so we parted and Abu Abdullah Mohammed left Córdoba, ostensibly as a free man, though one encumbered by heavy chains of guilt and sorrow.

Qasim Abdelmalik's grey mare ghosted up on Momo's left side. "I fear, my lord, this will not be a leisurely ride. We must cross the border under the cover of darkness, for your father's troops will be on the lookout for you. He's laid a large price on your head, you know, and while many will be on your side in their hearts, they'll be tempted by the money, or fear incurring his wrath. All the northern towns have gone over to him in these months; even Granada itself is torn in two."

Momo nodded coolly. "I know all this, but the situation will be reversed as soon as I arrive back in my kingdom, believe me."

The vizier appeared skeptical. "Sire."

"Tell me, sir, how was your mother when last you spoke?" Momo asked after a space.

Qasim stiffened. "That was a sorry affair, my lord, mistimed and ill-judged."

"Your comings and goings are less of a mystery than you would like to think. I understand how my son now lies in enemy hands."

My heart stilled: would I be the next accused? I waited for Qasim to give me up, but all he said was "Someone trustworthy had to do it. I apologize for the necessity from the bottom of my heart."

"That is a shallow trough indeed."

The vizier made no reply to this.

"Trustworthy!" Momo snorted. He held his hand in the air, signalling for the column to halt. Then he regarded the vizier full in the face. "I should kill you for your part in this miserable affair, but I'm going to need a man of your cunning and ability if I'm to rebuild my kingdom. Get down off your fine horse and pledge your fealty on your knees, or by God I will find a use for this pretty sword they have given me."

For a long moment Qasim hesitated, then in the dying light he slid from the back of the grey. His robe looked, even to my untutored eye, to be even more expensive than that the young sultan wore. I knew where his money from Isabella had gone. Indeed, we both wore our portable ill-gotten gains.

"There—" Momo pointed to the spot. "Kneel there."

A darker patch marked the place where a horse had just pissed. For a moment it seemed the vizier would risk Momo's ceremonial sword for the sake of his finery; then he dropped to his knees with a grimace and made his obeisance. When he clambered back up into the saddle, I saw Momo take note of the stain on the silk and how a tight expression of petty triumph flickered for a moment. But Qasim's face was suffused with blood.

It took a great deal to puncture the shield of urbane politeness the vizier held constantly before him and had just let slip. I knew Qasim's dark side better than most—importantly, better than Momo did—so, as much as for my own skin, I feared the consequences of this small piece of theatre.

We crossed the border in the dead of night. I was almost asleep in the saddle when Momo caught my arm.

"My banners!" he said with quiet satisfaction, and when I blinked and focused through the darkness, I saw his sigil rippling in the breeze. Three or four standards and beneath them just a handful of troops, barely more than the number who travelled with us already. That was all. Momo was craning his neck, but with a sinking heart I knew he would find no more: the rest had all gone over to his father.

Our homecoming was furtive. We had to make a great detour to avoid being spotted crossing the wide Plain of Granada by Moulay Hasan's lookouts. As we finally skirted the great promontory and crept into the Albayzín, I remembered how Momo's lance had broken against the gate when we rode out all those months ago. Maybe there was something more to omens and portents than I had reckoned.

Then I reminded myself that the spells I had contrived and hidden before we left the Alhambra had done their work: Momo had survived the battle, even if he was a shell of the man who had ridden out at the head of an army. Perhaps I should have been more careful in the composition of them.

23

They say that next morning, when guards ran to inform Moulay Hasan of his son's secretive but successful return to the city, such was his shock that he fell down in a fit, his limbs twitching and froth falling from his mouth. And that when he came back to himself, his blindness was complete. But I heard this from a travelling musician who had been at the royal palace that day, and I know only too well how little the word of such wandering people can be trusted.

What I do know is that coming back to the Albayzín was a miscalculation, though it's easy to say this in hindsight. Momo was driven by his need to see Mariam, to disburden himself of his guilt as much as by his love for her, dread forcing him on through the nights, through the windless days, through barrancas dense with Barbary fig and thorn, where the heat came at us off the rocks like the breath of a hungry lion; over forested hills where the pine trees wept sap whose pungent scent stung the eyes. We had passed abandoned shepherd's huts in hills that were sere and brown and in the valleys meagre flocks of bone-thin sheep and scrawny black goats, those few that had survived this hard summer. The peasants were thin too, large eyed with privation, though they cheered as we passed. "God's blessing on you, lord, for stopping this war!"

Some ran to kiss the hem of his robe, or his boot, or even the ground he had ridden over. By the time we came in sight of the city, tears had streaked a pale path through the dust on Momo's cheeks: he was already in a state of high emotions before his reunion with his wife and mother.

I was not privy to that reunion, for I had absented myself to get in and out of the bathhouse before anyone else. There, I paid the *hammam* attendant to leave me be and sat alone in the hot room, my sobs swallowed by the thick vapour.

Before the week was out Hasan's soldiers had stormed the Albayzín, and the common people, armed with only knives and stones, roof-staves and shovels, had rallied behind the young sultan to drive them out. Blood spattered squares where the day before children had played with dolls; it coated the cobbles of the back streets; bloody hands marked the walls where the wounded had attempted to stagger home. Bodies lay one atop another as elite guards in shiny breastplates and helmets collapsed upon shopkeepers and shoemakers, butchers, bakers and scribes. And their sons: beard-less young men not yet betrothed, though probably not entirely innocent of a girl's touch. After the soldiers had withdrawn, Momo wandered disconsolately through the alleyways, closing the eyes of the dead and helping to carry the wounded of both sides ("They are all my subjects") to a hastily constructed hospital tent at the top of the Albayzín hill. He, too, was covered from foot to helm in blood: I had never seen him fight with such ferocity.

"I can't stay here," he said that night.

"You can't leave!" The emira was appalled. "I've spent a small fortune shoring up our defences and housing our allies."

"As long as I stay in Granada, people will be butchered by my father's men."

"You know he has sent emissaries throughout the kingdom, proclaiming you traitor—even apostate—for signing the treaty with the enemy?" she taunted him. "He claims you're in league with the devil against him, that you've sold the good Muslims of Granada into Christian bondage!"

"I can't stop my father spreading lies."

"You can!" Her voice was shrill. "You can kill him—and that serpent of a woman whose evil spawn will claim your throne!"

"Mother." He took her by the shoulders, even braver now than in battle. "What point is there in fighting to keep a kingdom in which there are no subjects to rule? I will not see innocents slaughtered in my name."

She shook his hands off. "I'm beginning to see there's some truth in your father's poisonous words. You're a coward, not fit to rule! You are no king if you can't even keep your own city!"

Momo shrugged. "Maybe I am no king. But I care more for these people than my father does. I signed the treaty to save them from an endless war. But for what? So they could lose their lives fighting one another? My mind is made up. We'll leave for Almería."

Mariam was only a few weeks away from giving birth: she was as round as an apple. But her face belonged to another woman, not a young mother bursting with lush fertility. It looked grim and her eyes were sunken and dull. She had hardly exchanged a word with Momo since his return, clearly blaming him for the loss of their son as a hostage, and who could blame her? When Momo announced that she should pack only a few things to take with them to this unknown city, she burst into tears, and he ushered her away into their private quarters. I did not see either of them until another day had passed, but whatever wiles Momo had used to win her back seemed to have worked, for by the time they emerged once more her face was wreathed with smiles. Unable to rejoice in this, I went out and embraced my heathen origins. Not having to keep up the pretense of being a good Muslim, I got roaring drunk on a jug of the local rough red wine in a tavern for poor travellers out near the city wall and spewed my guts up in a side street where someone had daubed obscene drawings and slogans over the top of the dark, dried blood.

Almería. I have nothing good to say about Almería. It had been at the peak of its glory half a millennium ago and it was a dour place now, its massive keep crouching behind triple walls, its outlook the sullen sea. I hated the sea, with its endless succession of grey waves rolling in to the harbour below the alcazaba. I hated the way the ships bobbed at anchor, as if like me they could not wait to get away. I hated the acres of empty space it represented, of no use to anyone.

The empty space of the sea was partnered by the empty spaces inside the keep: miles of corridors lined with ages-old carpets worn almost threadbare by the passage of feet; cavernous chambers unrelieved by wall hangings or even furniture, where your voice echoed mournfully. The gardens had been tended by a small battalion of gardeners with no imagination and an overreliance on evergreens. Before a month was out I was sick of the sight of box and amsonia, basil and thyme, wormwood and mint. Oh, the mint. It was everywhere: you trod it underfoot and released its sugary sweetness into a cloud that seemed to follow you around.

"Where are the roses?" I asked the man who claimed to be the head gardener. "Where are the calendula and iris? The amaranth and jasmine?"

He spread his hands. "They don' like it 'ere. Too difficult." He stuck a finger to the sky. "Too much salt in the air." He paused, considering this. "Still, it keeps the djinn and their evil luck away."

It didn't, though. Mariam went into labour weeks earlier than she was due, and the whole palace flew into panic.

I went to find Qasim with a heavy heart, aware what was coming. "So, Blessings," he said, laying a hand on my shoulder. "It's inconvenient, but we'll have to make an adjustment to the plan. You will go to do the exchange and I will stay, since you will be less missed than I."

Thank you, I thought blackly. *Thanks very much.*

"A boy will have your horse ready. You know what to do."

"I can't do it." It would destroy him. How could I hurt him so? It was too cruel.

The fingers bit deeper. "You can. And you will. Or you know what will happen."

I swallowed. I knew exactly what would happen. Qasim would remove me, probably kill me, and bring in some other of his spies to do his dirty work. "It's for the best," I said at last, feeling like the worst sort of traitor.

"Of course it's for the best. You know that." He was already walking away.

"For Momo?" I called after him. "It's the best thing for him, isn't it? He'll be less of a threat to them?"

He didn't even answer.

My false foot, shining with its new gold, seemed to weigh like lead as I dragged myself back through the palace to my quarters. There, I garbed myself as we had agreed and, furnishing myself with a pile of swaddling clothes, made for the birthing chamber.

Long before I reached it I could hear Mariam's cries, hoarse and shocking. I turned the last corner, only to see Momo outside the door, pacing to and fro in anguish. I remembered how he had been at Ahmed's birth. I had thought that bad, but this was much, much worse. How could I pass by him unobserved? He would spot me even in this guise and then praise me for being so kind as to disguise myself thus to help his Mariam where he could not. His heart was too generous: I couldn't bear it. I hovered, desperate. Then, with perfect timing, the vizier appeared, bearing a sheaf of paper, looking agitated. There ensued a brief, intense conversation that I could not hear, then Momo followed Qasim toward the council chamber. Taking a deep breath, I slipped into the birthing room with the armful of swaddling clothes.

I had never witnessed a birth before. Mariam's bellows were urgent, guttural noises, like those made by a man mortally wounded on the battlefield, the sounds that drew crows. I felt like a carrion bird myself.

The women attending the birth were pale with fatigue: Mariam had been sweating and groaning for hours and they were afraid they would lose her, or the baby, or both.

"The baby's early—it should be easy to deliver," one whispered. "Something's not right."

"This place has a bad feeling," said another. "I've seen djinn here, in the night, eyes glowing with moonlight."

"Those were cats," a third woman scoffed. "They're everywhere."

The second speaker was not to be put off. "It's his bad luck. It follows him wherever he goes. I knew this child wouldn't come easily. It'll be a monster—if it ever does come out—just wait and see."

"I strewed salt across the threshold," said the local wisewoman they had called in to oversee the birth. "No djinn can enter here."

I tilted my good foot and scrutinized the sole of my slipper. Little white crystals were embedded in the soft leather: I had broken the line of salt and brought the bad luck in with me.

No. I *was* the bad luck.

It took another three hours until at last the baby was out—a lump of purple flesh with a slippery cloak of membrane across its head so that at first we all thought it had been born faceless, the monster some had expected. But the wisewoman knew better and the caul was soon off. The child was small, its first cry thin and reedy, but it punched the air with small, triumphant fists as if to proclaim its arrival: it would live.

I ran forward with the swaddling clothes once the wisewoman was ready, stood head down and obedient to receive the scrap of life into my arms. Then, as soon as they turned back to attend to the afterbirth and look after Mariam, I ran as if all the djinn in the world were after me.

At the postern gate I found the wet nurse, two guards in Qasim's pay and the promised horse. We galloped north and I prayed that the arrangements had been well made. *If he ever finds out, I am dead,* I thought, over and over, as the horses' hooves pounded into the ground. *Dead, dead, dead.* And then I caught myself in this selfish thought and made myself consider what Momo and Mariam must be feeling now: their elder son in enemy hands, their baby stolen from beneath their noses. What dark despair must they be in? I imagined Mariam wailing her heart out, Momo trying to comfort her. Or would he be out on his horse searching for the vile thief who had stolen his son, his mind full of murder? *If he finds out, he will kill me,* I thought again, and once more forced myself away from self-pity. I reminded myself it was a necessary step, that the removal of his heir would make Momo safer. But I knew I was doing something terribly wrong and my guilt felt as if it would engulf me.

The case should have been put to Momo. He should have been given time to come to terms with the need for it and to talk Mariam around to the decision, but Qasim was too impatient. "He will never agree to it, and that will bring war to our doorstep. They can have others," he had said dismissively.

Qasim had no wife. Children were nothing to him. Coming from him the words sounded so callous, so cruel. Then I remembered I had said the very same thing to Momo myself about Ahmed.

The vizier and the Special Guardian. The two who should have been his closest allies and his most trustworthy friends. Yet together we were betraying him in the worst possible way. And yet on I went with the precious scrap of life in my arms.

When we reached the appointed meeting place, they were there, the dark-robed men hiding their Castilian insignia—quartered castles and dragons rampant—the arms of the foreign queen, whose catlike contentment at holding one son had so turned my stomach. Now I was giving her a second. Would this one finally satisfy her? Or would she come calling for more, demand every child the doomed pair produced as hostage against their continued subjugation? Well, I was committed now. I handed over the child and the wet nurse followed as arranged. I was surprised when one of the foreigners brought forth a leather pouch. It was heavy, and its contents clinked. "The agreed price," he said in his ugly language. "You can count, check it's the right amount."

"What need?" said the second man. "Thirty pieces of silver is the same in any currency."

24

Kate

NOW

Abdou and Kate walked through the narrow streets of the Albayzín, almost touching, barely speaking, wrapped in their own thoughts. They had pored over the fragments of manuscript into the early hours, Khadija fetching down books and examining photographs of etched desert stones, then resorting to the Internet to download pages of alphabet charts tracking the language from its ancient roots to its current Unicode values. Together, they had tried to transcribe the separate words from the fragments and locate equivalent symbols on the charts, but the code—as Kate had come to see it—was complex and obscure. Every so often Khadija or Abdou would exclaim that they thought they had pieced together a word, only for the following phrase to prove indecipherable or to render the guessed word meaningless. At last the professor had sat back, rubbing her temples. "Time to bring in the experts," she had said with a yawn. "I'll make some calls. I know of a professor of Tamazight in Rabat. He may be able to help if I send JPEGS of the fragments to him. May I keep these for now?" Of course they had agreed, but secretly Kate had been disappointed not to have deciphered them right away.

Her heel struck a cobblestone and the sound ricocheted off the walls into the night air. She stole a sideways glance at her companion—it was what he felt like to her, a companion. Someone she could walk comfortably with, side by side, there being no need to speak. Then Abdou turned his head and caught her watching him. Moonlight slicked off his eye, caught the curve of his lips: he looked in that moment, she thought, almost demonic, and all thoughts of companionship fled, leaving her with a fast-beating heart and a sensation that flirted along the edge of fear.

She realized that they had stopped walking. Abdou placed the flat of his hand across the narrow alleyway, barring her path. Her first instinct was to push him out of the way with a nervous laugh and carry on; but there was no space without brushing her entire body against him, so she stood there, rooted and inert, waiting for the world to turn, for something to happen.

"My place is just up here," he said quietly. "You could come in if you like."

Kate shivered. Partly it was because of the cold. Mainly it was not. "I thought you were walking me home."

"Mine is closer." He left a pause. "But we could go back to yours if you prefer."

She knew she should feel angry at his presumption, but Kate blushed, and was glad that the darkness hid her discomfort. "It's fine. I know my way from here." Which wasn't entirely true. "It's a nice offer, but—"

His mouth upon hers was hot and sudden. She was too surprised to move, too surprised even to close her eyes: he was out of focus, a blur of dark hair and a gleam of eyes as he pulled away to look at her, before moving in again, this time cradling her cheek with one palm, tilting her face toward him, pulling her so close it was as if he would somehow absorb her through his skin. She meant to step out of the embrace, to push him away and walk quickly down the alley, but her tongue had other ideas, and her limbs had gone to jelly. She could feel him pressing against her now, hard and upright: in response a fire started somewhere below her belly button, turning her flesh molten.

At last the inability to breathe made her break away, gasping. "Oh," Kate said. "I didn't . . . I didn't want . . . I didn't mean to do that."

"Do what?" He leaned back against a wall, regarding her from the shadows, enjoying the turmoil he had caused.

"Kiss you. Or rather, kiss you back."

"You did, didn't you?" He sounded smug.

There was little point in denying it. "Yes, but, I shouldn't have. My life is complicated."

"Good. That's what life is for, complication. Without it there's no pattern, just straight lines and blank colours. That would be very dull."

She wasn't falling for semantics. "I meant, my life is already too complicated. There's no pattern to it, just mess and wreckage."

"I like mess. And if there was no wreckage, there would be nothing to salvage."

"You don't understand."

"So tell me."

"It's too late."

"It's never too late."

"I mean now. It's too late. It's—" She glanced at her watch, then tapped it, looked at it again. "Bloody thing. It's stopped."

He grinned. "Time has stopped, then. Come upstairs."

"Seriously, though, it's late. I must get to bed. My own bed."

"I thought you quit your job. No need to get up early."

"Even so, I need to sleep."

"'Our little life is rounded with a sleep': but the key word is 'life,' no?"

"For a man who can't write his own name in his mother tongue you're surprisingly literate all of a sudden," she said tartly.

He raised an eyebrow, surprised by her rudeness. "Ah, you have so many other surprises to discover about me."

God, she thought. *This is ridiculous. How am I supposed to resist a man who works with his hands yet quotes Prospero at me; who looks the way he does and kisses like that?* She could feel her hips being drawn toward his as if by a magnet. This was no good. Grappling with the potent mix of exhaustion and attraction, she quelled the instinct to close with him. "Honestly, Abdou, I really must get some sleep."

There was greed in his gaze, but also philosophy. At last he shrugged. "Okay, you must sleep, and so must I. Join us tomorrow at noon for some couscous?"

Was he being deliberately unthreatening, offering lunch, and with others present? It was the second time the same invitation had been made: how could she say no? "At the Tower of the Captive?"

"We can meet here. With my uncle and cousin and me, yes."

"All right." She turned to go, but her knees were a little unsteady and she twisted an ankle on the cobbles. At once he was there, a steadying hand beneath her elbow.

"I think I had better see you safely to your door. You never know who might be lurking around these streets in the dead of night."

A light musky scent drifted between them, a faint animal smell of promised sex. She could feel the heat of him through his clothing and hers as they walked together. *We are like lions*, she thought suddenly, *like hungry lions that know they will not eat tonight, but soon.*

At the entrance to the Calle Guinea, with the door to her apartment safely in view, she faced him. "I'll see you tomorrow."

"You will."

They stood there in the darkness, powerfully aware of each other, the air between them charged. For a moment, Kate's resolve wavered: after all, what harm would it do, really, to invite him in? She liked him, he liked her. And it had been so long . . .

She felt a sharp pain in her left arm, then another, and out of nowhere was assailed by the memory of James pushing into her with a groan— "Mine. Mine, mine, mine." She turned aside just in time. Vomit spattered down into the gutter, her stomach emptying itself in painful heaves, as if she were turning herself inside out, on and on and on. When she stopped, it was to find that Abdou was beside her, holding her hair out of the firing line. A folded tissue appeared and she accepted it gratefully, wiping her mouth.

"Impressive," he said. "Especially without the aid of alcohol. Like the eruption of a minor volcano."

"I'm sorry. I don't know why that happened," she lied.

"Father's cooking can have that effect on people."

"Oh, it wasn't that! I've had a lovely evening. I'm just tired . . . maybe it's a bug of some kind."

"A bug?"

"A virus or something."

He seemed to accept her weak explanation. Then he said, "You're shaking."

She was, and now that she thought about it, it got worse. Little black stars began to dance at the edges of her vision. She swayed, blinking them away.

"I can't leave you like this. I'll worry."

She breathed in then out. "That I'll erupt again?"

"Devastating the entire Albayzín."

They grinned at each other. "I'm fine now, really," Kate reassured him. It wasn't true. She felt shaky, both mentally and physically. Was this going to happen every time she thought about having sex? Damn James and everything he had done to her. Anger began to well inside her, displacing some of the nausea and faintness. "Give me your number and I'll call you tomorrow," she said, kneeling to fish in her handbag. She found her key, but where was her phone? She rummaged harder, till a spill of items tipped out onto the ground in front of him, her phone among them. Oh, not the condoms again. She swiped them up, hoping he hadn't noticed. Triumph soon turned to dismay: he had her passport in his hand, opened to the photo page, angling it toward the distant street lamp.

"Jessica Scott?"

Kate closed her eyes.

She did not tell him everything, but she told him enough. Some of it she could not voice, did not want to remember. Some of it was just too personal to share with a man she barely knew. But even the bare bones of the story were damning. "And that's why I'm travelling on my sister's passport," she finished miserably.

In the grey light of dawn, Abdou regarded her solemnly. Then he bent forward and took her hand, lifted it to his lips and planted a single hot kiss in her palm. He folded her fingers back over the place, as if to guard a secret. "I'm so sorry, Kate."

"I left Luke behind."

"At least he's safe."

"Yes, at least there's that." She paused, thinking. "I'm sorry I kissed you, I shouldn't have done that—led you on, I mean. I'm still a married woman. I think."

"You think?"

She shook her head, feeling awkward. "Though technically, you kissed me first."

"I'm not sure that kissing is a technical matter. Except maybe for engineers."

It was a poor joke, kindly meant. She smiled wanly. "I don't know why I got married. I never really loved James. And, you know, I didn't really want children."

"Not ever?"

"Not with him, anyway. Even as a kid I wasn't one of those girls who babied their dolls. I was the quiet one who pulled their heads off and buried them on the beach. It was always Jess who made little clothes for hers and sat them down for tea parties." She looked up at him, fearing the answer to what she was about to ask. "Do you hate me now that you know who I really am—a cowardly woman who fled from her husband and child?"

"Quite the reverse. I think you're brave, and strong, and beautiful. Most women I know would have sat it out, stayed married, stayed quiet about it. It takes a strong liver to throw everything away and make a new life."

"A strong liver?"

"It's what we say." He tapped his abdomen. "It's where all the deepest feelings come from."

"Not the heart?"

"The heart is a fickle organ."

Kate looked around at her bare apartment, which appeared all the more spare and impersonal in the dreary light. Yesterday's cups and plates sat on the counter, dirty, waiting to be washed, and she could smell the contents of the kitchen bin, which she'd forgotten to take out. "Not much of a life. Other than producing Luke, I haven't really achieved anything. I don't own anything anymore. I feel so transient passing through life with just a few necessities in a pack on my back."

"On someone else's passport!"

She laughed, rather sadly. "Yes."

"It doesn't always have to be that way, you know. I was a student for a time, and an activist when my grandfather was jailed. After that, I was on a list for a while in Morocco, so I drifted from job to job and place to place. I worked in garages, as a tourist guide, a cleaner, a driver. Till my uncle Omar took me under his wing and got me interested in restoration."

"I bet that made your mother happy."

"It did. It does. It makes me happy. It requires a lot of patience, and a lot of care, but I like to fix broken things, to give them back the best of themselves. It's satisfying." He ran a finger lightly over the little scars on her arm, making her shiver. "I've never tried mending a heart before, but I feel like I've spent all these years working up to it."

Kate smiled. "I think I'm pretty much beyond repair."

"No one's beyond repair." The look he gave her was direct, penetrating. She met it head-on, even though the touch of his hand caressing her arm was making her tremble.

"Why aren't you married?" The question came out before she could stop it.

He withdrew his hand, looked away. "I was."

"Oh. What happened? Or is it rude to ask?"

"She was the one thing I couldn't fix." His voice caught for a moment. "One day she was complaining of a headache, the next she was in intensive care with a shaved head and tubes coming out of her. It was just one big round of operations, chemotherapy and radiotherapy, a series of small hopes followed by terrible disappointments, and each time she was being worn away little by little, till there was hardly anything left of her. They gave her eight months: she lived for almost a year. It was a year too long."

Kate sat stunned into silence. All the words that she could think to say were not merely inadequate but offensive in their inadequacy. At last, instead of saying sorry she asked, "What was her name?"

"Sinéad." There was a pause as she took that in. "She was Irish. I met her when she was travelling. She said her name meant 'gift from God.' As they say, he gives with one hand, and takes away with the other. The day we buried her was the last time I went to a mosque."

"Oh, Abdou." She found herself reaching out and cupping his cheek, was surprised when he leaned into this small embrace. They stayed like that for a while, not speaking, until he straightened up. "I did not come in to talk about my troubles," he said. "There's nothing that can be done about those, and she is long gone. Ten years next year."

"And you've been single ever since?"

The look he gave her—at once knowing and mocking—demolished the question. "Sorry, I have no right to ask. But you never remarried?"

"A union blessed by God seemed to be tempting fate. He had already broken my faith: I did not want him breaking anyone else."

Rosy light had begun to flood into the little kitchen now; it warmed and humanized the place. Kate got up and made them both coffee, realizing as she did so that although she now knew more about this man than most, and having shared with him secrets she had told no one but her twin, she did not even know the simple fact of how he took his coffee. And yet she had the distinct sensation that their fates were bound together now. For a moment she stood still, feeling like a sailor at the bow of a ship looking out over an unknowable expanse of untraversed ocean. It would be so easy to turn back to the safety of port, but the mystery of him called her on.

25

K ate walked with Abdou through the Albayzín, then down
a way to a little street market she'd never come upon
before. She watched from the background as he went from
stall to stall, chatting and bargaining, and noted how everyone's
expression changed at the sight of him. There was much laughter,
always smiles. He was easy in his manner, teasing with the women,
respectful with the older men, exchanging greetings in such a plu-
rality of languages that she felt ignorant and undereducated. These
people were all polyglots, and no wonder: they had been traders
for generations, men and women for whom effective communica-
tion was a way of life, as well as of profit.

Soon it became apparent that, despite her attempt to stay out of
his limelight, she was under some scrutiny: while the men asked
cheerfully direct questions, the women were casting an eye over
her, assessing.

"*Eres hermosa*," one old lady remarked.

"*Bella, bella*," agreed her companion.

"Lucky man," said the jolly banana seller, winking at Abdou.

"Lucky girl," said his wife, grinning to show off her gold tooth.

"They all think you're my girlfriend," Abdou told her as they
moved away, cocking an eyebrow as he watched her reaction to this.

Kate tried not to smile and failed. "Well, I'm not."

"Yet," he said with undentable confidence, and bent to examine the ripeness of the peaches on the next stall.

Soon they had come away with bagfuls of colourful vegetables—aubergines and peppers, courgettes and carrots, butternut squash, French beans and red onions. It all seemed so delightfully normal, to be out and about, chatting with stallholders and shopping for meal ingredients with this charming man. It made Granada feel more like home than it ever had before, the people more like friends and neighbours than strangers. And there was a comfort to be had from the endless rounds of barter and chat; the sunshine; the prospect of the weekend, with long lazy meals and wine to be shared. Apart from the clothing the same scenes must have played out across the centuries—Moors and Jews and Castilians mingling in souks and markets to buy and sell and exchange news and gossip. Until, of course, the ambitions of powerful men set one against the other.

When you came down to it, though, people were much the same, she thought, watching a mother scold a small boy for taking an apple from the fruit stall without understanding the requirement of paying for the object of his desire. His howl rent the air, until the stallholder came around the stand to tousle his hair and hand him the fruit, waving the mother's coin away. Kindness was universal: a human default. She caught Abdou's eye—he had also watched the little sketch play out—and a wave of warmth travelled through her.

Thoughts of Luke shot through her and chilly guilt replaced the warmth.

"Are you all right?"

There was such concern in his voice that Kate almost burst into tears at how little she deserved it. "Fine," she said, pulling her cardigan tighter. "Just a bit cold."

If he considered it odd, he made nothing of it. Instead he said, "Here." He handed her a carrier bag. "Come and see how a proper Friday couscous is made."

They wove through back streets that Kate vaguely recognized from the night before. In the stark sunlight they looked different, calm and unremarkable; entirely unthreatening. Nothing lurked here, nothing moved. Bright geraniums popped their heads out of window boxes; hibiscus and bougainvillea spilled over walls. Rough whitewash, pantiled roofs, tiled doorsteps. By the time he led her up some steps to a door that offered more wood than paint she had no idea where she was.

He turned at the threshold. "It's no palace."

This proved to be an understatement. Abdou's apartment consisted of a single room under the eaves, where the air hung hot and heavy and undisturbed. He crossed it in three strides and threw open the shutters. Light flooded into the small space, illuminating his tiny but immaculate living quarters: a simple couch bearing a worn red blanket and two cushions, a small table and two mismatched chairs below the window, some shelving on which clothes were neatly folded. A curtain bearing faded roses concealed the kitchen area: an old porcelain sink and a two-ring gas hob sitting on top of a toaster oven. Kate had seen nothing like it since her student days. But there was no time to stare: Abdou thrust a chopping board and knife toward her. "Cooking is not a spectator sport."

Peeling and cutting up vegetables was easy and she had soon completed her tasks. By then, Abdou was engrossed in the matter of rubbing olive oil through a heap of couscous that he'd just lifted out of the steamer into a wide wooden bowl. She watched his hands moving rhythmically through the grain, rolling and separating, appreciating the conjunction of colours: the warm brown of his hands moving through the gold of the couscous. He caught her watching. "Onions." His tone was imperious, but edged with irony:

he was a magician calling upon the services of his assistant for an invisible audience.

He took the board from her and tipped the onions into the sizzling oil in the base of the steam tower, moved them around with a wooden spoon till the air was fragrant; then pinches and scatters from half a dozen unlabelled jars went into the onions, and suddenly her nose was twitching. Was that cumin? Cinnamon? Something sweet yet savoury, too complex to identify.

"What was that you just put in?"

"A little bit of magic." The rest of the vegetables went into the spices, and the couscous into the steam compartment above them.

"That's not very helpful!"

"I can't just give away my secrets. You have to earn them."

"I peeled vegetables!"

"You'll have to peel a lot more than that." He paused, calculating. "Four point five tonnes."

"I'm not that desperate to know."

Abdou shrugged. "Okay." Deliberately infuriating.

The smells were making her mouth fill with water. "Do you always cook on Fridays?" she asked.

"Not just Fridays. Why do you look so surprised? It's not so unusual. Everyone I know cooks. You have to eat, no?"

Kate thought about the men she knew. Left to themselves most would be living like hogs, eating straight out of the fridge, the microwave or the takeaway. She couldn't imagine any of them throwing spices into a pot in such a devil-may-care fashion.

"Food is an embrace," he said, casting her a sideways glance that made her stomach flip. "It's how we express love." He turned the gas off, wrapped a clean tea towel around the steamer and quickly washed, dried and put away the utensils and chopping board, till the place was pristine again. "Ready?"

By the time they had carried the pot of couscous up the long hill to the Alhambra, Kate was ravenous. In a little bit of the garden barred to tourists they found that Omar and Mohamed had spread a bright flatweave rug and set up a little portable gas stove between the citrus trees and roses. While Mohamed took the steamer from Abdou, Uncle Omar made a sweeping chivalric gesture that seemed to offer her the whole world of the courtyard. "*Marhaban*, Kate. Sit, sit." He ushered her into the shade beneath one of the trees. "To save your lovely skin."

Kate laughed. "No one's ever complimented my skin before."

Abdou paused in his preparations. "Really? England must be full of fools and blind men."

She watched the men pottering, stirring and sniffing while she washed her hands under the stream of water Mohamed poured from a big pewter kettle. She sniffed her hands. They smelled of roses.

"Roses!"

Mohamed opened the lid so she could see inside. Petals floated in the shadowy depth. "Alhambra roses," he confirmed, glancing shyly at her as he handed her a linen cloth. "I scavenged the fallen ones from the rose beds and added them myself." He seemed very pleased by her delight.

The men also washed their hands in the scented water and dried them on the cloth. Then Uncle Omar reached into some hidden pocket inside his capacious overalls and brought out a small jar. When he unscrewed the lid, Kate recoiled at the odour that sprang from it. "Good God, what is that?" She watched in fascinated horror as he approached the steamer. "Oh no, he's not— Please don't let him—"

Too late. A great dollop of the noxious-smelling substance fell audibly into the sauce. Uncle Omar stirred and stirred, then tasted the result and beamed. "Now it's ready."

"What did he just put in there?" asked Kate, suspecting manure or suchlike.

Abdou tapped the side of his nose. "Better not ask."

"I want to know."

"Curiosity killed the cat—isn't that one of your English sayings?"

"It smells as if the cat died a long time ago," she said, grimacing.

He laughed. "It's not that bad. It's *smen*."

For a moment she thought it was even worse than she'd imagined. "Say that again," she said, hoping she'd misheard; thinking that if it was what it sounded like, she'd be making her excuses and fleeing back down the hill.

"*Smen*," he said again. "Fermented butter. When a Berber child is born, our mothers take some of that day's butter and seal it in a jar. They keep it unopened until the child is grown, and only then, when it's safe, do they open the jar."

"Safe?"

"From the djinn." He took the jar from his uncle and dropped a spoonful of the contents into the earth at the foot of the nearest tree. "There: that'll appease them."

"They're easily pleased," Kate observed, wrinkling her nose at the pungent stench.

"Not at all. To them it's the height of luxury—like a cellared wine, or aged beef. This one is eighteen years old today. It's Mohamed's jar."

Mohamed beamed. "Today, I am man."

"Eighteen years." Kate felt a bit faint, imagining what eighteen years could do to butter.

"I look more old, I know," Mohamed said sagely, turning his baseball cap from back to more conventional front.

"Well, congratulations, Mohamed. I'm sorry, I didn't realize. I'd have brought a card."

"Is pleasure, Señorita Kate. That you here is best gift."

The smile he gave her was incandescent: the men of this family were frighteningly handsome. She'd bet Uncle Omar had been pretty devastating in his day.

Omar—clearly an old hand at this—spooned the couscous into a heap on an immense patterned plate, then tidied the edges till the grain formed a perfect golden dome. Upon this he arranged the vegetables, raying them out in green and red and orange from the centre in a colourful sunburst. Abdou produced from his duffel bag a single small plate and Omar carefully excavated a portion of the arrangement as a generous helping for Kate, and topped the small grain mountain with several spoonfuls of the aromatic sauce. Including the rank old butter.

All three men watched her expectantly. Clearly she was the guest and would thus eat first, but was it some sort of test? Bracing herself, Kate took a tentative mouthful, certain she would gag and have to force a swallow. The sauce sang in her mouth. Though symphonic in its complexity, there was no hint of the disgusting smell. It seared, it soared, just the right side of fiery. She closed her eyes, experiencing a kind of small ecstasy. "My God," she said when at last able to speak. "That's incredible."

As if she had uttered a benediction, *"Bismillah,"* Omar proclaimed, formalizing the blessing. They all tucked into the main dish, their hands busy among the vegetables, forming the couscous into little balls that they popped into their mouths as if performing a trick. Kate realized why she had been given a plate and spoon, and was grateful for Abdou's foresight.

Inevitably, once the last golden grains had been licked from fingers, there came the traditional ceremony of mint tea, accompanied by some of what looked like last night's almond biscuits in their little ⁊*ellij* shapes, and the peaches from the market, sun warmed and luscious.

Kate leaned back against the tree, replete. She could not remember the last time she had felt so content, so delighted by an experience. Not since she and Jess were young, after a picnic at the beach, falling asleep with her head on her mother's leg and her feet buried in the hot Cornish sand, with the sound of gulls and playing children melding into a single note above the soft *shooshing* of the waves as they washed up on the shore.

Jess!

The thought of her sister was insistent and electric: so shocking that she dropped her tea. "Ow!"

Abdou, quick as a cat, caught the glass before it hit the ground. "Are you okay?" He set the tea glass down and dabbed at her arm with the linen cloth.

She was about to answer, when her mobile phone went off, as if summoned by her thought. She retrieved it from her bag, swiped the green symbol and held the device to her ear. "Jess?"

But it wasn't Jess who answered.

"Damn you, Kate. Running to hide our son from me. How could you sin like that?"

The courtyard, the citrus trees, the three men, the scents of spice and jasmine evaporated like the figments of a dream and Kate felt as though she was falling endlessly through a cold, black void.

26

Blessings

ALMERÍA

1484

"Not like that, like this." I took the kohl wand from Rachid's fingers and, leaning toward the mirror, drew a fine line along the base of the lashes on my own eyelid. "See? It's just a matter of keeping a steady hand."

The boy giggled. He looked younger than his eighteen years, I thought from the lofty age of twenty, and younger still in the inexpertly applied cosmetic. It's an understatement to say I was bored. I was beyond boredom: I felt as if I'd been swallowed by a vast djinn down into the world of its stomach, a world so grey, featureless and inescapable. In the months since Mariam had given birth and lost her child a cloud of gloom had descended upon the court-in-exile, and particularly upon the young sultan and his wife. Mariam was hardly seen at all; Momo had taken to his bedchamber. As a result, I found myself, as now, at such a loose end as to be forced to spend time with his witless younger brother.

"Do you think me handsome, Blessings?" He batted his eye-lashes at me in a grotesque parody of female coquettishness picked up in the harem, where he sat for long hours at his mother's feet. It was for this reason that I kept his company, for he parroted to me every word she spoke behind those closed doors. It was how I kept abreast of the gossip. And how I earned my coin from Qasim, by passing it on.

"Very handsome, Rachid." I yawned. "A veritable Prince Ahmed."

"The one who went to Samarkand and bought a magic apple?"

We had been reading tales from the *Thousand Nights and One Night*. "The very one, just like you, the youngest son of a sultan. The one who rescued the Princess Pari Banu."

"I'd rather be her." He fluttered at me again. "And you should be Mercury Ali."

"Quicksilver Ali the Cairene? The trickster from Cairo?" Not very flattering.

He grinned. "You're from Africa. And Shahrazade describes him as beardless and well favoured."

I touched my chin, couldn't help it.

"Why don't you have a beard, Blessings?"

"You don't have a beard," I countered.

Rachid looked affronted. "I do—see?"

He came at me so close that I thought for an alarming moment he was going to kiss me.

"I see no beard," I said, drawing back.

"Are you blind?"

He was pouting now. He'd inherited some of Momo's beauty, but the lack of inner fire made him unattractive to me, even though he was so much more malleable and available than his elder sibling. Perhaps that was why he sparked no interest in me. Some people seem to love only what they cannot have. These are the same people who when they get what they have always wanted, want it no longer and seek to destroy it.

He took the mirror from me and tilted his head this way and that so that his glass earrings flashed in the candlelight.

"Well, I suppose my beard is very fine. But it's clearly there." He paused, considering. "Do all the men in your tribes wear kohl?"

"Yes," I said wearily. "But not for beauty, as I've told you before. Black is a protective colour: it wards off bad luck and evil spirits."

"I shall put some more on, then," he declared, twisting the wand in the little vial. "This place is full of bad luck."

I sighed. "Don't you have other friends?" I remembered how annoying I had found him as a boy. As a man he was even more so.

"They only want to hunt and ride and fight with swords. They are brutish louts who smell of old meat. None of them is graceful or elegant. Not like you, Blessings."

Was he admitting to a tenderness of heart for me? I got to my feet. Or rather, my foot. "Look, Rachid, you're a nice lad, but you're not my type."

He gazed at me like a kicked dog. Then his eyes narrowed.

"It's always my brother with you, isn't it? You moon around after him like some lovesick maid. Tell me, would you bed him like a woman or like a man?"

My whole skin went cold. My hands itched to take a dagger to him and stab and stab. "What are you talking about?"

"I have eyes. I've noticed the way you look at him."

So, he knew nothing. I took a step toward him and I think he must have seen the depths of violence I might sink to, for he backed away with his hands up.

"Sorry, Blessings. It's just . . ." His face crumpled. Tears spilled, spoiling the kohl even more.

Good heavens, where was his pride, his *asshak*? "Pull yourself together, Rachid," I said harshly. "Your brother is my king, and I am his Special Guardian and his most loyal subject. There is nothing more to it than that."

Then I pushed past him, banging the door on my way out. I climbed the stairs two at a time all the way to Momo's chamber. There, I did not even bother to knock but barged straight in. "Your brother is a bloody little worm."

Momo was sitting on the divan, his feet up on a tapestried stool. He was bareheaded and wore—or perhaps more correctly, half wore, a brocaded silk robe that had fallen from one side, revealing a golden shoulder and smooth pectorals. The sight of him unmanned me, putting my fury out as surely as water on a fire. He stared at me, then pulled his robe straight. "Rachid? He's harmless. Don't you knock anymore? I might have been doing . . . anything."

"You don't do anything up here," I said pettishly, sounding like the object of my earlier wrath.

"I've been studying." A pile of books towered beside the divan. "A king needs to acquire as much knowledge as he can. "I'm reading the *Picatrix*, trying to understand the nature of prophecy." He gestured for me to take a seat among the colourful floor cushions, and as I did so, straightened up, pulling the robe closed over his distracting chest; then he read at length from the book in his lap. I caught the words *convergence and diversion of planets, fixed stars as a reference* and *a woman wearing a red dress and rope* . . .

During this tedious stuff I fell into a doze and into a deep-buried memory in which the voice of Dr. Ibrahim threaded its way into my mind as I lay in my sickbed drifting in and out of consciousness, my foot swollen and rotting: "Blessings, such a cruel name." A hand lightly on the crown of my head. "Little one, how you have managed to keep your secrets all this time I do not know. Well, it is not down to me to make disclosures. I am a doctor, not a spy."

"Blessings?"

I startled, half in, half out of the memory.

"Are you listening? I thought I might learn more about the conjunction of the stars and how they can affect a man's fate."

The wretched prophecy again. "What use is it to know such things? We're down here and the stars are up there and there's not a damned thing we can do about the way they move," I said briskly.

"Something thwarts me at every turn. All I want is to do the best for my people. But what can I do from this godforsaken place on the edge of the sea? My father is squatting in the Alhambra, getting sicker and blinder every day. And here I am, with a mother who rails at me every day about taking my fate into my hands. Does she expect me to snatch back my kingdom with ten palace guards and a cripple?" He saw the look on my face. "Sorry, Blessings. I'm becoming as mad as a trapped rat in this place. I'll bite anyone who comes at me. How is your leg?"

"Still missing."

"I really am sorry—that was uncalled for. I am frustrated at every turn. Even Mariam won't talk to me. I can't remember the last time we—"

I felt like putting my hands over my ears and singing *La la la la* to drown him out, like a child avoiding a parent's scolding.

"Sorry," he said again.

"You don't need to keep apologizing. You're a sultan, remember? I'm just Blessings, a poor heathen cripple from the deserts of deepest Africa."

If he heard me, he gave little sign of it. He put his head in his hands and muttered, "Do the stars hate me, Blessings?"

"How could anyone hate you?" It was exquisite agony not to be able to put my arms around him and try to comfort him. But what comfort could I bring him? It was I who had betrayed him. "There must be something that can be done about Mariam. Have you sent her gifts? Perfumes and silks? Dishes of sugared nuts and little almond biscuits?"

He looked up. "My gifts come back unopened. I even sent troubadours to sing to her while she was in the *hammam*. She threw her pot of olive paste at them and screamed at them to be gone. She ate the treats, though. She's getting as plump as a goose. People have even started wondering if she's pregnant, but how can I tell them no, because she won't let me near her? Your mother was a wisewoman: don't you know any love charms?" he asked wryly.

I thought of all the talismans I'd made for him over the years. Small use they had been. "Magic doesn't work," I said sourly.

A frantic rapping at the door prevented further discussion, and Qasim put his head around before Momo could even bid him enter.

"Sire—" He saw me lying there among the cushions and stopped.

Momo waved a hand. "Say whatever you have come to say. I have no secrets from Blessings."

Ah, but he has plenty of secrets from you, said the narrowed glance of the vizier. "Visitors, sire. My spies report a dozen of them, all in black, on dark steeds, approaching along the ravine. I suspect they bring messages from your father. You should, uh, dress yourself, sire, and come downstairs."

Momo considered this. "Messengers? At this hour?" He sighed. "Well, I suppose they have had a long, hard ride. Tell the cook and have some rooms readied for them. And roust out the stable boys."

"Yes, sire." He turned to go. "Blessings, perhaps you could go to the stables?"

"Blessings will stay to help me with my turban," Momo said firmly, dismissing him.

Qasim flicked another look at me before closing the door behind him with a whisper. He did creep around so: he might not trust me, but I knew not to trust him.

"I don't like the sound of that," I said. "Official visitors don't come in the middle of the night. They find some place to camp and arrive at a proper hour."

By way of answer, Momo turned from me and shrugged off his robe. It shimmered into a heap at his feet, leaving me gazing helplessly at the way his long back tapered into the narrow waist then burgeoned into pale brown buttocks, their perfect roundness dented where the muscles clenched as he walked to where the samite robe and cotton leggings lay discarded on the bed. I forced myself to look away as he stepped into them, then waited for him to summon me to help with the turban, a tricky job: as a man claiming to be the true sultan his turban should be magnificent, and that involved acres of fabric and minutes of careful winding.

Noises outside. Horses' hooves and shouts. It seemed the visitors had arrived and someone was unhappy about something. Maybe the stable master yelling for his lazy staff— Then someone screamed.

The sound went right through me, as grating as steel on stone. I ran to the window. Dark shapes milled about in the courtyard below; then the clouds parted before the moon and I saw clearly men fighting, swords raised, horsemen hacking down palace guards. The fighting ceased as suddenly as it had started and the horsemen rode out of view to the right, leaving dead men in their wake.

"We're under attack!" I cried.

Momo ran to my side and stared down, and at that moment a riderless horse appeared, trailing harness and some black thing, and stood there, trembling in the moonlit square.

"I know that horse," Momo said. I eyed him, disbelieving. "Not everyone is like you, Blessings, who can't tell a horse from a cow."

This was an old joke, though now was not the time for it. On our way to his wedding in Loja I had pointed at some beast pastured in a distant field and claimed it would make a better mount than the wretched animal I was riding. Momo had laughed for three leagues, and had never let me forget it.

"That one comes from the stables in Málaga. I started him under saddle for the first time. You don't forget a horse you have that sort of bond with."

Málaga? Al-Zaghal's capital. The old bastard . . .

Momo grabbed his sword, propped casually in the corner alongside his cherished whetstone all the way from some place called the Ardennes. That was another thing he did up here on his own: you could hear the rhythmic *scrape scrape scrape* of the blade on the stone at all hours of the day and night when he was in a particularly dark mood. "Here!" He tossed me a dagger, and I snatched it out of the air. "And another!" It came sailing toward me. "You can never have too many!"

In two more strides he was at the door. But there he stopped, listening.

Another cry; then boot heels on the stairs.

Shit.

"Bar the door!" I howled. I scampered across the room and grabbed the turban cloth out of his cedarwood chest, then secured one end of it around the stanchion of the window and cast the other end out. "Remember the Tower of the Moon?"

"How could I ever forget?" He slung the sword around his back, hitched up his robe and looked down. The end of the turban cloth had not reached the ground, but it was the best that could be done.

Banging on the door, followed by shouts of "Come out, traitor!"

"Go!" I screamed at him. "Just get out of here!"

He straddled the windowsill. "You'll be right behind me, yes?"

"Yes," I lied. I couldn't climb with just one good leg and my feeble arms, and I knew it. But if I could buy him a few seconds, I would. Without him, there was nothing to live for anyway. His head disappeared from view and I took up a fighting stance, a dagger in each hand.

The noise at the door was terrifying now: crashes and bangs—sword hilts and boots. Little puffs of dust were coming out of the wood; then a big iron nail tore loose and went rattling to the flag-stone floor as a panel cracked.

"Blessings!" His hissed call could have been heard by anyone.

The wood splintered and I saw the gleam of a mad eye on the other side, and I knew there would be nothing I could do to hold up men like the owner of that eye. And my loyal friend would not go without me. Sheathing the daggers, I ran to the window.

Momo was on the stray horse, which was turning nervous little circles below the window. Whatever it had been trailing was gone, and he now wore a dark burnoose over the white robe. "Get a move on, Blessings!"

For a moment I wavered, half in, half out of the window. Then I got hold of the turban cloth, wrapped my one good leg around it and threw myself down.

27

He caught me. Of course he did. Then we were off at a gallop—not for the postern gate but in the opposite direction.

I held on to him, my arms around his waist, my chin thumping against his back. "Where . . . are . . . you . . . going?" It was hard to get the words out.

"Armoury," he said shortly, and seconds later he pulled the horse up and leapt down. "Just hold it there," he told me, as if I had any idea what to do with a nervous horse.

Luckily, he knew his way around the weapons store: moments later he was back with a short recurved bow and a quiver of arrows, a pair of scimitars and some throwing knives. "Here."

I took the bandolier of knives and stared at it stupidly. Did he not remember how poor my aim was? He'd be at greater risk than any enemy.

Momo vaulted back up behind me and, grasping the reins, held me in a strange embrace as he kicked the horse to life again. I could smell his sweat—sweet and salty at once—and felt drunk with the combination of it and my fear, drunk and delirious, so that I only came back to myself at the sound of a woman's scream.

Outside the royal private quarters, a group of people had been gathered inside a tight circle of horsemen. On every side lay bodies in palace uniform. The guards of the Almería alcazaba, unused to active duty, had proven no match for al-Zaghal and his battle-hardened assassins.

"Mariam!" Momo's cry was lost in the general pandemonium.

I watched as one of the horsemen dismounted to advance upon the group, which shrank from him in terror. Even at a distance, I could see that it was al-Zaghal himself: that hawk nose and jutting beard were unmistakable.

"Where is the traitor Abu Abdullah Mohammed? Where is the spineless little shit who signed away our sovereignty to the enemy?"

A woman broke from the group. She was dressed for bed in a billow of fabric and her hair floated free in a nimbus of silver-grey. Any ethereality lent by the moon was soon dispelled by a voice that bellowed like a bull's. "Get away from here, you old vulture! Go and join your poisonous toad of a brother where he squats in my palace! What sort of man are you to come here murdering innocent men and frightening women and children? A coward, that's what! My son is the rightful sultan of Granada and you are not good enough to lick his boots!"

Al-Zaghal took a step toward her, sword raised. Momo pushed me unceremoniously from the saddle and rode toward him, holding the horse between his knees as he nocked an arrow to the bow and let it loose. The missile glanced off his uncle's shoulder, spinning him round so that he lost his footing.

"Get up off your knees, Uncle!" Momo cried. "Fight me like a man, rather than terrorizing women. Or perhaps you remember the last time we fought and I put you on the ground."

Aysha ran toward him. "Don't be such a fool. You think this bastard will fight you with honour? Move any closer and they'll hack you to pieces and feed your parts to the crows! Don't give them what they came for. Your best service to your country and your family is to escape this damned plot and live to rule the kingdom when your father dies, which, *insha'allah*, will surely be soon."

"Shut up, you damned witch!"

Al-Zaghal had got himself to his knees. I saw Momo's gaze travel from his mother to his uncle and knew he was considering rushing in and risking all. But Aysha was not finished: she turned away from Momo, ran at al-Zaghal and spat at him.

I thought then she was sacrificing herself to save her son, that no man could withstand such an insult without reacting violently to the one who'd made it. But I had reckoned without al-Zaghal's cold fanaticism, and his sharp eye. He pushed himself upright, staggered into the group of women and emerged dragging one by the hair. His sword rose and fell in a flash, and the headless body dropped to the ground, spewing gouts of blood that spattered the hysterical onlookers.

How could a man who lived by the word of the Quran stoop to the unholy crime of murdering a defenceless woman? Mariam's eyelids fluttered and she crumpled where she stood.

Al-Zaghal calmly displayed the dripping head by its long black hair. Moonlight caught the dangling glass earrings. With a chill of shock I realized it was Momo's brother, Rachid.

"One less rat in the basket!" al-Zaghal shouted. "And you'll be next."

For a terrifying moment I thought Momo was going to ride him down, then die horribly at the mercy of the dozen Málaga horsemen who stood watching and wary. But he had decided to survive to fight another day, for he hauled his mount around and grabbed me up as he galloped past, and we thundered out of the fortress's gates, past the bodies of the bribed guards who had let these enemies into our midst—and had won eternal silence rather than gold for their act of treachery.

I don't know how we got away, but we did. Put it this way: the horse died under us a day later, keeling over without warning, so hard it broke the short bow in two. "I am sorry, old friend," Momo said over and over. For a moment I thought it was me he was talking to, but when I turned around, I saw him sitting with the horse's head in his lap, stroking its neck, tears streaming down his face in the pre-dawn gloom.

"We can't stop here in the open," I said hard-heartedly, scanning the hills for signs of the pursuit.

Wearily, he got to his feet. "He slaughtered my brother before my very eyes, and I let him do it. My wife wouldn't even look at me I disgust her so much. And now I've driven this poor animal to its death. What use am I? I should let them kill me and have done."

It was exhaustion talking, exhaustion and sorrow. I told him so and, taking him by the arm, dragged him into the cover of the trees. But no riders appeared on our trail then, or till the sun came up: al-Zaghal had given up the chase, knowing, no doubt, that all he had to do was put the word out and some poor peasant would happily lop off the young sultan's head for a fat bag of gold.

And so, in fear of being seen by anyone, we kept to unfrequented goat tracks as we followed at a distance the course of the River Andarax and made our way into the foothills of the mountains, sleeping by day and walking by night, drinking out of streams and eating whatever we could find along the way, which meant not a lot. How I regretted the breaking of the bow by the fall of our horse. By the third day we were starving and thorn scratched, and my poor stump was aflame. Coming down through the trees in a rocky barranca, we heard the unmistakable sound of a muezzin's plaintive cry shimmering through the greying air, and a few minutes later, where the pines parted as we met a wider path, saw a settlement ahead: a few dusty-looking houses in the lee of the cliffs. "I'll go and beg for food," I told Momo. "If they beat me for being a stranger, it's no large thing. And maybe I can discover if your uncle's men have made it this far and whether there's a bounty on your head."

He hugged me so hard I could feel his ribs. He had always been lean, but now he was worn to the bone, and when he held me away from him to say goodbye, I saw the hollows beneath his eyes and cheekbones. "I'll be back soon," I promised fiercely. I left him my sword, but tucked one dagger into the folds of my robe and another into the side of my false foot under its hem, and limped down through the scrub.

It was an hour or so after sun-up and already the village was astir. I could smell bread baking: my stomach roiled. A woman come outside to empty slops gave me a hard, black stare as I approached. I bobbed my head at her, but she gave no indication of acknowledgement so I kept walking, feeling her eyes on my back as I went.

In the small square before the mosque, men were appearing, having made their prayers. *"As-salaam aleikum,"* I greeted the first of them, and *"Wa-aleikum salaam,"* they responded in chorus.

"Lost your flock?" one joked.

I must look like some raggedy shepherd's boy. I managed a grin. "Just a poor traveller."

"Lost your mule, then," said another.

I nodded. "The poor beast died under me some leagues back."

The third man stared at my false foot, protruding from the hem of my robe. "Fancy boot."

My heart skipped. Was I about to be killed for my golden leg? That really would be a cruel jape by the universe. "Lost the other in a game of cards. There's some bugger chasing me to match the pair. You haven't seen him, have you?"

That made them laugh. "You're the first strangers through in weeks, but we'll keep our eyes open!" Which answered one of my questions, at least. The tallest of them clapped me around the shoulders. "You look in need of a good meal."

I admitted to this, and the other two wished me well and walked on, leaving me with Brahim, the tall man. I told him my name in Arabic, and he smiled. "It won't be anything fancy, just porridge and a bit of bread." It sounded like a feast to me, and I said so, making him beam.

His house was of crumbling *pisé*, with a low roof and a hole for a chimney. Dark smoke curled up out of it, bearing with it a delicious odour. He called out as we ducked to enter, "Mina, I bring a good luck with me! This lad is called Baraka."

His wife was small and dark, very pretty, and hugely pregnant. She covered her hair quickly at the sight of me, took my hand, raised it quickly to her lips, then released it and touched her hand to her heart. A lovely greeting, and unexpected. I was so touched by it that tears sprang to my eyes. I mumbled out my thanks for her hospitality and hoped she hadn't noticed.

The porridge was nothing special—a thick and largely tasteless gruel—but I ate two bowls of it before drawing breath and when I looked up from my bowl, they were both staring at me. I apologized hastily for my greed.

"What are you running from, Baraka?" Brahim asked.

I stopped with the spoon halfway to my mouth.

"It's clear from the state of you," Mina said. "Those rips in your clothing are fresh and there are some brambles left in the cloth, which is of good quality, better than anything we could afford. You've been walking at night, without a light—and no one does that in this hard terrain except out of dire necessity."

I let the spoon fall into the near-empty bowl and gazed helplessly at her.

"Are you really travelling alone?" Brahim asked quietly.

I wanted to lie. It was never usually a problem to me. But—maybe unmanned by their kindness and the sudden shock of food to my aching stomach—somehow I found I couldn't. "No. My . . . friend is waiting for me in the barranca."

"Have you or he committed some crime?" he pressed.

"No. We're fleeing from people who want to kill him."

Husband and wife exchanged a glance. Then Mina leaned forward and took my empty hand between both of hers. "You poor thing. You must love him very much that you choose to share his fate."

I almost fainted; then the tears came springing out. Brahim stared at her then at me. So this was all it took to break down all the defences I had built up all these years—three days' hunger and lack of sleep and a little kindness. "No one who knew him could fail to love him," I sobbed.

"Does he know?"

I shook my head, wordless.

"You poor thing. Love unspoken is the heaviest burden."

And that just made me cry all the harder.

Brahim got up and silently left. A few minutes later he was back with a bulging sack and two *gerbas*, goatskin bags, full of water. "Give Baraka the bread, Mina," he said.

Mina wrapped two hot loaves in a scarf of fine white cotton and pushed them into my arms, where they burned like little suns. "Go with God. I hope he's worth your love."

"*Tanmirt, shokran.*" I dipped my head. "I am not worthy of his," I whispered, truly miserable now.

Outside was a hobbled mule. "When you reach Abla, ask for a man called Tahar the Tall and tell him Little Brahim sent you. He's my brother. Give him the mule and say if he'll exchange it for a good horse, I'll pay him the difference. And if you meet shepherds along the way, tell them Mina sends her greetings. It'll be a rare herdsman between here and Abla who isn't a cousin. And be careful: you are running a great risk to take on such a disguise."

When I returned with the mule, the waterskins, the still-hot bread and the sack, which turned out to contain handfuls of dates, goat's cheese and strings of dried tomatoes and figs from the kind couple's cold-store, Momo's eyes became as round as plates. "You've really lived up to your name, Blessings."

After this, we met kindness after kindness as we went, as if the journey—despite the awful circumstances in which it had begun—was Granada's gift to its young sultan. And everywhere we went the story was the same: poor people struggling to survive, scratching a hard living out of the thin soil and bare pickings of an earth baked hard and dry by drought, from communities decimated by years of privation and war. Over and again—around campfires on mountains where goats baaed in the night from their makeshift enclosures, in valleys where the Andarax flowed out of the eastern Sierra Nevada, in scant woodlands in which no birds sang—we heard the same story: how the young men had gone away to war with the unbelievers and never returned. How wives were left widows and mothers bereaved; how there were none but old men for the young girls to marry; how families no longer had enough money to buy seed or fodder, let alone to pay taxes; how children were growing up wild and fatherless.

The power struggles for Granada's throne were of little concern to these people. No one spoke of sultans or kings, of battles or honour. Too far from the cities to care who was in charge of them, they talked of simple things: of sick babies and the price of flour, a broken plow or the merits of a fine bull.

Momo listened to everything, his eyes gleaming with a sort of sympathetic fanaticism, devouring it all as if to feed his starved soul. When we were alone, he said to me, "You see? I have always said it. It doesn't matter who is in control of the country, as long as there is peace. They have nothing these people, nothing but scraps. All they want is to be left alone, to love and marry and raise their children and their herds and crops, to go to mosque and make a Friday couscous: without the threat of war."

We made the promised exchange of mule for horse. As we left, Tahar the Tall came running after us with a fresh mule. "If my brother gave you a mule, how could I do less?" A prosperous man in comparison with his sibling, he added fresh clothes and some coin, despite our protests.

We headed ever north and west and I managed at long last to master the art of the throwing knives by skewering an unlucky rabbit that crossed out path: we dined like kings that night. A day later we arrived at a crossroads in open country I vaguely recognized, and here Momo halted his horse for a long moment, gazing west. He said nothing, but his eyes were misty; then we rode on. It was only later I realized it was the road to Granada, the one we had ridden years ago after Momo's escape from the Tower of the Moon.

We skirted Guadix, the town that had welcomed us in after that moonlight flit via the hills to its south, but we did not dare approach it. So many of those who had once supported the young sultan now paid homage to the old one. None of the nobles would welcome him with open arms now, except to capture him and send his head to his father or uncle and claim their reward.

And so, at last, we crossed the border, secretly, by night, close to where we had re-entered Granada after Momo's imprisonment by the Castilians. A boy was paid to carry a message; a token was returned.

The next day, the Great Captain, Gonzalo Fernández, rode out to accompany us into Córdoba.

We were given plush quarters in the royal palace. Yes, back there again: another capitulation, but there was no choice. Don Gonzalo requested an audience for Momo with Queen Isabella. She was polite and smiled often during their interview, but her eyes throughout were flinty. It was clear to me that we were captives in all but name and that no matter how well we were treated her attitude to any man, woman or child who did not truly espouse the Catholic Church remained unbending. Momo asked to see his son: it was one of the reasons he had voluntarily returned to this city.

"Alfonso is making great progress in his studies. It would be . . ." She fiddled with one of her pearl earrings as she sought the word. "Counterproductive to interrupt them." It was all I could do to translate without weeping as I watched Momo's expression change to one of utter despair. But worse was to come. The queen said something I did not catch, except for the word *infantil*: but how could I ask her to repeat it?

"What?" Momo asked. "What did she say?"

"I'm sorry," I said quickly, trying to keep my face immobile. "I didn't understand." Our audience with the queen ended shortly thereafter, and I went in search of more information.

The baby had died: unable to keep down the milk of the wet nurse, it had vomited itself into oblivion without even making it as far as Córdoba. The queen had been furious, storming around the palace, cursing all Moors and swearing she would have Momo's head. There were whispers that the wet nurse had been turned over to the Inquisition and burned as some sort of witch. I went outside into one of the tranquil little courtyards and could not choke back the tears. My soul was well and truly damned.

It was there that DonGonzalo came upon me. "What is it, Blessings? What's the matter?"

He held my upper arms and turned his wide, golden gaze on me. I told him and he nodded. "Yes, I know. It's very hard when a child dies. I'm very sorry for it."

"I can't tell him," I sobbed. "It's my fault and I . . . can't. All the palace servants were questioned. They never found the 'girl' who stole the child. He had men scouring the countryside when it was snatched. He has no idea it was given to . . . to . . ."

"The enemy?"

I nodded dumbly.

He shrugged. "Well, it can't be helped. He'll have others. And at least the boy is thriving and the queen has settled for just the one child."

"She won't let him see . . . Alfonso."

Gonzalo sighed. "He has to understand the lad is a hostage now, not a guest."

"Like us?"

That made him uncomfortable. "It's different. Still . . ." He brightened. "At least he's safe here, eh?"

Ironic, that the only place Momo could be truly safe was in the hands of his enemies. I pondered this often over the next months. Letters came periodically from Qasim Abdelmalik. They came unsealed, as he knew our captors would read the contents before allowing Momo to have sight of them, and sometimes parts of them were missing, as if they had been censored. He assured us that Aysha and Mariam remained "in health," but did not elaborate. We heard from other sources that sixty men had lost their lives in al-Zaghal's treacherous assault on Almería. He gave us news of enemy attacks on the towns of Álora and Setenil and told us that Christian troops had marched across the plain below the Alhambra, close enough to be seen by the lookouts in the towers. Apparently, Moulay Hasan—now reportedly fully blind, rising seldom from his bed—had sent out messengers bearing gifts to King Ferdinand and an offer to resume tribute and to honour treaty terms. All had been sent back with a terse refusal.

"The king scents victory," Momo said gloomily. "Now that he can smell it he'll accept nothing less."

In the spring, the enemy besieged the strategically important town of Ronda in the *taifa* of Málaga. The fortress, perched above a dramatic gorge, controlled the roads to the south. No army could move on the crucial ports of Marbella or Málaga without first taking control of it. The siege was short: we heard nothing of it till the action was over.

"'My liege,'" I read aloud from the latest letter from Qasim. "'It pains my heart to report that Ronda has fallen to the forces of King Ferdinand of the united kingdoms of Aragón and Castile after a thorough bombardment by their lombard guns, which reduced the outer walls to rubble, and brought ruination upon much of the populace.'"

Momo interrupted me. He was grey in the face. "Those walls were as thick as a man is tall. How in God's name could they be shattered? What necromancy is this lombard gun?"

'They call them 'the wallbreakers,'" I told him. I'd heard this around the palace.

"How could they destroy a city and the people within from a distance? What honour lies in such warfare, when a man does not face his enemy and fight him hand to hand but kills without even seeing the damage he does? Where's the chivalry in that?"

This, I could not answer. I continued to read from the missive: "'The elders of the city offered their surrender, promising to be loyal vassals to the Crown of Castile, to pay taxes and tributes and to release all their Christian captives. In return, the king has promised that those who wish to leave may travel in peace, while those who choose to remain may do so, and that the town may preserve the law of Mohammed.'" Here, I paused. "What does that mean?" I asked. "About preserving the law of Mohammed?"

He looked weary. "That they may continue to worship as they please and that the legal tribunals continue to hold sway. It's the least that could be promised in the circumstances. But it is something. I believe Ferdinand to be a man of his word: now we'll see if I am correct in that belief."

I scanned the rest of the letter. None of it was good news. But I read it out anyway: "'From Ronda, the enemy's army advanced southeast toward Marbella. Having heard the fate of Ronda, the caids, elders and citizens contacted the king, requesting the same terms as those applied there: that those who wished to stay to be allowed to do so as subjects of Castile, the remainder given safe conduct to leave.'"

Momo listened with his eyes closed. After a long minute of silence he stood up and paced to the window, rested his hands on the sill as he gazed out over the rooftops that once had been the houses of Muslims, Jews and Christians living together in relative tolerance and peace. "Next they'll march on Málaga," he said grimly. "They must take it if they're to stop reinforcements coming in from North Africa. But my uncle will never give up Málaga till every soul within its walls is dead. I must go back and rally my forces. I am the only one who can broker a true peace and prevent complete disaster."

But the campaign had taken a heavy toll on the king's resources, for the next month Ferdinand returned with the army to Córdoba to regroup and, I heard, to prepare to march again with his men and stores replenished in the spring. At once, Momo sought audience with him, asking that he be allowed to return to Granada. "I can be of greater service to you there than here," he told the king. "Wherever I reign, I can maintain our treaty and keep the peace."

It seemed to me that Ferdinand was not much interested in keeping the peace. He laughed and clapped Momo on the back, false hearty and impatient. "I'll give you an escort back to your kingdom," he promised.

It was only when we made our departure that we found out where our destination was to be. "Huéscar?" Momo could hardly believe it. I had not even heard of the place. "*Huéscar?*"

The captain of the guards assigned to escorting us was not best pleased by the task. "That's the better part of a month," he grumbled.

"It's in Murcia, not on the moon," Momo said shortly, but I could tell he was hardly any more pleased.

"It's the arse end of nowhere," the captain said.

By the time we arrived in Huéscar, I could not help but agree. I had thought Almería a backwater: this was little more than a village. I supposed Ferdinand had decided Momo to be a nuisance and wished to get him as far out of the way as possible, where he could do no damage and rally no troops. The people who came out to watch our strange parade into their town looked bemused, as well they might. There was no fortress here, no castle, just a lonely tower, a dilapidated mosque, two once-grand villas that had fallen into semi-ruin, broken capitals and pillars from some Roman site, a scatter of humble dwellings, an Arabic cemetery and an old plague-hospital. We did our best with the tower.

A few days after we'd settled in, Qasim Abdelmalik arrived. He looked grave and exhausted, and for a moment I thought it must be something terrible that had caused him to ride so hard he had almost killed himself—the news of Mariam's death. Or Aysha's. But it was a more momentous death altogether that he'd come to report.

Momo helped him down from his horse. The vizier grunted as he dismounted: he was not getting any younger and long hours in the saddle had made his hips ache. When he went down on one knee, I thought they had given way; but he bowed his head in formal homage. "Sire, accept my condolences, and my continued service to your throne."

I didn't fully understand what was happening until Momo raised him up. "When did he die?"

"A week past. I rode as fast as I could." Qasim sounded defensive.

"I thought he'd leave the kingdom to my uncle."

Momo looked alert and intent in a way I had not seen for months. Years.

"He did: before he died, he invited al-Zaghal to take the throne, and the old bastard marched into the city at the head of a cavalry column, their saddles garnished with the heads of a hundred Christians they ambushed on the way. He sent your father packing and the old man took himself off to Salobreña with Zoraya and their children and whatever treasure they could haul with them. But on his deathbed Moulay Hasan recanted and changed his testament. You are once more and without question the rightful sultan of Granada."

28

Loja

We stared over the battlements at the massed ranks of enemy troops down in the Genil Valley, and the large contingent on the Heights of Albohacen. Momo's mouth was set in a long, hard line. There was grime on his forehead, seamed into the furrows. He seemed to have aged a decade in the past short weeks and suddenly I could see his father in him. Which was not a welcome thought.

"What are those things they are setting up?" I inquired, but I had a nasty idea I knew. Whatever they were, hauling them up the road they had cut out of the hill opposite appeared to have required an entire battalion of men, a mile of rope, half a hundred horses and mules, and the determination of an enemy hell-bent on our destruction.

"Our doom," Momo said shortly, and turned away.

His moment of triumph following the death of his father had been all too brief. Before he could make the journey all the way back west from Huéscar to reunite with his family, re-enter the Alhambra and take up the reins of power, more news arrived. Violent fighting had broken out in the Albayzín and elsewhere in the kingdom between his supporters and those of his uncle, who contested the will of Moulay Hasan, claiming that his brother had not been in his right mind when rescinding the previous testament. As a result, a council of elders had, in these rare and dangerous circumstances, convened to declare that the realm be divided in two, with al-Zaghal taking control of the major cities of the centre and south of the country—Granada, Málaga, Velez-Málaga, Almería and Almuñécar—and Momo only the smaller northern region, centred here, in Loja.

Momo had stared at the rolled message in disbelief, rereading it over and again, examining the veracity of the seals. "They can't mean it. Surely they can't!"

But Qasim Abdelmalik just shook his head sadly. "They're cowards, sire. They've given in to pressure from your uncle to create a buffer zone between him and the enemy, with you in the middle. It's clever."

"This is wrong! The throne is mine: my father left it to me."

And all that was true, but as the vizier calmly and patiently explained, Momo had no choice but to bow his head and sign this miserable agreement. The council had spoken, and in any case he had neither the troops nor the finances to wage a war on his uncle, who had the men and resources of the richest cities in Granada behind him.

Momo took his fury out on the missive, grinding its wax seals to powder beneath his boot. He had come so near, but he was now further from his dream than ever before. "My uncle will fight till there is nothing and no one left to rule over. He'll drive the kingdom into the ground and every city will suffer the same cruel fate as poor Ronda, smashed to ruin."

His words looked to be prophetic.

On the day we rode through the gates of Granada, up the hill into the Alhambra, no birds sang where usually there were linnets and chaffinches, blackbirds and wood pigeons calling and cooing, as if they knew this was no occasion for celebration, and that Sultan Mohammed XII had come not to claim his throne but to sign the largest part of the kingdom over to the man who most wished to see him dead. But it seemed no one had told the famed roses not to bloom: their scent hung hot and heady over us as we dismounted and walked, in the midst of a heavily armed guard, into the Court of Myrtles and thence into the council chamber, where, with his anger simmering dull and quiet, he had signed the wretched agreement, then declined to stay another minute in al-Zaghal's presence.

The silent reflections in the beautiful pools, the elegant stone forests of pillars, the tawny towers and pantiled roofs, all seemed to mock us as we strode out, boot heels ringing on ancient stone.

"This place is poisoned for me forever," Momo said to me as we remounted, and his eyes glittered.

As we rode out of the city, set to retrace the route we had taken all those years ago when he had gone to claim Mariam as his bride, we came upon a small throng, and at its centre the thread-bare prophet from the Sacromonte. Seeing Momo, the old monster had cried out, and everyone turned to stare. "Look, there he goes, the Unlucky One! Keep the faith, young Mohammed: have no further relations with the infidel, for all they do is mine the ground beneath your very feet! Now you must choose: be a king or a slave, for you can't be both!"

Cheers and catcalls greeted this insulting pronouncement: I wanted to ride in among the rabble and sever the old greybeard's noisy head from his shoulders, but Momo held me back. "Why punish a man for speaking the truth? I really am what he calls me, the Unlucky One."

After that he didn't speak again in the two long days it took us to reach the fortress of Loja, where he and Mariam had been married, where La Sabia's poison had nearly done for me. Since the death of its lord, Mariam's father, old Ali Attar, at Lucena, where Momo had been taken captive, the people of Loja had increasingly blamed the young sultan for all the ills that had befallen the kingdom. As he rode in to make the citadel his capital, there were hisses and insults. Momo claimed not to have heard them, but I did.

I put on women's clothes and mingled with the staff to ascertain what threat there might be to him in this grim place. Many complained about the upheaval, others of having their jobs taken by newcomers. More worried that his arrival would bring the enemy down upon them, and that the wily old al-Zaghal had sent him up here to draw their sting, to be the idiot encouraged to put his hand in the hornets' nest. As once I had done for my mother, as all these years I had done for Qasim, I carried the whispers back to my lord, who put his head in his hands.

"The worst of it is, I suspect they are right, Blessings." And he handed me a letter that had arrived by courier from Córdoba.

I scanned the contents, frowning over one or two unfamiliar terms, then translated it for him, with a cold nausea feeling spreading through me like a deathly sickness:

"'By making this union with your uncle you have broken the terms of our treaty. Instead of acting as our vassal, you have now declared yourself an enemy combatant and as such have forfeited any and all right to our protection and forbearance. We have torn up that worthless contract and fed it to the fire, which was its only practical use. All Granada shall be ours: prepare to be attacked.

"'Ferdinand, king of Aragón and Castile.'"

That was three weeks ago: more than enough time for us to run away. But Momo had been determined. He'd organized defence work, getting his hands dirty with the rest of them, digging trenches and shoring up the weak points in the fortress walls; but until now I don't think he'd ever really believed Ferdinand meant what he'd said. Yet now here he was outside our walls, the enemy king, with his tents and banners, his cavalry of thousands and host of foot soldiers. And the damned lombards, his famed "wallbreakers."

"Ferdinand said he'd support me against my uncle." Momo glowered at the faithless enemy. "But he has traduced every promise."

I gazed out at the horrid scene. "He was just waiting for an excuse to declare the treaty null and void." *All Granada shall be ours.* I shivered. "You won't fight, though, will you?"

Momo dragged his glower away from the enemy and turned to look at me. Such exhaustion in his eyes. "I will not run," he said stolidly "I won't have them call me coward."

I wondered who 'them' referred to: the Castilians, or the people of Loja? If the latter, it was already too late, for they said little else, comparing him unfavourably at every turn with their valiant old dead lord. I hadn't told him this, of course; nor that they wondered where their beloved little Lady Mariam was, or mentioned their conjectures about his relationship with me, since they saw us always together. To my shame, the first time I'd heard someone say it my heart had swelled with something akin to joy.

". . . must choose."

Momo was eyeing me. "You weren't listening, were you, Blessings?"

I shook my head, ashamed to have been caught with my wits wandering.

He put his hands on my shoulders. "I said, we have to stop them before they have set up all their lombards, or they'll batter down our walls. I will ride out with our troops, but I won't order you to ride with me, as there's a very good chance you won't come back. You must choose."

"You can't!" I was aghast. "They outnumber us by—" My imagination failed me: I had never seen so many men together in one place.

"I know. And I can't say I'm not afraid. I've witnessed men die on a battlefield and it's not a pretty death. But neither will I meekly give Loja up, especially to this infidel king who clearly thinks I'm so weak that he can break our treaty with impunity." He paused, considering. "Actually, I'm ordering you *not* to ride out with me."

"But I'm your Special Guardian." The reminder came out like the bleat of a petulant child. It wasn't even that I wanted to fight: I knew I wasn't capable, and had contributed to his capture at Lucena.

Momo drew me to him fiercely, crushing my head against his collarbone. "You're a brave soul, Blessings. I know you'd give everything, even your life, for me. But I couldn't bear to see you hacked about by the enemy. It's selfish of me to forbid you to ride out. But I do." And with that he released me and ran off down the stairs, calling for the page and the armourer as he went.

Left dizzy by this unexpected embrace, I was slow to react. When I tried to chase him down the stairs, I couldn't catch him, hampered by my false leg and the press of attendants. So, in desperation, I hobbled out to the stables, my stump reminding me with every step why I couldn't go with him. There was his horse: a proud bay stallion. Not as flashy as the white that had been captured at Lucena, but well enough looking, I supposed. One of the standard bearers was holding it in readiness. "For the sultan?" I asked, and he smiled and nodded.

Out of sight of the flag waver, I slid a morsel of paper beneath the saddlecloth, against the spine of the stallion that would bear my beloved into battle without me. It was not much for a Special

Guardian to do: especially one who had rather lost his belief in the efficacy of charms.

I watched Momo ride out at a gallop across the Genil Bridge at the head of his cavalry: proud men on proud horses bearing the red-and-gold banners of the Nasrids and the green-and-gold of Islam. Proud, doomed men. I saw them charge the enemy and catch them unawares—for a minute, no more: then there was just a chaos of men and horses and swords and dust as they came together, and I could barely see a thing. For a moment the dust cleared and I saw one of our banners fall. Then another. I clutched the wall, straining my eyes for a sight of Momo: and there he was, sword rising and falling, the bay no more than a twisting shadow under him, like a djinni, I thought, but one compelled by my command. My charm was working—it was working: I saw one enemy after another tumble beneath his blade. No one could land a blade on him. No one—

And then I could not see him. The mill of fighting was too fierce, the light making a bright miasma of the dust churned up by hoofs and feet. Where were our banners? Where was our sultan? More of the enemy were joining the fight. I could see them charging down from the gun emplacement on the Albohacen, the light sparking off their helmets and weapons. The air was full of the sounds of men howling in hatred, in fury, in fear; in pain. The noise came at me in waves, but still I could not see him. I stared until my eyeballs hurt, and then the great mass of fighting men parted and a trickle of cavalry poured out of it, like water from a cracked bowl. Two banners still flying—two out of dozens. My heart jumped and stuttered as the survivors clattered back toward the bridge. There he was! I saw him slumped over his horse, his head lolling, pulled along by two of the *faris*. "Is he dead?" I screamed down with all the force I could muster, but my voice came out tiny and afraid, like your voice in a nightmare when you try to scream for help, and fail.

No one answered me. I tried again, but no one replied, and I began to wonder if it really was all a dream, a terrible one from which I could not wake. I ran down the stairs, my hands like claws from gripping the battlement so tight for so long, and at the bottom turned the corner and found a chamber stuffed with people running back and forth with water and cloths. The air was thick with groans and the smell of blood, and there he was, sitting half naked on the edge of a divan with a bandage around his head, holding one arm out as they examined his wounds. The next thing I knew, I was on the ground, my cheek smacking the cold stone with an audible *thwack*. The relief that he was still alive was so great that my knees had given way.

When I got up again, he raised a wan face to appease me. "Blessings, Blessings, don't look so aghast—it's just a scratch."

A scratch it was not. Neither was it a graze nor a cut, but a jagged gouge carved wet and red out of livid, bruised flesh. Whatever weapon it was that had done the damage had missed his heart by no more than a finger's breadth: I could see the glint of bone-cage. The sight made my innards quail: I'd come so close to losing him. "What have they done to you?"

He waved my concern away. "It was a mace, a lucky strike. They think I broke my collarbone, maybe a rib too." He winced as the doctor probed the area, pulling fragments of silk undershirt out of the mess. "I'll heal. I always do."

The patching up was making my gorge rise. I thought it likely I would lose my *asshak* by spewing in front of them all, but the doctor, a small Jewish man with a severe profile and neat grey beard, took me firmly by the shoulders and propelled me outside: "You're doing no good here, to him, or to anyone else. Let me do my work and he'll live, though he won't fight again soon."

This pronouncement cheered me somewhat. I hastened down to the kitchen and begged a number of ingredients from the bemused staff, mixed them up in an old pot, then went down to the front gate and scattered the mixture, grains and flour, some stinking, fermented butter, a handful of raisins and some chopped dates. A little cinnamon, some cumin seeds. No salt. Djinn abhor salt. I chanted the words my mother had taught me, and for good measure scratched the protective symbols into the sandy ground there. Then I went to the stables and asked after the sultan's horse.

"Over here, my lord."

No one ever 'my lorded' me. I wondered what he saw when he looked at me, this scruffy stable hand. He was dark skinned, and only a handful of years younger than I, dressed in a thick wool tunic stained and patched and too short at the wrists, while I stood half a head taller and wore a robe trimmed with fine embroidery. Was that all it took to distinguish us? And yet less than a decade before, I had been eking out a desperate living on the streets of Fez, a filthy desert orphan just as dark as this one, before the merchant found me—

". . . not a scratch on him."

His words broke into my thoughts and I realized he had guided me to the stallion, which stood in its stall cheerfully munching from a nosebag. Someone—probably the lad beside me—had removed the stallion's saddle and harness, though the embroidered saddle-cloth still lay on the horse's back. I ran my hand down the animal's hot neck while he tossed his head and blew noisily, as if I were aggravating him. The charm I had made was still in place and I palmed it, feeling uncharitable thoughts toward the beast as I did. *It was not meant for you*, I told the stallion in my mind, and as if in riposte, the animal kicked out and barely missed me.

"Come away, my lord. He's a bit on edge from the battle. But you can tell the sultan he's just fine." The lad adjusted the nosebag and rubbed the beast's poll with his rough hand and the horse thrust his head against him adoringly.

"More than can be said for his rider," I grumbled, and turned to leave.

"Sir?" The voice was tremulous.

I turned back. "What is it?" The question came out more curtly than I'd intended.

"He will save us, won't he, the sultan? From the unbelievers? I seen them things they're setting up on the Albohacen. My brother, he was smithing in Ronda when they used them machines to break the walls. Stonework that thick—" he spread his arms wide "— and they smashed it down flat. The noise were so fearsome it still rings in his head. And him used to the sound of iron on stone. Days of it, he said, on and on, like giants stamping on ants. He's never been the same, hasn't lifted a hammer since then, can't stand the sound of it. My big brother, he were a hero to me, and now he just sits at home and stares at nothing. There's hardly anything left of him now."

I spoke not a word, but it didn't stop him.

"They won't do that here, will they? Bash down the walls? I honestly don't think he could bear it again. And the horses too, sir: noise frightens them something terrible. The young sultan won't let Loja be smashed up and us all inside it, will he, sir?"

Momo had ridden out to try to stop the enemy setting up those guns, tried and failed, and from what the doctor had said he would not be riding out again: but how could I tell that to this lad, whose imploring eyes searched mine, as if I held any answers? "I'm sure he won't," I said, and left before he could see the lie in my face.

By the time I got back to the chamber where the wounded were being tended there was much noise and bustle but no sign of Momo. At the back of the room I saw the mounded shapes of men with just their feet protruding from beneath a white sheet and for a sharp moment terror gripped me. I stood there, sweating, staring at the footwear: scuffed riding boots, low brown boots, worn ochre babouches, grey shoes, boots with a curled toe; but no fine, soft red leather boots. Two corpses with yellowing bare feet. None was as finely boned as Momo's. And life was going on pretty much as normal, in a time of war. I reasoned with my panicking, illogical self that if the sultan had bled to death, or had fallen from a crisis of the heart, I'd have heard the ululations of grief all through the fortress. I found the doctor who had been tending him sawing through the shattered leg of an unconscious man. Transfixed by the vile spectacle of all that blood and bone, I thought: *They did that to me.* I had meant to ask the doctor where my lord was, but the horrid sight had unmanned me completely. Reeling, I threw up in a corner.

When I finished vomiting, to wash the foul taste from my mouth and restore my *asshak* I drank some of the wine they were using to clean wounds and went to look for Momo. There was no sign of him in his quarters. On the stairs outside, soldiers ran past me, their armour clanking, their boots loud on the old stonework. I expected someone to order me to fetch my sword and fall in, but no one did.

In the room the sultan used for conferences with the town elders, I found only a knot of old men hunched over glasses of herb tea, who stared at me with inimical black eyes then looked away, as if I were a ghost.

Like a ghost, I drifted up to the battlements, where I found a crowd peering over, wailing and praying. I elbowed my way between them, in time to see the tatters of a column fleeing back toward the side gate, not the one from which Momo had issued on his last excursion against the enemy, where I had strewn my offering to the spirits. With my heart in my throat, I gripped the top of the wall and peered and peered. Three horsemen, riding at full gallop, passed beneath us. None of them was Momo. Then two riderless horses, neither of them the mount the stable hand had been tending to—which was surely a good sign, wasn't it? "The sultan?" I clutched at the shoulder of the man beside me, my voice shrill above the racket. "Have you seen the sultan?"

For answer, he pointed. I followed his finger but saw no red-robed horseman, only some foot soldiers trying to break free of the press while four of our knights attempted to hold the enemy at bay. The soldiers were dragging something between them, straining, determined despite the threat to their lives. The something was red. And I knew. In that second I knew in the pulsing chambers of my heart the very particular shade of that red. Nasrid crimson: worn by the sultan when leading an army so that if he was wounded, the royal blood would not show and discourage his men.

I think I screamed. I know I ran. Faster than any one-legged thing should ever be able to, I scrambled down those winding stairs, my cries echoing off the walls. I arrived at the hospital room just as they carried him in like a dead weight, he who was so slim and slightly built, so agile and swift, so charged with energy and glowing golden with life. His head lolled, his helm missing. His eyes were closed, and his face—white as the sheet that covered the dead men—was ghastly with blood, which sleeked his neck and blended with the red of the marlota. His sword with *Only God is victorious* was gone; his fingers curled over emptiness. I could hear the cries of the women in the stairwell, their tongues shuttling relentlessly back and forth. They sounded like the djinn I had tried to banish. He had ridden out without my protection—without his Special Guardian, or the spells that would have kept him safe. The last of my reason fled me. I am told that I ran at the doctor, battered him with my fists until they pulled me off, and still I screeched that it was his fault for sending me away, his fault—anyone's but my own. I lashed out when they dragged me away, twisting in their grip like a wild animal, and locked me in a cell—for my own good, they said as they slid the lock across. I ran at the door. I kicked it with my false foot, kicked it with my good foot, fell screaming to the floor. And lay there, smashing my head against the flagstones until I died.

I didn't die, of course. I wanted to. But the spirits—or whatever rules our lives—wouldn't let me. I lay there in the hell that was left to me, a grim darkness of rumbles and roars in which the world shook and render powdered down out of the walls and distant cries filled the air, and prayed that I would die. I don't know how long I existed in this state between the living and the mad, but at some point light came into the room accompanied by a familiar voice— Qasim the vizier, chiding me in the tone he often took with me, impatience tempered with an edge of irony: "I see you're still with us, Blessings."

I thought he mocked me. "I don't want to be 'with you.' Leave me to die." My head throbbed like a pulped hand and when I touched it, I found it horribly crusted, as if I had grown a beetle's carapace over my face.

The shadow of Qasim's gaunt frame leaned itself against the door. I could feel his contemplation of me, like an insect on the skin.

"Oh, Blessings," he said, a verbal tut. "Such a mummer you are. They thought you'd gone mad, like a rabid dog, said one. People made the sign of the evil eye against you, said they should put you out for the djinn—and they would have if I hadn't put you in here. Such a scene! People bitten, kicked, insulted. Eardrums shattered by your screams, I have no doubt. And for what?"

"Don't you care that he is dead? Of course you don't." I answered my own question bitterly. "I see *you* are still in the land of the living and that's all that *really* matters."

That made him laugh. "Dear God, you really are a vicious little creature, aren't you? It's not surprising, I suppose. They told me as much when I bought you."

That stopped me. "You bought me?"

He tilted his head toward me. "Who did you think bought you as a companion for the lad in the first place? The merchant in Fez is my cousin. He thought I might be interested in you. Said you were 'a fine monster': I thought you might amuse the young prince. It never ceases to amaze me that he hasn't tumbled to the truth. Or just tumbled you, one way or another. It's been . . . entertaining, watching the pair of you dancing around each other: you so needy, he so naive."

The wasteland of the real world tumbled down around me once more. What did it matter that Qasim had been the one who bought me for Momo, now that Momo was dead? I sobbed, quietly now, into my hands, for myself: for him.

He dragged me to my feet. "Just pull yourself together. He's not dead, you unutterable little fool. God knows he ought to be, but he's not. An absurd stunt, to ride out like that when he could barely sit a horse, let alone wield a sword. A heroic charge, they're calling it. Heroic, but completely pointless: he didn't get anywhere near the guns, as even you could probably tell, given the bombardment this place took before we finally capitulated. And hundreds of good men dead—and women and children too—as a result of his wilfulness. A hundred more taken captive by the Marquis of Cádiz, so those ransoms will cost us a whole heap of money we don't have."

I wasn't listening to his merchant tally by now. My slow brain was working its way over and over those three little words. "He's not dead?"

Qasim sighed. "Come and see for yourself—he's asking for you."

He led me up out of the cells. Very quickly it became clear that I had been in the safest place during the enemy bombardment. Dust and rubble and broken glass lay everywhere, smashed pottery, strewn tapestries, shards of wood, pools of blood out of which trailed dark streaks and a mess of footprints. A hole had been blown clean through one wall: a glance out of it into what was left of the town below stopped me in mid-stride. The outer wall lay in ruins, the stables had been flattened; the smithy, the barracks, the grain store, all were gone, reduced to piles of stone and kindling. And over it all presided an eerie silence, as the survivors carried hastily shrouded bodies away for burial. Up on the Albohacen, barely in view, the guns that had wrought this destruction lay quiet. Over it all hung clouds dark with impending rain, casting further gloom on the scene.

"Blessings, you're safe! I wouldn't believe Qasim till I'd seen you with my own eyes." Momo spoke with a slur, lying on a divan, half propped up by cushions, half slumped, looking more dead than alive. A huge bruise covered half his face and his nose had clearly been broken. Someone had roughly stitched up a wound that ran from temple to chin. His left arm was encased in bandages that disappeared under the loose brocade robe that had been thrown over him: he held a pen in his right hand.

"I can read most of it, but some of the terms I'm not familiar with." He beckoned me near to read the document he had been poring over.

Surrender terms: and not just for Loja but for the whole of the northern region he had been vouchsafed by the council of elders. The people of the area were offered safe passage if they wished to leave; if they preferred to stay, they must swear allegiance to the Catholic monarchs and undertake to pay swingeing taxes. Ferdinand and his men would garrison the town; Momo would surrender his royal person and a select group of his nobles into the custody of the conqueror. With some effort Momo crafted the usual provisos: that the population who remained—be they Muslim or Jew—be allowed to continue to live according to their own beliefs, without fear of persecution or violent coercion or conversion, and that the Prophet's laws remain in place. Then eight surviving noblemen, and Qasim and myself, accompanied the litter bearing Momo out to the tent of the enemy king, which was pitched in a clearing on the other side of the Genil River. My prince leaned heavily on me as we made our way inside the tent, where King Ferdinand and his generals awaited us, seated behind a long trestle table spread with a damask cloth strewn with maps and scrolls. Seeing us, Ferdinand cleared a large space with an impatient flourish that sent papers flying. A stool was brought for Momo, but at the last moment his legs failed him and he went sprawling on the rugs, his robe open to show the bandages, his turban askew, and some of the enemy nobles sniggered. I helped him onto the stool and straightened his attire. They knew he'd been wounded, but I could tell from the way he moved how little he wished them to know his weakness and impotence, how much he hated their sneering.

There was a glint of satisfied amusement in the foreign king's regard, but he treated us with courtesy, until it came time for the signing of the treaty. Casting an eye over the amendments, he said something I could not quite catch to the man beside him. This gentleman had an ascetic look to him, his fine-boned face solemn, his dark clothing austere. Maybe one of the crown's inquisitors, I thought. He stroked his neat beard and sat back, and as he did so, I saw beneath his black cloak the shine of a breastplate.

Beside me, Momo drew in his breath sharply. "That is the man who wounded me, I am sure of it."

"I thought he was a priest," I whispered.

"Their priests are forbidden from shedding blood. But this one shed plenty of mine." He glared at the man in conversation with the king; watched as the latter energetically dunked his pen into the inkwell and made a great slashing line. The scoring of quill against paper rasped through the confines of the tent.

"There will be no infidel law in operation in any region under my control," Ferdinand declared with relish. "This proviso is rejected. You will sign here." He spun the sheet toward Momo and thrust the pen at him.

Momo refused to take it. "I will not sign unless I know the people will be left to live their lives in peace."

"Oh, I can assure you of that," Ferdinand said smoothly. "But surely you are aware that this little charade—" he waved his hand around the tent "—is a face-saving exercise. You are in no position to put up any further opposition. I'll admit you gave us something of a fight. Very chivalric, with your banners flying and your cavalry charging heroically at our guns. A pointless gesture: flesh and blood can't withstand missiles. Still, I'm grateful to you for granting me the opportunity to test our excellent lombards, which I think you'll agree are most effective." He showed his sharp little teeth in a wolfish half-smile. "My lord Boabdil, please pay attention to my words." Ferdinand enunciated carefully and looked to me as I translated. "I mean to take this entire kingdom back into the embrace of Holy Mother Church, with the help of my general, Don Rodrigo Ponce de León, Marquis of Cádiz—" The austere man gave us an austere nod. "And I'll brook no further resistance. I'm offering you and your retinue the gift of your lives, but never again shall you take up arms against me. And you're to keep well out of my way while I deal with your troublesome uncle. Agreed?"

He sat back, rocking his great wooden chair on its hind legs, and swung his feet up onto the table, presenting us with the worn soles of his boots. Was he aware of how churlish a gesture this was? How insulting to any Muslim, let alone to another king? He gave no indication of it if so.

"I will not sign."

Momo's face had gone white, his scar in livid relief. I could feel the fury boiling off him.

"Tell him he can behead me, string me up, strap me across one of his damned lombards, but I will not sign."

Qasim leaned in, one hand on Momo's shoulder. "Sire, you must sign: what else can you do? We should have surrendered Loja days ago, while it was still intact. Now it lies smashed to ruin, its population decimated, and for what? A little pride? I understand how hard it is for anyone, let alone a sultan, to be humiliated like this: but even a king's pride is too large a price for his people to pay." He left a pause, then added, "And remember: young Ahmed lies in the foreign queen's hands."

Momo fixed him with a murderous glare. "Do you think I forget that fact for even an instant?" He waited until Qasim gazed aside, then he turned to me. "Tell him I'll sign, Blessings." He might have looked wounded before: now he looked truly defeated.

That evening we rode out of the ruins of the once-defiant town of Loja, leaving behind us a fortress that had become a tomb to its defenders and was now home to its enemies.

29

Vélez-Blanco

Once more we were being taken into exile, this time into the *sharqiyyah*, the far east of the ever-decreasing kingdom of Granada.

"It's the back of beyond," I complained as we passed yet another ruined, unmanned watchtower. "It's like the land that time forgot."

Qasim shifted uncomfortably on his saddle. We were ten days out of Loja, and all our arses were raw from the long ride. "It's not so bad—you'll see."

"You've been here before?"

"No," he admitted.

"Then how do you know? There could be dragons and manticores living in those caves." I gestured toward the pitted hills. "These woods could be full of monsters, hungry for human blood. They're all around us—monsters—or so I've heard."

He winced at the bitterness of my tone. "I'm sorry I called you that, Blessings."

I knew he was not: he just wanted to placate me. I turned my face from him. Something had changed in our dealings since I had discovered his part in bringing me to the palace. My feelings had hardened, and there had been a subtle but significant change in the balance of power, as if this new piece of information had weighed heavily on my side of the scales. Qasim might have saved me from the merchant in Fez who had so ill-used me, but he had employed me unmercifully as a spy, a manipulator, a child-thief. What I knew could bring death upon him, and he realized this. Until now I believe he had thought I valued my own life too greatly to risk Momo's wrath in revealing our plottings; but now he had seen me at my most extreme, seen the urge to self-destruction that lay within me: I was a more fragile vessel for his secrets than he'd thought, and it prompted him to handle me with greater care.

Qasim grinned now, a forced expression that looked ghastly upon him. "The tales you come up with."

The tales I came up with were not mine at all: I had been reading to Momo as he rode in his palanquin, still too weak to sit a horse. I read to him from Arab scholars' translations of Pliny and Herodotus, about dog-headed men, people with the bodies of horses; about prophets who turned from men into women and back again; about tribes of women who lived as men, and men with their feet on back to front. I chose readings as far-fetched as possible to distract him from his gloom, and sometimes I made him laugh. "Such monsters in the world!" he would declare. "I wonder if we will ever come upon any of them."

"I wonder."

I fell back now to the palanquin and stuck my head through the curtains. "Would you like me to read to you?"

Momo lay there, propped on one elbow, staring into space, an open book in his lap. I recognized it.

"Hello, Blessings."

He beckoned me to join him, so I gave my mule into the charge of one of the soldiers and climbed in beside him.

"I've been thinking about the Trojan prince Hector," he mused. "How, despite being the best man he could be—a good husband, a father, a great and fair prince—he was made a martyr to his loyalties, trapped by his position in his family, worn down by his destiny. He was a wise man, Homer. Even if he was a heathen: like you, Blessings."

"He was just a storyteller."

"The ancients believed a man's life was dictated by three fates—Lotho, the spinner; Lachesis, the measurer; and Atropos, the cutter—who controlled the thread of life of every mortal from their birth to their death. Just as we believe that Allah has written the path of our fate in his Book. Strange, isn't it, how over the centuries different peoples have come to the same conclusion, despite their differing beliefs? Surely the wisdom of the ages must mean something, and the prophecy made at my birth must be true. That I would be the last king of this kingdom, that I was destined to lose it." His fingers ran back and forth over the scar on his face, as if he reminded himself of his own mortality.

With a little shiver I remembered my own strange prophecy then, made as I touched his blood, on the statue at the fountain's edge in the Court of Lions: "He will lose everything he loves." He had lost the Alhambra, his beloved home; and his two sons— Ahmed to the Castilian queen, and his unnamed babe too. Mariam still lived; and his mother, for whom his love had become a twisted thing. Could it be true, that fate had us in its grip? Before I could help myself, I asked, "Do you love me?"

He stared at me then, shocked out of his melancholy reverie. "What do you mean?" He sounded agitated, a little angry, as if my question was a stupidity. "Of course I love you, Blessings. You're my friend, my Special Guardian."

That should have made me glad, but all I could think was if there was such a thing as fate and true prophecy, then I too would die. The idea was unimaginable. "I don't believe in fate," I said fiercely. "Life is what we make of it: it's not written in the stars, or in some wretched Book."

He clutched my arm. "Do you really believe that, Blessings? Can I truly rewrite what has been written and save my kingdom?" His eyes burned into me. "But if I allow myself to believe that Allah is not all-mighty, then surely I am apostate? The Christians burn their heretics for less."

"They are a wicked people: cruel, treacherous and wicked. You are a king. If you can't make your fate your own, who can?"

After years in which towers had ruled our lives, now it was messages.

The lookout was a boy of barely fifteen, sweaty from running from the western watchtower in the hot sun. "There are horsemen approaching, sire! They wear the insignia of your uncle!"

Momo was on his feet instantly. "My sword and lance, bring them at once!"

Qasim stayed him with a hand on his shoulder. "Calm yourself, majesty: they're just messengers, I believe. They are armed, but only as you'd expect for dealing with bandits on the way. I'll send out the royal guard to intercept them." His spies were everywhere: I wondered why he had not informed us ahead of the official lookout.

The royal guard consisted of a couple of dozen local men who till recently had been more familiar with plowshares than swords. "I'll go with them, sire."

Momo looked panicked. "I can't lose you, Blessings."

"You won't!" I was already halfway across the chamber, my false leg rattling on the bare stone floor.

There were just four horsemen, and they certainly gave the appearance of messengers: they wore no armour, and bore two bags of jewels as a gift from al-Zaghal to his nephew and a rolled scroll fastened with his seal. When I demanded to see inside the bags, they smiled and nodded with seeming friendliness. "But of course, young lord. It's only right and proper that you should be concerned to protect your prince."

Their "young lord" did not fool me. I reached for the bag, but the man's gloved fingers closed over it. I suppose that had circumstances been reversed, I would have held on to it too: who was to say I would not grab it and gallop away, my fortune made? Who could you trust nowadays, with the kingdom divided and beset by enemies? People were out for themselves, making whatever they could however they could to have enough money to get their families to Morocco if all came crashing down.

The man eased the neck of the first of the velvet bags open to my gaze. Inside I could see the glint of gemstones and the soft nacre of pearls.

"Very nice. And the other one?"

Gold and silver—*doblas* and *maravedis*. The man carrying that bag shook it so that the contents shifted enough that I could see there was nothing more menacing within—no venomous snake or giant scorpion, or whatever threat I had been seeking, but still it seemed odd to me that the man who had tried to kill Momo in Almería and had in a fury of frustration lopped off the head of his little brother, Rachid, should now be offering him jewels and avuncular wishes.

I nodded at last to the head of the guard. "All right, let's take them in."

Inside the palace I watched them looking around, their scorn for our poorly furnished quarters barely disguised. They'd come from the most beautiful palace on the face of the earth, to this crumbling *kasbah* on the mountainside of the Sierra del Mahimón . . . It made a mockery of the greetings they offered, calling Momo "the lord of al-Andalus," "the flower of the Nasrids," "rose of the Alhambra," "defender of the glorious faith of Islam," "true heir of the blessed Hasan," "scion of the greatest of dynasties" . . . The praise rolled on and on. But as the head man offered the scroll on the palm of his gloved hand to Momo, I smelled, just for a fleeting moment, something acrid. In defiance of all royal protocol, I stepped between king and messenger.

"Don't touch the letter," I whispered urgently.

Momo stared at me in bewilderment. "It's just a letter," he chided. "What can you hide in a letter but words?"

"Use your eyes, my lord."

Momo scanned the visitors. They appeared nervous, maybe, but not afraid. His gaze returned to me. "Are you feeling quite well, Blessings? Perhaps you're sunstruck. You rode to meet them without a hat, no?"

I had. "You've answered your own riddle. Look again." And when I knew he'd understood me, I stepped aside.

Momo smiled at the messenger. "Be so good as to read the missive to me."

The man hesitated. "I was instructed to deliver it only into your hands, sire. Your uncle told me so himself."

"Even so." Momo reclined in his throne, watching, watching.

I saw a bead of perspiration appear on the messenger's forehead and begin to run down his nose. Unconsciously, he lifted a hand to wipe it away and the sweat darkened the leather of his glove. With a sigh he broke the seal, unrolled the scroll and read it aloud:

"Desirous as I am to forget the origins of our contentions for
the kingdom, and conscious that you alone are the lawful king,
by virtue of my brother's last will and testament, in which he

appoints you his heir, I wish to surrender the government into your hands as rightful king and master, requesting only for myself to be able to spend my days in some small part of this abode, to live content and to owe you due allegiance. This I require for Allah's and Mohammed's sake, that the kingdom not be destroyed by its internecine quarrels."

At this point the paper, which had been tightly rolled for many days, sprang out of his grip and obstinately refurled itself. The messenger struggled, and failed, to unroll it again, and through it all Momo just sat there, watching him through slitted eyes.

"Keep reading," he said sweetly.

The messenger wrestled manfully with the scroll until at last he mastered it. "It's fine, I've got it." He read on, stumbling here and there in his haste:

"Return, then, as sole king to this city of Granada as its lord and master. I sincerely lament the disturbances that have passed and desire to atone by my future conduct for the part I have taken in them.

From Granada, Moulay Abdullah al-Zaghal"

He held the scroll out to Momo, who made no move to take it.

"How interesting, and how humble," Momo said at last. "My uncle is admitting his error in usurping the throne that is rightfully mine. And seeks to offer me his loyalty." He laughed. "How uncharacteristically generous of him."

The second man bowed and stepped now forward, bearing the bag of jewels. "He sends you these gems to demonstrate his familial love and good faith."

"And these, sire." The third man made his obeisance and set the bag of coins with a rich chinking sound at Momo's feet.

Qasim made to pick them up, but Momo put a warning hand on his arm. "Don't." He looked to the messengers. "Would you take a glass of sherbet?" When they acquiesced, he sent a page running and the boy returned moments later with a jug and glasses of the stuff, the ice already melting in the short distance between the ice-house and the audience chamber.

"Come," he said, "make yourselves comfortable and don't stand on ceremony. Amin, take their outerwear."

Another of the pages ran in and retrieved the men's apparel from them; the fourth man—who held the letter—awkwardly shrugged off his cloak.

The light of comprehension suddenly dawned on the vizier's face. He turned and gestured to the captain of the royal guard. "Seize them!"

There was a scuffle, but nothing more: the "messengers" carried not even a fruit knife between them: we had divested them of their weapons—swords, daggers and a couple of boot stilettos—before they entered the audience chamber. Under questioning they soon capitulated, which took less time than you might have expected from men sent by the fearsome al-Zaghal. All but the leader. I stood before him. There was blood running down his face now, as well as sweat. I felt no regret at having caused it to flow: I knew well what mandrake poisoning could do to a man. It was a miracle I had survived, and I was sure al-Zaghal would not have gently dosed his missive and gifts.

"How did you know?"

There was hatred and madness in his eyes, eyes I had recognized as those of the man who had almost hacked down the door to Momo's bedchamber in Almería all those long months ago.

"You were all wearing gloves. On this, the hottest day of the year." I shuddered, remembering that long-ago chieftain's son writhing in agony. I wondered where al-Zaghal had found a poisoner

323

so clever as to be able to imbue paper and jewels with this terrible decoction.

Momo ordered that the messengers be beheaded and their bodies hung from the battlements. Their heads and a letter addressed to al-Zaghal were dispatched back to Granada. I had never seen him so coldly angry. He had changed, I thought, in the past three years. And when I considered what had happened to him in that time—his capture at Lucena, his imprisonment, the loss of his children, the coldness of his wife and the recriminations of his viperish mother, the loss of his throne and his home, the wounds to both body and soul he had taken at Loja—I supposed it was no surprise that he was a different man to the innocent lad I had loved.

Did I love him any the less for what he had become? Truly, I did not. If anything, I loved him more. And from that day on, I took it upon myself to smell and taste all his food and drink, to check his clothing and blankets. He never asked me how I knew about the mandrake: perhaps because his mind was not on me at all. But I feared what would become of me if he ever discovered my secrets.

Message to Abu Abdullah Mohammed,
rightful sultan of Granada
Jumada al-Thani 13, 891

Sire, I regret to inform you that the town of Íllora, the Right
Eye of Granada, has fallen to the infidel and the enemy then
moved upon Moclín. The women, children and the elderly were
evacuated for fear that the inhabitants of that town would suffer
the same fate as those poor souls in Ronda. God protected them,
but by ill chance a lombard fell upon the tower of the armoury
where our black powder was housed and the explosion was so
great that nothing but ruin remains. Queen Doña Isabella and
her daughter rode into what remains of Moclín to meet with

King Ferdinand, may Allah curse them all. The forces of the infidels now hold all the towns and castles west of Málaga.

Your servant,
Musa Ibn Abu'l Ghrassan of the Banu Serraj

Message to the rightful sultan of Granada
Jumada al-awwal 7, 892

Sire, the world goes in fear following a great shaking of the earth. Some say it is caused by the marching feet of the mighty army of unbelievers now heading for the port city of Málaga under the orders of the Christian king Ferdinand, others that God is trying to wake the faithful to the need to join together to fight to save our kingdom, the last bastion of Islam in the West.

Your uncle Sidi Abdullah Md al-Zaghal this very morning marched his troops out of the city of Granada to face the infidel. He will join forces with the garrison of Vélez-Málaga and with God's grace defeat the heathens. We will hold the gates of the city open for you.

Your servant,
Musa Ibn Abu'l Ghrassan of the Banu Serraj

Musa Ibn Abu'l Ghrassan of the Banu Serraj was true to his word: the gates of Granada were held open for us, then closed against al-Zaghal when he fled back to the city from Vélez-Málaga. The messenger he had sent was captured by the Christians as he tried to make his way to the city to give orders to coordinate efforts between the garrison and al-Zaghal's army. He'd given up his message easily: al-Zaghal had been lured into a trap by the Marquis of Cádiz, from which he'd barely escaped with his life.

Musa and Momo stood together on the battlements of the Alcazaba, watching as al-Zaghal and his straggler army were turned away—one tall and lithe and golden, the other squat and dark with a beard so vast it could house entire colonies of mice. Aysha screamed down at her brother-in-law, "You killed my beautiful Rachid, you black-hearted devil! May you fear the blade in the night and poison in your water! May you die alone in a place where no one even knows your name!"

Unsurprisingly, she and Musa had become great friends: Aysha, defying tradition by being determinedly present in even the public areas of the palace ("I have been a prisoner before, and it shall not happen again!" she had boomed when Momo had suggested she might be more comfortable staying in the harem). To me, they seemed much alike, the tribesman and Momo's mother. Have them switch attire and shear the old man's beard for the woman to wear and I swear you'd hardly notice the difference. Hard and unbending, they egged Momo on to see himself as some sort of saviour of Islam, a hero to his people. I did what I could to provide him with gentler distractions, like walking in the palace gardens where we had grown up together.

We sat now in the Courtyard of the Stained Glass, enveloped by the fragrance of jasmine and herbs. Momo leaned back against a lemon tree and closed his eyes, inhaling, the golden spangles of light from the candle lanterns patterning his cheek.

"Ah, how I love this place. It is balm to my soul," he said, after a long silence. "Look at it, Blessings. Take note of its sacred geometries, see the perfection of its dimensions, and how the pools mirror the scene above, making an exact counterpoint. Life and death, right here before us in the code of the mortal architect and the immortal one: their works a perfect shadow of the other. As above, so below."

All I could see was the inverted reflection of the Tower of the Moon, where he had been imprisoned by his father all those years ago. Now he was imprisoned again, by his own emotional ties to the place.

He turned to me, his eyes on fire. "The Alhambra was created as an earthly paradise. As sultan, my actions are designed to match the patterns God decreed: surely when he wrote my fate, Allah meant for me to strive to offer him my best." He shooed away a night insect that had the temerity to brush his cheek. "I must find a way to protect Islam in this peninsula. I am the only one who can do it, even if it means great sacrifice. The Alhambra has been trying to teach me this: it's been here all along, transmitting this message, but I've been too blind to see it. Here it is, the perfect symbol of our perfect faith, the physical embodiment of a spiritual truth. It must be saved, no matter the cost. I must fight to preserve it, don't you see, Blessings? Only I can save it."

He closed his eyes again before I could respond; but I had no idea what to say. The Alhambra was lovely, that much was true: it had been the scene of many atrocities, yet the serene pillars and elegant towers, oblivious to all the blood spilled, soared away from it into the night, indifferent to the sufferings of mere men. These buildings would outlive us all, I thought. And suddenly I hated the place with savage loathing. It was a cage, a beautiful cage, but a cage all the same. The kingdom of Granada was shrinking, town by town, as the tide of infidels rolled in inexorably: soon we would be cut off, without means of escape. The Alhambra would be an island in the middle of their bloody sea. The Christians would surround us, here on this little hill; then bring their terrible lombards to bear on its walls. They would batter down its gates and hang Momo from its battlements, for the carrion birds to pick clean, the way they had the messengers he had hung from the walls of Vélez-Blanco . . .

The vision seemed so clear to me, so graphic and detailed: his lovely body bruised and smeared, his head lolling, a crow upon his shoulder, pecking and pecking, like the crows on the battlefield at Lucena. I was so gripped by horror that it was some moments before I realized he was speaking again.

". . . the Nasrid dynasty. It is my solemn duty, before God. And surely my body will mend better now that we are here. Now that Mariam is installed in her apartments surely she will remember how it was when we were first together here, how sweetly we loved, and we will make more children, heirs to carry on the task God has set us." He turned to me as if beseeching the answer he needed to hear.

Spiritual sickness gave way to its physical counterpart and I had to swallow the bile that rose suddenly in my throat. I'd got used to having him to myself since he and Mariam had been apart. "I'm sure you'll heal better now that you're here," I said, then added, "but shouldn't you wait till you are hale before making advances to the Lady Mariam?"

He squeezed my shoulder. "I'm sure you are right, Momo: but I may not be granted the grace of such leisure. I have to stop my uncle before he destroys my people."

It was not long before we received a series of messages from the south that bore out Momo's worst fears: the governor of Málaga under al-Zaghal's orders had replied to Ferdinand's request to give up the city with a terse response: *I was sent here to defend, not to surrender*, and had promptly fired the bodies of several captured Christians back over the citadel walls into the enemy camp.

There had been savage fighting. The Christians had paraded throughout their camp the heads of the Muslims they captured; in retaliation, there had been an assassination attempt on King Ferdinand, though the man attacked had not been the king but some lesser noble who resembled him. The Christians had killed the assassin, chopped his body into pieces and catapulted them into the city, where the governor had ordered that the fragments be collected, washed, perfumed and sewn back together with silk thread, then given a martyr's funeral.

Supplies inside the city walls were running low: Ferdinand had blockaded the port and prevented any resupply—of either food or men—from the sea. The messenger reported stories that the people of Málaga had eaten every cow, sheep, horse and mule within the city walls and were starting now on dogs, cats and rats. "Soon they'll be down to the leaves on the trees and the bark on the palms," he said, and burst into tears. "I beg your pardon, majesty: my family are inside the city."

Momo dried the courier's tears with the hem of his robe.

"My God," he said when the man had been taken away. He rubbed distractedly at his forehead beneath the edge of the giant turban. "We must do something or Málaga will be reduced to rubble and its children will be dead of starvation." He summoned Qasim and beckoned to me to follow. Then he wrote a letter to Queen Isabella, for the Málaga courier to bear to her.

By the time he'd finished dictating it, he was shaking. I put my hand on his arm. Briefly he covered it with his hand, then returned it to me. "I must go to Mariam now. Our time here will be limited, and if we're ever to conceive an heir to carry on the dynasty, it'll be within these walls." He gave me a wobbly smile. "Wish me luck."

I returned him a wan reflection of his own smile.

Qasim and I watched him go. He looked not like a man about to joyously reunite with his wife but one walking to his execution.

The vizier rolled the letter tight and applied the royal seal. He did so with such alacrity I could tell he was relieved. "Where will we go?" I could not much bear the idea of returning to Almería, let alone Vélez-Blanco.

"Guadix, probably, once al-Zaghal has been dealt with."

Guadix was not so bad, I thought. I remembered our days there after Momo's escape from the tower. All those pretty young men;

though how many of them still lived if they had been pressed in his uncle's bloody service? "You think the Christians will leave us in peace there?"

He shrugged. "Who knows? But he'll be safer there."

In the end, it was taken out of our hands. The people of Málaga, in their desperation, surrendered, against the wishes of their governor and lord, and what followed broke every tradition of civilized warfare. The city's Jewish population was imprisoned for ransom—thirty *doblas* for every man, woman and child. Who was left to pay for them? Who could afford it? They had lived there in great extended families. One hundred captives were sent as slaves as a gift to the pope in Rome; others were parcelled out among other Christian rulers with whom Isabella and Ferdinand wished to curry favour. Christians who had converted to Islam were used for spear practice or were burned at the stake.

Worse was to follow. Instead of honouring the terms of the treaty, King Ferdinand marched on the towns of Vera, Mojácar, Vélez-Blanco and Vélez-Rubio; and all capitulated without a fight, having heard what had happened in Málaga. Momo's uncle continued to fight on, doggedly, furiously, fuelled by hatred.

Upon hearing of Ferdinand's treachery, I thought Momo was going to have a falling fit like his father. He mastered himself with difficulty. "It must be a misunderstanding. The king will surely return my towns to me once my uncle is removed from the field of play. This is his way of ensuring the land is withheld from him. Ferdinand is closing down his paths of escape; his hunting dogs are fanning out to run their quarry to ground. Yes, that's what he's doing."

I knew he didn't believe it; knowing the truth made him irascible, prone to headaches and small outbursts of temper. He threw a chess piece at me on a morning I'd heard Mariam crying in the harem, and though he immediately apologized and tended the wound with his own hand, it left a scar I have to this day.

Then five Muslim clerics begged audience with him. They did not make obeisance or even bow. Their headman went straight to the point: "We believe the emirate should be handed over to Moulay Abdullah al-Zaghal. Your father was clearly not in his right mind when he bestowed it upon you, as has been made abundantly clear by your many failures to defend our land and people."

Momo paled. Then flushed. His eyes went as hot as embers. "This is treason. Seize them!" he told the captain of the royal guard. "Hang them from the Gate of Justice." And when the man hesitated, he unsheathed his sword.

I saw Qasim's face in that moment. The vizier was never surprised by anything, but now he looked stunned. He'd thought the situation under control; that his clever stratagems for managing Momo were all working. Now he saw his error.

The guards dashed forward, secured the clerics and hustled them away. I heard they had taken them to the cells rather than executing them immediately, no doubt believing the sultan would change his mind.

He did not.

30

Kate

N O W

Abdou had taken her home, held her while she shook, made her sugar-laden tea—"For shock: you're in shock"— and listened as she raged and cursed over and over while trying and failing to get hold of her sister.

It was evening before Kate's phone rang, and when she looked at the number that came up on the screen, she did not recognize it at all. So when Jess's voice, shaky and seeming very far away, came out of it, she felt disorientated.

"Kate? Kate, are you there?"

"Where the hell are you? And where's Luke? James called me."

"I'm so sorry . . . James. Oh God, James. There was nothing I could do."

Kate went cold all over. "What do you mean, there was nothing you could do?"

"I'm sorry, I'm sorry. I just wasn't expecting him to turn up in such an out-of-the-way place. I thought Cornwall was the end of the world, but West Pembrokeshire, it's like the land that time forgot." She was babbling now.

Kate shook the phone in a sort of rage, but it was no substitute for shaking her twin, who sounded drunk or something. Slurring her words, talking too fast. "What the hell are you talking about? What are you doing in West Pembrokeshire? None of this is making any sense!" Her voice had risen to a shout that made Abdou, at the other end of the long salon, cutting something up on the wooden chopping board, turn and stare at her questioningly.

"Sorry, sorry, it's the medication. It's pretty strong."

"Medication? Why do you need medication?" Jess never took anything if she could help it: she even toughed out headaches. "Where are you? Where's Luke?"

"I'm in, ah, Withybush General, in . . . uh . . . Haverfordwest. Sounds like something out of *The Hobbit*, doesn't it?"

"Where's Luke?" Kate enunciated with furious care.

"Sorry, sorry, trying to remember. Luke, yes, Luke. James took him. He just turned up on the doorstep. I think, I think, yes . . . his mother must have phoned him after she saw Luke. That's right. She said he looks the spitting image of his dad at that age. She cried, you know. Said she hadn't known he had a son. Thought it was a daughter, but maybe her memory wasn't very good anymore."

Kate took deep breaths. "James has got Luke?"

"Yes."

"And that would have been the day before yesterday?"

A silence at the other end of the line. "Really? God, didn't realize I'd been so out of it for so long. Oh, Kate—"

"What the hell happened?"

"I went to Porth Clais, to that cottage you described. You know, the one you said James was standing outside as a little boy. I went there to look for his mother. But the cottage was empty, holiday let now, or something. Anyway, I asked around. God, this is making my brain hurt. Sorry, sorry, bear with me. I asked around in Saint David's if they knew anyone who lived at that cottage and some old dear in the grocer's said, 'Do you mean Margaret Hyde?' And I said I wasn't sure of her name, but she'd be around eighty now, and had a son called James, who was fifty-something, and the old woman clutched my arm and said, 'That'll be Maggie. She moved to Haverfordwest twenty-odd years back when her knees give her trouble and she couldn't do the walk anymore. You give her my love when you see her, tell her Olive asked after her, won't you?'"

"His mother's still alive?" But all this time James had said she was dead. What a thing to lie about. She felt faint as the reality of the situation began to sink in. Her husband—the man who had tricked her, lied to her, raped her—had somehow found Jess and taken Luke. She realized Jess was still rambling.

"I'm sure you'd have been a lot better at this than me, data analyst versus designer and all that, but I found her in the end. Age Concern, or was it the council—"

"Jess! Just tell me where Luke is! Where did James take him? Can you please focus?"

Her sister apologized again. "I'm sure it's the drugs, making me like this. Unless it was the punch."

"The . . . punch?"

"He punched me. James punched me. Right in the mouth. I lost three teeth. The doctors said it was lucky I didn't choke on them and die."

"*What?*"

"I said, the doctors said—"

"James hit you in the mouth? Jesus, the, the fucker!"

Jess let out a rough guffaw. "That's right. He is! A *fucker*. That's why I'm here, in hospital, in Haverfordwest. On—what is it? Sunday? Yes, Sunday. With concussion. So on Friday, two days ago, I found his mum and turned up on her doorstep with Luke, and when she saw him, she burst into tears and said, "How did you do that? Bring my lovely little James back to me before he fell into sin?" Then she sort of shook her head a lot and said, 'No, no, that can't be right. You can't turn back time, can you?' And I said, no, you couldn't, but was she James's mother, and was she called Hyde or Foxley? And she said she didn't know anyone named Foxley, but that yes, she was a Hyde. Maggie Hyde. I gave her the old woman's greeting—Olive, wasn't it—"

"I don't care about that," Kate interrupted impatiently. "Tell me about James turning up and taking Luke."

There was a long pause at the other end, then the sound of a muted conversation. Kate thought she heard a man's voice, then at last Jess came back on the line.

"Apparently, no permanent damage a good cosmetic dentist can't fix. Lucky not to have broken my jaw and swallowed my molars! They're just going to run a couple more tests, then I can be discharged."

"I'm coming back—don't go anywhere! I'll get the next flight— well, train to Madrid, then a flight—"

"Stop, stop! There's no point in you coming here. James is coming to you! To Spain! Sorry. He made me tell him."

Kate felt faint. "Before he hit you?"

"Yes."

"What did you tell him? What did he do to you?"

"Just that you were in Granada, working at a bar. Nothing else—well, I didn't know anything else. He, uh, tortured it out of me, I suppose."

"*Tortured you?*" Kate's outrage brought Abdou to her side.

"Ah, yes, I remember now. I'd better tell that police chap, what- ever his name was. William something. No, Williams, that was it. DI Williams. I filed assault charges, actual bodily harm, or was it grievous? I can't remember the difference. They took DNA and everything. It was fascinating. But I'd forgotten the abduction and stuff."

"He abducted you?"

"He stuck me in the boot of his car. Sounds ridiculous, doesn't it? Like something on TV. Yes, that's right. Must have been before he punched me. Or was it after? It's all a bit hazy."

"Anyway—"

"Anyway. He tied me to a chair in this house and burned me."

"What do you mean, *burned* you?"

"Oh hey, yes, that's why I've got a bandage on my *arm!*" Jess sounded bizarrely pleased to have solved this mystery. "He burned me with a cigarette."

"But James doesn't smoke," Kate said feebly.

"You don't have to smoke to buy a packet of ciggies and a lighter, do you? It doesn't say 'DO NOT TORTURE ANYONE WITH THESE' on the packet: they just show photos of the damage they can do to your own lungs and mouth and stuff . . ."

"My God, Jess. How many times did he burn you?"

"Three, four? No, two. Only two. I would have held out longer if I could have. But Jesus, it hurt. And he laughed."

"He laughed?"

"I could tell he was enjoying it. But he was enraged when he got the answer out of me. Shouted something about Arabs or infidels or something, couldn't quite make out what he was on about. And he called you a lot of names, and that was when I told him you'd probably run off because he was so weird in bed. You know, that thing you told me. Sorry, shouldn't have done that, I just wanted to hurt him back in some way. So then he hit me."

"Where was Luke when all this was going on? He didn't see, did he? Tell me he didn't," Kate pleaded.

"James left him with his mother, said he'd be back. She was the one took me to hospital after James had gone with Luke. She must have made him tell her where I was. I was in a right state: had pissed myself, blood all down my front. I think she thought he'd killed me when she saw me: she was crying and mumbling, 'Not again, not again,' or something."

"Not again?" Kate sat bolt upright. "Christ, Jess: do you think he killed his first wife? Ingrid, or whatever her name was? The one who fell off the cliff?"

A pause. "Well, I don't know. I'd forgotten about that." Voices again, then a rustle as if Jess was moving. "Got to go, Sis, more tests before they'll let me out of here. Aren't you proud of me for remembering this number?" And just like that, she was gone, leaving Kate staring at the phone.

"Is she all right?"

Abdou's voice jolted her. It wasn't that she'd forgotten he was there—he hadn't left since James's terrible call—but he'd done his best to be as unobtrusive as it was possible to be in such a small apartment.

"He hit her! And burned her arm with a lit cigarette, to find out where I was. He could have killed her. He may have killed someone else. My little boy, he's with a . . . a torturer, maybe a murderer! The bastard. The utter, fucking bastard!" Kate swore viciously.

Abdou did not touch her, just sat on the chair opposite, hands between his knees, his expression stern, and waited until she stopped. Then he said, "What did she tell him about where you are?"

"That I was in Granada, working in a bar."

"Except that you're not anymore."

"Thank heaven for that. The idea of him teaming up with Jimena is too hellish for words. But Jimena has this address. It's on my records."

Abdou blinked. "Then you come to my place. There's not much room, but I can sleep on the floor. It's no problem."

She grimaced. "You're really kind. But that's not the point. I have to see Luke. I have to *save* Luke. That means I have to see James."

For a whole day after James's phone call Kate had stamped around, furious, banging things about, swearing, fighting back tears, muttering "Bastard, bastard" over and over. Not once did she cry, which surprised her when she suddenly realized it. She didn't feel like crying: she felt alternately terrified and murderous. For his part, Abdou had pottered around her little kitchen, gone out to fetch supplies from the *supermercado* on the hill, made a stew that she had been unable to taste, though she'd dutifully swallowed some of it under his watchful eye. The next morning, after a restless night, she snapped awake, to a world in which James had stolen her son and punched the lights out of her sister and burned her deliberately, slowly and with pleasure, with a lit cigarette. She remembered, abruptly, the sensation of sharp pain she'd experienced in the back streets of the Albayzín that night when Abdou kissed her. It must have been at exactly the time James had been torturing her twin. And now he was on his way to Granada.

"At least there are no direct flights," Abdou had pointed out.

"What difference does it make?"

"It will slow him down a bit, give us time to think."

"Not us—me."

He looked hurt. "I can't let you face him on your own. He hit your sister, burned her arm."

"He's done worse than that," Kate said fiercely.

"Worse?" His face had gone very still. Then he looked at her arms.

"No," she said hurriedly, "that was me. Because of him, but he didn't do that to me, not directly."

"You don't have to tell me if it is too hard. I have no right to ask."

"You told me your hard story." She hesitated. "Forgive me, but there's so much I don't know about your culture. In some places in the world there's no such crime as a man raping his wife: it's regarded as his right."

"Rape is rape," Abdou said stonily. "An act of violence is an act of violence, no matter who does it."

Kate nodded. "Yes. Yes, it is."

"He raped you?"

"On our wedding night, and then every night till I ran away. The first time he made a strange ceremony of it, as if he were some kind of priest and I was a virgin to be deflowered. It was disgusting." She lowered her head so that she didn't have to see his horrified expression. She was repulsing him, she knew, but the story had to be told. Fiercely, she drove herself on, keeping her recital short and brutal, much like the act itself. "He tied my hands to the bed and kept grunting, '*Mine, mine, mine*'—as if it was all about him, and telling me he was making a son."

There was a long silence. Then Abdou said, "And you did."

"Yes. Luke. I can't really explain why I called him that, except that I knew Luke was the patron saint of artists and doctors. I think I was inspired by the foot."

Abdou frowned. "The foot?"

"The first thing James gave me: it was an artificial leg, made in Morocco or somewhere, but even though it was a prosthetic it must have been really beautiful when it was first made. Someone took such care in creating it—carving it with beautiful little arabesques and geometric patterns, just like some of the pillars and plaques in the Alhambra; and then they covered it with gold."

Abdou smiled. "A rich one-legged man."

"Or someone who loved him very much. I liked the idea of that, and the name just seemed right at the time, Luke. And now I can't even picture my own son. He's two years old. I haven't seen him in nearly fifteen months. I haven't seen how he has grown . . ." Only now did her face crumple.

"Don't. You saved yourself, at least. If you hadn't run, he'd have you both."

"But what if he hurts Luke?"

"Why would he do that? He hurt Jess to get to you."

"I'm going to make him give Luke back, to me or Jess."

"And if he won't?"

She looked pained. "Honestly? I don't know."

"Call the *poli*. Tell them what you've told me."

Kate shook her head. "I can't." She remembered the way the policeman had smirked at the sight of the condoms in her handbag. "I just can't. Besides, they have me in their records as Jessica Fordham. I've already lied to them: they won't believe a word I say. And James is so plausible."

Abdou held her gaze for a long moment, then shook his head. "He's hardly gone to these lengths to calmly hand your boy over to you and fly home. I can't stop you meeting him, Kate—that's your choice, and I understand it—but make sure you do it in a public place where I can keep an eye on you."

"You're a kind, lovely man, Abdelkarim" was all she would say.

When her phone rang that evening, she answered it with preternatural calmness as Abdou watched on with a grim expression on. "Hello, James. Yes . . . Yes, I'll meet you. Where?" She wrote it down. "At two tomorrow? I will be there. And Luke too?"

A pause.

"Good."

Another pause.

"I'll see you both tomorrow. Tell Luke his mummy sends her love."

Pause.

"All right, I'll bloody well tell him myself. Tomorrow."

So this was it. The worst had happened. She felt as if she stood in the eye of a storm, here in the heart of Granada.

The next day, Kate walked out into the Albayzín feeling as though she was going to the scaffold or to the stake. The sun beat down on her, the walls of the narrow streets of the city channelling the heat like a furnace: it had turned out to be the hottest day of the year. Rounding a corner to take a steep alley down the hill, she disturbed a cloud of bluebottles that had alighted on a fresh dog turd pressed into the pebble mosaic paving the alley. One of them touched her face as she passed and she batted it away in disgust: stepping forward, she was assailed by an awful stench that wasn't quite what she'd expected, and when she looked down, she realized it was not in fact a turd but a dead rat lying there, its yellow teeth exposed in a last gasp, its guts exploded over the cobbles. Farther down toward the Plaza Nueva, a striped cat streaked across her path, pursued by a small dog. Or was it a fox? It was gone, down steep steps, through a broken door into a courtyard, before she could tell.

Joining one of the wider streets that ran down to the Plaza Nueva, she had to step out of the way of a scooter and barked her shin on one of the little iron bollards that lined the pavement. "Ow!" It was her own fault: she'd been striding along in a sort of suppressed fury, her eyes trained ahead, not down. Such strangely shaped little bollards they were, too, like unexploded hand grenades. Oh. For the first time in all the months she had been here she had never really looked at them before: but now she saw that they were actually pomegranates, the symbol of Granada. And then she realized, *Granada–grenade*: the words shared the same root definition, the many-seeded fruit suggesting the fragmenting device.

Why had she never made that connection before? The thought struck her so forcibly it stopped her dead.

Then she decided: *None of these signs is good*. She almost turned back, but the furnace of the anger burning inside her drove her on. She had to be strong for her boy.

In all the time Kate had been in Granada she had not once set foot in either its great cathedral or the royal chapel. Having been forced into the Catholic faith, she felt nothing but distaste for its grandiose statements in stone, and for its dark and bloody history. But she knew where the cathedral was: you could hardly miss it, the great, hulking buttressed monster, squatting self-importantly in the centre of town.

As she turned the corner into Calle Oficios bells rang out, loudly discordant, overhead. It was two o'clock . . .

"Kate."

The voice came from behind her. She turned. He was just a shadow, a dark shape in the powerful sunlight, his form dense and silhouetted, and that alone was so suddenly terrifying that she almost screamed. But then he took a step forward and light fell from a different angle and she looked down and saw her son—Luke— the way she had never seen him in life: a proper little boy in red dungarees with a long-sleeved blue T-shirt underneath, his golden hair glowing like a halo. She felt a huge and reassuring wave of love for him, in the same instant as she thought: *He must be boiling in that outfit, in this heat*—which in turn transmuted itself into fresh fury against her husband. She fought the urge to rage at him and went down on one knee, concentrating all her mental energy on the toddler. "Luke, darling, are you all right? You look very hot."

He eyed her warily. Then he turned away, and buried his head against his father's trousers. Kate felt a physical pain, like a shard of hot iron inside her, and when she glanced up, James was smiling triumphantly, one hand possessively on Luke's head.

"He doesn't even know who you are."

He said it gloatingly, enjoying her pain. Then the splayed fingers twisted, forcing Luke's head to face her.

"This is your mummy. Take a good look at her. You haven't seen her in—what is it, darling, eighteen months? Or maybe you left right after the birth? Anyway, it's no surprise you don't recognize her. Have a good look. Go on. Look at the woman who ran away and dumped you like a bag of old rubbish. She flew away to the sun to have a lovely time without you. Because she's a terrible mother, a terrible wife, an unnatural woman. She has no concept of duty or decency, no regard for God's law or the natural order of things. She's a harlot and an unbeliever and we're here to make her repent her ways."

Luke struggled against his father's grip, his face reddening and crumpled.

"Stop it, James, for God's sake stop! Can't you see you're scaring him? Luke, sweetheart, I'm so sorry you're frightened. But everything is going to be o—"

"Yes, it is, isn't it? Everything is going to be just fine," James said fiercely. "Because we're going to make it that way, aren't we? For God's sake, indeed."

Letting go of Luke's head for a moment, he moved aside his scarf (a scarf, Kate thought, in this heat?), reached into his jacket and held something up. She blinked at it. A large iron key?

"This will be a special treat. We're going into the Capilla Real. There's something there you need to see, something Luke needs to learn: and a future for us to make together."

Behind them, the life of Granada went on—people out walking, doing chores, taking a shortcut; workmen in overalls, a priest in dark robes, tourists lining up their digital cameras on the Lonja de Mercaderes, the picturesque old merchants' meeting house, with its arched doorways and Solomonic pillars. Some of them stared curiously at this living tableau of a fractured family, enacting some eternal drama of their own in this monumental place. Kate felt their scrutiny as both discomfort and reassurance. The social embarrassment was excruciating, but at least it meant there were people around if she needed them. Despite all evidence to the contrary, she chose to believe that people were essentially good-natured and wanted to help others. You had to believe that, or where did it leave you? Desolate and in fear. Even so, she really didn't want to go into the mausoleum.

"Can't we go somewhere else?" she asked. "There's a nice park not far from here. I'm sure Luke would prefer that."

"Luke must learn that what he wants to do doesn't count when there are adults around, mustn't he—eh, Luke? If Daddy tells you to do something, you do it, don't you?' He gave the boy a small shake and Luke looked up at him uncertainly, lip wobbling. "Now then, Luke, what did I say about crying?"

"Mustn't," Luke said, barely audible.

"That's right. You're my little man now and men don't cry." This situation satisfactorily dealt with, he turned his attention to Kate. "Now, we're going into the royal chapel, and no arguing. It's a special place. A very special place indeed."

He reached out to take Kate by the hand, but she jerked it out of the way. His fingers closed around her elbow and she had to grit her teeth not to cry out or jab him hard in the gut. Actually, she thought, perhaps that was exactly what she should do. Hit him as hard and low as she could, grab Luke and run away with him . . .

But as if he knew her thoughts, James placed himself in front of the boy. "No, you don't," he said.

"I'm not going in there with you," she said firmly.

"Well, Luke and I are going in, aren't we, Luke?" And when Luke hesitated, he made the boy nod by the pressure of the hand he had spread across the child's head. "You see? Now, you can either come in with us. Or you can go to hell."

How could she leave her son alone with this monster? She glanced around, hoping that Abdou had indeed followed her, but found no one. Damn him. She would humour James for now: she had to talk to him if she wanted him to relinquish Luke. "All right," she said grimly.

Through the big arched double door they went, James ushering his wife and child in before him, then closing the door behind them.

Inside, the royal chapel was chilly with marble: huge pillars rose to vaulted fans that spread across the ceiling much as James's fingers splayed across Luke's head. Everything forced your eye to the silent stone figures lying on massive stone beds behind their cage of iron—to keep the living out, or the dead in? Kate wondered. Dead Queen Isabella and dead King Ferdinand and their dead daughter Juana the Mad, beside her dead husband, Philip the Fair.

James approached the grille and genuflected, as if at a saint's tomb. He beamed down at his son. "See here, Luke? This is where the finest woman in all history is buried: Isabella of Castile, who devoted her entire life, body and soul, to reunifying her country, to driving out the unbelievers and bringing the people back to the True Faith. She raised up Mother Church from the squalor of oppression by the infidel; she razed their vile temples, turned their minarets into bell towers and encouraged those who had strayed from the true path to see the error of their ways. She was driven by vision and faith that spread across oceans and brought undiscovered continents into the embrace of the Catholic Church. This—" he made a grand gesture toward the statue of dead queen "—this is the woman who financed the voyages of Christopher Columbus to sail to the New World, who channelled their wealth into the hands of Mother Church, who restored her dignity and pride and returned her to her rightful place, in control of the civilized world."

Luke pulled away from his father, uncomfortable in his grip.

"Stop, James," Kate said quietly. "Please stop. He's much too young for all this talk of faith and power."

"Nonsense: there's no such thing as being 'too young' to begin an education." He hoisted Luke up so that he could see the stone figure, lying there prone and silent. "See how Isabella's head rests deeper in the stone than her husband's. It's because she wore the weightier crown. Women are made for sacrifice and duty, whether they are queens or just mothers. Isabella loved her husband with the flame of passion sanctified by holy matrimony, and bore him sons and was true to him all her life. A mother, a wife, a queen, and a true servant of God. She was nominated a saint in 1972, when I was just a few years older than you. And see here—" He put Luke down and walked him to where they had a better view of the massive gold altarpiece. He pulled his son close and angled his head. "This scene carved on the lower bench is of the heathen king Boabdil handing over the keys to this city to Queen Isabella and her husband, King Ferdinand. And then they drove the wicked Muslims and Jews out of their country forever, and made sure those who remained accepted Christ by baptism. See there—"

Kate could bear it no longer. "Stop poisoning his mind! He's far too young to understand any of this—he's just a baby. But I understand. I understand all too well. These people—these Catholic Monarchs you respect so much—were monsters: cruel, fundamentalist monsters who caused untold terror and misery and countless deaths. It's no wonder you idolize these people: you're just like them! I can't believe you abducted and tortured my sister to find out where I was so you could come here and deliver this . . . this lecture on your weird, twisted morality!"

She'd expected fury from him, but all he did was to smile indulgently, and that was when she knew he was truly mad. James lifted the child down from his shoulders and set him on his feet. Luke promptly sat down on the stone floor and started tracing the patterns on the tiles. "But don't you see, Kate, that this is how it was meant to be? Even though you broke my heart, even though you fell from the true path and abandoned your family? You came here—to the city this magnificent woman chose to make her own. To the place where the pagan Middle Ages gave way to the modern era: this was where the dark tides were turned back and enlightenment began. This is where she chose to lie forever: she even designed her own marvellous resting place, this perfect architectural combination of pure Gothic with gorgeous Baroque. As soon as your sister said where you were, I knew we lay in the hand of divine destiny. 'God moves in mysterious ways,' isn't that what they say? It's an old cliché, but it's true. For some reason God's design brought you here, and brought Luke and me to be reunited with you in this sanctified place." His eyes were lit with fanatical zeal as he gazed at her. "Just look at our boy." Look at this miracle of life we made together. And now it's time to reunite our family, and give Luke the best gift a boy could have. A brother."

Kate's mind, for a long moment, was a white blank of shock. Then she thought she must have misunderstood, and waited for him to laugh, to make some sort of joke of it. When he just looked at her with a look she recognized too well, a look that had haunted her nightmares, she said, "You must be out of your mind."

"What could be more perfect? Here, where the blessed Isabella watches over us, where Luke's namesake sits with the disciples—see, carved right there, his parents both named for great saints: me for Santiago Matamoros, Saint James the Moorslayer; you for the blessed virgin Catherine, condemned to be broken on the vast spiked wheel—"

His words echoed around the marble vaults and it was only now that Kate realized they were alone, utterly alone, apart from the dead. No one else had entered with them. This was strange, in a city stuffed with tourists who had come all the way across the country to this place with no international airport, to see sights just like this one. She stared toward the great wooden doors. Had he . . . ? Were they . . . ?

As if he saw the cogs in her mind turn, James said mildly, "Yes, it's just us, in this beautiful chapel. Safely locked in." He patted his pocket. "For two whole hours. They always shut the chapel at lunchtime, but I had to be very persuasive to get the key. I made them a generous donation. A very generous donation—from the sale of your flat, in fact. You see what I mean about the divine plan? Everything happens according to God's will. We have this magnificent place to ourselves. No tourists snapping away at the blessed Isabella with their shitty little cameras. No gawkers. No witnesses. Today in this holy place we will make a new life together and call him—well, I had originally thought Matthew, but then I remembered that was the name of your drunken boyfriend—so maybe Mark, or John?"

Kate stared at him in disbelief. "For God's sake, James, this is crazy! You can't just rape me again, here, in front of a little boy."

"Rape? We're still married. Or had you forgotten?" He thrust his face at her, his aggression naked, and the scarf he had been wearing slipped, revealing a set of scabbing gouge marks.

Jess must have made those, Kate realized with a sudden horrible fascination. Before James had tied her into a chair and tortured her with a lit cigarette. The memory of what he had done to her sister shook her resolve. She bent to be on a level with her son. "Luke, come with me." He stared up at her, stuck his thumb in her mouth. Then, uncertainly, he offered her his other hand.

James blocked their way. She took a step back, then another, towing Luke with her, till the iron grille stopped her, the Catholic Monarchs at her back, mocking.

"You're my wife. Mine, remember? So I can do whatever the hell I like to you. Anything. And I will, believe me, I will. I've been thinking about it every day, every night since you left. I've imagined everything. I bet you've been over here fucking the brains out of every Arab who took your fancy, haven't you? Spreading your legs for them in dank alleys, or perhaps just dropping your jeans and bending over: I hear they like that, like boys, the filthy bastards. You whore, I can smell it on you, their stink—" He moved toward her.

Kate stepped in front of her son. "Don't you dare!" She would fight him; she would not submit to him. She would rather die than have him touch her, have him inside her again.

Spurred on by her defiance, James came on at a run, his fist raised to strike. And that was when a dark shape flew into view, arms spread like the wings of a great bat, and fell upon James, bowling him away. There was a cry, a scuffle, a whirl of movement and shouting, on the ground, then upright once more; then both shapes vanished from Kate's sight. Noises continued, muffled, distanced; thuds descending.

Then there was nothing to be heard but someone breathing heavily, a long way away, the sound amplified and distorted by the confines of a small space. At last came the unmistakable noise of feet on stone steps, drawing closer, closer . . .

31

Blessings

GRANADA

1491

It was a clear day, so clear that the air seemed to have been spread over the plain like a blanket of light, deceiving the eye, making distant things appear close, close things seem hazed and indistinct. The young sultan of Granada leaned on the battlements of the Alcazaba and gazed morosely out across the *vega* toward the enemy encampment, the hood of his white djellaba up over his head to keep off the worst of the sun. I had been looking for him for over an hour.

"So this is where you are."

He said nothing, didn't even turn at the sound of my voice. I tried again. "A messenger has arrived. Everyone is waiting for you in the ambassadors hall."

"I know what the answer will be," he said wearily. "It's always the same: everyone has an excuse. Tlemcen has made a trade agreement with the foreign monarchs so is sorry to say it cannot send us troops for fear of upsetting their merchants, because money means more than principle. The sultan of Egypt sends his apologies, but he is too occupied with the advances of the Ottoman Turks: the Turks beg my pardon, but they are too preoccupied with their conquests elsewhere to be bothered about what happens here. Or words to that effect. I saw the messenger riding in. He was in no hurry, his head was down and his mount wasn't in a sweat, and that tells me there will be no reinforcements from Morocco, or anywhere else. For whatever reason Mohammed al-Shaykh may have—from the lameness of his favourite horse to some tribal wedding complication three steps removed from the crown."

He turned to me at last. His amber eyes were dull and hooded: he looked ill, and I told him so.

"Well, I can't help that," he said. "I'm sick to my soul of this war, sick and exhausted. No wonder my uncle packed his bags and sold his lands and fled to North Africa. If even he—the most warlike of all of us—has had enough, how can I, who hates war with every bone in my body, be expected to continue to take the fight to these indefatigable zealots?"

"You're using long words again," I warned him with an attempt at humour, but he didn't smile.

The messenger had indeed brought bad news. The Moroccan sultan informed us that although he had tried to help, there was no safe port into which he could deliver reinforcements, as the whole coast was under blockade. The poor courier shook as Momo read this missive silently, then in quiet fury hurled it to the floor.

"There's more, sire," Qasim said. He gestured to the messenger.

The courier hesitated until the young sultan waved a hand at him impatiently. "Speak up, and hold nothing back. Things can hardly get worse."

But they could.

The messenger bowed his head as if waiting for a blow to fall. "They're building a city," he said indistinctly.

"What?" Momo said sharply. "I said speak up, didn't I? Does no one listen to me anymore?"

"I . . . uh . . . passed twenty or more carters bringing timber and stone across the *vega*, more of them the closer to Granada I came, and wherever I went the orchards that had existed had been reduced to stumps. The last time I rode past the enemy camp, majesty, on my way to Fez, it was just tents and firepits and trenches—the usual . . . uh . . . ramshackle arrangement you'd expect. But now they're building . . . something. They the unbelievers of Aragón and Castile—I mean. It looks as if they're building a city, sire . . ."

A wave of murmurs washed the hall, gathering in echoes among the cedarwood stars of the ceiling. "Quiet!" cried the vizier. "Go on, lad—tell us the rest."

The messenger dared a look up through his long dark hair at Momo, who sat glowering into space. "I was skirting the camp at a distance, majesty, when two men rode out toward me. I drew my sword, swearing I wouldn't give up the message to them: I'd see it destroyed before they killed me . . . But they were strangely friendly, and though they were armed, they didn't draw their weapons. Instead, they offered me water and sustenance. Of course I refused them for fear of poison; but the men pressed me to accompany them—not as a prisoner but so I could 'bear witness,' they said." He paused again, wiping a drop of sweat from his face. This time he darted a look not at Momo but at the vizier, who nodded brusquely.

"They took me into the camp. I rode right through it. It went on and on and on. So many men. They're building a walled city, majesty, with gates at every midway mark. A city with houses and streets. Proper ones, designed to last. What was timber and canvas is now timber and stone and mortar, and they're painting it all white—there are vats of lime wash bubbling all over the place, giving off noxious fumes. All except the main streets, and they're all red because of the colour of the earth here." He licked his lips, as if his mouth had suddenly run dry.

Qasim motioned to a page, who presented the courier with a cup of water, which the young man downed gratefully in three gulps.

"Streets, yes. There are four big streets, with an enormous weapons store at the centre. They're arrayed in each of the cardinal directions, sire, with each street named for the city it points to, with Granada the one to the south. So, uh, the city, is in the form of a cross. A great white city with a red cross running right through it, to make the symbol of their religion. And that's what they're calling it, majesty: the city of Santa Fe, the city of the Holy Faith. They told me that. Then they waved me on my way. It's like they wanted me to see it all, and to come here and tell you what I'd seen."

"Of course they did," Momo sighed. He thanked and dismissed the courier, instructed the pages to show the lad to the bathhouse and to massage him with scented oils, "to remove the stink of the enemy." Then he sat back in his throne and gazed fiercely up into the intricately carved rendition of the seven heavens, where the inscription read: *Oh, God, fighter of the devil, please help me.*

But no divine aid was immediately forthcoming. When he looked down again, I thought I had never seen him appear so fragile, not even when he was wounded at Loja; not even when I'd told him the enemy would take his son hostage.

"It's a message to us: a huge great message in stone and mortar, and it says: 'We're determined to drive you from your home, to be rid of you forever. Look!' it says. 'We're going nowhere: in fact, we're digging in and are going to stay the whole winter, then the spring and summer, until you surrender.'"

"Damn them," growled Musa, the words hardly making it through the thicket of his beard. "We'll never surrender. We will fight them to extinction, even our own. We will fight them in the streets and on the plains. We will fight them on the bridges and at the gates, in the fields and in the gardens. We will never give up. Fetch my horse!" he shouted to a slave at the door. "I'll ride out against them again, right now!"

He and Momo had ridden a dozen sorties from the gates of Granada toward the army camp. They had fought and withdrawn, fought and withdrawn. On one occasion they had even clashed with King Ferdinand himself. "I saw him," Momo had told me. "I saw the king with his damned standards, all done up in his armour. He had his helm on but his visor up, as if he wanted me to see him, and see he was not frightened of us. I would have ridden at him and challenged him to a duel, but they wheeled away at the last moment, as if mocking me."

"And Don Gonzalo, the Great Captain, did you see him too?" I had rather liked the young Castilian officer, with his lion's hair and open gaze. He had been kind to me. "Would you kill him if you met him on the battlefield?"

"I would kill any and all of them," Momo had said angrily. "And rejoice in their deaths."

"Then I will kill them all for you," I had replied loyally, baring my teeth in proper Banu Warith fashion. "Like the savage I am."

This had pleased him, as so little else did, these days. "Dear Blessings," he'd said, cupping my cheek fondly. "I can count on so few people now. I am surrounded by madmen and cowards, warmongers and collaborators, toadies and spies. It's impossible, sometimes, to see which is which. But you, dear comrade, are a constant in this sea of chaos. I always know where you stand."

"At your side, as your Special Guardian."

Ah, what a charlatan I had felt when he vouchsafed me these small moments of trust. What a snake in the sand . . .

I dragged myself back to the present. Momo was telling the

slave to stay where he was. Then he turned his attention to the chieftain of the Banu Serraj.

"Stand down, Musa, my brave friend. Every time we ride a sortie against them they lose soldiers and we lose soldiers. But our supply of men is limited, while theirs grows every day. Every day I thought we would have reinforcements coming—from North Africa or the Ottomans, or even my uncle. Now we know we fight alone, isolated and surrounded. And the enemy has built a city within sight of our walls and is either going to sit and wait for us to starve, or come against us with their guns, and there will be precious little we can do to stop them. Do I have the measure of the situation, Qasim?"

Qasim bowed his head. "It does rather seem that way, majesty." He took a deep breath. "I do humbly suggest that you make terms with these foreign monarchs: offer them handsome tributes, release the Christian captives in all our prisons and swear fealty to these monarchs."

Very slowly, very deliberately, Momo reached down, drew off one of his fine jewelled slippers and, with the precision of a man who has honed his skill at casting lance and spear for more than a decade, threw the babouche the ten yards that separated him from the vizier. The flat of its sole struck Qasim sharply on the head with a resounding smack.

The entire court held its breath. Qasim blinked, slowly as if in shock; then quickly, as if he sought to prevent tears of pain or humiliation from giving away any loss of equanimity. He took a deep breath, recovered the offending item from the floor and with a sweeping bow returned it to Momo's outstretched hand. The sultan bent and slipped his foot back into the pretty leather, then sat back as if nothing out of the ordinary had occurred.

Glances were exchanged, but no one spoke: no one dared. Ever since Momo had had the five clerics beheaded people were generally more alert in his presence, realizing perhaps that the olive did not fall too far from the tree and that the young sultan they had considered so pleasant and gentle had in fact inherited a measure of his father's unpredictability.

"My lord . . ." Qasim eyed him warily, in case the other slipper came to hand. "It is my duty to point out to your majesty that since the foreign king ravaged the Alpujarras, firing the fields, destroying the crops and capturing the livestock, our food supplies are . . . limited. We have, it has been estimated, maybe eight months' food for all the people of this city. And in the meantime King Ferdinand and his vast army will sit outside our gates and wait until the plight of Granada becomes that of Málaga. Why not negotiate terms now, before we are too weak to bargain well?"

Momo made an impatient gesture. "I know this. Do you think I don't know this? Why did we risk lives in an attempt to take back Salobreña and Adra? Because we were bored? Because we wanted to test our arms against the infidels? Of course not. We did it because we must find a way of being resupplied from the sea, since all other routes are closed to us. So we tried, and we failed: but by God we tried." He gazed upward to the seven heavens once more, his face drawn.

"Might I speak, majesty?"

Momo brought his gaze back down to earth, specifically onto the vast beard of Musa Ibn Abu'l Ghrassan. "Speak," he said. "But I beg you make it brief, for it feels as if my head is splitting."

The vizier and I exchanged a look: the illness that had finally carried off Moulay Hasan had begun with headaches. I was seized by a sudden terror then: what if Momo was suddenly struck blind, or fell to the floor in convulsions as his father had done? What if he died? The cloud that dogged me daily descended once more, cold and terrible, and I shivered.

"Let us work a deception on the enemy," Musa was saying.

"If we leave one or more of the city's gates open, those their spies would be most likely to see, perhaps we might tempt them to attack. Once inside, we close the gates and ambush them with the troops we've stationed there to meet them. Then we shoot the bastards full of arrows."

"That doesn't seem honourable." Momo frowned. "But they've hardly been chivalrous in their dealings with us, and if there's any way to lessen their number, it must be tried. Now I must take some rest." He pushed himself to his feet and the court bowed. "Do your worst, Musa. Do your worst."

I walked with Momo to his private courtyard and inside, to the great pillowed divan that took up an entire alcove in the stately domed chamber, feeling as I ever did the heavily ornamented ceiling bearing down upon me. "Ask the man to turn the fountain off would you, Blessings? Even the sound of the water hurts my head."

I ran to do his bidding. When I came back, he was sitting amid the gorgeously coloured cushions, watching a peacock dip its beak into the now-still waters of the fountain channel. The light struck its feathers, bringing the iridescent blue-green into startling relief against the pale marble. I passed the bird and it cocked its head at me, regarding me with a beady black eye, before continuing to drink as if I were no more bother to it than a passing butterfly.

"How can I give up all this, Blessings? All this beauty, all this serenity, the decades of craftsmanship and care that have gone into making it the loveliest place on the face of the earth? How can I let this paradise fall into the hands of the unbelievers, those who cannot treasure and comprehend it as I do? Who cannot read its sacred geometries and precious inscriptions, let alone take inspiration from them? But if I do not give it up, we will all die here and it will become forever and all time a gravesite, a final testament to the last Muslims who lived in this place and brought it to the peak of civilization. And that's if our enemies don't blow it to bits with their terrible lombards." He turned tragic eyes upon me. "I don't know what to do, Blessings. But you're the only one I can say that to. I must appear strong to put heart into our people—to encourage Musa and our soldiers, to reassure the people of Granada that I—their sultan—will safeguard them from all the horrors they've heard of elsewhere: the starvation and torture, the burnings and floggings, men used as target practice; women raped, children sold as slaves to God alone knows what monsters are out there in the so-called Christian world. And yet I know I'm not strong—I'm not some iron-willed, thick-skinned hero who will fight and fight till he has carved a path through the enemy ranks and taken on their king in single combat and screamed '*Y'Allah!*' while he did it. Oh, I know I make a good fist of appearing to do all that: I've shown them my warrior face and I've taken my battle wounds and flown our banners high. But I hate it. I hate the tearing rage and violence of it all. I hate to see men hacked about, limbs shorn off, heads caved in; men writhing in agony, waiting for the end to come.

"Last week when we rode out, I killed three men in a single sortie, and looked into their eyes while I did so. There is nothing in the world, Blessings, so terrible as to see the light dying in another man's eyes as you take his life. It butchers something in your own soul. It's a disgusting, inhuman, ungodly thing, taking a life. A life that God himself sent out into the world, whether he was recognized by the bearer of that divine spirit or not." He paused, thinking, and I saw a single tear leak from his left eye and track its way like a pale pearl down the side of his nose.

At last he spoke again. "No, there is a worse thing. As we turned back from one of those fights, I saw this horse—a fine black mare—standing shaking amid broken bodies where we had fought. She just stood there, head down, trembling, and I thought she was afraid of the blood—they don't like the smell, you know. But just as I was about to lean over to pick up her reins and lead her home, she suddenly coughed, and this great gout of black blood came spurting out of her mouth, and I saw there was a fine lance sticking out of her chest. It must have gone right through her rib cage and punctured her lung. She was drowning in her own blood, standing there, not understanding what was happening to her, not understanding anything. She coughed and coughed and struggled for breath, and then she just . . . fell in a heap. Collapsed on her side and lay there, her ribs heaving. And I could do nothing to help her. The Christians were on our tail: we had to leave to save our own skins. I . . . I am so ashamed that I left her there, like that . . . dying in a wasteland of corpses. For nothing . . ." He put his head in his hands and his shoulders began to shake.

I comforted him as best I could, which in truth was not at all. He went to Mariam that evening, and still she would not see him. Later that night I heard the screech of women's voices in the harem above the Court of Lions: it seemed Mariam had found her voice, for her raging cries drowned out even those of Lalla Aysha, Momo's redoubtable mother: "I will not sleep with him! He betrayed me and he betrayed our children: why should I give him more to sell to the unbelievers?"

I crept away into the medina to find some strong liquor. I did not have to look hard or for long: I was not the only one drowning my sorrows. Despair reigned in our city: word of the enemy's resolution to stay for the winter, until we starved or surrendered, had snaked insidiously out through its winding streets. I joined a blacksmith, a butcher, a livestock manager, two merchants and a man who would not speak, in downing small cups of some noxiously strong alcohol in a stable block past the mosque baths down near the Gate of Justice. We drank ourselves into a companionable haze into the early hours of the morning and beyond, when at last the mute man stood, nodded to us and left. A few minutes later the first call to prayer drifted out across the city, the singer's notes warbling uncertainly into the chilly air. The blacksmith caught my eye. "He's a good hour early."

It comes to something when your muezzin is driven to drink.

Musa tried his ruse. For three nights various gates were left ajar: and for three nights the enemy took no advantage. Our troops grew lax: late on the fourth night it seemed a small contingent of Christian knights had managed to slip past the so-called guards, for in the morning we found a crude wooden plaque with the words *Ave Maria* daubed on it in white paint, nailed to the door of the mosque. After that the gates were kept firmly shut. It seemed a small thing, but it cast Momo further into a pit of gloom. "They mock us. They mock me!" he cried.

He had grabbed his spear and ridden out with a band of our best knights, one of whom pinned the plaque beneath the tail of his horse, where the animal obligingly shat on it. I was convinced Momo would not return from this sortie, it seemed so ill-advised, so rash. As I had done at Loja, I gripped the battlements and stared through the dust kicked up by the battle, strained my eyes for a glimpse of him, alive or dead. He came back, though, covered in blood, none of it his own. In the courtyard of the Alcazaba he laid down his lance, likewise besmirched. Beside it he laid his sword. A little dust devil whipped up by the late-afternoon breeze swirled around the words on its hilt: *Only God is victorious.*

I made to pick them up to clean them, but he put a restraining hand on my arm. "No, Blessings. I shall not use them again." Then he turned and made his way toward the *hammam*, shedding pieces of armour as he went.

The next day negotiations began in secret for the surrender of Granada.

'Twixt us Qasim and I ran a dozen parlays between the Alhambra and Santa Fe, begging audience with the king and queen; and if gaining no access to them, with their secretary, Hernando de Zafra, and sometimes with the Great Captain and the count of Tendilla, whom Qasim seemed to know well, though I did not remember ever meeting him before. In each meeting we tried to persuade them to leave Granada be, to accept Momo as a vassal-king who would pay tribute as his father had done, and his grandfather before him, and his grandfather's father too—and his grandfather's grandfather: all those other Mohammeds and Yusufs down the centuries through so many other times of conflict. They had all paid protection money to the enemy—bribes of coin and released prisoners—so that they and their subjects might be allowed to live without the fear of being attacked and carried off as slaves, their wives and daughters raped, their houses fired, their livestock stolen, their wells poisoned.

We begged, we bargained, we wheedled; we made concessions large and small. All to little effect: the Catholic Monarchs—as they now termed themselves—held to a hard, unbending line. But one day during this tedious period I saw a man I recognized from his great bush of dark hair, sitting patiently in line with other petitioners awaiting audience with the monarchs. The last time I'd seen him had been in an antechamber in the palace in Córdoba, where we had both been kicking our heels. I remembered that he told me he thought it was possible for a man to sail right around the world without falling off, and that there was a secret way to Jerusalem and he was going to find it. But Jerusalem lies at the end of the Middle Sea, I'd said: something even children knew. He'd shown me charts proving, he thought, that it could be reached from the east, not the west if he could but find the funds to put together an expedition. And I remembered that I'd shown him my amulet and told him how my people used the stars to navigate the Great Desert.

Now when he saw me he leapt to his feet. "Don Baraka, isn't it?"

"Señor Colón!"

"Call me Cristoforo Colombo, like they do back home."

"My friends call me Blessings." We clasped forearms.

His Castilian was halting, for he came from Genoa by way of Portugal, and this made it easier for me to understand him; also, he had a little Arabic because he had picked some up in his trading days, and when studying to improve his charts had worked with a number of Arab scholars and sailors, who used a different system of map making and navigation. He was always avid for new information, as greedy for it as I was greedy for food: I liked that about him.

"I'm nearly there," he told me.

"Nearly where?" I teased. "You're right here in front of me in a city that is no city called for something that doesn't exist."

He grinned. "Hush, or I'll be forced to denounce you to the Holy Inquisition. No, I mean, I have nearly persuaded the queen to fund my expedition."

"What's the delay?"

"She says my expedition will be her next venture, but she can't afford the extra expenditure until the Granada campaign is completed."

"Completed?"

"Until you lot surrender."

"We're trying, but they won't accept any of our proposals. In fact, they're being extremely unreasonable."

"Ferdinand scents total victory."

"My sultan will never surrender the city unless his people are safeguarded, and their right to live and to worship as they will are guaranteed."

He shrugged. "I have the sense they think your sultan will capitulate pretty quickly when famine begins to bite."

"They underestimate the number and quality of gardens in our city," I said fiercely. "We have our own water cisterns, and we cultivate every fruit and vegetable you can name and then some you can't. If that's what they're waiting for, they'll have a very long wait and their resources will be well and truly depleted before our supplies run out."

Cristoforo Colombo made a face. "Is that true? If it is, then there's no chance I'll get my funding, and I'll have wasted years of my life. Perhaps I'll have to go back to England to talk to their wretched King Henry again." He grimaced. "But he won't give me what I need: he'll just try to cheat the charts out of me and send his own mariners." He looked despairing.

"Perhaps you could make mention to the queen . . . about the gardens?" And I regaled him with details of the grounds of the summer palace, where the peaches were so heavy and ripe they broke the branches of the trees on which they grew; of the peas and beans shooting up through the beds of rosemary and poppy; the squashes and melons so huge they could feed an entire family for a week; and everywhere the pomegranates that had become the symbol of the city. "It's believed our pomegranates trace their ancestry back to God's own garden. They say there's not a pomegranate eaten today whose seed did not come straight out of the Garden of Eden."

He raised an eyebrow. "She'll like that, Isabella. But won't it just make her all the more eager to conquer your city?"

"It might make her keener to sign an agreement on our terms, rather than have her husband destroy Granada."

"It might," he said, just as the Great Captain appeared and called his name.

Don Gonzalo seemed surprised to see the two of us—a Genoese adventurer and a desert prince-cum-translator—in conversation.

"Here again, Don Baraka? She will not see you, the queen, you know."

I smiled back at him. "I know."

They moved away toward the royal quarters; then Cristoforo turned around and whispered loudly, "Wish me luck, Blessings: I go into battle for both of us!"

The agreement was signed on the twenty-second day of the moon of Muharram, or by the calculations of the infidel, on the twenty-fifth of November. If we received no relief by the end of the year, Granada would be surrendered, with all swearing allegiance to King Ferdinand and Queen Isabella. Our Christian prisoners were to be released, with five hundred of them to be returned to the queen on signature of the document, along with hostages from the noblest families at court. No tribute would be paid for three years. The citizens of Granada and its outlying lands were permitted to stay in their houses and to retain their property; soldiers might keep their horses and weapons. All people had the right to worship as they chose, with no fear of the Inquisition: sanctity of the mosques was guaranteed, and there was to be no prohibition on what people wore or spoke or how they practised their usual customs. Sharia law would continue to pertain throughout the province. And Momo was to be given lands in the valleys of the beautiful Alpujarras in which to live; last, his son Ahmed would be returned safely to his care.

As surrender terms went, these were the most generous that could be imagined. I blessed Cristoforo Colombo, who appeared to have achieved with his silver tongue what Qasim and I had been unable to. But of course, it was still surrender, and that was painful. There were scenes in the throne room, and some hysteria. Musa Ibn Abu'l Ghrassan unsheathed his sword—which itself counted as treason in the presence of the sultan—and declared, "I'd rather have a grave beneath the walls of Granada, on the spot I died to defend, than the richest couch in some other palace, earned by surrendering to the infidel!"

Momo could have had his head for that, especially at the end of a long and trying day; but he was making an effort to remain as calm as possible, and in the end Musa put on his armour and rode out alone. What became of him I don't know. Some say he rode right through the enemy army, taking heads as he went, and kept on riding all the way to Guadix. Some tell that, set upon by Christian knights, he leapt from his horse into the river and was carried to the gates of heaven. All I can tell you is that Aysha, the sultan's mother, howled almost as loudly at hearing he had left as at the fact her son had surrendered Granada. Then she stormed around the harem, smashing vases and fretted screens and the beautiful bone-inlaid tables that had been created by artisans many centuries ago; and made a pile for burning of the precious carpets and wall hangings that could not be carried with us, shrieking that the infidel queen should not lay hands on them, that she would never again give up any treasure she owned to a Christian woman. By contrast, Mariam smiled for the first time in years at the news that surrender terms had finally been agreed upon, and laid out her prayer rug—also for the first time in years, I believe—to give thanks for the imminent return of her son.

At dawn on the fourth day of the moon Rabi al-awwal in the Hijri year 897, which the Christians reckon as the second day of January 1492, we took our leave of paradise, with all the portable treasures of the Alhambra packed into wagons.

"Ah, woe!" cried Aysha. "That it should be in the month of the Prophet's own birth that we deliver the keys to paradise into the hands of the unbelievers!"

"Hush, Mother," Momo said. He seemed very calm, almost serene, though his face was paler than usual, and he had eaten no breakfast. After morning prayers, I had helped him dress in the ceremonial clothes he had deliberated over long and hard. These consisted of a long silk shirt and cotton breeches under a figured velvet marlota in the crimson of the Banu Ahmar; a shining silver helm with a great shesh of white silk wound about it, one long tail fluttering down across his shoulder. Riding boots, of course, but of calf leather as soft as butter. A jewelled baldric and the sword he had abandoned those months back, now carefully edged and burnished to a fine sheen. *Only God is victorious.* "I will give it into King Ferdinand's hand," he said, with a glimmer of humour. "Perhaps it will make him more humble." Over the robe, a burnoose of heavy silk, its hems all gold embroidery; rings on every finger and a fine line of kohl around his eyes to ward off the evil spirits attracted by the view of so many. I had applied this last myself for him, and he had had to steady my hand.

"Come on, Blessings, you're shaking. If anyone should be anxious today it's me, for I'll be the one going down in history as the sultan who gave up the last part of a kingdom that's stood for almost eight hundred years." He looked around, and his chin trembled, just for a moment. "Farewell to this perfect little paradise, to the palace of my ancestors. Farewell to al-Andalus."

At this, I admit, I had burst into noisy tears, and he took me in his arms, and I stained his fine robe where my face was buried against his shoulder. That embrace was pure delight and at the same pure torment to me: but all I could do was to sob and shake until he gentled me as he might gentle a nervous horse, with quiet caresses and soft words.

We were sitting just inside the great carved doors of the sultan's hall, looking out onto the Court of Lions, where the fifth lion was spouting to denote the sixth hour. Swifts flitted here and there, catching the early-morning insects, as if today was a day like any other. The light was not the best, for the sultan's hall faces west, to make the most of the sunset rather than the sunrise, and it took everything I had in me to draw those lines of kohl straight and unblotched. "Now I dare not show my feelings," Momo said when I finished. "For fear of your kohl running down my face."

He stood up and walked to the courtyard lions, laid a hand on the nearest and sighed deeply. Then he called for the fountain master and told him to turn the water off and dismantle the device that controlled the timing of the flow.

When the sound of the falling water ceased and all lay still, he took a pebble and dropped it into the centre of the fountain's bowl, and we stood there for a long silent time, watching the ripples radiating out in wider and ever-degrading rings.

History tells that the young sultan wept: but I was at his side and I tell you he did not. Not when he handed his sword into the hands of the foreign king, sitting foursquare and triumphant in front of all his nobles, knights and cardinals on his big bay horse; not when he gave up the keys to the city to Queen Isabella, with her plump, catlike face, her small eyes burning with a fierce, sharp pleasure as the rose light of morning woke an answering red in the walls and towers of the fortress city she had just taken without further bloodshed. Not when he gave his ring of office into the hands of the Count of Tendilla, who was to be the new governor of Granada. Not when the cries of "*¡Santiago, Santiago, Santiago!*" And "*¡Castile, Castile, Castile!*" rang out through the clear air. He came close to it, though, when young Ahmed was brought forward between the Great Captain and Cristoforo Colombo, wearing a smart brocade suit and cap in the style of the foreign court (although I noticed his cloak was pinned at the shoulder with the amulet I had given his mother). The lad had shot up in the almost nine years he had been in the Christian court: he stood near as high as the adventurer.

"Ahmed, my son!" Momo cried, riding forward to greet him. "I am so happy to see you, I could burst with pride at what a fine young man you've grown into."

And at this moment Mariam, in defiance of all protocol, leapt out of the litter in which she had been travelling, hidden behind its curtains with the ladies of the harem, and, casting her veil aside, ran toward her son with her arms stretched wide to embrace him.

The boy stared first at the young sultan, then at his mother, in what seemed to me a sort of disgust. Then he turned back to Queen Isabella. "Do I have to go with these people?" he asked in flawless, unaccented Castilian.

"I am sorry, Alfonso, you must. They are your parents."

His disdain was horribly apparent. "But they are heathens."

The queen rummaged in her furs (it was a cold morning) and brought out a small black book. "Here. May the Word of God go with you always."

The boy accepted the book wordlessly, kissing first the queen's hand, which he held for a long time while she stroked his head, then the book. Then, stone-faced, he walked to his father, bowed stiffly and allowed himself to be led by a page to a waiting pony, which was far too small for his tall frame. He made an undignified exit from the city, his feet dangling on either side of the overburdened animal.

The mountains of the Sierra Nevada made a beautiful, snow-capped barrier between us and the past. The valleys of the Alpujarras region that had been given over to Momo and his family were lush with meltwater, the red-earthed hills dotted with evergreen shrubs and wildflowers, so that the place reminded me with a fleeting, strange, fierce nostalgia of Morocco. The hand of Castile had not reached into this place: as if it had been largely untouched since the Creation, for the people here lived lightly on the land, eking out some meagre sustenance from small plots arranged around flat-roofed, clay-walled dwellings that merged into the landscape like natural out-croppings. I took to walking for miles, seeing on my excursions only the odd skittering lizard, foraging herds of sheep and goats; a great-eared mountain hare, startled to paralysis by my approach, that so much resembled the ones I'd watched as a child dancing on our desert hills that I stood there gazing at it for a long minute till our connection was broken by the tears welling in my eyes.

To me, it seemed a great freedom to be able ramble at will like this, sometimes even staying out overnight with the stars spread overhead like a jewelled canopy and the jackals howling in the val-leys like the cries of wild muezzins, instead of being caged in by the careful beauty of the Nasrid palaces; or the current quarters of the royal court. Sometimes I thought of running away and living my life out in such a place: anything seemed preferable to the miserable atmosphere in our new home. The return of Ahmed should have reunited his fractured family, brought back some degree of har-mony between husband and wife; between father, mother and son; but it had quite the opposite effect.

Ahmed refused utterly to speak to his parents except through an intermediary in Castilian: to all intents and purposes, that meant me. And so, much against my will, I was dragged into their dis-putes, forced to witness Mariam's growing distress, and Momo's bewilderment at this strange young foreigner come back to us, who acted as more of an effete Castilian noble than any I had encoun-tered even in the Córdoban court. He would not speak Arabic, eat spiced food or wear the flowing robes his father offered him from his own chests; he threw the leather babouches his mother had lovingly embroidered in gold thread for him in her face, raising a welt, and when Momo chastised him for it, he sneered. "Who are you, anyway? They said my father was a king, but you are no king—look at you! And her, sewing like some peasant. Look at this place: it's a pigsty, and you are all pigs!"

I hardly dared translate: when I did, all the blood drained from Momo's face, and Mariam collapsed in a sobbing heap. The Lady Aysha had to be restrained she was so furious. "I'll put him over my knee and beat some respect into him!" she snarled. I'd have let her, given half a chance: the boy had come back to us a brat. All he could talk about was Queen Isabella—so wise and beautiful and brilliant and well read and devout—and King Ferdinand—so handsome and soldierly, so cunning and clever at chess; about the noble children with whom he learned grammar and archery, poetry and horse riding. And of course religious studies: he could recite whole passages from the Bible without prompting, fell to his knees morning and night to give up his prayers to a Christian god, refused absolutely to set foot in the mosque.

It was this as much as anything that broke Mariam: her faith had become her bedrock in life. While her husband was imprisoned by the enemy, she had devoted herself to learning to read the Quran. She knew each hadith by heart. All her energy went into charitable work through the imams of the local mosques. She prayed five times a day and had brought in a renowned religious scholar to establish the precise qibla in her chamber so that her prayer rug could be exactly aligned toward Mecca.

When Ahmed—who insisted on being called Alfonso—refused to go with his father to Friday prayers, Mariam's wails tore through the house: at night they had to dose her with poppy juice, to make her stop and allow her, and everyone else, to get some sleep. Day by day it got worse: the boy was trenchant in his views, determined to escape back to his "real parents." Momo cloistered himself in his own rooms or went riding with his hawks to avoid the weeping of his wife, the railing of his mother, the insults of his son.

To be honest, none of the signs for the future were good. Death had travelled with us: for rather than allow the remains of his Nasrid ancestors to fall into the hands of the enemy, Momo had ordered that their bones be dug up and brought with us, wrapped in new white silk shrouds, transported in baskets by mules that sensed the presence of the spectres of past kings, or the djinn they attracted, and kicked their heels and rolled their eyes.

Perhaps it was the proximity of the dead, or their djinn, that brought us such bad luck: perhaps something more corrosive, or contagious. In less than a year Mariam sickened and died, devoured by her own melancholy.

That was the only time I saw Momo weep in public: but surely there is no shame in a man's tears at his own wife's funeral. The men of our tribe pray to die before their wives, rather than bear the pain of their loss.

"I will never take another wife," Momo told me. "Mariam broke my heart as I broke hers. Why add to the sum of pain in the world?"

Perhaps this would have been the time to declare my love for him, to disclose my long-held, long-cherished secret. I look back now and wish I had. What did I have to lose? Except everything. But I lost that anyway.

For so long I had feared that if I told Momo, he would spurn me. For ours is not a culture that embraces difference.

There was a reason my mother named me Blessings. For among some of the people of the Kel Tamasheq, people like me, who come along rarely but not so infrequently that we are unknown, are regarded as specially blessed by the spirits. Doubly blessed: with both male and female parts. I have breasts—small, to be sure, but breasts all the same, with nipples that stiffen when brushed by a gentle hand. Still, there are men the world over with breasts, especially fat men.

I have curbed my appetite over the years to keep them as flat as possible. It's not easy, when you have known famine, to rein in the hunger that eats away at you even when you are full, but I have learned to do so. And then I bound them flat. And never bathed in the *hammam* with the others. We keep a certain modesty in our bathhouses, so my lower parts could be hidden; but my chest was more problematic.

And the rest? I have a cock of reasonable size that rises sometimes full of blood: it is an annoyingly intemperate addition. At its root two little hairy balls. And behind this boastful masculine trio lies a petalled slit as pink and complex as an Alhambra rose. I do not know if it leads to a chamber that will make children: I never found that out, or wished to know. I had rather not go into the details of that night in Fez, but suffice it to say the slave merchant took me as a man takes another male—or a child of ten or eleven, as I was then. It was the worst pain I have ever experienced. And then, after keeping me for a while to have his pleasure of me, he sold me as a "special monster"; to Qasim Abdelkarim, who made a gift of me to the young prince, and kept me as a spy. His little sparrow, his eye in the sultan's private quarters. His go-between in "discussions" with the Castilians. It makes me sick to admit the fear that drove me to allow him to use me so. Fear of losing Momo, of being discovered as the monster I am, and, discovered, being expelled from Eden. How much easier it would all have been had I not had the heart of a woman and lost myself in love.

So much for Blessings, bearer of the world's least applicable name.

After Mariam died, I never saw a man so sad. When Ahmed was taken by a fever, before he'd even relearned enough Arabic to bid his father farewell, it really felt as if the fates were determined to lay the last sultan of Granada as low as any man could go. Two months later we packed those things we could carry across the sea with us, including the coffins of his dynasty, and sailed to Morocco. There we were taken in by the sultan in Fez, Mohamed al-Shaykh, who had tried (he said) and failed to reinforce our forces: he gave my lord and his mother a small palace on a hill above the centre of that great city, set in wide and weed-strewn grounds. And there Momo devoted himself to recreating in as perfect detail as he could afford his beloved Alhambra.

And me? Fez was not for me. I hated the place: it held terrible memories, and now it was making for a terrible existence. Momo had become possessed by his need to replicate the palace in which he had grown to manhood, to the point of going without sleep and food. Even the death of his mother, shortly after we returned, had seemed no more to him than an inconvenient bump in the road, something to be negotiated swiftly and matter-of-factly so that he could continue with his journey. Every iota of his spirit went into the place, into overseeing the plaster makers and carvers, the carpenters and *zellij* men; the gardeners and the fountain engineers.

One morning I tried to exorcise my misery by writing it down. I wrote it in my own blood and in my own language, to imbue the words with all the power I could muster, making an inkwell of my left hand into which I dipped my pen. When I had finished, I sat there with the blood drying in my palm, and looked at the poem I had made. It was the saddest thing I ever wrote, and I lost my *asshak* completely. What was the use of staying here beside the man I had loved all these long years if I was not honest with him, did not open my dark secrets up to the light, make him look at who I really was, make him acknowledge my love and my suffering? How could I ever say I had given him a chance to return my love if I did not at last declare it?

Drying my tears, I took my courage in both hands, in the form of a scrap of paper. He knew enough now of my language to understand it, and to feel the rhythm and music behind the words. I went to find him. It wasn't hard to do: he was at his desk with the architect, their heads bent together over a series of drawings that more resembled mathematical problems than house plans, and arrived just as Momo said, ". . . for me, beside the *koubba* for my mother and our ancestors." So, they were talking about death again: the last resting place of the Nasrid dynasty, including his own tomb.

I waited for long minutes for the architect to be dismissed, feeling my courage turning to foolhardiness with each passing moment, taking in the changes in his outward form. He was not yet thirty-two: not even halfway through his life. But he looked a man thirty years older, his hair prematurely white, his face seamed with lines, his amber eyes sunken in pits as gaunt as a death's head. No flesh on it, or any of the rest of him, for the lack of food and the excess of nervous pacing and strange internal fires. The golden boy I had fallen in love with was long gone: but you don't stop loving someone just because their looks are gone. If anything, you love them all the more.

I closed my eyes, preparing my words. No, they all sounded so absurd, so hollow. I would just give him the poem, let him read my desperate yearning, and the awful truth behind it. Then we would see if he could love me, or would know me as a monster.

Finally, the man left, with papers in his hand, a smile on his lips and satisfaction in his eyes, and I was struck by the yawning parallel: here sat I with a paper in my hands, a tiny paper rather than the great sheaf he carried, with dread on my face.

"So, Blessings, come and see what we've designed," Momo said at last. "The Nasrid tombs will stand forever as a testament to the lost greatness of the kings of Granada. People will come from all over the Muslim world to wonder over them, and I hope offer their prayers for our souls."

I approached the table, my heart leaping in my chest like a caught rabbit. With a boldness I no longer felt, I put my scrap of poetry down, right in the middle of the drawings in front of him. All my life hung on that moment, on the few words I had so carefully inked there. And then cried over—I saw the last line was blotched.

I watched his hand move as if time itself had slowed. I saw his fingers brush the paper. I closed my eyes and waited for my fate.

There was silence, at least inside the room. Outside, life went on as normal: I could hear the cries of swallows over the noise of the workmen. I could hear the blood ringing in my ears, my own breath: *his* breath, slow and steady . . .

I opened my eyes. The poem lay half on, half off the edge of the desk, suspended in mid-air. He had brushed it away from his wretched plans, and was once more engrossed in them. I felt such anger then, such reckless fury. I reached out and took back the poem: he did not deserve it. Then I said, "I'm going away."

He looked up, though I'm not sure he saw me: for there were soaring pillars and vaults and decorations in his eyes. "What did you say, Blessings?"

I made a momentous decision that instant. "I'm going away, to sail the oceans. With the adventurer, Cristoforo Colombo."

He appeared puzzled. "Do I know him? I don't recall the name."

Had he actually heard what I'd said and understood what it meant? I wanted to reach across the table and grab him by the ears. But of course I didn't. I reminded him, as patiently as I could, about the man I'd met in Córdoba and then again in Santa Fe, the man who had been interested in how my people navigate across the Great Desert by the stars.

Momo nodded distractedly. "I do dimly recollect some mention of that. Well, that will be interesting for both of you."

I stared at him. "I don't know how long I'll be away, or whether I'll ever come back."

He looked pained, then faintly annoyed. "Don't say that, Blessings. Of course you'll come back. It is written."

It was written. On the paper I held in my hand. I closed my fingers over it. I closed my heart. "I'll pack my things and go this very day."

"Go with God, my friend. My friendship goes with you, no matter how far."

Was that a tear I saw in his eye? I don't know: he bowed his head and went back to his drawings. There seemed nothing more I could say. We hugged briefly, but it was as if I hugged a walking corpse.

Friendship is a fine thing. But it is not enough to keep a heart from withering.

I went to my room and sat there for a long time, staring into space, feeling bereaved. Then I stuffed the poem savagely down into my false foot and started to pack my things.

32

Kate

GRANADA

NOW

Kate held Luke close as the footsteps sounded on the stone stairs up from the crypt. Was there time for her and Luke to run for the door? They could try, but the entrance to the crypt stood between them and the exit, and Luke was head down and grizzling; she would have to pick him up and run: she didn't think she'd be fast enough. She looked around for a weapon, anything: but of course in such a place there was nothing she could use. Her hands ached from being balled into tight fists. *I will fight him*, she thought. *I won't let him terrify me, and I won't let him hurt Luke.* With a terrible cold dread she watched the pillar that hid the entrance.

The footsteps stopped echoing and became softer. There was a pause in the sound; then a dark shape ghosted around the pillar. It was not James.

He came toward her quickly, shedding his robe on the way. It lay on the tiles like a dead crow.

"Abdou—but how—?"

"I followed you. Are you all right? He didn't hurt you or Luke, did he?"

Kate, lost for words, shook her head.

Abdou dropped to one knee to put himself on a level with the toddler. "Hello, Luke. My name's Abdou, and I'm a friend of your mum." He paused, letting the boy take this in. Then he said, "Do you like chocolate?"

Luke gazed up at him in a sort of tear-stained wonder, then slowly nodded. Solemnly, Abdou held out his empty hand, and a small bar of Valor slid from out of his sleeve and appeared miraculously in his palm. Luke's eyes became round and a huge smile appeared on his face at this piece of magic. He grabbed the brightly wrapped bar, examined it for an opening and, failing to find one, tore into the foil with his teeth and started munching. The chocolate seemed to be all it took—for the time being—to restore a child's equilibrium. If only the rest of life could be so simple, thought Kate.

"Yes, I know you said not to follow you, but how could I not? When I realized he'd locked the doors, I called Saïd. His girlfriend, Pilar, works in the cathedral: there's a secret entrance into the crypt from that side. She got me a robe from one of the old chests in the vestry, let me in through the back door."

Abdou straightened up and Kate saw for the first time that he had a bruise on his jaw and a rip in his shirt. She reached out and touched his face, and watched him manfully suppress a flinch. "Does it hurt?"

"Yes, of course it hurts." He grinned. "But you should see him."

Instinctively, she looked over his shoulder. "What did you do to him?"

"I hit him with the crucifix that was on the wall down there. He's out cold, lying in state between the coffins of his wretched Catholic Monarchs. Better call the police before he comes around."

Eerily, at that moment Kate's mobile went off.

The next few days were among the strangest of Kate's life. A scant time after Jess phoned her, she had found herself back at the Granada main police station with her sister, a woman called Michelle Englefield, a diffident man in his forties who looked like an English professor but was actually from the National Crime Agency; and a smiling man with a greying beard and a Welsh accent, who introduced himself as Detective Inspector Alun Williams. James now languished in the police cells, awaiting the possible issue of an official Interpol Red Notice to extradite him to the UK. Everyone had given statements, through official interpreters, to ensure there were no linguistic errors that might later cause problems in court.

James had been charged with one count of bigamy (with a second count pending), and with the abduction of and actual bodily harm to Jess. The police had taken a DNA swab from him to check against the hair and skin sample removed from beneath the nails of a woman who had fallen to her death over ten years ago onto rocks in West Wales, a woman who had been unidentified at the time and remained so. "There had clearly been a struggle," DI Williams told Kate later. "But we couldn't identify the body, and the material under the dead woman's fingernails didn't match anyone we had in the database, so she went down as a cold case. But when we ran the results of the DNA under Jess's fingernails, it matched the evidence we'd found under the nails of the woman on the rocks; and Interpol has come back to us with a possible name for the dead woman: Isabel Villalobos, a Spanish national who'd been working in London before going missing. Her brother emailed us photos of her, and he's providing his DNA to police in Madrid as we speak. If everything matches up, James could be facing a murder charge as well."

It turned out that James Foxley had been born James Hyde, but it was as James Foxley that he had married Michelle Englefield, whom Jess had tracked down after Kate's tipoff message: she had been delighted to come to Spain with Jess to see James get his comeuppance, and "for closure." He had reluctantly allowed her to keep her maiden name after the marriage, she'd explained, seduced by the long and bloody history of the Catholic Englefield family. They'd had a child together, she added: a daughter called Catherine. "James was furious it wasn't a boy. He went almost black in the face with anger. Everything changed after that: he became so cold and cruel; but it was only after he hit Catherine that I left him and went home to my parents. I should never have married him in the first place."

"So clearly, he changed his name from Hyde to Foxley before he married you, since the Catholic faith doesn't allow divorce," Jess said to Michelle.

"And no doubt to distance himself from the murder of poor Isabel Villalobos, the bastard," Michelle said with relish. "Just in case anyone found and identified her."

"He must have expected she would fall into the sea, not onto rocks," Kate added, remembering that strange third date with James when he'd told her the story, with crucial details—like the location, and the name of his victim—changed.

The Spanish police had noted how alike all four women looked: Jess and Kate, Michelle and the dead Isabel. "He certainly has a type, doesn't he?" DI Williams said.

Michelle caught the train back to Seville to fly home the next day. Kate and Jess walked back through the Albayzín to Kate's apartment, where Abdou had taken Luke after he had given his own statement to the local police and been allowed to leave. "Are you sure?" Jess had asked, reluctant to be parted from her beloved nephew.

"Yes," said Kate. "There's no one I trust more in the world." It came out before she'd even thought the words, but she realized that what she'd said was true.

Jess looked remarkably chipper, Kate thought, for someone who had been through such a harrowing experience, including emergency dentistry ("Look—I have a temporary denture!" She grinned with glee at Kate's horrified expression as she waggled the false plate unnervingly). All the way through the old city, she'd stopped to exclaim over the prettily shabby doors ("Now, that's what I call the distressed look"), the tumbles of bright hibiscus and bougainvillea against rough whitewashed walls and over wrought-iron balconies; sighed over the picturesque vista of the great old Nasrid fortress on the hill opposite, backed by the distant snow-capped mountains of the Sierra Nevada. "What a place, Kate. I can see why you love it here."

At last they turned into the Calle Guinea. On the bare wall opposite her apartment Kate noticed that someone, apparently overnight, had spray-painted the words *Stop Machismo*. Though perhaps she hadn't noticed the graffito before amid all the drama. She stared at the words for a long moment. There were so many ways of being a man in this modern world, so many different definitions and expressions of masculinity. The balance between masculine pride and dangerous aggression had, she supposed, always been delicate: but you had to teach your boys the difference early in life, and explain that how they treated girls, then women, was a measure of their own worth.

She opened the door, to find Abdou lying flat out on the living room floor with Luke, playing jigsaw with dozens of pieces of multicoloured *zellij*. Their creation was not a pattern of unsurpassed beauty and symmetry like those in the palace, but at that moment Kate thought it was one of loveliest things she had ever seen.

After dinner that night—a tagine of chicken with olives and preserved lemon that Abdou had managed to throw together as the sisters talked and talked—Jess took Kate's passport out of her bag and slid it across the table to her twin.

Kate pushed it back.

Jess raised an eyebrow.

"Keep it," Kate said. "For now, anyway. Take Luke home. I'll follow in a while." Across the table, Abdou's face went very still and miserable. She reached out and put her hand over his. "There's a thing called a Special Guardianship Order. It's a law made under the Children's Act to provide for children who can't live with their birth parents for whatever reason. It's a sort of adoption order, but it doesn't end the legal relationship between the child and its parents. I'll always be Luke's mum, but I'd like you to be his special guardian."

Jess said nothing for a long time, but she couldn't help looking at Luke, now fast asleep on the sofa, wrapped in a white cotton blanket, drugged by a surfeit of sun, chocolate and Spanish fruit. Kate had over the past few days watched the lines on her sister's face soften every time she gazed at her son; had noted how Luke ran instinctively to Jess rather to her, no matter how alike the pair of them might appear.

"Are you sure?" Jess said at last.

Kate nodded. "I've seen how the two of you are together, and it only seems right to me."

Jess grinned. She looked at Abdou, then Kate. "I've seen how the two of *you* are together too. And that seems right to me." She leaned in. "So, have you swived him yet?"

Kate snorted out her wine. Then both sisters started to giggle like children, leaving Abdou staring, puzzled, from one to the other. At last Jess regained enough composure to say, "I love how you've been brought together by the poems you found."

"If they were poems," Kate said.

Abdou smacked his forehead. "I'm an idiot. Mother heard back from her expert in Rabat."

"Was he able to make any sense of them?" Kate asked, still pink in the face.

He grinned. "Of a sort." He got up, walked to the other side of the room and fished in his coat pocket, and came back to the table with a notebook, from between the pages of which he extracted photocopies of the two scraps of paper they had respectively found.

"This one—" He touched the photocopy of the fragment Kate had discovered in the garden wall. "This one says—" he peered at the notebook "—something along the lines of:

> *Save, oh spirits my beloved*
> *From every harm to his body*
> *I my blood give as pledge*
> *My body against his.*

Tears sprang into Kate's eyes. "Oh, how lovely. Is it a spell, do you think?"

Abdou shrugged. "If you believe in magic."

"And what about the second one, the one you found in the Tower of the Captive?"

"That one was much simpler, and written in walnut ink."

"What was the first written in?"

"They're not sure yet. They're testing it. But listen—this is what yours says:

> *He rides to war*
> *I go at his side*
> *Let not the enemy*
> *Take his life.*

"To war," Kate echoed. She looked up at Abdou, suddenly intent. She felt as if every hair on her body had stood on end. "My God, do you think this was written during the fall of Granada?"

He grinned at her. "Don't leap to such grand conclusions. Mother says they will try to date the paper and ink. That's why all I've got is the photocopies: the originals have to remain in Rabat for testing."

Kate gazed tenderly at the photocopies. "This is so special, so . . . wonderful. Imagine, loving someone and fearing for the person so much. Can't you just feel that love, arcing across the centuries toward us? I can." She shivered. "This place. It's . . ." There were no words. "You've got to see it, Jess. There's nowhere so beautiful on earth as the Alhambra. We'll go tomorrow, perhaps for the evening tour. It's so lovely by night." Then she remembered Luke. "Oh. Far too late for him. I really am a hopeless mother, aren't I?"

But Jess wasn't paying attention to what her twin was saying. Instead, she had reached across the table and pulled the photocopies toward her and was staring at them with a curious expression on her face. Then she suddenly pushed her chair back with a frantic scrape and got up. She came back with her handbag. Then she took something out of it and placed it carefully down in front of Kate and Abdou.

"Sarah found this," she said quietly, "when she was refurbishing that old wooden foot you gave me. It was jammed down in the toes . . ."

The three of them looked from the photocopied fragments to this new scrap of paper, which was much larger, and more clearly a poem, though some of the words had been erased by time, by folding and by might be water damage. All three pieces shared the same language and, surely, the same hand.

Kate gasped. Abdou put an arm around her waist and drew her close.

"Perhaps there is magic in the world," he said.

Epilogue

TWO MONTHS LATER

Extracted from a report by Professor Najib Tataoui of Mohammed V University in Rabat:

Paleography does not offer us much help in the dating of this manuscript, as we have no direct comparisons from which to draw parallels, provide context or give us rule of thumb. The fragment is not in the best condition, but once the dirt and cigarette ash were cleaned off it forensic examination and analysis of the paper by radiocarbon dating and microscopy suggest that it may derive from the late fifteenth or early sixteenth century, from an area that was highly cultivated, given the presence in the fabric of so many pollens, including those of jasmine, orange, myrtle, persimmon, pomegranate and mulberry, to name but six of the forty or so species identified. This in itself is surprising, given that the alphabet in which the text is presented is an old form of Tifinagh, which comes from the desert regions of Saharan North Africa, where it would have been quite impossible to cultivate such species at this time. We will continue to study and debate the fragment, but at this time it remains a fascinating mystery. I have, however, pieced together an attempt at transliterating the contents, reproduced below. And whereas the previous fragments I examined appeared to be some type of enchantment or spell, this third and longer manuscript is quite clearly a love poem.

It is worth noting, in addition, that we have deduced the inscription to have been written in human blood.<end ext>

Both man and woman
Is poor/cursed blessings
Made by the djinn
A monster they . . . [illegible]
. . . [illegible] *sun rises*
in the eyes
Of one now diminished
There is beauty in stone
But cold marble has no blood
Let me be the one
To bring sweet joy and . . . [illegible]
[illegible] *to your life*
Chieftain [*amghrar*—the Tuareg have no word for king] *of my heart*
I your slave
As the peacock drinks
From the fountain pool
So I . . ./[illegible] *from you*
Two hearts beating
As one

Author's Note

I first visited the Moorish palace complex in Granada—the Alhambra—over twenty years ago and, like everyone who walks beneath its graceful arches and gazes upon its serene pools and lacy, geometric stonework, fell under its spell.

We all think we know the story of the fall of Granada, that great hinge point in Western history, beginning the momentous year of 1492: how, after handing the keys over to Queen Isabella and King Ferdinand, the young sultan turned for one last time to look upon the city he loved; how his mother derided him for "weeping like a woman for what you could not hold like a man"; how that spot is called The Moor's Last Sigh. But when I started in on some serious research, I soon discovered that this was largely made up by Antonio de Guevara, bishop of Guadix, for the benefit of Emperor Charles V when he visited Granada on his honeymoon in 1526, and that history—from both the Christian and Muslim perspectives—had treated that young sultan, Abu Abdullah Mohammed, known as Boabdil, cruelly. So I wanted to tell his personal story, as well as recount the great sweep of events leading up to the fall, which the poet Federico García Lorca described as "a calamity, leading to a new dark age."

The book was shaping up to be a straightforward historical epic, but one day in 2013 the producer who was interested in making a film of *The Sultan's Wife* told me about a discovery by restorers in the Alhambra. While moving one of the great doors, they had come upon a scrap of paper that had been hidden deep in the intricate latticework of the wood. It appeared to be an ancient love letter: but the provenance of the note and the identity of the scribe remain a mystery. The movie deal sadly stalled, but the story was a gift, and I remembered another Lorca quote: "In Spain, the dead are more alive than the dead in any other country in the world." And that got me thinking about how the past and present arc toward each other, and how love is an eternal force. And I thought: *What if a series of tiny notes (love letters, maybe; or spells) written in the fifteenth century were to come to light in the twenty-first century?* And *Court of Lions* turned into quite a different book to the one I had originally envisaged.

And so the story of Kate Fordham wrapped itself around and through the tale of the young sultan growing up in the most beautiful palace on earth, yet at the heart of a terribly fractured family, providing echoes and parallels and points of contrast, and a mystery focused on the enigmatic scraps of paper found in the walls.

Who wrote those mysterious fragments? I needed a viewpoint character, one who could wander the fifteenth-century stage, taking us behind the scenes and into enemy territory in a way young Momo simply could not, trapped as he was in his role—as royal heir, pawn in the great game, king and political prisoner. I could have used the vizier, Qasim Abdelmalik, and thus given the novel an even more unreliable narrator: but I wanted the story of the last sultan of the last Moorish kingdom to touch readers' hearts, and so Blessings came into existence, an abused, enslaved nomad child transported across a continent, given as a companion to a boy of a similar age, thus—I hope—tingeing an already tragic tale with further sadness and frustration—of unrequited love, of yearning and nostalgia for a golden age about to be lost.

Blessings is, of course, fully my own creation, his false leg inspired by an obscure piece of folklore surrounding a golden foot discovered in excavations. Certainly, there would have been companions for the young sultan as he grew up in the Alhambra—sons of nobles and allies sharing his time and education. But they would have given me no angle from which to view Momo, being too similar in background and upbringing. Making Blessings a desert nomad meant the hidden notes could be written in a language no one else could read, so adding dramatic tension to the modern tale. The Granadan court would certainly have contained both Tuaregs and Berbers, albeit fewer during this final era of Moorish history in the peninsula.

In truth, the golden age of the Moors in Spain was already long past. It had reached its apogee under the great Abd al-Rahman III in the tenth century, while the rest of Europe was regarded as being in the Dark Ages. Then, Granada truly was the golden realm Momo talks of as he rides into Córdoba, the city that was the fount of all knowledge and the ornament of the world, a place where scholars, merchants and poets from all backgrounds and cultures gathered to trade knowledge, arts and crafts. Power ebbed and flowed, as power will, and the emirate of Granada was nibbled away over the intervening centuries, surrounded as it was on all sides by the ever-increasing kingdom of Castile. But in the latter part of the fifteenth century circumstances conspired to make the long-desired Spanish reconquest of Granada possible.

The accession to the Castilian throne of Isabella—strong-willed, fierce and devout—and her marriage to the martial Ferdinand of Aragón brought renewed determination to the quest to eradicate Islam from Spain, a crusade funded in large part by the pope in Rome. Persuaded of the royal couple's devotion to the Catholic cause by their establishment of the Inquisition, he donated a tenth of the Church's revenues to their crusade. The medieval prophecy *Woe to the World*, which told of the coming of a messianic hero, or "Great Bat," who would defeat the Antichrist, was enthusiastically espoused by Ferdinand, whose Aragonese heraldic device included a bat. (Although, ironically, the sign of the bat was originally derived from a Muslim Sufi symbol.) The monarchs were also exceptionally lucky to be able to call on the talents of one of the finest soldiers of the time: Gonzalo de Córdoba, the Great Captain.

History—and often fiction, too—has glorified Isabella and Ferdinand as a result of their lauded reunification of Spain, but in truth they were a pair of genocidal religious fanatics whose intolerance of diversity forced vicious persecution upon a mixed population that had lived in reasonable harmony under Muslim rule.

The surrender terms agreed between Isabella and Ferdinand and Sultan Abu Abdullah appeared to be fair and equable. They stipulated that once the sultan gave up the keys to the city all Granadans "great and small, men and women" would be accepted as "vassals and natural subjects" to the Catholic Monarchs and were guaranteed the right to remain in their "houses, estates and hereditaments now and for all time." The "common people, great and small" would be allowed "to live in their own religion," and it was promised that their mosques and muezzins would not be taken from them: "nor will they [the Catholic Monarchs] disturb the uses and customs which they observe."

The sultan negotiated the treaty in good faith: but the Catholic Monarchs had no intention whatsoever of abiding by its terms. As soon as they entered the Alhambra, they began to draft an Edict of Expulsion for the entire Jewish community, which decreed that Jews had three months to leave and that any persons harbouring a Jew would forfeit everything they had, even their lives. All assets that could not be carried had to be sold: but Jews were forbidden to take into exile with them gold, silver, jewels or coin. A perfect double bind. Family houses were exchanged for donkeys or mules or bolts of cloth, and Spanish coffers swelled. The Inquisition swung into cruel, Daesh-like action and the Jewish population of Granada—which had been the most brilliant, talented and erudite in Europe—was destroyed.

When Cardinal Ximenes de Cisneros, the inquisitor general, took over responsibility for Granada from the considerably more tolerant count of Tendilla, his first act was to burn every Quran in the city, then the contents of some of the greatest libraries in the world, the culmination of a thousand years of scholarship, in the Plaza Bib-Rambla. There followed massacres in the Alpujarras, including Ferdinand's slaughter of three thousand prisoners of war (echoing the atrocity of Richard the Lionheart's massacre of prisoners at Acre) and the blowing up of six hundred men, women and children taking refuge in a mosque near Andarax.

In 1502 the Edict of Conversion was published: all Muslims must convert to Christianity or go into exile, any Muslims remaining in Spain to be enslaved and made subject to the Inquisition. But the Catholic Monarchs were not content with just this. In 1511 Moorish converts were forbidden to carry arms or even knives. Tailors were forbidden from making Moorish-style clothing. Property could no longer be passed from father to child, nor could former Muslims sell their property. And finally, in 1526 came the Edict of Granada, which prohibited all Moorish customs. All bathhouses were closed; Moorish music, dancing, rituals and ceremonies were all forbidden. Any contraventions of these rules were handed over to the Inquisition: between 1492 and 1530 fifteen thousand people were tortured, over two thousand executed.

It was another expression of the Catholic Monarchs' fundamentalism that launched the expeditions to the New World. Not content with driving the infidel out of Iberia, they wished to launch a crusade to take back the Holy Land from the Muslims, and in this fervent wish were joined by Columbus, who stated in his diaries that he intended to find gold and spices "in such quantity that the sovereigns . . . will be able to undertake and prepare to go conquer the Holy Sepulchre and . . . spend all the profits of this my enterprise on the conquest of Jerusalem," the only city that exists twice: "in heaven and on earth."

And so we come back to that other earthly paradise: the Alhambra, the expression in the divine symmetries of stone and water, light and shade, pillar and tree of a sacred paean to Allah, the architect of all things. The Catholic Monarchs made their royal court in the palaces and converted the mosque to a church. They are buried in the Capilla Real, adjoining the Cathedral of Granada, according to their decree: "We ordain that in the Cathedral Church in the city of Granada a worthy Chapel shall be built where, when it pleases Our Lord to call us, our bodies shall be placed."

Isabella may have loved the beauty of the Alhambra palaces, but no matter how hard her engineers tried to figure out the mechanism of the fountain in the Court of Lions it never worked again.

Abu Abdullah Mohammed lived to old age in Fez, a dependant of the Merenid sultan, concentrating all his efforts and what little money he could beg or borrow on recreating the palace in which he had grown up. He died in 1534 and was buried in the city in a *musalla*, a mausoleum. Some sources claim he died in battle during the war between the Merenids and Saadians; others that he died peacefully in his bed. Some sources say he was dark; others that he was light skinned. Some that his sons outlived him; others that they predeceased him. Almost every historical chronicle refers to him as "weak," "hapless," "foolish" or "unfortunate." My view is that he was a man raised in the most beautiful place made by human hands in a family riven by jealousy and hatred, and that he wished for nothing more than a peaceful life for himself and his subjects under the best terms he could possibly negotiate. That all his efforts came to nothing and his people were betrayed and persecuted makes him for me neither a fool nor a coward but a tragic figure.

Jane Johnson
Cornwall, May 2017

Further Reading for Court of Lions

Brenan, Gerald. *South from Granada*. London: Hamish Hamilton, 1957.

Dodds, Jerrilynn D., ed. *Al-Andalus: The Art of Islamic Spain*. New York: Metropolitan Museum of Art, 1992.

Downey, Kristen. *Isabella: The Warrior Queen*. New York: Anchor Books, 2015.

Facaros, Dana, and Michael Pauls. *Cadogen Guides: Granada Seville Cordoba*. New York: New Holland Publishers, 2011.

Grabar, Oleg. *The Alhambra*. London: Penguin Books, 1978.

Harris, Katie A. *From Muslim to Granada: Inventing a City's Past in Early Modern Spain*. Baltimore: John Hopkins University Press, 2007.

Harvey, L.P. *Islamic Spain: 1250–1500*. Chicago: University of Chicago Press, 1990.

Irving, Washington. *Tales of the Alhambra*. New York: Lea and Carey, 1832.

Irwin, Robert. *The Alhambra*. London: Profile Books, 2004.

Lane-Poole, Stanley. *The Story of the Moors in Spain*. New York: G.P Putnam's Sons, 1896.

McGilvray, Donald. *Granada: The Seizure of the Sultanate*. Leicester: Matador, 2012.

Morris, Jan. *Spain*. New York: Harcourt and Brace, 1964.

Nicholl, David, and Angus McBride. *Granada 1492: The Twilight of Moorish Spain*. London: Osprey, 1998.

Nightingale, Steven. *Granada: The Light of Andalucía*. London: Nicholas Brealey, 2015.

Núñez, Agustin J, and Aurelio Cid Acedo. *The Alhambra and Granada: In Focus*. Granada: Edilux S.L., 2006.

O'Callaghan, Joseph F. *The Last Crusade in the West: Castile and the Conquest of Granada*. Philadelphia: University of Pennsylvania Press, 2014.

Reston, Jr., James. *Dogs of God: Columbus, the Inquisition, and the Defeat of the Moors*. New York: Doubleday, 2005.

Rubin, Miri, ed. *Medieval Christianity in Practice*. Princeton: Princeton University Press, 2009.

Tremlett, Giles. *Ghosts of Spain: Travels Through Spain and Its Silent Past*. London: Faber and Faber, 2006.

Acknowledgements

Thanks first of all must go to Susan Cherian, for that long-ago conversation that sparked to life a magical chain of ideas; and to Abdel Bakrim, whose help with the Arabic source material, support and encouragement throughout the writing of the novel was invaluable. Warm thanks and gratitude also to professors Gabra and Fotopoulou, to Philippa McEwan, Lucy Vanderbilt and my agent, Danny Baror. To the guides, gardeners and conservators at the Alhambra who put up with my many curious questions; to Claire and Tony Morpeth, Lizzie and Chris Hopkins, and Lucy and Nick Howe for their serendipitous company in Seville and beyond.

But a manuscript has a long road to travel before it becomes a published book, and for her insight and guidance and cheerleading along the route I must thank my marvellous editor Zoe Maslow and all her colleagues, particularly Kristin Cochrane, Amy Black, Val Gow, Kelly Hill, Jessica Cooney and Melanie Tutino at Doubleday Canada.